MW00451566

The Resistance

Dear Allison,
Dare to Dream)!
Rock On,
S. L. Scott

S. L. SCOTT

The Resistance
First Edition

Copyright © S. L. Scott 2014

The right of S.L. Scott to be identified as the author of this work has been asserted by her under the *Copyright Amendment (Moral Rights) Act 2000*

This work is copyright. Apart from any use as permitted under the Copyright Act 1968, no part may be reproduced, copied, scanned, stored in a retrieval system, recorded or transmitted, in any form or by any means, without the prior written permission of the publisher.

This book is a work of fiction. Names, characters, places and incidents are either a product of the author's imagination or are used fictitiously. Any resemblance to actual people living or dead, events or locales is entirely coincidental.

ISBN: 978-1-940071-14-5

Cover design: Sarah Hansen of Okay Creations
http://www.okaycreations.com/

Cover Model: Michael L. Ceorgoveanu

Cover Photographer: Sean Nicholas Amey Photography
https://www.facebook.com/SeanNicholasAmeyPhotography

Interior Design: Angela McLaurin, Fictional Formats
https://www.facebook.com/FictionalFormats

Raves and Reviews

"*The Resistance* is a fun, sexy read that you don't want to miss! This book pulled me in from the first sentence, and I couldn't put it down. Jack Dalton is hot, and Holli is just the type of protagonist that I like to root for.
~**R.K. Lilley, New York Times and USA Today Best Selling Author**

"The Resistance is a unique and refreshingly sexy twist on the usual Rock Star Romance. If you love hot sex, rock stars, and a heroine who is strong and capable, this one is for you!"
~**Lisa, Rock Stars of Romance**

"5 Stars—another must read from S. L. Scott, who continues to wow me with her ability to suck me into a story and make me feel that I'm standing on the outside watching everything unfold."
~**Heidi McLaughlin, USA Today Best Selling Author**

"The Resistance isn't just a book about a Bad Boy Rocker. It's about finding your true north, learning how to cope with the past, finding a way to navigate the present... In the end it's a ride you won't want to get off."
~**Jennifer, Wolfel's World of Books**

Prologue

I'm a fucking fool.

I'm not even sure how I got into this mess, but I know I need to get myself out of it. I look down at the hand on my thigh inching up higher and my stomach rolls. Squeezing out from between the tight confines of the third row in this van, a girl on each side wanting a piece of me, I fall over the seat into the cargo area and move away from their astonished stares. They're speaking German and I don't know what the fuck they're saying, but I've been in this type of situation enough to know how it will end, if I let it.

Everything has changed... or sometime around my last birthday I changed.

I didn't invite these chicks. Dex did. He'll fuck'em all before the night's through and the bad part is, they'll let him. Thinking they're special, that they'll be the one to tame him. They'll let him do what he wants just to be close to him.

Beyond this set up being predictable at this point, it's really fucking old or I am, probably both. I ignore their taps on my shoulder and them calling my name. I ignore everything to do with them and focus on my phone.

On the inside, I'm freaking the fuck out that I'm sitting in the cargo hold of a huge van in Germany with attractive girls willing to do anything I want them to, but I prefer to look at a photo of a little blonde with hazel eyes. Freaking the fuck out might be an understatement.

I'm a player or was, supposed to be, maybe still am. I don't keep score or anything like that, but I've slept with plenty of women, sometimes more than one at a time. I used to blame my lifestyle, but more recently, I realized I'm the common denominator in the bad relationships I've had.

The car comes to a stop and the driver rushes around to the back to let me out. I stumble while climbing out, and hurry inside away from the sound of my name being called. The girls will be upset when they realize I'm not staying to play, but Dex will be thrilled—more pussy for him.

Cory hops out from the front, and follows me. "Wait up," he says, jogging to catch up.

When we reach the elevators, we look back. Dex is helping the girls out of the vehicle one-by-one. With a cigarette hanging from the corner of his mouth, he's sloppy, already drunk. He never lacks for female companionship. By the way he acts, I don't see the appeal, but I don't think that's why they're hooking up with him anyway.

Cory looks at me and nods once. "What's up? What happened back there?"

The elevator doors open and we step in, pushing the button for our floor. "Over it. Over it all."

"The girl from Vegas?"

"She's not from Vegas, but yeah, I've kind of been thinking about her."

When the brass doors reopen, we walk down the hall to our rooms. Cory and I don't do small talk. We've been friends for years, best friends if I think about it.

"Maybe you should call her," he suggests as we open our doors.

"Maybe I will."

"Night."

"Night," I mumble and shut the door behind me.

1

Holliday Hughes

"Comfort zones are like women. You have to try a few before you find the one that feels right." ~*Johnny Outlaw*

That damn lime and coconut song has been playing on a loop in my head, driving me nuts for hours. I make a mental note: Fire Tracy in the morning for subjecting me to that song twenty-thousand times yesterday. She called it inspirational. I call it torture after the first two times.

Rolling over, I look at the time. 4:36 a.m. I have four hours before I need to be on the road. This may be a business trip, but it will still be good to get away for a few days. I need a break. I've been in a bad mood lately. The spa and I have a date I'm really looking forward to. The thought alone relaxes me. I close my eyes and try to get a few more hours of sleep before I need to leave for Las Vegas.

I get two tops.

I tighten my robe at the neck. Just as I open my front door to get the paper, I hear a male voice say, "Hello?"

Peeking through the crack, I hold the door protectively in front of me just in case I need to close and lock it quickly. "Hi."

"I'm your new neighbor. I just moved in last week. I'm Danny."

Curious, I slowly stick my head out to get a better look at this Danny. Strands of my sandy blonde hair fall in front of my eyes, so I tuck it behind my ear and get an eyeful. To my surprise, he's quite handsome and has a big smile. "Oh, um," I say, dragging my hand down the back of my hair, hoping to tame the wild strands. "Hi. I'm Holli. Welcome to the neighborhood."

He nods toward the paper on the bottom of the shared Spanish tiled steps that lead to our townhomes. "I'll get your paper since you're not dressed."

"Thanks." I watch him. He looks like he just got back from a run or workout—a little sweaty, but not gross, in that sexy kind of way. Or maybe Danny's just sexy. He's well built with short, brown hair and when he bends over, I notice his strong legs and arms. Well-defined muscles lead to—*Oh my God!* Not just my face, but my entire body heats from embarrassment. Hoping he doesn't say anything about me checking him out, I turn away and start picking at a piece of peeling stucco near my house number. "Um, so are you settled in, liking your place?"

His chuckling confirms I was busted. But he's a gentleman, so he acts as if it didn't happen. "I like the neighborhood. The place is great," he says. "I like all the space, especially the patio.

I'm thinking of having a party to break it in, maybe in a few weeks after I finish unpacking." He hands me the paper and takes two steps back. "You should stop by."

Nodding, I look into his eyes. I think they're brown, lighter than mine, more honey-colored. His offer is friendly, not a come on, which is good since we're neighbors now. "Thanks for the invitation."

Walking back to his door, he steals one more glimpse over his shoulder. "Have a great day. See you around, Holli."

"Yeah, see you around."

I shut the door, paper in hand, and fall against the wood with a smile on my face. One of my golden rules is not to date where I sleep, but I still appreciate that my new hottie neighbor is easy on the eyes. He might know it, but he doesn't seem arrogant.

I lock the door and get ready to leave.

Los Angeles is hot, smoggy, and grey at this hour and I have a feeling it won't be much different a few hours from now. I close the patio door and lock it, double checking for safety. After pulling the drapes closed, I take one last look around to make sure I'm not forgetting anything. I text Tracy and let her know I'm leaving. She doesn't reply, but I'm not surprised. Her boyfriend proposed last night after six years of dating. Being the kind boss and friend I am, I let her out of this trip, so she could spend the weekend with their families to celebrate the engagement.

There are selfish reasons as well for letting her off the hook. I really don't think I can handle hours of sitting in the car with her as she reads bridal magazines and plans every detail of her big day. After too many dud dates in the last couple of months, I'm not in the right frame of mind to plan her happily ever after.

With my garment bag in one hand and my suitcase in the other, I click the button, disarming my car's alarm as I walk to my parking space. I've lived here a couple of years. I wanted a place near the beach that also had space for my office, and I was fortunate enough to find both in this townhome.

A meme I created went viral three years ago this month. Who knew a snarky-mouthed fruit would be the way I make my fortune. I took it though and ran with the brand, building it into a small empire I named Limelight. The company is lean and I keep my costs under control. My fortune has grown by a few million in the last year alone.

I back out onto the street and take the scenic route, one block up to the beach. Driving slowly along with my windows down, I let the sound of the waves and the smell of the ocean center me. At the first stoplight, I take one deep salty air breath, roll the window back up, and leave for Vegas.

An hour into the trip, Tracy calls. I answer, but before I have a chance to speak, she asks, "Can I please tell you all about it again?" Happy laughter punctuates her question.

"Of course. Tell me everything." I'll indulge her wedding fantasies because that's what friends do... and because I have four hours to kill in the car. Listening to her takes my mind off the time and the miles stretching ahead of me as she relives every last detail of the proposal. Fortunately for me, she skims over the engagement sex.

Her excitement is contagious and because I've known her and her fiancé, Adam, for so many years, my happiness exudes. "Congratulations again."

"Thank you for letting me stay home this weekend. You'll be great and don't be nervous. It's just a rah-rah go get'em presentation and cocktail party. The rest of the time is all yours."

"You know how much I hate these kinds of events."

"You don't have to prove anything to anyone. Your company's success speaks for itself."

"Thanks. I'll try to remember that."

"Drive safely and squeeze in some fun."

I laugh. "You know I'll try. Bye." When we hang up, I turn on some music and let the miles drift behind me.

After a stop for gas half-way and a coffee later, I enter the glistening city in the desert. Pulling up to my hotel, I valet my car and take my own luggage to my room after checking in. I like this hotel because of the amenities, but the men aren't bad to look at either—a little edgy, a lot sexy—lucky for this single girl.

I spend a couple of hours checking emails and work on a proposal before I realize the time and need to get ready for the night. It's Vegas, so I mix business with some sexy. I pull on a black fitted skirt that hits mid-thigh, an emerald green silk camisole with spaghetti straps, and a short black jacket. I slip on my favorite new pair of stilettos and after one last check of my makeup and hair, I head out.

The meet and greet isn't long, but I slip out at one point to use the restroom. As I'm walking back toward the ballroom, I'm drawn to a man standing with a group of people nearby. His magnetism captures me. He might just be the best looking man I've ever seen—tall, dark hair, strong jaw leading me up to seductive eyes aimed at me. His head tilts and for a split second in time, everyone else disappears. I break the connection by looking away, everything feeling too intense in the moment. When he laughs, I add that to his ongoing list of great attributes.

When I pass, the feel of his gaze landing heavy on my backside warms my body. With my hand on the door, I pause, wanting to look back so badly. I resist the urge, open the door, and return to the party. The presentation portion of the evening is interesting. Despite that, my thoughts repeatedly drift back to the hot guy in the corridor—fitted jeans, black shirt, leather wristband. *Damn I'm weak to a leather wristband.*

I'm mentally brought back to the presentation when my company is recognized as one to watch. The acknowledgement is nice, and it feels good to be among my peers.

The dinner becomes more of a party as everyone wanders around instead of taking their seats. I'm not hungry and need to psych myself up to mingle. Tracy is awesome in these types of situations. Me, not so much.

The ballroom is dimly lit, I'm guessing to set the ambiance, but since this is business, I can do without the romance. I head straight for the bar just like everyone else—one big cattle call to the liquor to make the rest of the night a little more bearable.

"I usually hate these things," I hear from the guy behind me. When I look over my shoulder, he gives me a half-smile—half-friendly, half-creepy. "But they don't usually have attractive women either."

I roll my eyes while turning my back on him and his cheesy pick-up line.

"I'm sorry. That was bad. I know," he says with a weird nasally laugh.

His breath hits my neck and I jerk back. "Do you mind? Ever hear of personal space?"

"Sorry. You're just really pretty." He shrugs as if that makes everything better. "Your beauty is making me stupid."

"You think?" *Big mistake.*

He actually takes my sarcastic comment as a conversation opener. "Yes, I do. But I can't be the first to be dumbfounded by your beauty."

Standing on my tiptoes to see how many more people are in

front of me, I exhale, disappointed by the long line. One person in line would have been too many at this point. "Excuse me," I say and slip out of line. I find the table with my name tag on it, set my purse down, and take off my jacket. This hotel ballroom is crowded and too warm.

Saved by a friendly face, I see Cara, a marketing strategist I know from L.A. Weaving between the tables, I sit down in a chair next to her. With her eyes focused on the paperwork in front of her, I ask, "Working during the party?"

She looks up, smiling when she sees me. Opening her arms, she leans in and hugs me. "Holli, it's so good to see you."

I went with a different company than hers for a campaign a while back and glad she's not holding it against me. "Good to see you again."

"Congratulations on your success. Well deserved."

"I'm not sure if a smartass lime deserves the success it's gotten, but I'll take it."

She taps my leg. "You deserve it. It's funny and quite catchy. Just take the accolades."

"Thanks."

Looking over my shoulder, she leans in and whispers, "I'm skipping out of here early, but I'm meeting a few people for dinner tomorrow. If you're still in Vegas, you should join us."

"I'd love that. Thanks."

She stands up and grabs the papers in front of her. "Fantastic. I'll text you the details tomorrow. I'm so glad we ran into each other."

"Me too. See you tomorrow."

I'm left sitting alone. When I look around the room, like Cara, I'm thinking that skipping out early might be the way to go. If I do, I know Tracy will kick my ass, so I decide to suffer and give this party one last chance. But I definitely need a drink and the line for the bar in here is still way too long.

I head for the doors to buy a drink in one of the many hotel bars—any bar without a line. Guy from the bar line jumps in front of me as I try to exit, startling me. "Hey, hey, hey. You're not leaving already, are you?"

Since my glare and earlier hints didn't work, I reply, "I'll be back, no need to worry yourself."

His head starts bobbing up and down, confidently, and a big Cheshire cat grin covers his face. I start walking again as he keeps talking... again. "Cool. I'll see you later then."

I feel no need to respond to the come on, and will try to avoid him when I return. Following the wide-tiled path through the casino, which reminds me of the Yellow Brick Road, guiding me to what feels like Oz, a bar in all its gloriousness with no lines in site. Inside the darkened room, the sounds of the casino fade away as current hits play overhead. Still on a mission for a cocktail, I step up to the bar and wait.

2

"I've enjoyed a drink or two. Alcohol gives you perspective without the lecture." ~Johnny Outlaw

Leaning his palms on top of the sleek black bar, the bartender smiles, and asks, "What can I get you, beautiful?"

Dressed in a button up and vest, he fits right in with the vibe of the bar. His smile is flirty and I bet his looks work well for him and often, but not on me tonight. After the jackass in the ballroom, I'm in no mood for another BS line, and just order my drink, "An Old-fashioned with extra orange please."

"Coming right up. But first, I'll need to see your ID. *Please.*" He flashes his smile again, bright white teeth, as if that will ease the blow that I'm still being carded at my age.

I reach down to my lap for my purse, then look back up to the bar top, and to the floor under my feet. *Shit!* I left my purse at the table in the party. Holding my finger up, I start to stand, and say, "I left my purse in one of the ballrooms. I need to go get it."

"Don't worry about it," he says with a lazy shrug. "It's cool. I trust you."

I sit back down and say, "You can charge it to my room."

"Sure thing."

"Rules are made to be broken, but laws, breaking laws can get you into a lot of trouble. Hate to be a dick, but I'll need to see your ID." Two barstools down from me, the hot guy from the corridor sits smugly with a cocked up eyebrow and a wry grin firmly in place.

Stunned, I tilt my head to the side and ask, "Are you being serious?"

He puts his hand up when the bartender starts to protest. "I'm undercover and if she's underage, your ass is going to jail." Turning back to me, he says, "Dead serious."

"You're a cop?" I ask, eyeing him again. He's clearly too hot to be a cop, so I'm taken aback by his tone because he actually seems serious. "You don't look like a cop."

"I didn't say I was a cop. The hotel hired me. Now about that ID..."

I take the time to look him over before I give into his demand. Up close, I can see his shirt is tailored by the way it fits, his hair is messy in that sexy, just rolled out of bed way, and there's a lightness to his eyes that leaves me wondering if they're green or blue. It's hard to tell in this dark bar.

The bottoms of his jeans are a bit frayed, and he's wearing brown Doc Marten's—not the boots—naturally distressed, not bought that way.

He's an arrogant son-of-a-bitch, but I'm starting to think that small dimple in his chin gives him that right. It really is kind of hard to resist, and emphasizes just how intriguing he really is. Not how I usually imagine hotel security.

"You're really going to make me walk across the hotel to get my ID just to prove that I'm older than twenty-one? Do I look that young?"

"It's Vegas. I can't be too careful. Wouldn't want this bar to lose their liquor license."

"Fine." I quirk an eyebrow. "I've got nothing to hide, but you're buying the drinks if I have to walk to that ballroom and back just for you."

"Get to walking, sweetheart" he says with a nod and a smirk.

Huffing, I slide off the stool and start to leave, but I can feel him watching me. I can feel it. I stop and glance back. "Does your job also include watching my ass as I walk?"

"Nope" He's rubbing his thumb over his bottom lip and winks. "Just a perk of the job."

He almost had me with that bottom lip action, but he lost me with the wink. I roll my eyes and continue out the door and through the casino, regretting wearing these shoes and this tight skirt to the event tonight. Even after giving them a rest at the bar, my feet still hurt.

Walking back into the dimly lit room, I go straight to the table and grab my purse. When I turn to leave, Mr. Relentless is standing there with a flask in one hand, and is apparently drunker by the way he sways to the side. "You're back," he says. "I knew you'd want me."

"Real charming," I reply. "Now excuse me." I duck too fast for a drunk, which means I move at my normal pace, side-stepping around him, and rush back out into the main casino where the sounds of slot machines take over. When I enter the bar again, the bartender smiles as he dries a glass.

Hot dimple guy reaches forward when I flash the license. I start to hand it to him, but with my own smartass smirk, I show the bartender instead. The bartender eyes the other guy and then hands the ID to him for his approval.

Needing a cocktail more than ever, I ask, "Can I get my drink now?"

"Sure," he says, and gets to work.

"Happy?" I ask the guy with my license. He's rolled his sleeves up and his well-defined arms draw my attention to a pin-up style hula girl tattoo. The coloring is faded, revealing there's a history there. While he analyzes my card, holding it up at different angles like he expects it to be a fake, I'm left fascinated watching the hula girl move rhythmically with his muscles.

He looks up from my license, all cocky with a wry grin, and a waggle of the eyebrows that I find sexier than I should. "Very happy, Holliday Hughes. Thanks."

Right then I figure out what game is being played and I get pissed that I fell for it. Although I'm facing the bartender, the other guy knows I'm talking to him when I say, "You could have just asked me my name." Somewhere along the line he crossed over from doing his job to enjoying the fact that he knows my details—*all of them*—including my weight or the lie I told them at the DMV.

Sitting back, he seems to be enjoying this way too much, and asks, "What's the fun in that?"

"It's called etiquette, not fun."

"Depends on which end you're on—"

"The receiving end of your bad pickup line is lacking the finesse I prefer in a date."

"So I'll start over."

I swivel in my chair and eye him up. "Start with the truth. Did the hotel really hire you?"

He smiles. "Yes, they did."

There's an innocence to his smile and an honesty to his tone that makes me drop my guard... just a little. "Okay. What's with the hula girl tattoo? Someone you know?"

He takes a swig of his drink before answering, "Maybe somebody I'd like to know—"

"Maybe somebody you hooked up with once."

That makes him laugh. It's a good laugh, deep and real, sounding a little raw. "Maybe," he says, making me smile.

"That's two maybes and no real answer."

"The truth?" When he asks this, I take the opportunity to get another good look at him. Even in the low light his hair is dark. It's not quite black, more like a really dark brown.

"No, lie to me."

"You're a hard ass, you know that?"

Keeping my eyes steady on his, I say, "You should know since your eyes basically felt up my backside a few minutes ago."

The drink is set down in front me, but Mr. Tall-Dark-Hottie security guy says, "Put it on my tab."

"Yes, sir," the bartender replies.

"You didn't have to do that."

"Wasn't that part of the deal? If you showed me your ID, I'd buy the round?"

I notice a small scar near his right eye. Makes me curious to how he got that little imperfection. I'm so used to the pretty boys of L.A., that to see a real man is a total turn on. Feeling too much for this guy already, I direct my focus and scan the bottles lined against the back wall, choosing to tease instead. "You're mocking me."

"No, I'm buying you a drink and if you'd let me, maybe *more*?" The insinuation of his offer is not lost on me.

"Just like that? You give me a hard time. I give you a hard time, then you want to buy me *more*?"

With a nod, he says, "Exactly like that."

"I don't even know your name, so *more* than a drink might be a bit presumptuous."

He sticks his hand out. "Jack Dalton. I was named after my dad's favorite writer and there are rumors," he says, lowering his voice and looking around before his eyes land back on mine, "that we're distantly related to the Dalton Gang. It's nice to meet you."

"Jack Dalton." A warmth covers my cheeks and down over my chest when our hands touch. It's ridiculous that at my age I still blush, but I do and I might be falling for his overly-confident act, something I would never do back in L.A. "So you're an outlaw, huh?"

Dropping the smile, he looks away briefly, as if checking the surroundings for eavesdroppers. His expression lightens when he turns back. "I guess you could say that, but I prefer Jack."

"Jack. I like Jack, but I think I'll call you Dalton. Seems more fitting."

Chuckling, he says, "I can handle that." He takes a sip of his drink, then looks me over. "Holliday is a beautiful name."

My heart starts to race from his sweet words and the sincerity in his eyes. "My mom was a little quirky. I think she heard it on a soap opera once or a Christmas special. My friends call me Holli. It's more normal."

"Normal sounds boring and there's nothing boring about you."

There's still a barstool between us, but I find his charm

enticing and lean a little closer. "Thanks. Guess Holli just seems easier."

Taking a sip of my cocktail, the ice shifts. He doesn't take his eyes off me. I feel him watching even when I'm not. The moment of silence between us is filled by the music changing, a new song starts playing and I listen, enjoying it. "I love this song. Have you heard it?"

His head tilts up and he listens for a second then shakes his head. "This band sucks."

Running my fingertip over the lip of the glass, I say, "I think there are a million women who would argue otherwise."

"Maybe more," he adds, chuckling.

"Probably. The Resistance is very popular. You don't like their music?"

He leans in, taking a quick peek around, then says, "I heard the lead singer is a total asshole."

Intrigued, I whisper, "Really?"

Spreading his arms wide, he says, "Big ego."

"Seems like that happens a lot when people get too rich and too famous too fast."

"Yeah. I can see that." He takes a couple of sips, then asks, "Would you like another drink?"

"I'm good. Thanks." I shift, wondering if I should return to the party. But when I steal another glance, catching sight of his strong jaw and broad shoulders, I decide to stay a little longer. He's much more interesting than anything that ballroom holds tonight anyway. "Are you working all night?" I ask.

"Some of it."

When I slip off the stool, there's a sudden panic in his eyes. I quickly reassure him... because I'm having too good of a time not to. "I'm going to use the ladies room."

He nods, looking straight into my eyes. "You're coming back?"

"Yeah." Turning on my heel, I say, "I'm coming—" I'm grabbed, a loud gasp escaping me before I finish my sentence. My purse falls from my hands, landing on the barstool from the sudden commotion.

"I've been looking for you. You're a tough girl to track down," Drunky from the party slurs, the alcohol on his breath hitting me in the face as his hand tightens around my arm.

It all happens so fast, the commotion just a blur. One second I hear a barstool scrape loudly against the hardwood floor, the next Dalton is standing in front of me and the drunk has released my arm. Dalton warns, "Don't touch her again."

With his hands up in surrender, the guy says, "Back off, buddy. I didn't mean to scare her. I was just happy I found her after searching the casino. So excuse me while I buy her a drink." His eyes meet mine over Dalton's shoulder and he adds, "Or we can get a nightcap in my room. I paid for the upgrade and the view is great."

I see Dalton steal a glance my way when I answer, "No."

"Just no?" the guy asks, astonished. "You're not giving me a reason? I thought we were sharing something special in there." His head bobs a little—losing his common sense to the booze. If he's invited to this conference, he's a successful businessman, but he can't hold his liquor worth shit and he needs to learn some manners.

"You need to walk away while you still can," Dalton says, unflinching.

Holy shit. Dalton's protecting me. I've never had anyone stand up for me like that before. I'm instantly drawn closer to him, grabbing hold of the back of his shirt with one hand, his arm with the other. Feeling brave, I say, "I don't owe you a thing."

"What a little bitch. You're a tease just like the rest of th—"

"You have your answer," Dalton says, his words a snarl that vibrates his chest.

The confrontation I was trying to avoid is now in full swing. After a heated moment of hard glares between the two of them, the drunk looks away. "Whatever, Asshole," he spews. In his haste to take a shot at Dalton, he stumbles, spilling the remainder of his drink on him. "You can have her. She's a fu—"

Dalton doesn't back down though his shirt is wet. Standing strong and tall, his eyes locked on the other guy. "You should walk away while you still can," Dalton says, keeping his voice low between us. "Because if you finish that sentence, you'll be leaving on a stretcher. Your choice."

Two large security guys walk up behind him, but they wait. After a few more profanities, the guy meanders off without another word, out the door and disappears into the crowded casino.

A camera flashes in the corner of my eye and I lower my head toward Dalton, hoping the camera wasn't aimed at us. I'd hate to end up in an online story saying I got into a bar fight.

"C'mon, we're leaving," he whispers, taking possession of my hand. Moving fast, he tosses a large bill on the bar and tells the security guys, "Thank you for your assistance."

Our fingers lace naturally, his grip tight, confident, but intimate. Looking down at me, he asks, "Now that you know my name and the fact that I might be related to criminals, how about that *more* we spoke about earlier?"

I grab my purse, anxious to see exactly where 'more' leads me. "Okay," I reply, not putting up much of a fight... *or any fight at all.* Maybe it's because I just gave him the answer he wants or maybe it's because he feels he might get to second base, but his arrogant smile is becoming less cocky and more endearing the more time I spend with him.

On the way out, whispering is heard throughout the bar. *"Is that who I think it is?"* The chatter makes me paranoid. I'm not used to the attention and it's unsettling. Tracy says I need to get used to being in the limelight the more PR I do, but I'm not there yet.

Dalton notices when I tense, and asks, "Everything alright?"

I shake it off. "Yeah, everything's fine."

He leads me out and around the walkway to the right instead of through the casino. While riding the escalator, I feel the need to say something. "I'm sorry about that jerk."

"Not your fault. No need for sorries." He gives my hand a little squeeze.

At the top, we take a right toward a security guard behind a podium. Dalton doesn't flash his room key like I've had to do every time I come back to my room. I guess since they both work for the hotel, they know each other. The guard smiles at him and tells him to have a nice night. Dalton returns the gesture, but keeps walking until we stop in front of an elevator. He pushes the button and the doors open immediately.

When we step inside, I ask, "Are you taking me to a hotel room?"

"Yes," he replies, still holding my hand. "I want to spend time with you privately." With his other, he inserts the key card into the slot, then waits to push the button. "Are you okay with that?"

"Yeah." Maybe I should've said no, but when he pushes the button for the top floor, I let it ride just like in roulette "I don't do one-night stands," I announce with my chin in the air. *Anymore*, I add silently.

His eyes meet mine and there's a vividness to them, a sly happiness shining in the green. *Ahhh, green.* "Who said anything about just one night?"

3

"The ones who anger you the most may turn out to be your most trusted ally." ~Johnny Outlaw

If the doors hadn't opened right then, distracting Dalton's eyes away from mine, he would have seen my jaw hit the elevator floor. He walks, but gets jerked back when my feet stay firmly planted inside the vestibule. When he looks at me, he laughs. "I was kidding." He raises his eyebrows, his eyes reflecting his mischievous side. "Unless you don't want me to be."

My breath deepens as a debate sparks inside. I shouldn't be doing this, but he's too damn enticing not to.

The worry creasing his brow disappears when I step forward, but he teases, "Just so I'm clear. Do you want me to be kidding or you don't want me to be kidding about the one night?"

I walk past him with a determination in my stride, and casually reply, "I need food. Let's order dinner and go from there."

When I look back, his smile returns. "That sounds good." He rubs his stomach, his T-shirt lifting just enough for me to catch a glimpse of hard abs and a sprinkling of dark hair that leads to naughty and stimulating places. "I can eat."

Failing to mention he was taking me to a penthouse suite, I have to ask, "How do you have access to the penthouse?"

"Perks of the job." Double timing his footwork to get in front of me, he opens the door wide and waits. "After you."

I hesitate just outside the door, peeking into the large suite. "You sure do get a lot of perks." One glance at Dalton and his words from earlier tonight run through my mind. Rules are meant to be broken—*maybe he's someone worth breaking them for.*

The penthouse is bigger than most apartments in L.A. Definitely bigger than the last one I had and maybe even my townhouse.

Dalton disappears into a bedroom off to the side, but I remain by the front door, a little nervous to disturb the opulence. When he returns, he's changed into a dry T-shirt with sleeves that have shrunk up a little more on one side than the other. Two more tattoos are partly revealed—one is a number, the other is the bottom of a flag. He walks out onto the crescent-shaped balcony and grabs a cigarette from a pack on the table. With the cigarette in his mouth, he glances at me over his shoulder, and asks, "You have a light?"

I shake my head, and ask, "You smoke?"

"Bad habit. I know, but I picked it up a long time ago."

"Can you quit?"

"Anytime."

His confidence is sexy, but still makes me skeptical. "Really? Anytime?"

"Sure. Yeah, I might get the shakes from the withdrawals and gain a few pounds, take up the bottle to replace one bad habit with another, but yeah," he says, shrugging, "I can quit."

I want to say so much to that smartass reply, but I think he needs the cigarette after that rant, so I'll let him smoke in peace.

After blowing the smoke into the air, he leans against the railing and adds, "Sorry."

"No need for sorries," I repeat his phrase from earlier tonight. "I get it. I wasn't lecturing, so you know. I was just curious." I stand and walk to the kitchen and search for a glass, thinking I need the distraction.

I fill a glass with water and stand at the kitchen counter, taking sips, and beginning to doubt my decision to come here.

He approaches from behind and presses his chest against my back. I try to control my swallow, but I'm sure he hears my gulp.

His lips touch the top of my bare shoulder and he kisses me gently, causing me to swallow hard again. Fingertips tap against my skin, then drag the spaghetti strap of my silk top to the side until it drops. When it comes to bad boys, I've always been a sucker when accompanied by a handsome face and sweet gestures. And I have a feeling Jack Dalton is a very bad boy.

When I turn around, his arms trap me and our noses touch, making my heart race. I place my hand on his chest to feel, without him knowing, if he's having the same reaction. His hand covers mine, and he whispers, "I feel it." When I look into his eyes, I see his every intention clearly set, but his words surprise me. "I lied earlier."

"About what?" My tone may not be as comfortable as his, but I keep it low to match the intimacy of the moment.

"When I said I'd replace smoking with drinking. I think you already know I drink since we met at a bar."

He makes me smile. Feeling bold, I move my hand up from his chest and around his neck. "We all have our vices."

"What's one of yours?" His hands are near my waist, his fingertips barely touching me... and I want more.

Looking down, and feeling shy, I reply, "Hot guys with tattoos that I meet at bars on vacation."

When I look back up, he's smiling. "So this is something you do often?"

"Let's not go that far. Makes me sound easy. Oh wait," I say with a devious grin. "I guess I need to confess my own lie now, huh?"

"And what is that?"

"I've had a one-night stand before... maybe even a few."

With laughter edging his tone, he says, "Eh, who hasn't." His warm breath covers my mouth, making my insides swirl in anticipation. I need to slow down before his lips are pressed against mine. Because once that happens, there's no stopping.

"Now about that vice of yours," he asks, "you think I'm hot?"

Wow, he caught that, but I guess that's what I get for opening my mouth. "Yes, I think you're very hot."

"I think you're beautiful, Holliday, and you have a fucking great ass. So it seems I was in the right place at the right time to indulge that vice of yours."

I'm about to say something really clever, but his lips are on mine and the witty comebacks I might have had disappear. His hands grasp my hips tightly as he presses his against mine. There's no hiding his reaction and I begin to hope we can get into a little trouble together. But then his lips still and his hands drop. He pulls back and starts walking away, but I grab his arm before he's out of reach, and ask, "What just happened?"

"I don't think we should do this," he says with his back to me as his hand scrapes through his hair. I release his arm, but he stays. When he turns around, he looks me in the eyes. "You may have had a few one-night stands, Holliday, but that's not how I see you."

"You don't know me." I try to tamp down the defensiveness in my voice.

"I want to."

My eyebrows go up in surprise, revealing everything I want to say without the necessary words.

He crosses his arms over his chest and tilts his head, amused. "What? A guy can't want to know somebody before fucking them?"

"Sounds like your own personal demon."

A heavy sigh escapes him as he stares at me, perplexed. "So you just wanna fuck then?"

Doubt rears its ugly head and I walk around him, keeping my eyes focused on the balcony and the burning cigarette he left in the ashtray out there. I sit down on a chair and kick my feet up on the railing, looking out over The Strip a block away. His footsteps echo as he walks outside, taking a seat on the other side of the table.

"Are we playing games?" I ask, leaning my head back on the chair. I roll my neck to the side, and watch him. "I admit, I thought agreeing to come up here for *more* had the potential to lead to that, but, you got me all worked up and now you're changing the game on me."

"You're from L. A."

The direction of this conversation makes me pause, but then I play along. "I'm from Texas."

He narrows his eyes. "No, you're not."

"I was once."

"But not now."

"No, not now. You know this about me already since you saw my license."

The legs of his chair squeal in revolt as he pulls it forward to lean his elbows on the table, staring at me in analysis. "I don't want to learn about you from a license. I want you to tell me. Where are you from, Holliday Hughes?"

"Why do you need to hear me say something you already know?"

"I want to get to know you from you, the real you."

"Next time, just ask the first time." I look away. When I turn back, I say, "Los Angeles."

He chuckles as if he knew I'd give in and tell him. "That wasn't so hard, now was it?"

"A little painful, but no, not *hard* at all," I emphasize the hard in memory of a few minutes earlier. "How about you? Where are you from, Jack Dalton?"

"You don't know?"

"How would I know?" I touch his shoulder, lifting up his sleeve enough to get a better look at his flag tattoo. "This flag might be a clue," I say, shrugging. "But maybe you just lost the love of your life in the great state of Texas."

"You know, not every tattoo has to be about a girl or lost love."

"So you're claiming they're not?"

"No, not the love of my life, but I lost myself along the way."

"You've got a dark side that creeps out every now and then. Do you want to talk about it?"

"Creeps? Ha! I've got a dark side that slaughters hopes and dreams on a daily basis."

I should be concerned, but for some reason I trust him. "Slaughter is a strong word. What did you once dream of that you're not doing now?"

Getting up from the chair abruptly, he walks to the railing, standing with his back to me. The action feels intentional and hurts a bit. Braving the possible rejection, I join him, covering his hand with mine, but keep my gaze averted to our surroundings. I'd love to read verse upon verse of what makes this man so intriguing, but I fight that instinct and stay silent, letting him answer when he's ready.

He doesn't disappoint, his vulnerability drawing me in once again when he says, "I once dreamed of being a professional ball player."

This is such an unexpected response that he catches me off guard. An innocent dream revealed in the middle of Sin City.

"Don't laugh," he adds, side-eyeing me with a grin.

"Okay, I won't laugh. A little smiling, but no laughing here." I sneak a glimpse of him again, enjoying his playful expression. "I'll share a secret with you since you shared one with me." He leans a little closer as I go on. "When I was a kid, I dreamed of being a fireman, a fire*woman,* technically. I once saw a fireman save a dog from a burning house and I wanted to do that. I knew I could. I was the fastest kid in the fourth grade in the fifty-yard dash. I'd get in, save some lives, and get out. That was the plan. I told everyone I would be a hero one day."

"You still can be."

"How? Do you know someone who needs saving?"

His gaze penetrates deep. "Yeah, I might know someone."

The air is dry, but the atmosphere has thickened. This time I give his hand a little squeeze before dropping mine back to my side.

Tilting his head to the side, he eyes me. "You hungry?"

"Famished."

"Room service okay?"

"You want to stay in?"

He nods. "I like the privacy."

"The suite's not bad either."

"No," he says with a chuckle. "The suite's not bad either."

Inside, I take a seat on one couch and he sits across from me on the other, and asks, "What do you want to eat?"

"Where's the menu?" I look around, but don't see one.

"Anything you want." He moves closer to the phone on the table. "Just name it and they'll make it for us."

"Why do I get the feeling that your job entails more than busting minors trying to score alcohol at the bar?"

He doesn't bother answering, but says, "I'm ordering a burger."

"You can order anything you want, even stuff not on their menu, and you want a burger. Interesting."

"I'm gonna get fancy on you, order cheese on it too. You might want to note that down."

"Noted. I'll take the same."

"A girl who lives in L.A. and eats meat. That's impressive."

"I'm chock full of surprises."

With the phone pressed to his ear, he says, "I just bet you are." He places the order and hangs up. Sliding down the cushion looking exhausted, he closes his eyes. "Thirty minutes. What do you want to do in the meantime?"

Too busy admiring him to respond right away, I follow the hard lines of his arms down over his body. Although he works in security, he's definitely not a donut eating cop. He stays fit and the way the thin material of his shirt stretches across his stomach, I can see a six pack. Might be more, but I'd need a closer lick... er, look, to determine that. I linger, admiring as my gaze rolls over his chest to his jaw again—scruff, cut, strong, and masculine. When I reach his eyes, they're already on me. Catching me in the act, he asks, "Did you ever decide if you wanted me to be kidding or not?"

Here we go again... He sits there, waiting for an answer, so I reply, "In all honesty, it's not what I thought I'd be doing when we left the bar. At least not a hundred percent what I thought we'd be doing."

"We both know I wasn't kidding. Here I sit, across from a beautiful woman in a private suite. I can't seem to take my eyes off her except when I force myself, attempting to keep her from feeling uncomfortable. But she has this delicate curve where her neck meets her shoulder that I can't stop thinking about, curious to what it feels like to trace it with my finger, and then with my tongue, remembering just how sweet her lips tasted." Motioning between the two of us, he says, "Whatever you decide, won't change the fact that you're feeling what I'm feeling."

I release a long held breath, swooning inside while desperately trying to hold onto my sensibilities. All my willpower goes out the window. I stand and walk around the coffee table that divides us, and sit down next to him. With no space left between us—thigh against thigh—I lean forward and press my lips to his. "You remember what I taste like?"

His hands touch my face in such an intimate way, that I feel his warmth in my knees. With a small inch or two between our mouths, his words are just a whisper. "I want you, but there's something about you that makes me want to *know* you even more. That will make it even better when we do *come* together." I catch the double entendre just as his thumb softly grazes across my cheek, tempting me to give into my body's wants, but I look down and his hand falls away.

The back of my legs are pressed to the couch, so I slide to my left, slipping out. I cross my arms over my chest and sigh, loud enough for him to hear. "You mean that, don't you? You really do want to get to know me?"

"I do. I didn't bring you up here to have sex. I know you won't believe me, but I was having fun with you at the bar and wanted more—"

"*More* time?"

"More than a half-hour downstairs."

"I'm confused, Dalton." I walk to the kitchen and take a sip of my water, then say, "I'm not gonna play dumb here. Once I knew we were coming to your room I figured *more* might happen and I wasn't fully against that. We talked and ordered food. Things slowed down, then you started the flirting back up. I start to give in. You pull away. Why am I here? Because I'm not sure anymore."

"I wanted you alone. I wanted you without any eyes on us. I want to get to know you better."

"You make me feel slutty for wanting what I thought we both wanted. You brought me to this fancy penthouse, started talking about where we're from, and long-forgotten dreams. So forgive me if I've read this all wrong, but what you're saying and how you're acting sends two different messages." I walk toward the door. "Maybe I wanted to play," I say, but stop, and look him in the eyes. "But I don't think I want to anymore. I'll let myself out."

"Wait. Don't go. Stay. Whether we have sex or not, I just want your company." His expression appears sincere, but he seems to have several sides to him.

With my back against the door, I keep my eyes on his. "Look. I don't sleep around... much. But I have slept with someone just because it was Wednesday." I shrug. "So I'm not innocent over here, but I work hard and I have a pretty crappy social life because of it. Sometimes it's nice to feel a warm touch that vibrates with excitement instead of a cold one that's battery-operated." I step forward as if I owe him more, more of an explanation, or more of me, I'm not sure. "Judge me if you must, but I'm in Vegas and now officially on vacation. And despite what you may think, I've only had the one drink so far today, so I'm not drunk. I'm a grown woman who appreciates a handsome face and the artistry of a tattoo that has meaning to the person wearing it. I actually thought we'd have dinner and a good time. All that came from somewhere pure, somewhere that now feels dirty, a little tainted. So I'm going now and if one day you find yourself not so lost in Los Angeles, you know my information."

I don't wait for a response or apology. I don't know Dalton well enough to know if he'd offer one anyway. So I go without looking back, passing the room service waiter on the way, and hop in an elevator that's for the exclusive use of the two penthouses.

Half expecting to hear him call after me, my finger hovers over the Lobby button, but I count to ten and when I don't hear anything, I push it. The doors start to close when a hand reaches in, stopping them. Dalton peeks around the corner with a big smile in place, and says, "Can we start over? Stay for dinner?"

"Why?"

"Because I like you. I like your honesty and I don't get much honesty in my line of work."

"You're an undercover narc. Of course you don't get much

honesty. Isn't that why you got into the business?"

A sly smile crosses his face, revealing a small dimple in his cheek. A light sparks from within, reflecting in his eyes, and with a nod of his head, he says, "Come back. I'll feed you and give you the sex you came up here for. Because it's a Friday and while Friday may not be hump day, it's still a damn good day of the week."

My mouth drops open. "The sex? You'll give me the sex because it's Friday?" I roll my eyes while huffing, and then push the lobby button twice.

Stepping inside, he blocks the doors from closing and a buzz is heard from overhead. With his arms stretched wide, he looks into my eyes. "No. I mean, if you want the food that's currently getting cold inside, you can have it. If you want to have sex, let's fuck. You can have anything you want."

The elevator starts buzzing even louder, escalating its level of warning. Dalton spreads his feet apart to hold the doors open and reaches for me. "I'll even call you Holli since that's what you prefer."

He's sexy and when he's flirting with me, even sexier. I can't give in too easily though. I should make a few ground rules, or at least one. "I'll only come back on one condition."

"Name it."

"You still call me Holliday because I like the way you say it. I'm still going to call you Dalton though, because I like the sound of that."

"Deal, Holliday."

I accept his hand and just like the first time we came up here, he holds onto it until we're inside. The same tingle of excitement courses through my veins and I can tell by the smile on his face, he feels it too.

4

"Don't discount foreplay. It's not only about the act itself, but the build up as well." ~*Johnny Outlaw*

"I'm so stuffed," I say, rubbing my belly and moan while sprawled across the couch.

"Told you they make a great burger," Dalton replies from the other couch.

"I could totally sleep right now." I pull a blanket from the back of the couch and cover up before closing my eyes.

"You look comfy. You planning on staying a while... *or even the night?*"

"I'm becoming quite partial to the palace in the sky." I yawn, my food coma coming on fast.

He shuffles around the table and picks me up. My eyes go

wide, and he says, "Let's move this to the bedroom."

He carries me into the room and I don't resist, but I do tease. "You do remember that I have a reputation of being a sex-crazed hussy, right?"

With a hard chuckle, he tosses me onto the fluffy, white bed in the middle of the extra-feathery down comforter. "I'll take my chances. Now hop in." He walks into the bathroom and shuts the door.

I'm not a shy person when it comes to stripping down to my bra and panties. They cover just as much as most bikinis, and living in California, I'm in a bikini quite often. After undressing, I scramble under the covers before Dalton comes back out. I fall back on the mattress with the pillows anchoring my head and attempt to pose all pretty, propping myself up at an angle with my hand behind my head. It feels wonky, but he walks out too soon for me to readjust and try a different position. Eyeing him, I say, "Maybe I shouldn't trust you. What if you were trying to fatten me up all along so you can have your gluttonous ways with me?"

Wearing only a fitted pair of boxer briefs and all of his tattoos finally revealed, he slips under the covers and rolls onto his side, breaking into laughter. "I'd say you watch too many scary movies or read too many fairy tales. If I was your friend, I would have advised you not to come up to my room. As for me, I'm glad you came. At this point, you've had plenty of opportunity to escape; I'm not holding you captive. I would however be disappointed if you left."

"I'm already feeling a little captivated."

"I'm a little captivated myself."

"Just a little?"

"*More* than a little."

"*More* seems to be a running theme between us."

"I like more," he says, looking very relaxed. *"More's* good."

Fighting the shyness sneaking in, I reach over and run my finger over his shoulder—the one with the Texas flag and just below it, the number forty-four which is much smaller. The hula girl is centered right on his bicep. He has a tiger over his heart; it's very detailed and seems familiar, but I can't place where I would have seen it before. "You have three tattoos on this arm and none on your other," I say, noticing.

No long response or explanation. Just a simple reply, "Yeah."

Moving on, I drag my finger over his abs to his other side. He rolls onto his back so I can get a better look at the tattoos on his ribs. Three guns, identical, slanted downward. As I rub my finger over them, I ask, "Did these hurt?"

His eyes follow my finger as I trace. "The guns?" Out of the corner of his eyes, he looks at me. "No. I got them at different times."

"No pain. Impressive."

"I was drunk," he says, "I didn't feel much of anything at the time. The next morning was a total bitch though."

Looking back at the guns—old-fashioned with black barrels and brown-handles—my curiosity is piqued. "What kind are they?"

"They're .45 Colts."

"Why did you get them? What do they represent?"

He smiles—sleepy, but amused. "That's for another time. Are we gonna sleep?"

I move closer and his arm comes around me. "Yes, let's do this and get it over with so I can start that long walk of shame across the hotel to my tower later."

"The walk of sex-less shame? Is that what we're talking about?"

"It's happened before... to someone, not me, of course, until now, but it happens. It's real. The shame and humiliation a girl will carry with her from the rejection associated with a guy tempting her to his room with the insinuation of sex, but instead gets her to eat a huge, delicious cheeseburger and then to top it off, sleep with him, but not the sex sleep but real sleep."

He kisses my forehead. "There's no shame in this."

My cheeks heat and his words make me smile. "None whatsoever."

Then he pulls me closer and we fall asleep...

5

*"It's easy to believe in Hell. It's
Heaven I'm not sure exists."*
~Johnny Outlaw

I snuggle closer, the depth of my dreams becoming shallow as light starts to invade the back of my lids. My senses are enticed by warmth and the scent of comfort surrounding me. My thoughts shift from cloudy to clear as I wake up in Dalton's arms. Peeking my eyes open, I see his handsome face—his eyes still closed, his breath hitting my cheek softly. Details of him come back as his strong arms tighten around me. *Vegas. Convention. Dalton. Works at the hotel. Dinner. Penthouse. Sleep.* I think that about sums up my night. By the shining lights outside streaming in, I check the time. It's only been an hour, but feels like longer. He's cozy.

"I'm glad you stayed," he whispers.

"Mmm." I turn and face him. Dalton has a gentle smile on his face, but his eyes are still closed. He's fighting the reality of dealing with what comes next for us as much as I am. And if we both open our eyes, we have to deal, so I close mine again and snuggle in, enjoying this way too much to give it up just yet.

When I feel a kiss on my forehead, I smile and open my eyes again. "Hi," I say, not sure if anything else fits the occasion.

He leans down really close, looking deep into my eyes, the moment granting us more than lighthearted niceties. His lips press down on mine and I close my eyes again, savoring the feel and enjoying the build-up that has lead to this. But just as I squirm around to free my arms so I can wrap them around his neck, a thought occurs to the contrary. "I thought you said you wanted to get to know me."

"I know you. I know your name, your address, your height, your clothing size, your eye color, your hair color, that you grew up in Texas, and most importantly, that you're trusting me when I haven't earned it. You sleep with your mouth open, which is very fucking tempting," he says, moving his hand to my hip and sliding it back and forth. "And your heart races, even in your sleep, when I touch you right here."

I'd like to say that I stood my ground on the sleeping with my mouth open part, but I'm too distracted by his green eyes and the lustful way he's looking at me. This is what I came up here for in the first place, I remind myself once again. Or is this how I'm justifying having sex with him after meeting him only hours before. So keeping my mouth shut, open, or however he finds it most 'tempting' is exactly what I'm going to do. Lifting up, I kiss him and that is the moment when everything changes...

My wrists are pushed up and held tight above my head as his

body maneuvers on top of me, his eyes locked on mine as my breathing deepens. Every movement is calculated and smooth, covering me in a way that only intensifies my desire. His lips barely touch mine, his voice low and intimate as he whispers, "I want you, all of you. I want to be inside of you and feel the peace you've found, even if just for a short time."

Pushing my head further into the pillow, I pull my arms forward and stroke his cheeks. "I can't battle your demons, Dalton."

He rubs his nose along mine, closing his eyes while I hold him. With his forehead pressed to mine, he says, "Be my angel. Just for the night."

The only answer needed is my mouth on his. He relaxes on top of me as one of his hands explores down my waist over my hip and then back up. My breath catches, proof that he does know me better than I thought. Our initial connection at the bar was not based on depth of character. It was based on attraction. We aren't a couple in love. We're a couple of people in lust where he can be my demon and I'll be his angel for the night.

My lace underwear doesn't block much and his briefs don't hide much. It's almost pointless that we're even wearing barriers, but this is how things are supposed to be. I can't demand more from him, that makes me slutty. If he demands more, that makes him a player. So we move along with the sensations that have been stirred from within. An unseemly moan escapes without my approval and he slides over to the side.

With his arm resting across his head, he glances my way. "You said you didn't want to play games. I don't either. I like you, Holliday. You're gorgeous and your body's rockin', but that lingerie you're wearing is fucking torturing me. I want to rip this fucker," he says, tugging on my panties, "from your body and suck your nipples until they're hard. Then I'll take ownership of your pussy—first with my mouth, then with my cock. So let me ask you, do you want to keep your bra and panties?"

"I—"

"Shhhh." His finger covers my open mouth. I suck it in, swirling my tongue around the tip and then wrap my lips tightly over it. His right eyebrow twitches up once, revealing how much I affect him. I like the power. He centers his expression back onto me, no tells or weaknesses left to be discovered. This is sex in its most raw form—the act itself not a production, but the emotions he's created engulf the room, swallowing us with it. I'm heady with lust and as much as I want to checkmate, his move wins. I want him inside me, filling me just as much as he wants to be there. His voice is controlled, low and serious. "If you say yes to keeping them, I'll be nice. I'll make your fantasy Prince Charming come to life while we make love. But if you say no, I'll rip them to shreds and fuck you so hard you'll never forget I was here," he says as he cups me between the legs and squeezes. "Choose wisely."

"There is no choice. I knew what I wanted when I agreed to come up here." Silence fills the space between us, but I don't just break it, I shatter it into a million tiny pieces when I say, "Rip'em."

I gasp, startled, as my bottoms are ripped from my body, leaving red marks on my hips where the lacey sides were stretched just below my own tattoo. My head drops back, the sting of pain and the pleasure of his desire forging across my body. The bra is ripped down the center, the silk and lace no match for his passion. I smile, admiring how sexy he is, turned on by his strength. The man I met downstairs is not the same one ravaging my body now. Freed from all clothing—the barriers that once divided our desire—I lay bare before him, giving into my own carnal needs.

One swift jump and he's on his feet, his briefs dropping to the floor. He's not shy about his body. He obviously works hard to stay in shape, and I imagine many others have appreciated his efforts. Everything about him exudes experience, a master in the field of sexual stimulation. I'm not a novice and I've learned a few tricks as well as earned a few bedpost notches of my own. Being an attractive single girl in L.A. has its perks, but when my eyes follow the line from his waist down that muscular V to his prominent erection, I realize being a good-looking girl in Vegas is a total windfall tonight.

"C'mere, you," I say, reaching over and grabbing his hand.

With one swift tug, he falls forward, catching himself before he lands flat on the bed. Dalton crawls over me and lengthens his body along mine, then rolls over so I'm on top. "Ride me, Angel."

He stretches his arm to the side and grabs his wallet. Opening it, he pulls a condom out, and tosses the wallet carelessly to the floor. Sitting up, he drags me on his thighs up higher on the bed. After ripping the package open, he takes the condom and rolls it down his cock. He slides back down and lifts me by the hips. The man knows what he wants and I'm happy to oblige.

I'm just about to adjust on top of him when he says, "Wait." He reaches to the nightstand one more time and grabs his phone. Scrolling, he smiles when he finds what he's looking for. With one push of the button, a song I'm all too familiar with begins. I know every word and every riff. "Stairway to Heaven" was the soundtrack to a lot of trouble I got into back in high school. "Led Zeppelin?"

With a smirk in place, he nods. "This is great fucking music."

"Great fucking music or great music for fucking?" I ask as his hands squeeze my breasts.

"Both." He lays back, his hands sliding up the outside of my thighs, and says, "Take me to that place that keeps you from getting jaded. That place where you find peace without the demons destroying everything you thought you wanted. Take me there."

Darkness fills his eyes, his gaze alluding to everything he doesn't have to be any longer. I lift up and sink down on him, my hands pressed flat against his chest, wanting to smother the dark and cover it with light. Slowly rocking back and forth like the tempo calls for, his words lyrics to my ears, invading my thoughts. I drop my head back as his hands grab my hips, holding me down. The resistance causes inner turmoil as my insides begin to coil. Wanting more, my hands fall behind onto his legs, balancing me on top of him as we move against the other.

I let my mind drift with the melody, the fullness of him overtaking all other feelings. The music builds and my body reacts to the rhythm he's creating inside me. The song becomes our anthem, a soundtrack to our moans and heavy breaths.

When I look down at him, his eyes are open, watching me, one hand roaming my body freely. The other caressing my tattooed skin.

The song speaks of winding roads, shadows and souls... I'm flipped onto the mattress. Dalton's inside me again, moving over me. Our bodies become slick with sweat, emotions begin swirling between us. Feelings that this could be more than just one night plant themselves like seeds in the depths of my mind.

I close my eyes to block the thought that I might actually be able to save this beautiful man from his demons. *The here and now. Focus on how amazing this man makes you feel and the passion he puts into every thrust. The here and now.* He pushes my hair back from my cheek and leans down to kiss it. Slowly sliding down my chest, he takes a nipple into his mouth, sucking.

The here and now.

The here and now.

My eyes fly open as a sharp pain shoots across my skin as I realize he bit me.

"You still here?" he asks.

"I'm here," I say, my voice coming in raspy, making me want to clear it, but I resist.

Dalton moves back up, but doesn't break our connection. He's starting to feel like he was always a part of me. His kisses are gentle. I open my mouth and our tongues meet. It's not our first kiss, but this time feels different, more real. The fun of this fling feeling less like a temporary good time, the line blurred along the way.

Running my nails down his back, I stop when I reach his ass and encourage him to start moving again. He does as he moves his hands into my hair and around to the back of my neck, lifting me so my head drops back onto the pillow, leaving my throat exposed to him. His tongue licks me from the base of my neck to my chin. Holding me close, he rolls over placing me on top. Gripping me by my ass, he scoots up the bed, putting his back against the headboard while I straddle him.

I take hold of the headboard and as he tastes the tender skin between my breasts, I fuck him. We make our own music, sounds derived from pleasure and bare skin sliding together.

Wrapping his arms under mine, he holds onto me and slams harder, but I want faster and fight his strength. I can tell he's close just like me. It's his expression—the one that teeters between pain and gratification—that sends me, my orgasm hitting hard and I cry out his name. My body trembles around him and he grinds harder. I catch sight of him. He's biting his bottom lip and his eyes are squeezed shut when he calls out, "Angel. Fuck."

Continuing with a few more small gyrates, he holds me just as tight. I rest my forehead against the headboard and bring my hands down to his neck, moving up until I'm cupping his face. Leaning back just enough to look him in the eyes, I see cloudy greens lending themselves more toward hazel in the aftermath of our activities. I kiss his lips. Then again.

And once more.

Dalton holds my face between his hands and brings me lower, closer, and kisses each of my eyelids then my nose, and stops against my lips. "You showed me Heaven," he whispers.

"And you gave me Hell," I reply with a lazy grin.

He smiles and it feels like the most genuine moment we've shared. While I know intimate details about Jack Dalton, I don't know *him* at all. The man is shrouded in mystery and his protective armor is thick. But in this moment, we're just a girl and a guy sharing something special, something spectacular created from our union.

The phone vibrates on the nightstand and he picks it up to read the message. With the phone in hand, he sighs heavily, his gaze drifting back over to the clock beside the bed. Our moment is lost, the façade of whatever cover he gave me earlier back in place. My disappointment was inevitable.

"I need to leave soon and I have to shower," he says, looking away from me.

I remain, still situated on top of him, waiting for his eyes to meet mine. The seconds pass and I don't want to be the cause of any awkwardness.

Lifting up, I swing my leg over and walk to the bathroom.

Trying to sound like tonight didn't change me, I say, "Yeah, no worries. I'll get out of here. Maybe I can borrow your robe?"

"Take the robe. Keep it."

I shut the bathroom door and fall back against it, willing the tears to stay away as I try to swallow down the lump in my throat. I don't understand my emotions being caught up like this. Jack Dalton is not my first one-night stand and he won't be my last. So I need to push away the desire to see him again and get back to my life.

Grabbing the robe from the hook, I put it around me. The collar smelling like Dalton and I find some comfort that I'll have this piece of him and the memories of our rendezvous long after I leave Vegas.

After freshening up, I walk out. No sappy emotions remain dwelling on my face. My normal confidence is back in place. He's got jeans on, hanging low, the fly only half-way buttoned-up. His right arm across his chest as he holds his left shoulder and all signs of light in his eyes are dark like the room. Outside the large, picturesque windows, the Strip still sparkles like it did when I came up here, like nothing has changed.

My torn panties dangle from his hand. Lifting them up, he asks, "Can I have these?"

His voice makes my insides twist. It's deeper and more steady. Very different from the playful tone of earlier, confirming once again that there's more than one side to this paradigm standing before me.

Digging into a conversation of why he wants my underwear is not good for me. They will be sacrificed for my greater mental state and the little bit of dignity I have left. "Keep them." I drop the robe onto the bed, standing there naked before him as he watches me. I take my skirt and slip it up my legs, wanting to show him what he'll be missing. I'm playing a stupid game that I mentally admonish myself for playing, especially after telling him how much I hate games of the heart. I usually lose. I pull my top over my shoulders and let it fall into place before wrapping the robe around me again, tugging the belt tightly at my waist.

I walk out of the bedroom, find my shoes, and slip them on. Grabbing my purse from the coffee table, I'm ready to beeline it out the door, but he's in my way with that same baffled look he had on his face earlier. "This is awkward. Not how I thought it would be at all," he says.

"We're adults here. We knew what we were getting into, so no need for awkward." *It's so awkward.*

"I like you, Holliday."

Putting on a reassuring smile for him, I say, "I like you too, Dalton." I pat him on the shoulder like an old pal, hoping he believes the act.

"You're mad."

"I'm not mad."

"Okay."

He looks down and I repeat what he said, "Okay."

When he looks back up, the greens are clear, but a sadness prevails, "I'd forgotten about this thing I have to do for work... sometimes these meetings run late and—"

Walking forward, I raise my arm and shake it to dismiss the guilt he's feeling. "No, no, no. Don't worry about it." I shrug. "I'm busy anyway tonight, so..."

Right when I pass him, he takes my arm and holds me still as he comes close, really close to me. "This was amazing."

Humor is the defense I use to protect my delicate heart. This time will be no different. "I bet you say that to all your one-night stands."

His hand tightens around my arm, not to hurt, but getting my attention for sure. "I don't. I don't say stuff I don't mean. You're amazing. I want you to stay." He releases me and takes a step back. "I feel like shit for leaving. I don't want to and while I want you to stay, I feel rude asking you to wait for me."

"I appreciate that, but I should go before things get messier than they already are." *Protect my heart.* Our eyes are locked, saying way more than either of us could express with words. The truth lies there. I nod, letting him off the hook, no one needing to feel guilty. "I had fun. Thank you."

Saying anything more seems a disservice to that truth, so I walk out, shutting the door behind me and leaving my heart a little more damaged than it was prior to meeting Jack Dalton. It makes me wonder how a man I just met seems to be making an impact that no one else has in years.

6

"I have a very good life. There are no maybes anymore. The only answer I'm given is yes." ~Johnny Outlaw

The ride down the elevator gives me enough time to get pissed. Jack Dalton is the exact reason I'm single. It's not because I'm unwanted, but because nobody I've met deserves me. Yeah, fuck that. I'm a successful woman. I can take care of myself. So what if that entails using battery-operated assistance sometimes. At least that gets the job done quickly and efficiently without any messed up emotions to go along with it. *Carnal.* That's what a vibrator is—carnal pleasure, nothing more than getting off to feel human again. I can't believe he convinced me I was the one who wanted the sex in the first place. *The sex.* He's already rubbing off on me.

When the elevator doors open, two guys—early twenties—are

standing there. They're cute, but too young for me. The way they're eyeing me reminds me I'm dressed in a robe and high heels. Probably looks like I'm naked underneath.

I grab the collar and tighten it closed at my neck while checking to make sure the knot in the belt is still solid. Backing into the corner, I give them a wide berth to step inside.

As soon as the doors open, I rush out, bobbing and weaving through the slot machines and poker machines, trying to avoid the main walkway since I have no panties on. I feel exposed even with this huge terrycloth robe wrapped around me. Seeing my bank of elevators ahead is like seeing the light. I might have even heard angels singing.

Angels.

Angel. Fuck.

That name, the word itself will haunt me for days if not weeks to come—the way he deemed me his savior, his hope that I could save him. He didn't see me clearly and our time is already up.

Hopping inside another elevator, I hit the button for my floor. The doors start to close and my heart skips a beat wishing Dalton would surprise me, and block the doors from shutting like he did before.

The doors close, and disappointment invades my chest.

The Rolling Stones' "Paint It Black" is playing in the elevator, a song befitting my mood. When the elevator doors open on my floor, Tracy is standing there. "Hi," I say, shocked to see her.

"Well, hi there, stranger," she responds, her suitcase next to her. "I thought I was gonna have to go back to the bellhop station and check my bag."

When I step out, I hug her tight. "I'm so glad to see you. But why are you here? I thought you were celebrating your engagement?"

While hugging me, she says, "I know how much you hate these events and wanted to save you." She releases me and her brows knit together. "I called you several times and looked for you at the party... Why are you in a bathrobe in public?"

I don't have but seconds to come up with an answer she'll consider suitable. The girl has never had a one night stand. Hell, she wouldn't even sleep with her fiancé until they had dated several months. I start walking down the hall to my room. Keeping up with my fast pace, she asks, "Where've you been? Don't tell me you skipped out on the conference."

"No, no. I went. It was great. They even acknowledged the company."

I stick my key card into the slot, and push the heavy door open with my hip.

"So you left early to wander the halls in your robe?"

"Um." Damn, I've got nothing. Oh wait, yes I do. "I was at the spa."

Tracy follows me inside setting her bag down just inside the door. "Okay. It must have been bad or you really needed a break." She walks over to the bed that still looks fresh and flops backwards, lying down. "You mind if I barge in on your weekend?"

"Of course not. I'd love the company."

Rolling onto her side, she props up her head in her hand as I unwrap my robe and toss it onto the bed without thinking.

"You went to the spa dressed like that?"

I look down, and reply, "I went straight from the party. I'm gonna take a shower."

"Sure. I'll settle in unless you want to go back out and party?"

"No, I'm done for the night, but you can if you want. Don't let me hold you back."

I walk into the bathroom just as she says, "No, I'm good. I'm tired from the drive anyway. We have all weekend to party."

When I come out again, Tracy is in her pajamas tucked in bed with her laptop out.

"It's late. You're working?"

"Just catching up from what I missed today while driving."

I climb under my covers, punch the pillow twice, then lay down, looking at her. "So what's the real reason you left L.A.? And don't tell me you did it for my benefit because you missed the event."

She rolls her head to the side, appearing exasperated as she looks at me. "Stop seeing right through me."

I smile. "Well, just know I'm here for you when you're ready to talk about it."

"Thank you, Holli. I know you are and that means a lot to me."

"Goodnight."

"Sweet dreams."

I wake up too early. I can feel it's early and going to bed by eleven always guarantees I'll wake up by five in the morning. I check the bedside clock. 5:05. Damn. I was hoping to sleep in. After changing positions, I try to fall back asleep.

Tossing and turning, worrying about what I did last night and who I did it with owns every thought fluttering through my mind. I get up at six, needing to clear my head. The heavy blackout drapes are closed, and it's dark in the room except for a dim light in the corner. I immediately head over to the curtains and peek out. The sun is starting to rise, a golden glow lights the distant mountains from behind. With amazing things like that existing in the world, it's hard to feel sorry for myself. Life is pretty fucking awesome and I refuse to consider what I did with Dalton a mistake. A lesson, yes, but not a mistake. The sex was way too good to make me feel bad, despite the outcome.

"Holli?" a groggy voice calls from behind me.

I look over my shoulder at Tracy. "Sorry. Did I wake you?"

"Kind of. Why are you up so early?"

"Couldn't sleep." Dropping the curtain closed again, all the light gets trapped back outside. "I think I'm gonna go workout."

She yawns, then mumbles, "Sure. I'm going back to sleep."

After turning on the bathroom light, I dig through my suitcase and find my workout clothes and sneakers. I change quickly and make a fast exit. With my keycard in hand, I head to the hotel gym and spend the next hour rotating between the treadmill, the elliptical, and a stair-stepping machine. The burn in my muscles reminds me of last night, images of being on top flood my mind. Today I'm sore, but I've always relished that feeling. It makes me feel alive, wanted, even pretty. I shouldn't let those kinds of superficial emotions affect my self-esteem, but it feels good to be sexually desired.

Tired and weak from the workout, I search out coffee on the casino floor only to find vacuums humming in between the machines. Vegas is sad at this time of day. So vibrant at night, but so desolate in the morning.

I find the café by the pool and order a latte and an English muffin. Taking a seat at a nearby table, I watch as a few people start to stumble their way to stake claim to a pool lounger with their towel and then disappear again, probably going back to bed.

Standing up, I set my mug down and head back to the room. Even after having coffee, I'm feeling tired again. It's probably as much an emotional exhaustion as a physical one.

Hoping not to wake Tracy, I'm quiet when opening the door. "Good morning, Hols." *Guess she's awake.*

"Morning."

"How was the workout?" She sits up, adjusting her too large of frames for her face glasses to the top of her head. The curtains are open, so I can see everything.

"Good. I think I might shower and go back to bed."

She nods, looking like she's got more on her mind than me working out this early in the morning.

"Spit it out, Tracy."

"I was just wondering something," she starts to say while looking down. "If you were really at a spa last night. It is kind of odd to go straight from a party to get a massage." She looks straight into my eyes.

Damn, she's good. Really good.

"Can we talk about this after I shower? I feel gross." Disappearing into the bathroom without waiting for her response gives me ten extra minutes. I don't like to lie and I'm not really in the mood to play twenty questions, but I'm also not sure if I want her to know about last night either.

When I return to the main room, I have my pajamas back on and slip under the covers.

She's persistent—one of the reasons I hired her. "You don't have to talk about it, reveal any secrets or anything. Just doesn't seem to add up is all."

"I'm going back to bed."

"Alright. Alright. I got the hint, but you know you can trust me, right?"

"I do trust you. Just need a little more time to think things through." As soon as I close my eyes, I hear her clanging around and look up. The delicious smell of bacon hits my senses and makes my stomach growl. "You ordered breakfast?"

"Nope." She shakes her head and takes a piece of bacon from

the plate sitting atop the room service cart. There are several other plates covered with silver domes, a bottle of champagne, orange juice and berries.

I sit up. "You didn't order room service?"

"Nope, I didn't."

"I can assume that this food did not magically appear. It was delivered while I was in the shower?"

"You would assume right though it felt pretty magical since I didn't order it."

"If you didn't order it, then who did?"

She holds a note in the air and with a mouth full of bacon, waves it around. "Good question. Maybe we should ask your secret admirer since he sent it to you."

Jumping to my feet, I immediately snatch the card and jump back in bed, huddling under the covers. I flip it open and read: *Here's hoping fresh starts can replace bad endings. One more chance? D.*

"Who's D?" Tracy asks.

I try to distract. "Why'd you leave L.A.?"

Watching her, she sets the lid back down and walks to the window. With her arms crossed over her chest, she says, "Like you, I need a little time to process something." When she turns and looks back at me, I nod. "Thank you for understanding." She takes a deep breath and releases it, her whole demeanor changing and a smile appears. "I'm gonna catch some desert rays. Get some rest or join me by the pool... or maybe even give this D another chance."

I laugh. "That's the bacon talking."

Shrugging, she says, "I'm weak to bacon. What can I say?"

"Who isn't? Toss me a piece please."

She does, then goes to the bathroom to get ready. From

across the room, I stare out the large window, Vegas coming to life outside of it. Five minutes later, she's out the door and I'm left lying in bed with a handwritten note card pressed to my heart. Flashes of Dalton biting his lower lip as he came comes to mind. And just like in the bar last night, I find him impossible to resist.

7

*"Regrets? Sure I have them, but
doesn't everyone. I don't think I'd
change anything if I could though.
Some things are meant to be. You just
don't find out until much later."*
~Johnny Outlaw

It's amazing what bacon can do. It actually makes me forget how mad I am at Dalton. I owe him a thank you. The man did send me breakfast, after all.

After slipping on jeans, a T-shirt, and flip flops, I tuck my room key into my back pocket. I grab the cart of food and wheel it down the hall, down the elevators, through the casino, and up another elevator to the podium where the guard stands protecting his set of guest elevators. I stop in front of the security guard. "I want to deliver this to Jack Dalton's room."

Scrolling down his screen, he looks back up and asks, "Name?"

"Holliday Hughes."

"You're cleared. Go ahead." He follows me to the elevator. When it opens, he sticks his keycard in the slot and presses the penthouse button. "Have a nice day."

The doors close, reopening on the penthouse floor. I continue my journey and push the cart of food to his room. With a solid knock on his door, I hold my breath. I'm trying not to freak out from the anxiety of being back here and the possibilities of what might happen once I walk into that suite again. I see the peephole go dark and then hear the bolts undone. The door swings wide and Dalton smiles. "I didn't order room service."

Leaning my head to the side, I return his smile, and ask, "You sure about that?" I start to pull the cart backwards, teasing him. "I can take this away if you're not interested." I shrug for emphasis.

"Oh, I'm interested alright. I'm very interested. Now get in here." He pulls the cart through the door and I follow him inside. The door shuts and he pins me against it, his arms trapping me, his lips just a quick breath away from mine. "I'm sorry," he whispers. "Will you forgive me?"

"No sorries, remember?" His hand leaves the door and slides into my hair, tilting my chin up. His lips touch mine, feather light. No kiss, just breaths exchanged; my chest rising against his with each taken, falling away when released.

I react with a shiver, pressing my hands hard against the door to keep from ripping his clothes from his body and ravaging him. I silently count to ten to calm myself.

One.

Two.

Three.

Four.

Five.

Six.

Seven.

Eight.

Nine.

Ten...

In a flurry of frenzied desire, my arms wrap around his neck, my legs around his waist, and my lips smother his instantly. Pushing forward, he presses his body against mine, my back slamming against the door with a loud thud. His hands hold me by the ass, my body still wrapped around his, and he turns. Maneuvering to the couch, he drops me down and strips his shirt off. I do the same, dropping mine to the floor.

Crawling over the arm of the couch, he pushes my knees apart and settles between my legs, his erection pressing against me. Looking down at my body and back up to my face, he says, "I don't know why you insist on wearing bras. Your tits are too fantastic to keep hidden from view."

I giggle. "You want me to show my tits off in public and get arrested?"

He doesn't laugh. Instead, he thrusts hard between my legs and replies, "I'm feeling quite possessive over your tits actually. So let's agree that they're not for public consumption. They're only for me."

"Only for you," I repeat, lifting up enough to unfasten the clasp and take my bra off.

Dropping lower, his bare chest slides against mine, the heat magnified when he kisses me hard, taking my breath away along with any willpower to say no. Our feet hang off the end of the couch, my knees still draped over the arm, but he still manages to balance on top of me.

Dalton's hips begin to move, deliberate thrusts hit me just right and I pull back to take in air. The feeling overwhelms when his hands squeeze my breasts as his mouth tastes my neck. I begin moving, needing, wanting, craving the sensation that's building. Holding him tightly to me, I move with him, against him, despite him, because of him. I do everything to keep this feeling alive and growing inside. "God, please," I beg for more.

We lose time to kisses and strokes, thrusts, and moans. Thrusts go from gentle and rocking to harder and erratic, uneven like his breath in my ear. "I'm so close." His voice is just a murmur.

"Close. So close," I say, encouraging him to keep going, to keep creating the magic between us.

"Shit!" His words are harsh, but his hands are gentle while kneading my breasts. His grip tightens and he pushes three times.

The seam of my jeans rub and I succumb, giving into him, and come. A moan, the only credit offered him for giving me such pleasure. It seems to be enough as he lays heavy on top of me, relaxed, and happy. A small smile tugs at the corners of his mouth and he laughs lightly. "We just made out like teenagers."

While he rests his head on my chest I run my fingers through his hair lackadaisically. "Yes, we did. I liked it."

When he lifts up, he looks me in the eyes, and says, "I liked it, too."

I caress his cheek and smile, admiring how his face looks even more handsome when calm and relaxed. "You're very charming, Jack Dalton."

"Not always. I want a redo on how things ended last night."

"I thought we just did or re-did?"

The right side of his mouth curls up, his brow rising with it. Pushing up and off of me, he stands at the end of the couch and offers me a hand. "You came back?"

He pulls me to my feet, our bodies landing together as we stand. "I really had no choice. You sent me bacon... and I had a bra in need of ripping. By the way, I'm a bit disappointed about it still being in one piece." I drag a finger down his nose and tap him on the chin before I slip to the side and head for the bathroom.

"Ripping can be arranged. I thought you might be running low on bras in your suitcase though. So the sacrifice was made on my part because I chose to be a gentleman, but we can change that now if you'd like."

"You're so cocky," I say, laughing.

Just before I close the bathroom door, I hear him call from the living room. "That's what they all say."

"Ha!" I just bet they do since that cock of his is not lacking in any way, shape, or form.

8

**"I choose to stay out of the limelight.
Ironic, considering the name of my
company."** *~Holliday Hughes*

"What are you doing in here?" I ask, walking out of the bathroom to find Holliday sprawled under the sheet on the bed. She, at least, had the courtesy to leave her tits exposed for me.

"I'm sleepy." She acts dramatic, putting the back of her hand against her forehead and sighing. "You wore me out."

"And here I thought we were just getting started."

Her head pops up. "What? Started. No. I'm too tired. After last night and then, you know, the teenage make-out session we just did in there... I need rest. You don't?"

"I always need sleep, but I've gotten used to the lack of it over the years." I climb into bed next to her. The long night taking its toll on me. I wrap my arm around her, her skin soft and warm against mine as she snuggles close.

"What time did you return to the room last night?" She tilts her face toward mine, her eyes wide with innocence, so unsuspecting. *I fucking love it.*

"Right before I ordered you breakfast."

Her body tenses momentarily and I know her mind is searching, trying to determine what time that might be. Her heavy gulp gives her away. "Thank you for doing that. You didn't have to."

"I wanted to. I'm glad I did. Honestly, I thought I'd never see you again."

"Me too," she says with a soft laugh. Her tone changes. "So you were out all night?"

She tries to put some distance between us, but I hold her tighter. "It's not what you think. I wasn't with another woman." When I feel her body relax, I explain more, but just enough to keep her in the dark a little longer. I like how things are too much to ruin it. "It was business, strictly business. But part of that business is going out, so we went to a few clubs."

"Going out to clubs? So you bust minors all over Vegas? I thought you only worked for this hotel."

I stroke her hair back and kiss her forehead. "My job is complicated. Hey, I thought you were tired?"

Her fingertips scrape lightly across my chest, drawing figure eights, which reminds me of her tattoo and how fucking sexy it is on the curve of her waist. Definitely unexpected from how I first sized her up at the bar—defensive and a little prissy, but a cool calm surfaced once she let her guard down. Her feisty attitude was unexpected in more ways than I first imagined... all in good ways.

She yawns, then says, "I am tired and don't have enough brain cells right now to work through complicated, so I choose sleep."

"Ugh!" My eyes bolt open and start burning from the lack of sleep as something hits me in the stomach, waking me from my dreams.

"Get up, you lazy fuck." Dex says, walking toward the door. "We have soun—"

"Shh!" I don't know what time it is, but I recognize the annoying voice. Holliday stirs, her breath shows she's teetering between sleep and awake. I have more plans for her before she leaves, so I want her to sleep for now. I whisper, "I don't know how you got in here, but get the fuck out, Dex."

"Tommy told me to drag your ass down there if I have to."

I glare at him, in no mood for his shit today. "Now you listen to Tommy? You're never on time. I'll be down later."

"Dude, it's a broad." He digs in his pocket and holds up a silver coin. "Dime meet dozen."

A sweet voice from next to me chimes in, "Why is there man in the room?"

Looking down at her, I reply, "Ignore him. He's leaving."

When I turn back to Dex he's holding his hands in front of his chest and says, "Nice jugs."

Holliday gasps in horror and throws the covers over her head. I grab the closest thing I can reach, which is my wallet, and strike him in the face before he even sees it coming. Credit cards and money go flying everywhere, and I yell, "Get the fuck out! Now!"

His hands cover his face and he groans in pain. "Ever since you gave up drugs, you've become such a dick, Outlaw." I freeze when he calls me Outlaw. My heart stops as my gaze drifts to the woman hiding next to me. He storms out of the room and I hear the front door slam.

Holliday peeks out, the sheet covering everything but her eyes. "Is he gone?" She sounds mad, and I'm not sure if it's because Dex was here or because she now knows the truth.

I nod once, my breath caught in my throat still waiting for a sign that she knows.

"He saw my breasts! What the hell? Why was he in here?" She looks pissed, and sounds it as she continues. "I can't believe he barged in here like that and called you a dick. Do you work with him? He should be fired for intruding like that."

"Yeah," I reply, clearing my throat.

My tone must sound off because she looks up at me, her eyebrows knitted together. "Are you okay?"

"Yeah," I repeat my other answer.

"How'd he get in here anyway? That was really unprofessional of a co-worker to barge in like that."

"He needs to learn some manners. I apologize for what he said to you."

"You don't have to. It's all on him. He was rude." She looks past me to the clock next to the bed, and says, "I hate to do this because it's so warm and cozy in this bed with you and I would happily stay here all day if I didn't have someone waiting on me."

She starts to climb out of bed, but I take her hand, tugging her back to me, and ask, "I need to go too, but can I see you later?"

Her expression turns sweet. "I'd like to see you later. I have a meeting to go to and then a dinner I've already scheduled, but I'm free after that."

I can't set a time without going through my schedule of obligations with Tommy first. "Can I have your number? I can text you when I'm done and we can meet up later."

She takes the phone I hand her and types her number in, then gets out of bed. I do too, grabbing some jeans from my suitcase and putting them on. I stop to watch her get dressed, the act more appealing than she realizes. I catch one last glimpse of her tattoo before her shirt tumbles down and covers it.

At the door, she pulls me by the fly, closer, until our lips meet. Licking my lips afterwards, I taste her, realizing she gave me a kiss to remember. Watching her drag her teeth over her bottom lip, I smile, knowing I gave her a kiss she won't forget.

"So you promise to text me?" she asks, so oblivious to how sexy I think she is.

"I will. The moment I'm free. It might be late."

"Late's okay. We're in Vegas, after all."

I open the door for her and she walks out, stepping backward. With her finger pointed at the tray of food she brought over, she laughs, and says, "You owe me another breakfast."

"I think I can handle that."

"Bye, Dalton," she says with a little wave and a smile.

If I didn't have to leave, I'd be tossing her over my shoulder and fucking her again. But I do, so I watch her and that great ass until she reaches the elevator then go back inside to get dressed.

9

Holliday

"Some shows, I walk out on stage and can tell it's gonna be an awesome night. Other times, I leave it to fate to figure out." ~Johnny Outlaw

I should eat because I'm starving, but I want to get back to the room and check on Tracy. The day has disappeared; Time slipped away when I was with Dalton.

When I walk in, she's there, putting on her makeup. She stops and our eyes meet in the mirror, then a smile appears and she says, "So you chose the second chance, I see."

Sitting down on the bed, I flop backwards with my arms wide open. "It might have been a third chance technically. It's hard to keep track." I giggle. "But I did and I'm so glad. Feeling this good should be criminal. Criminal. Ahhh. Dalton."

"Dalton with a D. Mystery solved." She turns around, leaning back on the dresser. "Do I need to be concerned you're this deeply involved with a criminal?"

I laugh. "He's not a criminal," I say, sitting up. "Although I think he might have stolen my heart." I flop back down in hysterics.

"Oh my God, what has he done to you?" She rushes over and pulls me up to shake me. "Holli? Are you in there, Holli?"

"Stop it." I swat at her. "I'm just feeling giddy. It's silly I know, but I haven't felt like this in so long that I'd forgotten I could."

Smiling, she says, "You deserve giddy. Now when do I get the details about Mr. D and this second technically third chance romance?"

I stand and walk to the window. Like Dalton, we also have a view of The Strip. "Tonight," I reply. The sun is lower in the sky and I check the time. 4:36 p.m. Seven hours with Dalton felt like thirty minutes. Turning to get my phone, I check my texts. Two from Tracy and one from Cara: *Dinner at seven, meet at Maestro.*

"Remember Cara from the marketing meetings?"

"Cara who didn't get our account, Cara?"

"The very one. She invited me to dinner. Want to go?"

"Guess she's not mad she lost the account."

"Nah, she was nice last night."

"I'll go," Tracy says, "I'm almost finished with my makeup, so I just need to get dressed."

"We've got time. I'm gonna shower." The tension in my shoulders eases under the heat of the pounding water and I close my eyes and move my head under the spray. "Stairway to

Heaven" intermingles with memories of Dalton's hands on me—
caressing me, taking me, making me his. I glide the soap over my
body noticing there are no physical marks to match the ones he's
left on me emotionally.

It's all too much, so I rush through the rest of my shower and
go about getting ready for a night out with friends while trying to
block those green eyes, the light and the dark, the two sides of
Dalton that he lets me see. One side is so open and friendly,
bright as the desert sun. The other, burdened as a darkness
overshadows him. Dalton has secrets. Secrets I'm intrigued
enough to want to explore and discover, but I need to forget all
that. I've got his name and his room number, and not much else.

Tracy grabs her clutch and walks to the door. With the knob
in hand, she says, "I'll meet you downstairs at the bar near the
elevators. I need to make a call."

I'm worried about her. Something happened after the
engagement or she wouldn't be here in Vegas with me. "Sure," I
reply, giving her the space she needs.

Because I'm in Vegas—anything goes, so I pull on my
skintight couture black dress, the one that shows a lot of leg. I'm
not normally conservative, but this is really pushing the
boundaries for me. *I wonder if Dalton would like it on me.*

We walk into the restaurant right on the hour and I see Cara
sitting at a large round table in the corner. She waves us over.

After she introduces us to everyone, we take the remaining
two chairs and are sandwiched between two men in suits. The one
next to me is named Jack—I do a double take when we're
introduced because of the name alone. My reaction piques Cara's
curiosity, but she doesn't say anything about it. This Jack is mid-
thirties, shaves his head completely, and is wearing an expensive
suit and watch. The man next to Tracy is European and must be

well into his fifties with a dark spray tan and blinding white teeth. She elbows me when we sit. I chuckle under my breath.

Conversation around the table picks up as we start looking over the menu. "I saw you at the banquet last night. Congratulations on the recognition," Jack says.

"Thank you. It came as a surprise. I probably looked dumbfounded. I'm not good in the limelight."

"Limelight. That's clever."

"Well, I didn't mean my company, more the spotlight."

He nods and smiles. "It was funny though. What are you drinking tonight? I was thinking about a bottle of Cabernet. Will you join me?"

Shaking my head, I say, "I'm not a big red wine drinker. It gives me headaches."

"Maybe you haven't tried the right one," he says and I get the distinct feeling we're not talking wine anymore. When I don't say anything, he does. "I highly recommend this bottle." He points to the wine menu.

Not wanting to be rude, I say, "Sure. I'll try a glass." One glass then I was done. Like the man sitting next to me, the wine is overrated. Fortunately, the pasta isn't. It's delicious.

Cara taps her glass twice to get our attention. She stands, and I can't help but feel the formality is a bit over the top for a dinner that is supposed to be a group of friends. "I wanted to thank you for coming tonight. I'm so thrilled to have shared a night with great company and food." We raise our glasses in a toast. "And because we're friends, the dinner is on me. I can write it off," she adds, proud of herself.

This dinner is not a group of friends. It's a business dinner full of men and I'm getting the sneaking suspicion she wanted us here as her wing-girls to help her out. Naturally, she's sitting between two hotties and the rest... yeah, not gonna happen.

Jack's nice, but not my type. My type might share the same name as him, but they couldn't be more different. My mind wanders back to Dalton and I check my phone. Sneaking it out of my purse, not wanting to be blatantly rude, I start to get anxious to meet up with him again. But I'm bummed there are no texts or missed calls. It's still early though and he said he'd be late, so hope remains.

Jack leans toward me, and asks, "Do you have plans for the rest of the night?"

Cara stands up again and with her phone and a message displayed on the screen, she announces, "I have great news. I just got us into the concert tonight. My company is a sponsor and I pulled a few strings to get us tickets."

"What concert?" Tracy asks.

"The Resistance," Cara replies, sitting down.

I look at Tracy, and say, "I think our night just took a turn for the better." Then I turn to Jack. "Guess we're going to a concert."

"Oh my God, Holli. I'm freaking out inside. They're one of my all-time favorite bands. That giddy you were feeling earlier, it's contagious. I've caught it now. I seriously cannot believe we're gonna see The Resistance in a private performance." She squeezes my hand because she's so excited and I must say that I'm pretty damn excited myself. I have a couple of their CD's and from what I remember from some magazine, they're hot.

Tracy stands and says, "Dinner was wonderful. Thank you for inviting us. We're going to freshen up and we'll see you at the concert." She looks at me and says, "Come on."

I stand, giving my thanks. Jack stands, setting his napkin on the table in front of him. "I'll see you there."

Tracy grabs my hand, and says, "Move it, lady. I've got to pee and I don't want to miss any of the show."

"And here I thought that quick getaway was for my benefit."

"It was... you and my bladder equally."

"Gross," I say, amused.

Heading into the bathroom, Tracy goes into a stall and I straighten my dress in the full length mirror. Opening my purse for lipstick, I see my phone and check for messages one more time even though I know I shouldn't. I don't want to be this hung up on a guy that may or may not even contact me again. I barely know him anyway? Well, I know him, his body and a few... Instead of analyzing everything I remember so vividly about Dalton, I bypass the phone and get my lipstick out and reapply.

"You okay?" Tracy asks, "That guy really got to you, huh?"

With a sigh, I say, "I get sick of guys feeling like they have rights they clearly don't. I think Jack is used to getting what he wants by flashing his money around. I'm not impressed."

"Because you're a success all on your own. Feel good. Feel proud about that."

"Thanks. I appreciate that."

When we stand, Tracy does a little hip wiggle, and says, "First round is on me at the show. We need to live it up tonight. Tomorrow we go back to being responsible. Tonight we party like rock stars."

"Just like rock stars," I say, feeling the excitement of what's ahead overtaking all the rest.

10

*"The leaves are truth. Secrets are the
roots buried beneath the surface."*
~Johnny Outlaw

The venue is intimate; the size of this club is not a place to hold a huge concert. That makes this show even more exciting because of the access we've been granted to see such a famous band. It's also really smokey in here. I wave my hand in front of my face to clear some of it away while following the group to an open area at the bar. Leaning over the bar's edge to shout over the loud music, I order, "Three top shelf tequila shots."

The bartender nods, then lines the shot glasses up. Grabbing the Anejo, he pours then pushes each one forward. "Ten each. Yours is on the house," he says with an arched eyebrow.

I lay down the cash and a good tip. "Thanks."

Tapping the top of the bar twice, he says, "Make sure to visit me again tonight."

He's flirty. Kind of cute, too, but ever since Dalton happened, it's hard for me to see anyone else as a possibility.

After handing the drinks to Cara and Tracy, we hold them in the center, each glass touching. Cara takes the lead. "Ladies, tonight we're partying Vegas style, so here's to hot guys and wild times."

"I'll drink to that." I down the shot then bite the lime to ease the harshness of the alcohol, catching Jack and the other men from dinner watching us. With a smile, he nods.

Tracy squeals and points to the stage as the drummer kicks into a steady beat and the bassist joins in. The crowd starts cheering. The lead singer, with his back to the audience is wearing a black T-shirt and jeans. He strums his guitar with an intensity that highlights the muscles in his arms as the music builds. "We scored getting in here." With a laugh, I tell Tracy, "We owe Cara a few more cocktails for hooking us up."

"God, I'm about to die. Johnny Outlaw is so fucking hot," Cara says with a dreamy look in her eyes. "We should try to meet the band after the show. I've met the drummer a couple of times. His name is Dex. He's from Brentwood and took one of my friends to prom when the band was starting out."

"That's our in because I'm totally onboard with meeting them." Tracy adds, "Liquid courage and we'll go for it."

Cara high-fives both of us, which feels silly, but this night has become full of unexpected fun.

The audience is getting louder and I start swaying to the rhythm. The girls squeal loudly, grabbing my hands and holding them in the air just as the lead singer turns around and starts singing into the microphone.

His green eyes are haunted, the bright lights obscuring his view of the crowd idolizing him as he gets lost—in the music, in the club, in the moment as he sings a song I've probably heard a hundred times on the radio.

All at once... I'm hit with reality.

The girls release my hands as I stumble back, my shoulders hitting the wall behind me. It's not the alcohol that's hit me so hard. *It's him.* I recognize the tattoos on his arm: Texas flag, number forty-four, hula girl. As my gaze scrolls over his body, I can place the tattoos by memory even the ones the audience can't see—a tiger on his chest just over his heart and three guns over his ribs.

Lines, lies, fake names, real names. Suddenly I feel humiliated for believing his pickup lines and stupid for not knowing who he really is. *Did he play me or was he being real?*

Johnny Outlaw is live, and in person, singing from his soul and The Resistance is a band I would pay money to see, but I didn't expect this. Now I've got thirty emotions fighting to overturn my current reaction as I try to reason through everything I thought I knew.

Jack Dalton is Johnny Outlaw, the lead singer of one of the most famous bands in the world. He's also the man I've been having sex with over the last twenty-four hours.

"Hey, you okay?" Cara asks, glancing back over her shoulder.

I wave my hand in front of my face, acting like it's nothing. I must be a good actress because she turns back around and gets into the music again.

Tracy seems to be drunk already and doesn't realize what's going on. I can't keep this to myself though. "Hey," I whisper into her ear. "That's Jack Dalton."

"Who?"

I yell louder than the music to be heard, "Jack Dalton."

"What? I have no idea what you're talking about. That's Johnny Outlaw."

I put my arm straight out and point. "No, Tracy, it's the man I've been hooking up with. He told me his name is Jack Dalton. He sent the food this morning."

She bursts out laughing. "Oh shit. Really?"

"What oh shit?" Cara asks, stamping her foot because she's not in on our secret. "Who's Jack Dalton?"

Leaning against the wall next to me, Tracy looks at Cara with her cocktail straw pressed against her lip. I shake my head at the girl who's five sheets to the wind drunk at ten o'clock at night. The only saving grace she has to be this drunk is that we're in Vegas, which is the gold standard here.

"Jack is," Tracy starts, her voice louder than necessary to fight the loud music, but the song stops just in time to further my humiliation as she shouts, "Holli had sex with Johnny Outlaw today."

"Tracy!" My cheeks flame with anger and embarrassment. I drop my face into my hands. Now I sound like a groupie to the world.

Peeking out from between my fingers, Cara is staring at me. "Is that true, Holli?"

I debate answering, wondering how much of a lead I can get on them if I take off running now. With the heels I'm wearing, I'm thinking not that far, so I answer. "It's true. I guess I slept with a rock star."

"You," she says then looks back to the stage briefly before lowering her voice. "You slept with Johnny Outlaw? Why am I only finding this out now?"

"It's not like that. I didn't know he was Johnny Outlaw when I had sex with him."

People are staring. When my eyes meet the bartenders, he sets down another shot, and says, "Thought you might need this."

"Thanks." I down it knowing it won't ease the mortification that a portion of this room now knows I slept with the band... or at least the lead singer, which kind of feels like the same thing right now.

The band is only three songs in and I'm being swarmed with questions from the girls while other girls I don't know are glaring at me.

Cara looks at Tracy and asks her, "How did this happen? I need details and if she won't give them to me, you will."

"I don't know any details," Tracy says, shrugging. "She hasn't told me anything either."

Both of them turn to look at me, curiosity and impatience written on their faces.

"I don't know Johnny." I look back at the stage and I start questioning everything he told me, our conversations running through my head, wondering if I missed something or he just blatantly lied to me.

I've seen him on TV winning Grammys and walking the red carpet with famous models. *Who knew I'd ever meet him in person?* Was I that caught up in my own work to actually pay attention to the man on the screen in front of me? It makes no sense that he's the same man I've been spending time with.

Seeing him now, and knowing him so intimately, I hear the same passion I heard through jagged breaths. He holds the microphone like he held me, caressing it with care.

Beautifully tortured, there's a dark aura projected through the pain on his face as he sings about lost dreams and faded nights. His body is defined, his hair styled, image intact for everyone to see the star he is—the star he was always meant to be. Keeping my eyes on him, I say, "I don't know the man on stage. I don't know him at all." I watch, fascinated like the entire room of fans, staring at the man who owns all of their adoration.

With a nudge, Tracy says, "You should talk to him after the show."

My heart pounds, not knowing where anything stands between us while starting to feel betrayed, tricked. "I don't know. I feel weird about things now."

"You didn't do anything wrong."

I glare at her. "I may not have done anything wrong, but I was an idiot. He must think I'm so stupid. I slept with one of the most well know bachelors in the world. Someone who every woman wants and I thought he was an undercover security guard working for the hotel."

Her expression says it all, but just in case I misinterpreted it, she says, "You would have sex with a security guard?" Her nose is scrunched in disgust.

I point at the stage again. "Need I remind you that the security guard we are talking about looks like that?"

"Good point."

We spend the next couple of songs in silence, listening, every song's lyrics have new meaning to me and feeling like he might be singing just for me, kind of hoping he is. When I remember I have no messages, I know he isn't. He can have any girl in this room, so I don't expect to hear from him anyway.

The crowd is clapping, the band deserving the ovation. Cara says, "Show's over. Let's try to get backstage."

My heart begins to race. "I don't think so," I say, shaking my head. "I don't want to barge in on him. He said he'd message me."

The band hops off the side of the stage and disappears and my heart calms. I should go with her and see Dalton... *Johnny*. I should, but I'm confused by the lies he told me or untruths or whatever he's gonna call the fact that he led me to believe he was someone different altogether.

"C'mon. We have to try." Cara grabs my hand and pulls me out the side exit into a hotel hallway that leads to a door backstage. I pull free from her tight grip and shake my head again. "No, I can't. Not right now. Not with a crowd around."

"Holli, you had sex with him. He'll want to see you." Her determination makes me wonder if she's doing this for me or herself. "We need to get back there before everyone else figures out where they are."

Tracy stands close, taking my side. "This is about Holli. Not us, so I don't think we should do this."

"We shouldn't," I add. "You're welcome to see them if you want, Cara, but I'm not gonna turn into a groupie for him." Turning on my heel, I start to leave, but stop when I hear Dalton behind me.

"Holliday?"

11

*"Fame brings out the worst in
everyone, including myself."*
~Johnny Outlaw

*What am I thinking? Why did I stop? Fight your instincts and
move forward like you didn't hear your name roll of his slick
tongue like honey. Go. This is the last chance to save your heart.*

Closing my eyes, I drop my head down, willing my feet to
move, but my heart's desire is too strong.

He's so close. I can smell him, reminding me of this
afternoon. "Look at me, Holliday." I turn, lifting my head and
opening my eyes, meeting his. His hands are close, so close to
touching me, but he pulls back. "What are you doing here?" he
asks.

"I came to see a concert," I say, looking around at the people passing by and staring at us, at him.

He turns his back to them and moves closer. "Can we talk about this privately?"

"Holli? You okay out here?" I look to my left and see Jack from dinner standing there looking pensive, his tone stern.

Dalton eyes him, probably sizing him up. In the meantime, Cara steps forward and introduces herself, "I'm Cara Leeds. I'd love to talk about marketing opportunities over dinner sometime."

My mouth is wide open until Tracy whispers, "She's a shark."

"Johnny, Dex sent me to get you," some sleazy woman with fake everything says while trying to pose provocatively against the door that leads backstage. "We're waiting for you."

Dalton doesn't acknowledge them, fully focused on me. "Please,' he asks, "can we talk?"

Glancing at Tracy, she slowly nods. She's the only one I trust here, so I take a deep breath then sigh when I release it. "Fine."

Abruptly, he turns and I begin to follow him. "I'll be back. Wait for me," I whisper to Tracy over my shoulder.

Cara steps forward and asks, "Can we come?"

But Tracy handles her. "They want privacy."

Dalton leads me down a side corridor to a door that blends in with the wall, no doorknob. He hits it twice with his fist and it opens. A very large man eyes us and then signals us in, moving out of the way to let us pass. We take a right and then the first left into a room with a paper sign taped to the door that reads 'Johnny Outlaw.'

"You're Johnny Outlaw," I read aloud, astonished, the sign finally solidifying the information. "You're a rock star."

He stops in the middle of the room and looks me straight in

the eyes. "I'm more than that, Holliday," he says, putting his arms out to the side. "I'm also Jack Dalton."

"Hardly."

"I didn't lie to you. I am Jack Dalton. That's my real name."

"This is an age old quandary. Is leaving information out lying or just a simple omission? Why didn't you tell me?"

"I liked you. I liked that you didn't know. You didn't recognize me and you didn't question."

"Guess I should have but asking someone if they're famous isn't usually on the first date agenda."

"That's my point. You liked me for me, the real me, not the stage me. Don't be mad."

My voice automatically rises because he doesn't seem to understand how stupid I feel. "I'm upset because as much as you think you gave me the real you, you didn't. You kind of left out a major detail."

When he comes toward me, I take a few steps back. I don't want to be sweet talked into giving in. I have a feeling that tactic works way too often for him.

"I trusted you," he says, his voice quieter. "I told you things—"

"You told me you were from Texas. The damn tattoo can tell me that. You gave me nothing authentic."

He looks down. "That's not true."

When he looks up again, I say, "It is. It's truer than the few moments of intimacy we shared. The sex was good, but now I doubt the sincerity behind it. Did you think I would tell the world about you? Was that why you pulled away from me last night? You made me expose more of myself than I normally would and in the end, for what? A fucking hookup on vacation? You protected yourself and your image, but left me here to feel like a complete fool. I'm so stupid I didn't know and you let me feel that way to save your great Johnny Outlaw's imag—"

"That's not true. I never thought you'd talk to the press. Fuck! Why are you making this so hard? Why am I apologizing to you like I did something wrong?"

"Because you did," I say, stomping my foot in frustration. "And if you don't see it then there's no point in us continuing this conversation." I turn and open the door to leave.

He grabs my arm suddenly, surprising me. When I turn back to him, he says, "You're ungrateful when you should feel special." Anger tinges his eyes, a flame flickering in his irises. "You had sex with Johnny Outlaw. You know how many women would trade places with you?"

I yank my arm free and step out the door. With one last look back, I say, "Having sex with a rock star doesn't make me special. It makes me a groupie." I slam the door and walk away. Something hits the back of the door and breaks as I walk back toward the big guy on guard. "Open it." All my niceties have been used up today.

The door opens but closes just as quickly behind me, leaving me standing in the middle of a group of girls begging for entrance into the great Johnny Outlaw's dressing room. I lift my chin and work my way through the groupies. *Groupies*. Ugh.

I'm not worried about Dalton coming after me. He didn't last night and now he has his idolizing fans to entertain him.

Tracy rushes to my side, Cara flanking my other. "What happened?" Cara sounds edgy, realizing she has no chance of hanging out with the band. "You have something against famous, hot rock stars? They're not your type or what? Because they're totally mine. Did he mention me?"

"Ha!" I give her an evil eye. "Sorry to disappoint you, but you didn't come up in conversation." I stop walking. "And rock stars are what legends are made of, not fairy tales, so I left. Let's go, Tracy." I loop my arm around Tracy's and leave Cara standing there in her disappointment.

Approaching us from ahead, Jack from the restaurant, says, "Maybe I can call you sometime back in L.A."

"Maybe not. Goodnight."

We walk forward, our pace quickening. "What happened, Holli?"

"I just want out of here. This was a mistake. I made a huge mistake, Tracy."

"No, you didn't. You had fun. Isn't that what it was all about? Don't be so hard on yourself. You fell for a hot guy and his lines. You didn't do anything wrong."

Leaning against the wall, waiting for the elevator, I feel regret sinking in. "I think I might have started falling for him..." I just drop that there between us and wait for her reaction.

"You know Adam and I met at a frat party, but did I ever tell you that we hooked up that first night?"

I stand up when the elevator arrives. "You never told me that before."

"I was embarrassed for being easy, but what I've come to realize is that I wasn't easy, Adam was just the right guy."

As we ride up to our floor, I ask, "So you think I just left the right guy for me back there with a pack of the wrong girls?"

"I don't know if Jack Dalton or Johnny Outlaw is the right or wrong guy for you, but is it such a sin that he didn't reveal his fame?" We exit and walk to the door. "We need to talk. I think it's time you heard some hard truths."

"Can I get comfortable before this gets any heavier?" I walk into the room and start to undress. I slip on a pair of jeans and a soft heather grey T-shirt with my logo on it, finding comfort in my little lime design.

Tracy sits down on her bed, leaning her back against the headboard. "Here's how I see it. You're a great catch, Holli. Too great for most men, but you settle on these pricks who on paper seem to fit what you want or need. But they suck."

"Geez, don't hold back, Trace."

"I'm not going to. Not anymore. You need to hear this. Everything about you shouts single girl who doesn't need anybody. But you do. You do need people, companionship, and more. And guess what? That's okay. We all do. You've just gotten really good at hiding it, even from yourself. I'm not like you. I can't be alone. I know this about myself. I'm not brave like you."

"You have Adam, so you don't have to be brave by yourself. You have a partner to share that responsibility." Lying back on my pillow, I say, "I don't like it. I've just lived with it for too long."

"Holli, let me ask you something and I want you to be honest not only with me, but with yourself."

"Okay."

"Why are you up here with me when you have a rock star downstairs?"

"How do I answer that?"

"You don't have to. Just think about it."

I sit up and look at the bright lights out the window. Twisting my hair into a ponytail, I glance over my shoulder. When I look at her, she asks, "Do you want me to go back downstairs with you?"

"He knows my room number and name. Hell, he knows my address in L.A. The man knows how to contact me if he wants."

"What do you want to do then?"

I stand up. "I want to wash this heavy makeup off my face."

"Chicken."

"Bock. Bock." I walk into the bathroom and start cleaning my face. When I come back out, Tracy is asleep curled up on the bed. She never could hold her liquor... and I hope she never can. I like her just the way she is.

Picking up my phone from the dresser, I check for messages. Sitting down at the desk, I prop my feet up on the window ledge. I look at the sparkling lights of The Strip, my reflection staring back at me from the glass. Maybe she's right. Maybe I do keep dating the same type of guys and that's why it never goes anywhere. But can it really be more than sex with a rock star? I highly doubt that Johnny Outlaw is a relationship type of guy. So why bother? Why set myself up for heartache?

I close my eyes, feeling the weight of the emotions drain my energy. I wake to a double beep and the phone in my hand vibrating. I look down and see a message from Dalton. *Third chance a charm? Meet me at the Eiffel Tower restaurant at midnight. I'll be the one with remorse on my face.*

Tracy shuffles. I look over as she's getting up, and tell her, "He sent me a text."

She stops and sits back down on the corner of the bed. "He did?"

"He wants to meet me at midnight at the Eiffel Tower Restaurant."

"What do you think?"

"I'm not gonna go, because if I do, I'll probably end up forgiving him and wind up in his bed again."

She doesn't look convinced, but her face lights up. "Well it's my last night in Vegas and I haven't seen the water fountains," Tracy says. She looks tired, but stands up. "I heard the music is synced to Sinatra. Can't get more Vegas than that."

"You don't want to go to sleep?"

"I got a cat nap. I'm good to go. Wanna go with me?"

Feeling more awake than I should, I say, "I'm always up for an adventure." I slip on my shoes as she changes clothes.

A ten minute cab ride later, we're there. We walk down the long descending sidewalk from the hotel and meander along the front of the fountains. The water is dark and unmoving, no big displays of spouting, booming, or dancing water is found. "We missed it," I say, disappointed because I really needed something wonderful to happen.

"They'll have another show," she says, looking at her watch. "But in the meantime, don't you have a date?" She points across the street at the Eiffel Tower anchoring the Paris Hotel to The Strip.

With a smile and a sideways look, I ask, "I was set-up, wasn't I?"

She nods, proud of herself. "I'm afraid so. Hope you're not mad."

"I'm not mad at you, but it doesn't change the fact that he lied to me." The realization sobering as I lean against the cement railing, my fingers holding tight. "I don't think I can go."

"I don't think he lied, Holli. I think you're looking for reasons to end it. I can tell you like him, but for whatever reason you've decided everything that happened between you was built on false pretenses. Maybe it was. Maybe it wasn't. You have a chance to find out and I think you should take it."

"Third chance a charm," I repeat his message. I narrow my eyes at her. "Just so you know, I'm kind of hating you right now."

"I'm good with that. Now go."

"Fine," I say, my stubborn side coming out. I'll go just to spite her because she thinks I'll chicken out.

"I can stay and wait if you want."

"No, it's okay. Thanks." My mind starts going into overdrive with the possibilities of the pain I'm setting myself up for. What if this is a ruse? What if he doesn't show? Maybe he'll change his mind and after what happened, he might be as done with me as I was with him earlier.

Crossing the street, these thoughts make each step heavier, my heart being dragged behind me. While walking up the hotel steps, I consider turning around, knowing it's not too late to catch Tracy before she leaves. When I look back, she's gone already. As much as I want to start swearing her name up and down to high Heaven for abandoning me, she accomplished her mission, which was to get me here. The rest is on my shoulders.

Inside, I stick to the edge of the casino floor. I'm nervous and there's no hiding it as I quickly wipe my hands on my jeans before approaching the hostess. She's set up behind a podium, guarding the elevator doors that will lead me up to the restaurant. "Hi," I start, but she cuts me off.

"We're closed for the evening. If you'd like to make a reservation you can call in the morning. We open tomorrow at eleven."

"Closed? But..." I want to argue that she must have her facts wrong. Dalton wouldn't do this to me. Would he? Would he play a sick game like this? "Okay," I say, "thank you." Tears sting the corners of my eyes, threatening to fall, so I turn away to leave, hiding my disappointment. And to think that for a moment in time, I almost thought...Well, it doesn't matter what I thought. The restaurant is closed.

12

"What do I know about keeping a woman happy? I haven't had a relationship that lasted. The one thing I have learned though is an apology should be genuine or it's pointless." ~Johnny Outlaw

"Mademoiselle, wait. Is your name Holliday Hughes by chance?" The hostess asks after tapping me on the shoulder. Startled, I turn around and see fascination written all over her face.

"Yes," I reply, sucking down my disappointment that Dalton's not here.

"I'm sorry. I was told the woman would be wearing a black dress." She smiles and says, "Mr. Outlaw is waiting upstairs for you."

"He is?"

She continues smiling as the elevator doors that will lead me to the restaurant open. Swinging her arm out for me to enter, she says, "He is."

Just before the doors close, I ask, "What about Mr. Dalton?"

She tilts her head confused, but the doors close too soon for her to respond. *It was rhetorical anyway.*

I grip the railing as the elevator takes me up. When the doors open, I hesitate and take a deep breath before walking out. I go to the bar, instantly spying Dalton across the room standing near the large windows. The Bellagio Fountains are lit up, as if on demand, as the man they're performing for watches. His silhouette is dark against the bright and choreographed water rising high into the sky. Even with the dancing water, he outshines it all.

Walking slowly across the room, I'm not sure what I'm going to say. John Mayer is crooning through the speakers above and it feels out of place for the French setting. I stop next to Dalton, watching the fountains move across the lake, and whisper, "Hi."

Dalton's eyes flash to mine. "Hi."

With both of us watching the fountains outside, I say, "I didn't take you for a John Mayer fan."

"I'm taking notes. He's a king at romancing the ladies."

"I hear he's gifted in other ways as well." I turn to look at him, really look at him. "Not that I would know or anything."

"Drink?" he asks.

His drink is on the table next to him, it looks like whiskey or bourbon—either will do. "I'll have what you're having." I pick up the glass and take two sips.

He chuckles under his breath. "Literally, you mean, you'll take what I'm having."

I shrug. "Figured since we've swapped spit already, what does it matter now."

His tone turns serious. "I'm sorry."

"For what?"

"For not telling you who I was."

Guess it's better to deal with this now then to beat around the bush. "I've been thinking a lot about it, trying to understand why you didn't tell me."

"It wasn't to hurt you," he says.

I turn back to appreciate the fountains before the show ends. "But why lie?"

He's next to me watching the show, but his hand crosses the divide and takes mine in his. "I didn't want to ruin it."

I whisper, "You didn't."

His hand goes flat against the glass and he says, "It's magical."

"The Fountains?"

"No." He doesn't say more. He doesn't have to. I feel it too.

I place my hand flat on the glass next to his, our thumbs touching. "What now?"

When he looks at me, light reflects in his eyes, and he smiles. "I thought we'd eat, then move on and cover a few what-ifs you might have."

"Hope you've got some time because I have a whole slew of what-ifs to cover."

"I've got all night, but my flight is at ten in the morning."

"You're leaving Las Vegas?"

"We were only here for meetings and the gig. Are you going back to Los Angeles tomorrow?"

"Yes, back to the real world."

"This world is real, Holliday. It's my world and I'm asking for it not to end here, for us to get to know each other better."

Every girl dreams of hearing someone like him say that to them, but as I look around, it's not just words with him. He means it. "Tempting. You did rent an entire restaurant just for us, after all. That's quite the romantic overture."

"Guess it's a good thing you came then," he says. The lake across the street goes dark, the show officially over, leaving us lit by a flickering candle in the center of the table. He takes my hand down from the glass and faces me. "Maybe we can start with a meal. Will you stay for dinner?"

"Only if I can apologize first?"

"For what?" He repeats what I said to him earlier.

"For letting my own insecurities judge you instead of taking you for who you've shown me."

His hand touches my cheek gently, and he says, "No need for sorries. I'm new at this too."

"You're new to dating?" I ask, joking with him.

"No. Just new to dealing with real feelings."

Silence, as my breath is taken away, stolen by him just like my heart. I want to kiss him, but I don't.

Moving behind me, he reaches and pulls out my chair. After sitting down across from me, he subtly bites his bottom lip. I remember him doing that last night and liking it.

A waiter introduces himself and I place my order, "I'll have another one of these please."

Dalton orders the same, then leans forward, and whispers, "Thank you for coming. I didn't know if you would. You look beautiful."

"Thank you." I glance down and pull my napkin into my lap. "I'm glad I did, but why did you want to meet here?"

"I hated how things were left. I did that. I'm sorry. Our time together meant more to me than you know, you mean more. Already." He chuckles to himself, embarrassed. "I feel crazy thinking stuff like this much less saying it."

"I'm just a girl. There's nothing special going on here." I lean forward to whisper to him, but the waiter arrives with our drinks, setting them down in front of us.

"We'll need a minute more before we order. Thank you," Dalton says to the waiter.

Watching him speak, it's hard to imagine he's the same guy who was singing on that stage tonight. His body is relaxed and I sense he feels calm, safe around me.

When we're alone again, I say, "I'm not fishing for compliments here. I can get a date, but you're trying so hard. What are you trying to convince me of?"

"I don't know," he says, looking into my eyes. "I trust you. Even though you're not fishing for compliments, I have a million I can give you." He spins his glass slowly between his fingers with noticeable strength and agility. I don't fill the moment between us, wanting to hear more. "You're different, Holliday. I don't need a week to know that. I knew the minute I met you." Shaking his head, he smiles. "I still can't believe you agreed to leave with me."

"I'm in Vegas and you know what they say when you're here."

"That's not how I see you."

My tone comes out flatter than I intend. "You keep saying that, but that's who I wanted to be this weekend, just for a weekend, someone else, someone carefree again."

"I wanted to be Jack Dalton again."

And with that simple comment, my heart melts for this man—a man who just wanted to be who he is on the inside. I get up and walk around the table. He slides back in his chair unsure of what I'm going to do. I straddle him, not caring how it looks to the few people working. After wrapping my arms around his neck, I kiss him, leaving him no outs or choice in the matter. He wants the same. Wrapping his arms around my waist, he pulls me closer and deepens the kiss. Our tongues meet and slowly mingle; my hips start a slow gyrate.

"I want you," he murmurs against my mouth, refusing to give up the kissing for words.

Moving up his cheek, I place kisses all the way to his forehead and down on top of his eyelids. His hands hold my hips against him and I feel him grow beneath me. A moan escapes as I drop my head back, enthralled by the feel of him between my legs.

"Shhhh," he whispers in my ear. "They can hear you."

My eyes open and I take a deep breath. "We should leave." I maneuver my leg from over him, standing up. "Like right now."

"Fuck, let's go," he says anxiously. He grabs my hand and turns me fast, pulling me behind as he rushes toward the bar where the waiter is stationed. "We're gonna go. You have my card. Give yourself a big tip and thank you."

"No dinner, Sir?" the waiter calls after us, confused.

Dalton's pace never slows as he heads for the elevator. "Nope. Thanks."

I keep my mouth shut, fighting all the tingles bursting beneath my skin while trying to regulate my breathing. I don't think I've ever been so hot for someone in my life and the thought of a cab ride... damn, it adds to the whole experience. *How am I not going to have sex with this man in that cab?* That will be the tricky part.

The elevator doors open. I'm swung inside and he presses me into the corner. Dalton's pelvis is against mine as he kisses me, holding me in place. My only thought is that I totally want to have sex with him in this elevator.

One of his hands squeezes my breast as the other squeezes my ass. I lift one leg up, wrapping it around his thigh and he begins to grind into me. The elevator doors open and we hear a clearing of the throat.

We jump apart, Dalton flying to the other side of the elevator trying to act nonchalant. "Okay," he says, walking forward and talking in a business tone. "We're here."

"Yes, Mr. Outlaw," the hostess says with a huge flirty smile. The top button of her black blazer seems to have popped open revealing the very low cut vest she's wearing underneath. "I hope you'll join us again."

He slips her money, and says, "Thank you for staying and working late."

"My pleasure. Can I be of service to you?"

Whatever she means by that, that's my cue and I take his arm, sliding mine around his as he replies. "No, that's all. Thank you."

After a kiss to my temple, he says, "I need to get you to bed."

"I'm liking this idea a lot."

We start walking toward the doors that leads to the cab line, but I stop him, pulling him just past the exit.

He looks at me, questioning. "What?"

I pin him against the wall and kiss him again. With my hands on his chest, I say, "I don't care who sees us or what anyone thinks of me. I want you, Jack Dalton. I want all of you. The good. The bad. And the rock star. No holding back on me. Okay?"

A devilish grin appears. "Fuck you like a rock star?"

I lick my lips, as I stare up into his green eyes. "Exactly."

"No more wasting time. I'm either getting a room here or we're heading back to the hotel. Your choice."

"Let's go. I have a few dirty ideas planned for that cab ride back."

His eyebrows go up. "Damn, woman," he says, adjusting his erection. It's impossible for him to hide. "We've gotta go now."

We hurry outside the doors, rushing between the luggage of hotel guests coming and going, but when we see the cab line, it's too long. Dalton stops and waves a bellhop over. "Any cars for hire?"

The bellhop's eyes go wide as he stares at him, speechless.

Dalton smiles and says, "Hey man, any limos or sedans available?"

"Holy shit! You're Johnny Outlaw."

We look around as a few people glance our way. Fortunately, none stop.

"Yep. You want to take a pic or something?"

"No way! For real?"

"For real, but then get a car for us. Okay?"

"Yes, sir, right this way," the bellhop says, checking me out and giving Dalton an approving smile.

Dalton snaps his fingers to get the guy's attention. "Keep your eyes up here."

I blush, finding his jealousy kind of attractive, but I'll never admit to such a thing.

The bellhop signals a Town Car over and opens the back door wide. "He'll take you wherever you need to go."

I slip inside the car and Dalton slaps my ass. "Don't get too cozy in there without me," he warns.

The bellhop pulls his phone out and they take a picture together right before Dalton jumps in and shuts the door quickly. With his hand on my knee, he greets the driver. "Evening. The Palatial please."

"Yes, Sir."

The privacy glass goes up and I'm grabbed by the hips and pulled down. My T-shirt is pushed up and his mouth is on my stomach. While grinding against me, his sweet kisses turn feverish as the skin of my middle is covered. When he reaches my tattoo, he stops and lifts up. Looking at it, he smiles, and says, "I didn't think I'd see this beauty again." As my fingers run gingerly over the colorful design, he places one delicate kiss on it. "Have I ever told you how fucking sexy I find this tattoo?"

"You haven't told me a lot of things, but we have time."

With a wry grin, he pushes my shirt up even further while pulling the cup of my bra down, sucking in a nipple with the fast action. His pelvis starts moving again, his hardness pressing between my legs and I drop my head back, my mouth coming open. The car is hot inside, the windows steaming up.

I love the feel of his mouth taking me so passionately. He bites just enough to send sparks through my body. My hand flies to the window to anchor myself as he pushes his body harder against mine.

Moving to the other breast, he repeats the beautiful torture, my hand losing leverage as it slides across the wet window. The car comes to an abrupt stop and we slide off in a heated heap onto the floorboard. "Shit. Are you okay?" he asks as the car's horn honks loudly.

"You broke my fall," I reply, starting to laugh. I climb back onto the seat and look out the window to see what the commotion is as Dalton gets up. "Traffic jam."

"We're only to Aria. Damn it." He looks at me and I can see a plan forming by his expression. "You up for an adventure?"

That's the second time I've been asked that tonight. And I

give him the same answer I gave Tracy, "I'm always up for an adventure."

"C'mon." He slips out the door, then helps me out.

The driver's window rolls down and he starts apologizing, begging us to get back in. Dalton waves. "No worries, man. We'll leg it from here. I left money on the seat."

I look back and there's two hundred dollars on the seat we just vacated. The driver waves just as Dalton takes my hand, and we run to an island in the middle of The Strip. "We're not supposed to stop here," I say, worried we'll get in trouble, or worse, hit by a car.

It's barely wide enough for the two of us to stand there, but he says, "I know, but look up. Look around, Holliday. We're in the middle of it all, the entire Strip."

Holding tight to his side so I don't fall off the small curb, I look up and then around and smile. "Wow. What a view."

He surprises me by kissing me all of a sudden. And if I didn't know better, I would swear in that moment in time, the entire world revolved around us.

13

"If I tell you all my tricks they won't work anymore. So let's just say I like to surprise my dates and do something unexpected, something special just for them." ~Johnny Outlaw

"I've never been on a date to a 7-11 before," I say, squinting under the bright fluorescent lights of the convenience store.

"Sadly," Dalton says, looking at me over his shoulder, "I have."

Checking out the goods he's eyeing up, I laugh and hand him a Twix. "I'm getting hungry."

"I offered to buy you a fancy French meal earlier, but you..." He leans down and kisses my neck adding a little sucking action that gives me goosebumps. "... decided you were hungry for other things, like me." He stands up all proud. "Not that I'm complaining."

"I still am. So get your treats and let's get out of here. You've got me all worked up and I'm starting to feel like everyone is staring at us."

"It probably just feels that way." We both scan the place. "Correction," he says, "everyone *is* staring at us. Just follow me and stay close."

"That sounds so ominous. Are we robbing the place?"

Chuckling, he says, "Get your sweet ass up there and let's buy this stuff. Do we have everything?"

"More than we need, but if they had Big Red, I'd be all over that."

"Wow, I haven't had one of those since I was a kid back home."

"I crave them sometimes. Reminds me of my childhood."

"Who knew a soda could hold that much power," he says, as we step into line. When it's our turn, Dalton dumps all the junk food onto the counter. Other than one can of Monster Energy, a Gatorade, a Twix bar—large, an extra-long Slim Jim, and a big bag of Bugles hitting the counter, the entire store is silent and still staring at us.

He pays and grabs the bag in one hand, my hand in the other and we hurry out the door. "We should get going or people will follow us."

We choose to walk down a dark alley on the back side of a large hotel, lurking in the shadows where occasional car lights find us.

I stay close to his side, a little nervous. "Do you think this is safe? I mean, you may be famous, but we could still be attacked back here."

Stopping, he pulls me closer to the building. We keep walking, but he explains, "I'm not afraid, Holliday."

"What if they have a knife or a gun?"

"Then we should walk faster."

"Real comforting."

We take a right onto a main road where the sidewalks are wide and not crowded. There are enough people around to make it feel a little less dodgy, but vacant enough that one of the biggest stars in music today can go without notice. We share the Monster drink as we walk, passing it back and forth, and talking about our pasts.

"When did you lose your virginity?" he asks with a sly grin aimed in my direction.

"Upstairs, earlier... with a security guard," I deadpan.

He follows a loud laugh by saying, "You're such a liar."

"Okay," I say now laughing too. "It was high school. Senior year, after prom."

"No way," he chuckles. "That's such a cliché. I expected something more unique from you."

"Don't hold back or anything. Sorry to disappoint," I reply sarcastically. "How about you?"

"The back of my Ford truck. I set it up with an air mattress in the back and parked in a field. I stole a bottle of red wine from my parents and played Barry White on the recommendation of this guy Steve from school who scored with all the girls."

I smile. "I love that you went to so much effort. Tell me about her."

"You want to know about my ex-girlfriend?" He seems surprised.

"I want to know about you and she's a part of your past, so tell me about her."

"Okay. Her name was Patty O'Toole. She was head cheerleader and with a name like that, she was lucky she was hot. Every guy in school wanted to date her—"

"But you got her."

"I got her because I was a right fielder and star player. After I was injured, she started dating Ricky Brouchard, my best friend and replacement on the ball field."

"So did the Barry White work?"

"I think it was more the wine. There was nothing smooth about my moves back then. We had sex and then I puked over the side of the truck bed."

"Very romantic."

He chuckles. "I've learned a few things since then."

"I can vouch for that." I take a drink from the can and then see the hotel sign ahead. "There it is."

Anxious to get back to the hotel, he takes my hand and we pick up our pace. I can tell he wants to continue what we started in the restaurant as much as I do.

As we approach the parking lot of the hotel, he stops us, and says, "People will recognize me in here. If we get separated or get crowded in, go to my room and wait for me." He pulls his room key out of his wallet. "Here, take this."

Sticking it into my back pocket, I say, "Will you be alright?"

"I'm used to it, but I don't want you hurt and I can never judge how these things will go."

"I'll take the bag so you have your hands free." He hands it to me and I ask, "Why does it feel like we're going into battle?"

He doesn't answer, but looks ahead. I see his eyes focused forward, his shoulders tensing as if on high alert. "Meet me at the room. Promise me."

The situation hovers over our heads like a rain cloud. "I promise."

Under the hotel carport, the chatter starts. It grows as we approach the doors. *Then they descend.* Out of my peripheral, I see him swarmed. Dalton stops, his eyes connecting with mine for a brief second before he turns his attention to signing shirts and anything else people shove his way, including their bodies. I see the transformation before my eyes. The Dalton who was just holding my hand is now all business and in full Johnny Outlaw mode—laughing, posing, owning everybody's attention in the vicinity.

Keeping my promise, I go, slipping inside undetected by any of his fans.

Just as I step into the elevator, a couple walks in behind me. He's in a T-shirt that has the sleeves ripped off and wearing a bandanna around his head. She's dressed very risqué, but we're in Vegas where anything goes.

On the other hand, I catch a glimpse of myself in the shiny brass elevator walls as I'm entering Dalton's keycard and pushing the button. The guy does the same but pushes the floor below mine. I stand there mortified that I'm just now remembering that I washed my face before I went out with Tracy tonight. I have no make-up on, my hair is pulled back into a ponytail, and I'm wearing one of my old T-shirts. And yet, this guy smiles at me.

If I could ball up nice and tiny and disappear right now, I would. I just look down at my slip-on espadrilles and pray they are too busy making out to notice me.

"You with Outlaw?" The guy's voice is rough, like he smokes too many cigarettes.

When I look up, they're both staring at me, the girl's expression a lot less friendly than his.

"You're with Johnny?" she asks as if it's the most shocking thing she's ever heard, or disgusting. I'm not sure.

My defenses kick in, so I stand a little taller. "Yes."

The guy smiles, lazy like a stoner. "Dude."

I'm not sure what that means, but it seems like a good thing. The doors open and he walks out. She's draped on him like a pelt, but takes her time to glare at me in disgust one last time when she passes. *It does wonders for my ego...*

The doors close and I get off one floor higher. I let myself into the suite and walk to the bar, setting the junk food bag down. There's a fruit tray along with a basket of fruit on the dining table with a note.

Dear Mr. Outlaw,

Fantastic show. Thanks for coming to Las Vegas.
We hope you enjoy the rest of your stay.

Sincerely,
The Palatial Hotel Staff

Not sure when Dalton will walk in, I set the note down and dig into the platter. I'm hungry and can't imagine he'll take this with him tomorrow. I slip onto the table, letting my legs dangle, waiting. As the minutes pass, I start to feel a little ridiculous, a little stupid, and doubt starts creeping in.

Dalton enters, startling me when the door flies open. It bounces back from the impact and closes behind him. His energy is different than when he performs, more like coming down from an adrenaline rush rather than riding high on one. His eyes lock on mine and he comes toward me as I bite into another strawberry. He tosses a handful of condoms on the table beside me. I gulp.

With strawberry still on my lips, I glance at the condoms, then ask, "How many girls were you planning to sleep with this weekend?"

"I wasn't. My bandmates gave them to me because we already used what I packed."

My mouth is licked and the strawberry stolen from between my lips. "Fuck, Angel. You're delicious." The tray is pushed across the table and the fruit basket knocked off entirely. Leaning over me, he asks, "You ready for me?"

Surprised by the commotion, I nod, suddenly turned on and food forgotten.

"Get naked. Now," he demands. Leaning back on my elbows, I tilt my head to the side and start to pull the rubber band from my ponytail, but he grabs my wrist. "Leave the hair up."

Shit.

I unbutton my jeans, sliding the zipper nice and slow, the sexual tension already thick in the room. Music starts playing as he sets his phone on the bar behind him and I lift my ass up off the wood tabletop, balancing on my elbows. He takes my shoes off and then my jeans, yanking them off by the hem, pulling hard enough for me to end up straddling his waist. Dalton looks down at my exposed lace panties while rubbing his thumb across his bottom lip several times in a calculating fashion.

When his eyes meet mine, my desire flares to life, and he asks, "So I'm going to ask you nicely, do you want to keep these panties?"

I know how to respond this time. "No."

"Right fucking answer." He rips them on one side and then the other, exposing me. Bending down, he licks me, his tongue slips deeper and my head hits the table with a thud. He squats at the end of the table and pulls me even closer, draping my legs over his shoulders. His tongue double thrusts inside me while sucking where I want him most.

My fingers weave into his hair and pull unintentionally as he continues pleasuring me with his mouth. Closing my eyes, I feel every nerve he flames and hear his every breath and moan mingling with mine. My hands grip as he holds me tighter. He doesn't relent. He sucks, and with my back arched, my orgasm hits me hard.

I squeeze my thighs together, his head trapped between until the vibrations cease. I fall back, my body weak from the release. I hear him undoing his belt then unbuttoning his jeans. It's not going to pretty or graceful. He's going to fuck me just like I asked him to earlier, and my body trembles in anticipation from the thought.

When I look up, our eyes connect and we still, only for a quick moment, and I read something deeper in his expression than either of us would say. He takes a condom, putting it on before his fingers slip between my legs. Bringing them back to his mouth, he slowly sucks them in. Reaching down, he touches me again and guides himself inside. Grabbing hold of my outer thighs, he pushes forward until his pelvis is pressed against mine. A sharp breath is forced out. I take a deeper one, then encourage him, "Move."

His eyes are closed, his face is contorted in his own sweet agony. When told to move, he starts moving. Thrusting. Fucking. He gives no reprieves, takes what he wants, what he desires and needs. His hands plant firmly down on the wood surface and I hold the edge of the table while wrapping my legs around him, holding me in place. His shoulders are strong, every muscle in his arms working toward the common goal. "Fuck, you feel good, Angel."

I grab onto his shoulders and he lifts me up, still inside of me and moves us to the edge of the kitchen counter. I push against him, our rhythm out of sync, making me feel every thrust even deeper. The sound of our bodies together is an aphrodisiac for all the *more* we spoke about.

Suddenly my hair is grabbed and pulled back, exposing my neck to him. His body quickens as his teeth scrape along the front of my throat and downward, his tongue teasing the dip at the base. "I'm gonna come so hard," he says. I'm getting close, but by his erratic movements, he's closer. He grabs me by the ass and slams into me, feeding his orgasm. "Fuck!"

His body stills against mine then he drops forward, resting his head on my chest. "Fuck," he repeats. Stroking his hair from his forehead, I kiss the top of his head. Turning, he puts his chin on my chest and says, "Be careful. I can get used to this."

"It could be habit forming," I reply.

He helps me down, holding my arm as my legs adjust. After a few minutes in the bathroom, I come out and see him lying on the couch. I crawl under the blanket and snuggle to him. Our breathing hasn't regulated yet, though it's calmer than before. I rest my ear on his chest, loving the sound of his thumping heartbeat.

A few minutes pass before I peek up at him and whisper, "I really lost my virginity junior year in the parking lot after at a Puddle of Mudd concert."

His smile shows his struggle not to laugh. "You lied about losing your virginity?"

"I was embarrassed that you'd think I was a slut for being seventeen, and worse, having bad taste in music."

"You slept with me just hours after we met, so there's that."

"Nice," I reply with a giggle, hitting him on the chest.

"And I'm definitely judging you by your choice in music." He pulls me close and kisses the top of my head. "But you're still fucking sexy as hell and I have a feeling your musical taste has improved since then."

"It hasn't. I still have one of their CD's that I sneak and listen to sometimes and I have a couple from this little known band called The Resistance." I smile against his chest, rubbing my finger over his abs.

"You already know I think that band sucks. I hear The Rolling Stones might tour. If they do, I'm taking you, so you can hear real music."

"It's a date." Leaning my head back on his forearm, I ask, "Wanna fuck again?"

"You had me at fuck." He moves over and kisses me with gentle pressure.

This round we take our time, reacquainting ourselves in a new way, learning each mole and scar, the sex torturously slow, but amazing. I feel everything—all of him inside of me and all of him above me, learning all I can about the two sides to this man who's trying to be all he can for me.

Rolling on top, I rock back and forth, savoring each time he hits that special spot buried deep inside. His eyes stay open, watching me, his hands running over my hips and up to my breasts, kneading them. I lift up, but he pulls me back down, grounding me to him in more ways than just physically. Time passes with exaggerated ticks on the large watch wrapped around his wrist, a subtle reminder that we have tonight, only tonight and to make the most of it.

Though I want this to last all night, it doesn't. The power of our attraction, our needs being met, and feeling too good to last, we end up in another heap of satisfaction.

"You're really fucking fantastic," he says, holding me.

"Best sex ever."

"I don't just mean the sex."

Oh. "I feel the same about you," I say, trying to be open without freaking him out. "You want to move into the bedroom?"

"Yeah. It will be more comfortable."

Lying in bed together, facing the window where The Strip beckons with colorful signs and lights, he has his chest to my back. His finger traces my tattoo, covering even the smallest of details hidden in the design. "This is the sexiest tattoo I've ever seen," he says, keeping his voice low. "Did you sleep with the artist?"

Rolling onto my back, I run my hand down his neck and over his shoulder, stopping on his flag tattoo. "Why do you want to know that?"

"The lines are clean and the shading impressive. The way the colors blend like the ocean and sky. He took his time with it and he knew your body well enough to play off your curves."

Rubbing his cheek, I say, "I didn't sleep with him."

"Did you fuck him?"

I swat his shoulder. "No. I didn't sleep with him or fuck him. But I shopped around. I did the design and had it made into a temporary tattoo and lived with it before I ever laid down on the table."

"You designed this?"

"Yes."

"Tell me what you do for a living?"

His interest is genuine, so I tell him the story. "I was partying with friends one night three years ago. We were doing tequila shots and I started pretending, in my drunken state-of-mind, that the lime kept saying bite me."

"You're kidding me, right?" Dalton sits up, staring down at me like he can't believe what he's hearing.

I sit up, pulling the sheet up to cover my chest. "I'm not kidding."

"You designed the Bite Me Lime?"

"I did. You know it?"

"Who doesn't know it? Everybody fucking knows that lime. You seriously just blew my mind, Holliday Hughes."

I smile and laugh. "Yeah, most people are pretty shocked when they find out I'm the woman behind the lime."

"I bet." He lies next to me and I slip back down into his arms. "I'm impressed."

I pretend to pop my collar. "Well, I'm not a rock star or anything..."

Rolling on top of me, he says, "No, you're better and completely fucking hard to resist."

"Who said anything about resisting? Hope you're not getting tired on me. I'm having way too much fun to stop now."

With a light chuckle and a cunning look in his eyes, he smiles. "Don't worry. I'm just getting started."

14

"A woman who blushes even after being made love to might just be the sexiest thing ever." ~Johnny Outlaw

The water cascades down Dalton's body as the spray of the shower hits the top of my head. I take him in again, deliberately slow because I know he's close. He grips the small ledge he's leaning against with one hand, the back of my head with the other.

The shower stall is steamy, but there's no shortage of hot water. Pressing one hand against the marble for support, I hear a muffled moan just as his head hits the wall. His tremors stop and I swallow around him.

"Shit, don't do that," he says, his voice breathy. "My dick is sensitive."

I slide back—hands on thighs, mouth closed, eyes wide, kneeling before him. His tone, like his expression, is serious when he says, "You're going to be the fucking death of me, Holliday. You, the way you look at me, makes me want to stay here with you forever."

When I stand up, I rub my chest against his, remaining pressed firmly against him. "Nothing lasts forever. You'd grow bored."

I expect a witty comeback. That's our thing. I don't get snark. Instead, his arms come around and pull me into an embrace, my cheek to his chest—the gesture kind and loving after such heated activities. If I'm not careful, I might confuse this for something more, something deeper, something I would be able to count on.

Relying on a musician to be faithful is not the plan. Do I think it might be nice to see Jack Dalton on a regular basis—yes. But as for Johnny Outlaw—he's more unpredictable. And I don't handle unpredictable very well. My life is organized, scheduled to the minute, planned, and synchronized with my growing business. I don't have a life outside of work. I'm single. I take care of myself and my company. It's better that way. Nobody gets hurts, especially me.

"Relax," he whispers. "You're so stiff. You're over-thinking this. Enjoy the now."

My shoulders drop and I close my eyes. "What are we doing?" I ask, feeling like I'm on the verge of developing feelings for the man that fucks me one minute then holds me tenderly the next—giving me the best of both worlds.

"We're having a good time."

Moving away from him, I press my back against the opposite wall of the shower, my hands behind me. You can't get much more exposed than this, vulnerable, with no barriers to hide behind.

"A good time," I repeat, nodding and looking down.

"A really great time." When he speaks, he draws my attention back to him. "I'm not going to feed you lines, Holliday. You know my lifestyle now. It doesn't work well for most women."

"And here I thought I was special," I say with a laugh while rolling my eyes.

"Why do I get the feeling I could tell you all the things that make you special, but you'd still think I'm feeding you a line of BS?"

"Because you already know me well enough to know that's true. How about one?"

He smirks. "I thought you didn't fish for compliments."

I shrug. "Sometimes a girl needs an ego boost."

"You have great tits."

I laugh, the noise sounding good even to my ears. Dalton may not be able to make me any promises, but he knows the right thing to say to make me see the good in the moment. "Thank you."

"You're welcome, but really," he says, dropping his hands on either side of me and kissing my lips. "I should be thanking you."

"Go on."

A chuckle echoes deep in the shower stall then he replies. "I'll go on alright. And on." He kisses down my neck and across my collarbone, his fingers settling between my legs.

Resting my arms on his shoulders, I close my eyes and feel, feel everything he wants to give me, each sensation playing a part of the melody our bodies create together. The water rains down around us as his breath heats the skin of my neck. It's just a whisper that could have been so easily lost in the sound of the shower, but I hear him. I hear him and my heart clings to the words when he says, "You'll always be my angel."

His fingers thrust, eliciting every desire I tried to hide, the emotions that have been blooming inside. I will always be his angel. Though we'll leave this room, our own little world created in the middle of desert chaos, we will have the memories. In this space, I own all of Jack Dalton and have tamed Johnny Outlaw. In this space, I've rid his life of demons and showed him Heaven. With his hands on my body and his lips to my skin, I convince myself this will be enough.

I can't stay still, everything feeling too good, almost to the point of overwhelming, so I give into it all and free fall. When I resurface, the blurry lines of reality sharpen. My eyes meet Dalton's clear greens and I see a smile that can rule the world— maybe it already does. Mine for sure.

"That was amazing," I say, still a little breathless.

He kisses me on the forehead, then says, "You're amazing to watch."

My body is already heated from the hot water splashing down and the sexual adventures, and now my cheeks flame under his sweet attention and words.

"I like seeing you blush. It's sexy."

"I don't blush for just anyone, you know."

"I'm counting on that."

Grabbing the body wash, I squeeze some into our palms, and smile at him. "Saying such things might give me the wrong impression. I might actually start to think you like me."

Lathering my chest, he pays special attention to my breasts, rubbing until they're nice and soapy. His hand slides down my stomach and between my legs again. His lips touch mine, but he doesn't kiss me. "I more than like you,

Holliday. If I could give you more, I would."

My knees go weak as my heart starts pounding in my chest. When I look up, I know my expression is filled with questions and hope, but I feel fragile for letting him see that side.

He stands straight up and smiles. "Don't get all weird on me, okay? So I like you more than a little."

"But less than a lot?"

We rinse our bodies off, and he whispers, "More than a lot."

Standing behind him, I kiss his back three times, satisfied with 'more than a lot.'

15

*"Revelations are hard to come by,
but when you do have one, they're
usually worth the wait."*
~Johnny Outlaw

The Bugles are gone, the Slim Jim devoured after we had sex on the couch. The Twix remains and I'm not liking the cunning look in Dalton's eyes, so I settle the issue. "The Twix is mine."

"I thought we were sharing everything?"

"You said you wanted the Slim Jim."

"But you ate half of it," he states, crossing his arms over chest.

He's got me there. "Good point." I walk inside to the bar and grab the Twix from the counter. When I return to the balcony, he's looking out over the city of Las Vegas.

"Sin City is where dreams come to die," he says, a somber tone taking over. Even after the short amount of time we've spent together, I'm starting to get used to his moods. It's fascinating how you begin to read people, becoming accustomed to their habits and traits when you spend any real amount of time with them, especially like we have.

"Did your dreams die in Vegas?" I ask, sidling up next to him.

He wraps his arm around my shoulders, and says, "No. My dreams died in Texas when I was eighteen."

I'm surprised he seems to feel his current life is a back-up plan. "Tell me what happened."

A long pause leads him into a deep breath and a loud sigh before he says, "We were in our last game of the season. If my team won, we'd go to the playoffs. If we lost, the season would be over. I had played some of my best ball that game. I caught two balls in the outfield and hit a homerun by the fifth inning. The second time I was up to bat I hit a fly ball. It was an easy catch, an easier out, but they missed. They fucking missed it and I thought I was home-free. But the other pitcher sucked and when he threw the ball into home plate to strike me out, he hit me instead. Imagine a seventy-five mile an hour baseball hitting you squarely on the shoulder." His hand rubs over the number forty-four tattoo like it still bothers him. "The impact from the hit fractured my humerus, just under my rotator cuff and busted up some of my bicep muscles, which ended my season on the field with me flat on my back." He looks at me and says, "We scored, won the game, and I was helped off the field, my career in baseball over."

I'm unsure how to proceed with this information—condolences or reassurance. He's probably been drowning in everyone else's sympathy for years, so I just ask, "Was forty-four your number?"

"Mine and Hank Aaron's. About the only thing we ended up having in common."

"How'd your team do in the playoffs?"

"We were slaughtered in the first round."

"Fine, you win. You can have half my Twix." I hold one of the long cookie bars out for him.

Biting off the end, he smiles as he chews. "I knew I could get you to give up the candy with a sob story. Girls are so gullible."

I punch him in the arm. "You made that up to get my candy?"

He's laughing, and ducking from my swings as we move around the furniture on the balcony. Hiding behind a lounger, he has his hands in the air, holding up his half-eaten candy bar in surrender. "Stop. C'mon. I give up. I didn't make it up. It's the honest truth. That's what happened." He pauses for a second, then says, "But did I use the story to get your candy? Sure did." He takes another bite flaunting it in front of me.

He smiles. His face is as bright as the stars in the dark desert sky at night. It makes me giggle. He doesn't even realize he was played. Since his dark mood is gone, I won't rub it in that he's really the gullible one. I'll just enjoy the time we have together instead.

I sit down in a chair, but Dalton remains standing. He looks at his watch, the silver face reflecting from the light inside the room. "It's late."

Leaning my head back, I look his way, feeling tired when the time is mentioned. "How much time do we have left?"

"About four hours."

"Then you're off, jetting into the great blue yonder to who knows where." I close my eyes, feeling my body relaxing against the plush cushions.

"I'm going to Germany." Opening my eyes, he's in front of

me. He squats down so he's eye-level. "I'll be there for a week and then I have no idea after that. I think I come back to L.A. in three or four weeks, but I'm not sure."

My suspicions are growing and I wonder if he's feeling the same as me. "Why are you telling me this?"

With his hands on my bare thighs, his thumbs rubbing my skin gently, he says, "I want you to know where I am. I have your number and now you have mine. I don't want us to end tonight."

Tears form in the corners of my eyes as I watch him laying his heart on the line.

Reaching up, he soothes my cheek with the warmth of his palm. "I didn't mean to make you cry."

"No worries. It's the happy kind." I lean forward and hug him, the coarse hairs of his beard scratching my neck, but it feels good. I stop the tears from falling, my heart soaring from the sentiment. "You want to call me after tonight?"

"I do, and since I memorized you address already, I might also want to stop by one day too." He stands, pulling me up with him, and wraps his arms around my waist.

"You can, anytime. I'd say I'll be waiting, but yeah, that's probably too much too soon."

"Since you already put it out there, I'd like to take you on a real date when I return."

"We sound like we're in high school. Next you'll be asking me to wear your letterman's jacket."

"Maybe my class ring?" He smiles and I swoon because yeah, he wants to date me and for me to wear his class ring and stuff.

"How about we start with sleeping together?"

A look of hope crosses his face. "And here I thought five times was a pretty solid start. Damn, Angel, you're insatiable."

I push him playfully. "I'm too tired to banter. You've worn me out. You win, rock star."

He winks. "Well, you did request the special—a royal rock star fucking."

"That I did," I say, turning from him and walking inside, "and I have absolutely no regrets."

"What about complaints? Any complaints?" He asks, following me into the bedroom.

Climbing to the middle of the bed, I'm so sleepy, I flop face first. When I roll over he's next to me. "Only one," I say.

His expression changes, his voice lower. "What's that?"

"That you're leaving me in four hours. I could spend days in bed with you and it wouldn't be enough. I could spend night after night listening to you hum, the way you do when you're deep in thought. So four hours is not enough time to memorize the two million, three-hundred and fifty-six thousand other things that I wanted to learn about you."

Silence.

The silence makes me uncomfortable, so I turn onto my side and snuggle into his. "Are you okay?" I ask nervously. "Are we okay?"

His arm tightens around me, and he whispers, "I've never had anyone say anything like that to me before." When I look up at him, sliding my cheek against his chest, he smiles at me. "We're more than okay."

A yawn escapes and my eyelids are heavy.

He adds, "We should get some sleep."

I snuggle down. "You can sleep on the way to Germany."

"I'd rather sleep with you. You wouldn't happen to be free for the next week would you?"

My eyes open wide. "You're inviting me to Germany?"

"Yes. Private jet, five-star hotel, Michelin rated restaurants. You know, all the perks of being famous."

I kiss him on the cheek, loving the offer, but disappointed because I know I can't say yes. "I won't bore you with my schedule for the week, but I have three meetings I can't reschedule."

"The offer stands. You're invited if you want to come. I'd like you with me. I'd like to get to know you better."

"I had to move a meeting for this weekend to happen." Moving up, I press my lips against his ear and whisper, "Your offer means the world to me."

He turns and kisses me on the lips. No more words are needed tonight. We close our eyes and sleep takes over.

Sunshine fills the room, the bright desert blinding me through the large picture window. The fluffy comforter is cozy, so I snuggle under, avoiding the reality of day for as long as I can.

Daylight! My eyelids fly open and I sit up abruptly, looking around the room for Dalton. He's not in bed, so I call for him, "Dalton? You here?" Flipping the covers from my legs, I slip out of bed and hurry into the living room. "Dalton?"

I scan the balcony and look for clues to where he might be. Then I see it... and try to gulp down the dread lumping in my throat.

A note sits on the bar, a pen next to it. I walk closer, trepidation filling every step. I don't pick it up. I don't even touch it—my heart and head both fearing the worst. When I'm close, I take one last look around the suite for any signs he still might be here. When I don't see any, I look down and read:

Dear Holliday,

Please don't hate me for not waking you. No reason both of us should suffer without sleep. Anyway, I'm terrible at goodbyes. I'd rather you remember our goodnight.

Dalton

I stand there rereading the note countless times before I take it, grabbing my phone from the counter, and go back to the bedroom. After climbing back into the middle of the large bed, I pull the covers over me and hold the note to my chest. Then I lose my mind and do crazy girl shit. I smell his pillow. I bury my face straight down into it and do a full inhale. When I come back up, I decide right then and there that the pillow is coming home with me... that and the fruit basket that was knocked off the table last night. Also the Gatorade because I'm thirsty and after all the sexual fun we had over the last twenty-four hours, I probably need some electrolytes replenished.

Noticing the time, I know I should get up and go back to my room. Although I texted Tracy to let her know I wouldn't be coming back last night, she still might be worried. I crawl out of bed twenty minutes later and start gathering my clothes that are scattered in various locations around the suite. My T-shirt is in the bedroom though I distinctly remember it coming off in the living room. My jeans are under the dining table next to the one remaining unopened condom package. My lace undies are in shreds with pieces in the kitchen, dining area and on the balcony. I find one shoe, but after an exhaustive search, I give up on the other.

I get dressed and walk the around one last time, remembering how in this room, being together, it felt like we ruled the world.

Making sure to grab my note from him, I tuck my phone into my back pocket and go to the door. It feels sad as if the goodbye meant for Dalton is transferred to the room, heavy emotions coming over me. "Goodbye."

When I open the door, I spot my shoe just outside on the floor. I slip it on, not quite sure how it ended up out there, but it allows me to walk away from this love nest a little less shamefully and with a smile on my face.

16

*"It's easy to lose yourself if that's
what you want. I don't."*
~Johnny Outlaw

This is ridiculous. I barely know the man. The excitement I felt from our weekend together in Vegas has been replaced by a strange dull ache, much like heartburn, but antacids won't make it go away. A little warning about these changes in emotion would have been nice, but I got nothing from Tracy on our drive back. Maybe nobody knows because nobody has felt the way I feel about Dalton. At least that's what it feels like to me.

I'm an independent woman. I shouldn't be letting some guy run away with my more sensible side. Yet here I sit staring at my computer on Monday afternoon, the Bite Me Lime dancing across the large monitor in front of me, and I realize I'm being utterly ridiculous.

Pushing back from the desk, I realize I'm useless. This isn't good. I don't get like this over guys. Guys are for my entertainment. I leave *them* wanting, not the reverse.

When did I become *that* girl? I stand at the window and wonder when I became one of *those* girls—you know, the type of girl whose life revolves around a man—the type of girl until now, I've judged as weak. The answer is obvious but I refuse to acknowledge it. I make myself a cup of chai tea instead.

My Lime-itude greeting card line is due and I only have ten of twenty cards finished. Sitting out on the patio, I hear the ocean breaking in the distance. I should take a walk to clear my head and get the creative juices flowing, so I slip on my flip flops, grab my phone and head out.

The beach is three blocks away from my condo. It's a nice walk, the streets lined with palm trees and flowering shrubs, but there's just something about when I first lay eyes on the ocean. It gets me every single time—the realization that the world exists beyond my online community. It's a nice reminder that life happens beyond the stucco of my sanctuary. I take a deep breath and appreciate the awesomeness of this life I'm so fortunate to lead.

Finding a bench to sit down on, I pull my knees to my chest and rest my chin. Dalton is half way around the world from me and my heart seems to have packed a bag and joined him.

I haven't called him, but it's been a struggle not to. The thrill of this new relationship and what might be is too exciting not to dream about. But I'm a logical girl, one everybody relies on for a reason. Sure I can be spontaneous and fun, but it feels like that was the me of many yesterdays. The success of my business has taken a toll and I'm starting to think I'm its first victim. I love it too much to give it up, so I'll learn how to balance.

Maybe dating a musician who's on the road all the time is the kind of relationship that will work best for me. I can be me, and he can be him, and when we find ourselves in the same city, we can be together.

I'm not sure anything works out that easily. My heart's got a wager on the line that says yes, but my head still has doubts.

My phone rings and I pull it from my pocket. I stand up and start walking when I answer. "Hey Trace."

"What are you doing?"

"I'm at the beach." The sun is high, the temperature nice.

Her tone shows her surprise. "You are? You're taking a day off?"

I laugh. "No, you know me better than that. I'm just taking a break and getting some fresh air."

"This is Los Angeles, Holli. We don't have fresh air here. Smoggy air—yes, but not fresh air."

"You know what I mean," I say, smiling. "What are you doing?"

"Eating a salad. I've been thinking about what you said on the drive home yesterday... Or maybe more about what you didn't say. I'd like to hear about Jack if you want to share."

"I do, but not today. I feel weird and need time to process the weekend. It still feels surreal, like a dream to me." I take a deep breath and exhale loudly. "I'm afraid if I start to believe it was real, I'll jinx it. Does that make sense?"

There's a sigh in her tone, the kind where you know the other person feels sorry for you. Then she says, "When you're ready, I'm here to listen. I should go. I have a ton of work to do and I'm trying to make yoga class tonight. You should come."

"I can't tonight, but I'll be there Wednesday."

"Hey, Holli?"

"Yeah."

"He's real and I know you'll see him again."

"You're always the sentimental type." Looking back at the waves breaking before me, I say, "Never change. Okay?"

"Okay," she says with a laugh and then hangs up.

Only time will tell. I just wish I had more patience.

At the corner, I cross the street to head home. Sea air, the ocean view, and people watching are things I love and usually helps center me before putting in long hours of work. But not today. Dalton isn't easily forgotten or I'm not easily diverted from the memory of his strong arms, how he bites his bottom lip, and the way he looks at me after sex. He's altogether too distracting.

I close the door, walk straight to my bedroom, and flop on the bed. I rest my head on his pillow—the one I stole from the penthouse in Vegas—the one that still smells like him and close my eyes. I like the closeness, but it still doesn't alleviate the ache.

Work is the best course of action. I'll trudge forward. After heading into my office, I have one foot propped up on the seat and the other pushes off my desk and I do a slow spin around. *Funny fruit anecdotes. Comedy. Sad Fruit, Happy Fruit.* I try to think of more greeting card quips. My eyes target my phone with each pass I make, so I grab my keys and wallet and go for coffee down the street.

Standing at the end of the coffee counter, I wait for my name to be called. My phone rings and I see the name I've been dreaming about all day. "Hello," I say, trying to sound casual, but the fluttering I'm feeling gives me away.

"Holliday Hughes." His voice is low and seductive, making me a little weak in the knees. "How are you?"

I press the phone a little closer and lean my head down for privacy. "I'm good."

"What are you doing?"

"Dalton, half-caf toffee-nut latte." I hear my order being called and look up at the barista, hoping Dalton didn't hear what I named my coffee.

"I'm getting coffee. I needed a break from the office. I can't seem to focus on much today."

"I hope I have something to do with that."

I smile, and maybe blush a little. "You might. What are you up to?"

"I'm watching a talk show in German with no subtitles."

"Is it good?"

"I'm not sure. The canned laughter tells me I should find it funny, but... you know what, I'm not really into it. I'm just killing time. We leave in forty-five minutes for the concert."

"Is it a big show?"

"Regular."

"What's regular?" I ask, wondering if he means five or twenty thousand people.

"I think this arena holds fifteen thousand people."

"Holy Hell, that's a lot of people to perform in front of. Do you ever get nervous?"

"Every time." His answer is quick.

It makes me wonder if I shouldn't have asked. Will asking make him more nervous? "I'm sorry. I'm being nosy and it's probably annoying to answer these kinds of questions."

"It's okay. I like this, this normal conversation we've got going on here. I've been thinking about you—on the flight over and today," he replies easily.

"What were you thinking?"

"About your hot ass, and I'm still a little bitter about the Twix."

"Dude! I will buy you a Twix and won't make you work for it this time." Smiling, I ask, "And what about my hot ass?"

"I think I was getting used to having it around."

"Oh, Mr. Dalton, you're such a charmer," I tease, but I love that he's thinking about me too. Makes me feel a little less crazy.

"Know what else I've been thinking about?"

Feeling like this conversation is about to get a lot more intimate, I lower my head, keeping my voice quieter as I walk out of the coffeeshop. "What?"

His voice is low, a deep confidence emphasizing the words. "I've been thinking about how good it feels when I'm inside you."

I stop on the sidewalk, my breath catching. "You have?"

"When I close my eyes, I can feel your breath against my chest while you sleep. I can hear your laughter when we walked from the 7-11 back to the hotel, and I can see your face when you come. You're hard to forget, Holliday."

My body yearns for him in ways I haven't felt before. "I remember the feel of your wet body against mine in the shower, the taste of your skin. But when you kissed my hip and left a mark over my tattoo, I will never forget the feel or sight of you doing that to me, Dalton. Never."

Muffled voices on his end, draws his voice away and he shouts, "Alright."

I wait for him to return, curious to what's going on.

"Hey?"

"Yeah?" I ask, lowering my voice to match his, a seriousness overtaking him.

"I need to go, but I want you to know, we may be playing, just joking around with each other, but I meant what I said."

We're dancing around our feelings, but the meaning is caught. When I remember the sincerity in his eyes when he would say such sweet things to me in Vegas, I smile again. "I meant what I said too."

"And I'll kick any guy's ass that comes within twenty yards of you. Have I mentioned my fierce jealousy streak?"

Now I laugh. "You must have overlooked that little detail."

There's a silence that spans more than a few comfortable seconds as I walk inside my home. "I should go," he says. "I need to."

He hangs up and I'm left with a racing heart. I start a slow spin in my chair again, back at square one and my whole world revolving around the emotional dependency I've developed for this man.

Two hours later, I've gotten two greeting cards done and with that, I'm ready for my first of three meetings scheduled for the week. I call it a day and go to meet Tracy. I didn't think I'd make yoga, but decided I need to go.

When I arrive at class, I toss my mat down next to Tracy, which causes her to look up. She smiles and whispers, "Didn't think you were coming."

"I need to clear my head and workout after this weekend of debauchery."

She's shushed by the instructor when she giggles, which also causes me to giggle. "We'll talk after," she mouths.

We walk down the street for drinks after class, hoping to burn some bonus calories before consuming more. The margaritas are set down and as soon as the waitress walks away, Tracy says, "Tell me every single detail. And don't hold back. You had sex with a rock star and I need to live vicariously. My God, talk about a fantasy come to life."

"You get to have sex with Adam."

She rolls her eyes. "We're a boring couple and..." She looks away, the smile leaving her face. "I'm not ready to go there."

Sensing the change in her demeanor, I tap her hand. "When you are, I'm here for you."

"Let's get back to the fun stuff like you and your hot sex life."

My cheeks heat under her gaze. I touch my hands to my face to cool them down, but it doesn't help. Flashes of taut abs, kisses down my stomach leading to other wonderful places, and seeing that number forty-four flex as he thrusts down and then back up fill my thoughts.

"You've got it bad," she says. "So was the sex better before you knew he was famous or after? Because I would totally think after would be better."

"Dalton is different than I expected. I think I'll leave it at that."

"Nicely dodged, my friend. Guess I'll ask that again when you're drunk." She laughs. "Why do you call him Dalton anyway? Why not Jack or Johnny?" she asks, resting her chin on her hand.

"He introduced himself as Jack, but it didn't seem to fit his personality."

"Can't believe you fell for that ID pickup line."

"I didn't *fall* for it. I just didn't want to make a scene. If he was a legit security guard, he had rights to ask for my ID," I try to justify.

"He's smooth. I'll give'em that." She looks at me and asks, "So what now? He has your number, you've got his. Is there a future here?"

Looking down at the table, I touch the screen of my phone bringing it to life and smile. He took a picture of him touching his tongue to my ear while I slept and made it my screen image. It makes me smile every time I look at it and I've been looking at it a lot. "Am I stupid if I hope there's more than a one-night expiration date on us?"

"No one can answer that but the two of you." She takes a long sip of her cocktail and says, "Anyway, he'd be a fool to let you go."

"You say that every time."

"And every time they're fools. Face it, Holli, you date idiots...until now."

"Why do you think Dalton is so different?" I ask. "Everything about him shouts complicated and inconvenient."

"It's not Dalton. It's you. You're different this time."

17

"The tabloids think they have me all figured out, so I like to throw them a curve ball every once in a while."
~Johnny Outlaw

It's been too long. I have plenty to keep my mind occupied, but I don't want to focus on those things. I want to talk to Dalton. We have only talked once over the last week. He left a message last night, but only said, "Be ready for me," and I haven't heard from him since. I tried to call him back, but it went straight to voicemail. I want to hear his voice, so I've been listening to The Resistance as a substitute for the real thing. I turn off my music and pull up his number. After taking a deep breath, I call.

One ring.

Two rings.

Three rings. My nerves go into overdrive, worried he won't answer.

Four rings.

Fiv—"Hello?"

"Dalton?"

"You have amazing timing."

"I do?" I ask, walking downstairs to get a glass of water. My doorbell rings and I detour.

"Yes, you do. I sent you something."

A surge of excitement fills me. "I think it's here. Hold on. Let me get the door." With the phone to my ear, I unlock the bolt and open the door. My mouth drops open and my phone falls as my eyes land on the sexiest man I've ever seen.

With quick reflexes, Dalton catches my phone before it hits the ground, but all I see is the smirk on his face and his sexy body as he kneels before me. When he stands up, I jump on him, giving him a long kiss while loving the feel of his arms around me. He pulls back, enough to look me in the eyes, and with a cocky grin on his face, says, "Guess you missed me."

"How are you even here right now?"

He gets a good firm squeeze of my ass before setting me down, and says, "Well, there's this thing with really big wings. It's not a bird, but a—"

"Shush it and get in here." I grab him by the shirt and pull him inside.

"I thought you'd never ask." After picking up his duffle bag, he follows me inside and kicks the door closed behind him. Dropping the bag, he takes a look around.

I poke him. "I can't believe you're here. I thought you had another week or so before your break?"

"We have a two day break until our next show, so I've got twenty-four hours with you."

My eyes go wide and my mouth drops open again in shock. "You flew back for twenty-four hours?"

"No." He pauses, shaking his head and then looks at me, really looks at me, and says, "I flew back for you. But I wouldn't have cared if I only had two. I wanted to see you." Glancing over his shoulder toward the door, he signals with his thumb. "I can go if you want."

"I don't want you to go," I say, taking his arms. I pull him close, anchoring him to me.

Looking me straight in the eyes, he asks, "What do you want then?"

"You." I move to him, closing the gap, and kiss him. His breath is minty, his body hard, making me want more than politeness allows since he just got here. *Screw etiquette!* This man makes me want him in very un-ladylike ways, so why pretend. Surprising him, I push him back, but continue fisting his shirt.

"What?" he asks.

"Get your ass upstairs. It's time I show you just how much I really missed you." I dash upstairs, and by the commotion–his heavy steps following close behind me—he's just as anxious as I am.

Once we're in the bedroom, we hurry to undress. A mischievous look colors his expression as he unabashedly checks me out head-to-toe. I climb onto the bed and roll onto my back, tempting him to come to me by calling him to me with my finger and a slight parting of my knees.

With a lick of his lips, a look of lust appears. "It's so fucking sexy that you weren't wearing panties. Might make me jealous though when I'm not with you." After pulling his boxers down, he climbs onto the bed and hovers over me. "Tell me what a good girl you are when I'm not around."

My breaths deepen. The feel of his warm skin against mine, teases, making me crave him even more. "I'm so good."

"How bad are you gonna be now that I'm here?"

Watching him ready himself with a condom, I'm anxious to feel him inside me again. "Fuck me, Dalton," I say with a breathy whisper.

"God, you've got a dirty mouth sometimes. So fucking hot." His lips cover mine as he spreads my legs further apart. He leans down to my ear, and whispers, "Now show me how much you missed me, Angel."

I gasp as he thrusts forward. I close my eyes as my back arches up, driving him for more. We both push and pull, taking and giving until our bodies are tired and gratified, trying to catch our breath.

The noon sun streams in through the sheers. My eyes are heavy, my body weighted to the bed in exhaustion, but I can't take my eyes off of him, still astonished he's here and even more so that he's here just for me.

"Is the sex that good?" I whisper with a smile.

"I didn't come here for 'the sex' but the sex is pretty damn awesome." He rolls over to face me. "Wait, let me clarify that. I did come for sex, definitely hoped to get laid, but I knew there was no guarantee of it." With a sweet smile, he asks, "How do you like your surprise?"

"Best surprise ever." Running my finger down the defined muscles of his arm, I say, "I still can't believe you're here."

"It wasn't a selfless gesture by any means, Holliday." He closes his eyes, looking like he could fall asleep, but he reopens them and says, "I've been in this business long enough to know how things play out, but you, you might just be a game changer."

I snuggle closer, resting my head in the nook of his arm, running my fingertips over his other bicep. "You're supposed to be player. Now what use does the infamous Johnny Outlaw have with a simple girl back in L.A.?"

He chuckles lowly, his breath hitting the top of my head. "Johnny Outlaw is all image stuff. Who I am for real is the Jack Dalton I'm giving you. As for a simple girl from L.A... there is absolutely nothing simple about her. Everything about her screams complicated with strings attached." He whispers, "And she completely fascinates me." He kisses my cheek. "I've been meaning to ask you, who was that guy back in Vegas?"

Surprised by the change in subject, I slide my head up to see his eyes, and ask, "What guy?"

"The one in the suit after the show. The one chasing you."

I try to remember who he's talking about, placing the time. "Oh, Jack."

"What?"

"No, not you. His name was Jack."

He's not amused by the coincidence. "Was he your date? Were you with him?"

"No, I was at a dinner and we were seated next to each other. He was at the show with the group. It wasn't a date."

"He wanted it to be," he states flatly.

Exhaling, I sigh. "I think he wanted it to be."

His hand rubs my arm, warming my skin. "So I've got to

worry about you being stolen out from under me while I'm gone?"

"I could ask the same thing of you."

It's a breath released, a whisper on the tongue, but I hear him. "You don't."

Somewhere between showing my ID to a hot guy at a bar and finding out he was famous, I could see a difference in Dalton. What I thought I was getting and what I got has intensified, changing both of us. "You don't either," I say, feeling it deep inside where no one else has been for a long time.

Needing fresh air to clear the heavy away, I ask, "You want to go to the beach?"

"We can try."

"What do you mean?" I ask, sitting up.

"Paparazzi follow me, Holliday. I don't think they followed me here, but I can't do the normal things you're used to without attention."

"Would you rather stay in?"

"I'd rather go to the beach if that's where you want to go. You just need to know our trip might be cut short if they do show up."

Twenty minutes later we're walking down the sidewalk with a few feet between us, neither of us talking. I find myself scanning the area as if looking for spies. He keeps his attention forward, but I have a feeling he's also checking out the area behind his sunglasses. He's just less obvious than me.

"This is nice," he says, regarding the neighborhood.

"I like it here. It's quiet for the most part."

"How do you feel about holding hands?" he asks. A small smile slides onto his face.

"Holding hands is nice. You held my hand when we left the bar in Vegas."

With a laugh, he adds, "I didn't want you to escape."

I bump into his arm with a giggle. "Little did you know, I wasn't going anywhere without you."

"You sure did put on a show about going up to my room."

"Eh, a girl can't come off too easy."

"You made me do a little work."

"You had it easy. Or maybe I'm just easy." I laugh. Reaching over I take his hand and with the warm breeze blowing, we swing them between us. The connection is not just easy, but also wonderful.

18

"I take risks—in business and in my personal life. Sometimes it pays off and sometimes I get royally fucked over. But where's the fun in playing it safe?" ~Johnny Outlaw

Jack Dalton fascinates me. He has so many sides to him and I want to discover every one of them. Sometimes I feel anxious, like if I don't get to know all of him right now, I might lose the chance. Being at the beach is one of these moments.

"You live close. Do you come down here a lot?" Dalton asks as we cross the street to the beach. He walks straight to the ocean, kicks off his shoes and lets the water cover his feet.

"Every day if I can," I reply. The sun is lower and from this position behind him, his body is silhouetted much like when he's on stage.

"You're lucky," he remarks, looking around.

"Is your life that sheltered?"

"Sometimes." Turning back to me, he asks, "Can I buy you an ice cream?"

The innocence is so darn charming. "Sure."

He takes my hand and picks up his shoes and socks with the other, and we start walking. "What do you like to do, Holliday? For fun, when you leave work behind?"

"I like meeting friends. I would rather hang out with a small group then party at a bar with all of L.A. What about you?"

"This might destroy any illusions you might have had of me, but I like to have video game tournaments with my friends. Pretty geeky, but since going out is... complicated, it's easy to hang with friends at home or somewhere private. Favorite cocktail? Old-fashioned like you ordered in Vegas?"

"I needed something strong that night," I say, laughing. "There's no way I could have survived that event sober. I like margaritas if I have a choice. There's this restaurant down the street that makes really good ones. It's a neighborhood place, very low key. I should take you there sometime. What's your favorite drink?"

"A good lager, but whiskey does a better job most of the time." He stops, causing me to stop, and stares ahead.

"What is it?"

He starts walking again and replies, "Nothing."

I follow the direction his eyes have narrowed on but all I see is a couple taking pictures of each other.

When we reach the sidewalk, he sits, putting his shoes back on while I order ice cream from a cart. "What do you want?" I ask, glancing at him over my shoulder.

"Nothing." He's next to me and his response is clipped as he hands a five to the ice cream man. "We should go."

Taking me by the elbow, he starts to leave. I grab the popsicle from the guy just before I'm dragged away. "Okay, okay, Dalton. I'm coming. Geez, let me get the ice cream."

He stops abruptly and turns to me. "Go straight home. If you're followed, go somewhere else, somewhere public like a shop or a restaurant. Just anywhere other than your place. Okay?"

"What? Is someone following us?"

"The paps are here. Just go. I'll meet you soon. I'll call if it's going to be longer." He walks away from the nearby food carts and meandering people, leaving me standing there with a melting popsicle and fear growing inside my chest.

Fortunately, nothing weird or suspicious happens, but this cloak and dagger act is worrisome. A couple of hours later, I watch him, much like I did earlier at the beach. He might realize I am because I'm not exactly hiding the fact, but he's letting me without making it weird... or so I thought. "Are you just going to stare at me all night?" he asks with his arm stretched out, remote in hand, as he channel surfs.

Shrugging, I say, "I like staring at you."

"Everyone stares at me. Makes me feel like a freak show sometimes."

I look away, pretending to busy myself on my laptop. When he gets up, I take a peek again as he sits on the arm of my chair. "I kind of like when you do it."

My grin is big as I laugh. "How do I do it?"

Kissing my temple, he slides his hand up the front of my shirt finding my breast and squeezing gently. "You," he starts, his breathing changing, his mood dictating his actions, "see beneath all this. You see the real me."

"I only see what you give me, Dalton."

"Lies. All lies." There's a tease to his tone, but his voice remains direct. "You're wiser and more observant than you let on. I know this because I watch you too."

Leaning back, I give him easier access. His hand slips inside the top of my bra, his palm hot against my skin. He perks my nipple, then the other, and whispers. "Come with me."

In the bedroom, we take our clothes off, the act itself routine at this point, but the anticipation just as strong as the first time in Vegas. Standing at the end of the bed, he takes a quick look around. When his eyes come back to me, he moves closer and kisses me. His hands are strong on my neck, with pressure he slides them lower to my hip, digging just enough to feel a claim being made.

I slide my hands around his middle to the spot where the muscles indent in his ass and squeeze, staking claims of my own.

We move to the bed, and he asks, "Any requests?"

I'm not usually vocal with my sexual preferences, but with him, it's different. "From behind." I turn, climbing onto the bed and position myself on all fours. Looking down at the rumpled duvet, I wait.

And wait.

I'm tempted to look behind me, to find him, and figure out why he's keeping me waiting, but something in the room, something with the thickening tension, tells me to keep my eyes forward.

His hand covers my ass and my breath catches, memories of telling him I don't like to play games never included the ones of the sexual variety. I gulp just as his other hand rubs small circles on my hip, distracting.

Thwack!

I jump, my breath knocked from me as his other hand meets my ass again, the spot rapidly heating. I jerk around and am about to say something, but his eyebrows are raised and a small smile plays on his lips, which makes me hesitate.

He waits, keeping his eyes directed on mine. The corner of his mouth goes up as his hand rubs my sore ass. "Just testing."

I release a breath, much calmer than seconds before, and Dalton climbs onto the bed behind me. "Did I pass?"

Caressing me, he presses himself against me, a slow movement of his hips against my backside. His hands slide up my sides and grabs hold of my breasts while his hardness inspires me to wiggle. With his mouth pressed to the shell of my ear, he whispers, "You most definitely passed."

I close my eyes, wanting to feel, wanting my senses filled with all of him, wanting to experience everything. Cold air covers me and he disappears. I remain in place, waiting for his return, secretly yearning for more.

The sound of a package ripping open, causes me to grip the covers beneath, preparing. "Feel Like Making Love" starts playing as warmth invades my insides, my breath forced out. Erratic and out of control, he plays, toying with my body, testing boundaries by touching forbidden places. I leave no room for misunderstanding of what I like and what I don't. His body falls forward, his chest against my back with quickening thrusts and jagged breaths that foreshadow his release.

Fingers slip around and down my stomach until they find that place I'll never turn him away from. His rhythm found is my reward. As I tremor, he comes. Moans fill the bedroom before we collapse, exhausted.

Twenty minutes later, we're soaking in my jetted tub, bubbles covering our bodies and I ease back, resting against him.

Dropping my head back on his shoulder, I close my eyes. The sudsy water makes my skin feel silky and his hands roam. His sweet words cover me as he pushes water up and over my chest, "You're incredible."

"You're pretty incredible yourself," I say, returning the compliment. When his hand dips, I wiggle. "I think I might need a little recovery time."

Bringing my hand up from under the water, he places my wet palm to his mouth and kisses it. "I'm sorry. Was I too rough?"

"Not too rough. I enjoyed it, but I'm starting to feel the effects."

Strong arms wrap around my middle and a kiss is placed on my cheek. "I can give it time."

While drying off, I admire his tattoos, running my finger over his ribs. "You told me you'd tell me about the gun tattoos one day."

"Each one represents an album that hit number one."

"Three guns. That's impressive." I wrap the towel around me and stop, shocked I didn't know he's had that much success. "How many records have you recorded?"

"Four," he replies, tucking the towel around his waist. He chuckles. "But our first was complete shit. We were so fucking arrogant and wouldn't listen to our producers. They did the best they could. We just sucked back then. That album should have never been made."

I slide onto the bathroom counter, leaning against the mirror and watch him. "What about the hula girl?"

"Wish I had a cool story to go along with it, but I don't. That was just a drunken night in Hawaii."

"You're lucky it turned out so well."

"Damn lucky."

I don't ask about the tiger tat on his chest. I love to lick the skin of that tattoo in particular and don't want to find out he got it on a dare or something ridiculous like that, tainting it.

After changing into pajamas and pulling my robe on, I walk downstairs and find him in the kitchen.

Dalton holds a big box in the air, and says, "I love that you buy the family size frozen lasagna." I barely notice the box because he's standing there naked except for a pair of boxer briefs, and frozen dinners don't compare to how good he looks. I watch as he reads the directions and starts the oven. "It's getting late and these take almost two hours to cook."

"I can wait if you can. Do you want to watch TV to pass time? I blew off work earlier and need to return a few emails." I straighten the belt of my robe at the waist.

"Can I hang out with you?"

"And watch me work? Ummm—"

"I want to watch the magic happen."

"There's no magic," I say, laughing. "Just a lot of wasting time online, looking out the window and praying for inspiration to hit."

He feigns offense. "It's okay if you don't want me in there. I can hang out here." Adds puppy eyes, and says, "I probably have a few emails and messages to return too."

Tugging him closer by the waistband, I say, "Join me in the office when you're ready and we'll work together."

Dalton is noisy. He also has trouble sitting still. More insight is good, but Mr. Wiggles-Around-A-Lot is distracting. Kicking his feet up, he flops back on the couch in my office and starts playing drums against his legs.

I can't concentrate. I should be annoyed, but he's too cute to be irritated by. When he reads, he whispers and responds aloud. I don't think he even realizes he does it. When he huffs, I ask, "Everything alright?"

"A wedding invite," he replies, keeping his eyes on his phone.

"Whose?"

"An ex."

Wow. Okay. *Guess they left on friendly terms.* "Impressive that you remained friends."

"We didn't."

I get up, walk across the room, and sit down next to him. He's bothered. I can tell by the way his forehead is crinkled. I'm curious, so I ask, "Why would she invite you then?"

"I have no fucking clue other than she's crazy." He looks me in the eyes. "I mean like a nutball, out of her mind, batshit crazy."

"I see the attraction."

"Ha! Yeah."

Curling my legs under me, I lean closer to him, and run my fingers along his neck and into his hair. "Tell me what it's like for you to date."

"Why do you want know that?" His tone is even, but his expression curious.

"I want to know you and how you ended up single in Vegas with me."

He smiles. "I'm a player... or was, *am*, supposed to be. Something like that. I don't keep score or anything, but I've slept with a few women, sometimes several at one time. I was always free to do it, even when I was in relationships if that gives you any indication of how dysfunctional they were."

"That won't happen with me." I don't bother beating around the bush. "That's cheating in my opinion."

"Good to know." He seems to make a mental note, but deep down, I don't think he's the same guy he was back then.

"How many serious girlfriends have you had?"

"Serious. Hmmm. Tricky."

"Rephrase. How many girlfriends have you had?"

"Three in the last seven years." He sighs. "Women date Johnny, not me. I'm just the baggage that comes along with the image and fame they desire. One was an actress. She forced me to go to these big Hollywood events, would do a lot of schmoozing, and eventually started landing small roles." His eyes meet mine, and he raises an eyebrow. "When I say schmoozing, I mean she did anything to get the job, *anything*. She broke up with me when she hooked up with her much more famous than me co-star. The dude was twenty-two years older than her and recently separated. He's since dumped her. When she turned twenty-five, he traded her in for a nineteen-year-old lingerie model from Eastern Europe. It was a big tabloid scandal. I almost felt bad for her. *Almost*. She's the one who sent the wedding invite. I didn't even know she was dating anyone."

"Maybe she found true love."

"Maybe she found an asshole who fell for her tricks."

"You fell for her."

"But I'm an asshole."

I laugh and hit him on the arm. "I'm hoping you're not. I've dated enough of those to last me a lifetime."

"And I'm hoping you don't turn batshit crazy on me."

I kiss him. "Guess we'll find out, now won't we?"

"That's half the fun, right?"

I giggle. "Totally. Now carry on and tell me about the others."

"The other two were models—big mistake. I figured since my relationship with the actress went south, maybe hot models were the way to go. The thing about hot models is they're hot and everyone wants a piece of them. I ended up dumping one when she couldn't kick her blow habit. The other, I caught in bed with a famous photographer. He walked away with a bloody nose and a broken camera. She treated me like I was the bad guy. The crazy one for flipping out on them."

"So you could sleep with whomever, but she couldn't. This is starting to sound a bit like a double-standard."

"I couldn't fuck whoever I wanted. I could fuck my girlfriend and whoever she brought home to fuck. There's a difference."

I roll my eyes. "Okay."

When I lean back, he reaches for me, and I can tell he senses the distance I'm putting between us. "You asked me. I was honest. This is the past, the distant past, so don't hold it against me. I've changed a lot since then."

The oven timer sounds, drawing our attention toward the door. I stand up, but he grabs my hands. "I'm asking you to trust me, Holliday."

Although relationships and boyfriends don't come with guarantees, I look into his eyes, seeing his truth and believe he's changed. "I trust you, Dalton. I do."

He stands up, still holding my hand tightly in his. With a kiss to my head, he says, "Thank you."

We've been asleep for hours when I feel the bed move and the warmth of Dalton pressed against me disappears. Rolling over, I sit up when I hear him rummaging downstairs in the fridge. I head down to join him. The fridge door is wide open and he's standing next to it. "What're you doing down here?" I ask, rubbing one eye.

"I was hungry," he says with the leftover lasagna pan in his hand. "Want some?"

"That's why I buy the family size. Let me get you a plate," I say, taking it from him. I serve up two portions and heat his up in the microwave first, then set it in front of him at the bar. "It's good cold, but better warm."

"It is good. Really good." He looks around while chewing. "How long have you lived here?"

"Almost two years," I say, sitting down next to him.

"I like it." He takes another big bite. When he's through, he says, "It's been a long time since I've sat still and listened to nature. I can hear it here even with the windows closed. I can hear seagulls and the wind. Not much traffic. That's nice."

"The sound of breaking waves is my favorite."

"Why did you buy blocks away then?"

I look at him. "Nothing was for sale in this area that was located on the beach and I couldn't afford Malibu." I'm not offended he asked, but it does feel like he's a little out of touch with reality.

"Yeah, I like your place," he says, pushing his plate away. "I didn't know what to expect, but it really suits you and it beats being stuck in a hotel suite, isolated from the world."

I take him by the hands and pull him to his feet. "Let's go back to bed."

We curl up under the covers together and he kisses me—deep and needy, sweet and sexy all at once.

Our lips part and I smile in the dark. "If I get more kisses like that, I may never let you leave."

"You'd have to deal with some angry fans, so maybe it's best if I just sleep on this side of the bed," he teases, scooting away from me. "You know, for your safety."

"Your kisses are worth the risk. Now get your ass back over here."

Reaching over, he pulls me to him. After a long, hard kiss, he rubs his erection against me and says, "There's more where that came from."

With a giggle, I say, "I was hoping you'd say that."

19

"My dad used to say 'Never assume anything. Everything comes with conditions and a price to pay.' He might be right." ~Johnny Outlaw

We're easy, almost too easy. I'm starting to worry that maybe I went into this relationship with Dalton blinded by the instant attraction instead of taking the safer, slower get-to-know-you route. He left L.A. five days ago and completely planted himself into my thoughts, demanding all my time and attention. I guess I can't blame him for that, but I'm not used to being this into a guy. At this rate, I'll be checking myself into the Johnny Outlaw Rehabilitation Center for Once Functional Women.

I bet there's a waiting list a mile long for that rehab program.

A knock on my front door coaxes me out of my head and back

to the present. I spin around my desk chair and get up to answer it.

Looking through the peephole, I see my new neighbor. After unlocking the deadbolt, I open the door and say, "Hi, Donny."

"Hi, ummm, it's Danny," he says with a smile and little awkward two finger salute.

I mentally admonish myself for the mistake. "Eeks, I'm sorry. Danny, yes, Danny. It's been a crazy few weeks. Sorry about that."

"It's okay. Sooo," he continues. "I'd mentioned a party when we spoke last. It's tomorrow night if you're interested in coming. Just wanted to extend the invitation again."

"Tomorrow?" I ask, sounding surprised and a bit ridiculous when my voice goes up an octave. "I umm, yeah, I'll stop by."

"Great!" He claps his hands together as if his job here is done, and backs down my two steps to the shared landing. "Around eight?"

"Sure. Eight. Can I bring anything?"

"No, just you."

"Okay, see you then. Thanks."

He smiles, revealing two small dimples in his cheeks. "See you then."

I shut the door and get back to work.

When Danny says a party, he means a party. I can hear the music through the walls and muffled voices through the open doors of my patio. It's not even nine o'clock and his place is packed. *Popular guy apparently.*

I should have invited Tracy over. I haven't seen her all week. We've talked business on the phone, but I still haven't gotten the lowdown on why she came to Vegas and blew off the family celebration of her engagement. I'm gonna get her to spill at Sunday brunch tomorrow. In the meantime, I have a party to attend that makes me all kinds of nervous. I won't know anyone there except Danny and I don't know him at all.

Dressed casually in jeans and a fitted shirt, I grab my gifts and head next door. I knock three times and wait, but no one answers. Just when I start to open the door, it's pulled open and I go stumbling right into Danny. "Oh!" I say, surprised.

His hands grab hold of my arms and we steady ourselves. "Hi there. Glad you could stumble by," he says, chuckling.

"I knocked... three times, but no one answered." I shake my head and the incident off, following him just inside the door. With a smile I offer up my goods. "Welcome to the neighborhood." I hold out a bottle of champagne and a measuring cup full of sugar. Fortunately I put plastic wrap over it or it would be all over his steps right now.

"Thank you and ummm..." He looks at the cup of sugar, his eyebrows pulled together, perplexed. "Sugar?"

"Yes. You know, to save you the trip when you run out. Now you have it."

He smiles, and it's sincere. When he looks at me, he says, "That's the most clever gift I've gotten in a while. Thanks."

I hand him the last gift, which makes him laugh. "You got me a Bite Me T-shirt. Awesome. Thanks."

"It's my company."

"It is?" His face shows his astonishment.

"Don't be all impressed. It's really just free advertising if you wear it. I'm totally just using you," I joke.

"I dig it and you can use me anytime. Hold this." He hands me the T-shirt, sets the cup and champagne on a side table, and then unbuttons his shirt.

"You don't have to wear it now," I say, looking around at anything other than his tan and very toned body.

165

"I want to and thanks for the new duds."

Stripping it off garners everyone's attention, almost to the point of hearing a needle skid across a record. When I look back at Danny, he takes the shirt from my hands and pulls it over his very fit stomach. Not that I notice his abs or that defined V that his muscles make. Nope, didn't notice any of that.

He nods toward the kitchen. "Let's get you a drink."

Fifteen minutes later, I'm standing on his patio and some guy whose name I forgot is talking my ear off about something, but he lost me on differentials. Holding my finger up, I say, "Excuse me. I'll be back."

I escape, my glass already empty, the fast consumption of my drink needed to get through a conversation with that guy. Walking back to the kitchen I notice every female here is pretty, but not just average pretty—model pretty. Danny's a good looking guy but doesn't he know normal looking women? Oh wait, maybe that's my role at this party.

"Can I refresh your wine?" Danny comes up behind me.

"I'd like that." As he refills the glass, I ask, "Is every woman here a model or what? I have to say I'm a little intimidated."

"Not all of them, but most," he says matter-of-fact. He tops off my glass. "And you have nothing to be intimidated by." He licks his bottom lip while looking into my eyes.

After sipping my wine, I ask, "Do you only date models?" I lean against the counter, hoping to steer the topic away from me.

"No. But I have dated a lot of models, most are more or less friends these days."

The wine is starting to go to my head. I should have eaten dinner before I came over. "Most of the women here are friends you've dated?" I briefly question if that even makes sense.

Laughing, he smiles, tilting his head and looking amused.

"Ummm... I kind of meant, most of the women I've dated I'm still friends with." He looks around as if taking a tally. When he turns back to me, he says, "I'm not currently having sex more or less with any of the women at this party."

"The night's still young."

"It most definitely is," he adds just as a woman in a skin-toned dress wraps her arms around him.

"You've been avoiding me, Danny," she slurs.

He takes her arms and in one smooth move, he turns, freed from her clutches. "Not avoiding, just playing host to all my guests."

She eyes me up and says to him, "Come spend some time with the gang in the living room. We're your guests, too."

With a roll of his eyes, he smiles, then chuckles under his breath. "If you'll excuse—"

"It's fine. Tend to your guests." I raise my glass to him.

Looking over his shoulder, he asks, "You're staying, right?"

"I'll stay a little longer."

With a nod, he turns and walks with her into the other room.

I rummage around the dining table snacking on hors d'oeuvres and pretending to be completely comfortable in my aloneness. A waif of a girl breezes up to the table and takes a cracker, eats one bite and then disposes of the rest before pulling a cigarette from her bag and heading out to the patio. I set my plate of food down, feeling guilty for eating now and decide to drink more wine.

Moving out to the patio, the night is nice—clear skies and cool, but not cold. I can hear the ocean in the distance and lean on the patio wall toward the water. His patio overlooks mine, which needs a good sweeping. Maybe something I should do tomorrow or maybe not.

"I love the location," Danny says, leaning his back against the wall next to me.

"Worth every penny."

"I think you got a better deal a few years ago, but yeah, still worth every penny."

I tap my glass against his beer bottle. "Let's hope I did. Ha!"

"You're not home much or you're a very quiet neighbor. Do you travel a lot?"

"I travel a little. Not much for work if I can help it. I went to Vegas recently."

"I'm still amazed I live next to the woman who created the Bite Me Lime. That's so cool."

"And what do you do?"

"If you listen to my agent—"

"*Ahhh*," I say, "You have an agent."

"Hey, hey. Not so harsh."

I laugh. "Sorry. Go on."

"Well, according to my agent, I'm an aging underwear model..." My eyebrows go up as he continues, "...But now I'm a photographer most of the time, location scout sometimes. It pays the bills and I love what I do. Something different every day. I never get bored."

"I bet not. Sounds interesting."

"Do you mind if I ask you something personal, Holli?"

Even in the soft light of the living room that's seeping outside, I can see his eyes fixed on me. Makes me want to blush from the intensity. I laugh instead, my usual comfort reaction. "I think you have every right after what I asked you in the kitchen."

"Well," he starts, but pauses to glance down. "I've been wondering... if you think I should upgrade to hardwoods through the lower level."

I burst out laughing and hit him on the arm. "You had me going the way you were so serious. You have a sick sense of humor, you know that?"

"I do," he says, laughing. "Actually, I was wondering if you have hardwoods I could see?"

"Yep, I do. Stop by anytime."

"How about now?"

I look at him and then to my patio, trying to remember if I straightened up earlier. "Sure."

As we walk over to mine, he asks, "I'm thinking dark wood, but being near the beach makes me want to go light."

"I went light." I unlock the door, and walk inside.

He stops just inside the door. "Wow, for the same floorplan, your place is a lot nicer."

"I've done a little renovation here and there. Make yourself at home." I close the door and follow him around.

"Can I see what you've done upstairs or is it off-limits?"

"You can peek in my office, but not in the bedroom please. I have issues with hanging up clothes, so they end up on the floor and in my chair, piled high."

He makes his way up and I go into the kitchen to get a glass of wine since I left mine at the party. My phone buzzes on the counter and Dalton's name flashes. I hear Danny talking to friends at his house from my patio when I answer, "Hi." I feel like I should join Danny, but stay in the kitchen.

"Hi. You're up?"

"Yes, I'm still up."

"What are you doing?"

"I've missed your voice," I say, not realizing how much I have until I hear it again.

"You do?"

"Yeah."

"Good. I miss everything about you. Especially that tattoo... and your pus—"

"Cool digs," Danny says, startling me when he walks into the kitchen.

"Oh, thanks," I reply, my attention divided. I raise my finger to let him know I need a minute. He nods and walks into the living room. "Dalton?"

"Holliday, who's there?"

"My neighbor stopped by to see my hardwoods."

"*Hardwoods?* Is that code for something?"

I burst out laughing, but suddenly realize he's not joking. "No, it's only code for flooring." Trying to bring him around, I lighten it up by saying, "I know how sexy the topic of flooring is, but no, it's not code... I don't know where I was going with that."

"Not at all," he says, chuckling. "Get rid of the neighbor and let's get back to talking about what I miss about you."

"I like that idea a lot. Let me call you right back."

"K."

When I hang up, I join Danny in the living room. "Do you like what you see?"

He nods, a small smile appearing. "I do."

"So you're gonna go for it?"

"I might. It's hard to decide. Sometimes you want to know for sure before pulling the trigger, so to speak."

Leaning against the sofa, I'm suddenly thinking we might be talking about two different things entirely. Feeling the need to clear the air, I say, "Danny, I just started seeing someone."

He plays it off as he heads for the door. "Oh, yeah, sure," he says, "no, um, flooring. We were talking hardwood flooring, right?"

"Yeah, right." I take a deep breath, hoping the uncomfortable tension escapes the room when he opens the door wide.

"I should get back. You in for the night?"

"I think so," I reply, kicking off my shoes.

"Thanks for coming and for the housewarming gifts. I'll have to come up with an excuse other than needing sugar to pop round."

"There's always eggs."

"True. See you around."

"See you around." I walk to the door and close it after he enters his apartment without looking back. With a deep breath, I sigh. Danny is my neighbor. I don't date where I sleep and if my calculations are correct, we have about 2 feet between where our heads lie. That's too close for comfort. Anyway, I have Dalton.

I pick up my phone and call him back. He's on an adrenaline rush from the show and we both benefit from the good mood as he catalogs everything he loves to touch on my body and exactly how he loves to touch it. Since he's not here, I replace his hand with my own and he replaces mine with his. It's not the same as him, but with his dirty words and breathy moans, we both end the night on a high.

20

"Relationships are tricky. You bring a carry-on into it and end up with major baggage." ~Johnny Outlaw

Sitting down across from Tracy, I drop my bag in the seat next to me, and say, "Hey there."

She looks up from her phone as if she doesn't even notice the whirlwind of an entrance I just made. "Hi."

"Sorry, I'm late. I got held up at—"

"It's okay." She holds up her hand, no further explanation needed. "I ordered coffee. We should get you something."

"Why are you drinking coffee? We drink mimosas or screwdrivers at brunch. Even a Cape Cod occasionally, but never coffee? You okay?"

"Yeah," she says, waving the waitress over. Clear sign she's diverting.

I lean forward, concerned. Tracy is never rude or impatient. "What is it? What's going on?"

She straightens her shoulders and tilts her chin up as if she's steeling herself for an argument. "I broke up with Adam."

"What?" I say this way too loud, drawing attention from nearby diners. Lowering my voice, I whisper, "What happened?"

Snapping her fingers in the air for the waitress, Tracy orders two Screwdrivers when she arrives. "But hold the OJ," she adds.

The waitress, not amused by Tracy's treatment, asks, "So you want two vodkas, straight up? A bit early, don't ya think?"

Tracy glares at her. "My fiancé has been cheating on me, so judge away."

"Oh, honey," the waitress says, her tone changing completely. "I'm so sorry. I'll get the drinks."

Tracy stifles a sniffle, but stops her before she leaves. "And I'll have the pancake platter with an extra side of crispy bacon, two scrambled eggs with salsa on the side, and a muffin. Do you have blueberry today?"

The waitress answers, "Yes."

"I'll have the blueberry muffin then. Also, do you have those big olives that you put in your Bloody Mary's?"

"From the bar? Yeah."

"Can I have a few of those on the side," Tracy adds as my eyes start bugging out. I guess we know what kind of griever Tracy is— comfort food is her friend, soon to be best at this rate.

They both look at me. "Oh, ummm." I scan the menu quickly. "The Eggs Benedict please and a Mimosa."

"She'll have a vodka with me and make them shots," Tracy interrupts. "And maybe I'll also have the Eggs Benedict too.

Seems fitting considering I've been in a relationship with a traitor."

"I'll put a rush on your order," the waitress says, then hurries off.

I immediately lean in, still shocked by the bomb just dropped, and ask, "What do you mean Adam's been cheating on you?"

She crosses her arms, and looks away from me. "Sure, Holli, take his side."

My hands fly up in front of me. "I'm not taking anyone's side. I'm just shocked because I know how much Adam loves you. I'm so surp—"

"If he loved me he wouldn't have cheated on me with some ho-bag five years ago on Spring Break in Mexico."

Sitting back, I digest what she just said. "Five years ago?"

"That doesn't make it right just because it was a long time ago."

I huff. "Stop twisting my words. I know it doesn't. It just sounds—"

"You're siding with him again."

"Tracy, calm down. I'm not siding with him."

"You're not siding with me either. I need you in my corner."

I reach across and cover her hand with mine. "I am in your corner. This is just out of the blue. When did you find out? How did you find out?"

"He told me a couple weeks ago."

The pieces seem to fall into place. I raise my eyebrow and look her in the eyes. "That's why you came to Vegas."

She nods. Our drinks are set down in front of us along with a little bowl of olives and a muffin for Tracy. She takes a big bite of the muffin, and with tears in her eyes, says, "I didn't know what to do, so I left."

Despite the pastry-filled confession, I understand every word. I pick up the vodka and hand her the drink. With my glass in hand, I say, "Bottoms up." I shoot the shot and shake my head in disgust afterwards. "Why are we shooting vodka by the way?"

"I couldn't think clearly. I needed something stronger than coffee."

I set the glass down and try to find reason in the insanity. "Okay, let's talk this through. He told you. That's a pro in my book. Maybe poor timing. He should have told you when it happened or even better, not have done it. That's a con. But it did happen. Did he tell you why he cheated?"

She stays quiet when the food is set down in front of us. When the waitress leaves, Tracy says, "He shouldn't have done it. Period. But he did, so I've been trying to remember everything about that spring break. I stayed on campus because I had to work. He ended up on a boys' trip to Mexico having sex with some college sophomore he met from Rochester. End of story. Con. Con. Con."

"I'm sorry." My heart hurts for her, but I can tell this isn't something that's going to be solved over vodka shots and Eggs Benedict. "If you need a place to stay, you know you can come over to mine until you figure things out."

"No, it's fine. Adam went over to one of his friends' apartments, but thank you." She sips her coffee, leaving the second shot of vodka untouched as she stares out the window of the restaurant. When she looks back, her tone is steady, but lower. "He's apologized to me every day through email, text, and voicemail, sent flowers, and he even serenaded me one night. What should I do, Holli?"

"Oh Trace, I suck at relationships. You know this. So I'm not sure I have any words of wisdom on the subject."

"Tell me as a friend. Don't be logical and give me pros or cons, but from one girl to another."

"What does your heart tell you?"

"To forgive him. I miss him, but it pisses me off that I miss him after what he did."

I drag my fork through the hollandaise sauce. "I've been cheated on. It's not pretty and it's not easy to get over. I stayed with one guy. I broke up with another, but anyway you look at it, I'm not with either now. Was it because they cheated? I don't know anymore. I may have thought that at the time, but looking back now, I'm not so sure. I had issues in both of those relationships. The cheating just magnified the problems."

She sets her glass down and says, "Things have been so good the last few years, heck, I thought all six years were, but was it just a charade he was putting on for me?"

"No, Adam loves you. You can see it. Everyone can see it. Don't doubt what you've shared. It was mistake he made a long time ago."

"But I do. I doubt everything now."

"Do you love him?"

"Of course, I do. So much. Still, which makes me mad."

"Then it sounds like you need more time."

Glancing down as more food is set in front of her, she says, "I guess I do." When she looks back up at me, she smiles. "You're gonna eat some of this with me, right?"

I reach across the table and steal some bacon. "Absolutely."

We continue eating as I fill her in on the party at Danny's. "Sounds like he likes you in more than a neighborly way," she says, raising an eyebrow up suggestively.

"What is the neighborly way anyway?"

Tracy shrugs. "Maybe it's when you share your old eggs—"

"Don't talk about my eggs like that. They might hear you and shrivel up and die."

"That's gross, Hols. I was talking about the eggs in your fridge. They're like two months old or more. But maybe he does want your eggs." She drops her fork. "I think I'm done eating. This conversation has taken a turn for the worse."

"This conversation is a lot ironic by the way. The last thing I told him is I have eggs if he needs any."

"Is that what the kids are calling it these days?" she teases. "Sharing eggs?"

"You and Dalton with your code words. I think I'm a little more straight-forward than that. Now stop. I don't even know how we got started talking about sharing old eggs."

"Back to this neighbor," she says. The girl's got tenacity, that's for sure. "You say he's a model?"

"Was."

"Are we quibbling about was or is a model? Does it matter? He was an underwear model. Holy hotness. And why didn't you invite me to this party?"

"I thought you were busy with Adam."

She snorts and shoots the second shot before ordering another round for us by twirling her finger in the air. She might be drunk. "I don't want to talk about me and Adam."

So instead of Adam, I tell her about the models and how Danny is 'more or less friends' with them. That makes her giggle but I think the vodka is helping the sillies along as well.

When she stops laughing, she asks, "And Johnny? How's the tour and that going?"

"Life feels like I'm peeking at it through a looking glass, so surreal. It is normal to fall into a funk after someone you like leaves?"

"It's surreal because you hooked up with a rock star. As for the latter, I've been in a funk too, so I'm thinking it's normal."

I'm starting to giggle, the booze affecting me. Fortunately, I biked here. "Good to know I'm not crazy."

"You still might be a little crazy—crazy over a guy named Johnny Outlaw."

"That's what I'm afraid of," I reply with a sigh.

We leave after another round of mimosas, both of us in better moods. As I bike home, my mind goes to Dalton, like it always does. I can finally admit to myself that I am crazy—crazy in love with Jack Dalton and crazy in lust with Johnny Outlaw.

21

"A lost soul doesn't have to wander forever." ~Johnny Outlaw

Weeks later, Tracy and I repeat our brunch date, vodka and mimosas and all. She hasn't made up with Adam and he hasn't stopped begging for forgiveness.

Unlike what I thought would happen in my own relationship, I'm not missing Dalton less, but more. Things between us are good, really good, and mostly effortless. A simple phone call to say hi usually turns into a two-hour conversation, but weeks of touring Europe is wearing on him. I can tell by how rundown he's starting to sound. We miss a few calls when he's too exhausted after a show. It doesn't bother me, not like I thought it would. Despite the newness of our relationship and the distance separating us, I trust him. I don't know when I developed this new found comfort and faith, but I like it. I like me better because of it too. The stresses that past relationships caused don't seem to exist between Dalton and me. *I wonder if I should I be worried?*

I slow down as I approach my place, my bike coming to a stop on the sidewalk out front. When I look up, I see I have a visitor sitting on my stoop and my heart momentarily stops. Sight for sore eyes doesn't define how happy I am to see him.

Dalton stands, shifts his weight and smiles. "I had an unexpected wanderlust."

Putting the kickstand down with a flirty smile on my face, I say, "You have the heart of a poet, Mr. Dalton. So were you just in the neighborhood?"

"I was nowhere near your neighborhood."

I walk up the steps and he walks down a few and we meet in the middle. Our lips and bodies coming together. I roam over his shoulders and back up again, testing to make sure he's real and I'm not dreaming. "I like your surprises." Taking him by the hand, I invite him in. As soon as the door closes, he presses me to the wall, showing me how much he missed me, a feeling I'm becoming all too familiar with.

"I missed you, too." I lean against his chest and listen to his racing heart as it syncs with mine. "Stopping in for the day or do I get you longer this time?"

His chest move as he chuckles. "Only one day."

"That's why you're traveling so light," I say, referencing the backpack.

"I sent my luggage to Mexico City. I've got a free day. Wanna spend it with me?"

Tilting my head in confusion, I ask, "No meetings?"

"No meetings."

"Just a random free day?"

"Just a random free day I'd rather spend with you then cooped up in a hotel in Mexico." He shrugs like this isn't the most romantic gesture ever.

I sigh, pretending to be exasperated. "I had a feeling you were going to say that."

"Did I screw up?"

"No," I say, tugging on his belt loops. "I just had this whole list of things I needed to get done today and now that's all shot to hell." I slide my hand under his shirt, his jacket still on. While feeling the muscles of his stomach, his leg slides between mine, adding pressure. I don't mean to gyrate, but he does this to me, makes me lose control. I also like to get a rise out of him, and selfishly, it feels good.

He grabs a hold of my waist, pushing up the side of my shirt he knows my tattoo is on, and rubs his hand over it. His voice is strained, when he says, "I can go."

With a deep breath, tingles take over and I close my eyes. Slipping away, I try to collect myself. He watches me as I get a glass of water from the kitchen and drink, keeping my eyes on him. I set the glass down and lean against the counter. "Nope," I tease, "the damage is already done, but we should go ahead and have sex because you're here and I missed you. Truth is, I won't be able to think about anything else, so we should just get it out of the way now."

With a grin on his face, he teases right back. "You're a horny girl and I like it."

I say, "Damn straight," and walk past him up the stairs.

A "Fuck," is muttered before he says, "A woman who knows what she likes. Be careful, I might fall in love." Inside the bedroom, he kisses me, leaving me breathless, then he does it again and adds, "I missed you."

Reaching up, I touch his cheek, feeling warm inside. Such sweet words, that this time, I lift up and kiss him before turning and starting to undress. With only my bra and panties on, I wiggle my ass to tempt him to follow me to the bed. He's fast, rushing in and taking me down onto the mattress in an embracing tackle. Hovering over me, he says, "I missed you, but I really fucking missed that freckle on the inside of your left thigh. Mind if I visit it?"

Everything about him feels amazing. He makes me feel amazing. "The freckle would be disappointed if you didn't."

Taking his phone from his pocket, he scrolls through his music. I'm used to the routine now. His song will dictate his sexual appetite.

Nine Inch Nails' "Closer"–*Oh fuck me.* It's like he's speaking straight to my libido.

After setting the phone on the nightstand, he slides back down. His erection is against my body until his feet touch the ground again. Standing at the end of the bed, he takes my knees and pulls them apart, not gently, but like he can't wait any longer. I know the feeling.

Dalton's mouth covers the spot where I can only assume a freckle resides, and I close my eyes in ecstasy. He sucks, leaving a physical reminder of his presence, and I let him, wanting it.

Lifting up, I unhook my bra and toss it aside. He looks up and uses both hands to grab my breasts, squeezing them, forcing a heavy breath out of me. He suffers from the same lack of control I do when it comes to him.

"I wanna fuck you so hard," he says, climbing back on top of me. "I want to devour you. I want to fucking own your body. I want all of you, all of you—body and soul." He pushes me back on the bed, then strips my underwear off before he focuses on my pussy. "You're mine, Holliday Hughes. Are we clear?"

"Yes." I gulp. Reaching for a condom in the nightstand, I hand it to him. Right when he's about to take it, I pull it back. Using it as leverage. "The same goes for you, Jack Dalton. You're mine. Are we clear?"

A hard stare is shared—testing me by the way he narrows his. When I don't relent, he replies, "Yes." With that verbal agreement, I hand him the condom.

I watch as he drops down again, his arms landing on either side of my head. He licks his lips just as I do, then aligns himself, pushing forward. His head drops down, his forehead landing on the bed next to me. My breaths stagger and heave, uneven and shattered like my thoughts. Nothing makes sense but the urge to give and take more.

I do. He does too.

He starts thrusting harder and I groan, the pleasure too encompassing to hide a natural reaction. My back arches, my head falling back. My nails scale his body and then slide down his back, digging in, taking possession. He moans and jolts in response, my body reacting to the sound of him, pleasure bordering on pain.

"My angel," he murmurs.

My skin is set on fire, my face feeling flushed and he smiles, cocky written in that wry grin as he fucks me. I arch my back again, exhaling his name with every thrust, "Dalton." Everything about this moment feels too great as prickly sensations cover me from head to toe and I give into it.

"Get on your knees," he demands, no time to soak in the afterglow of my orgasm.

I roll over, getting on my hands and knees, and he's in me. Fingers dig into my hips, as he takes me over and over how he wants—rough and hard. The sounds of him taking me from behind fill my room, his groans penetrating my body and turning me on.

He quickens, slamming into me four times in fast succession then holding me against him as he comes.

"Lay down," he says, his voice much raspier than before. We both fall to the mattress and I close my eyes, loving the feeling of what we shared. He looks exhausted next to me and I run my fingers through his hair.

Rolling onto my side, I drape my thigh over his leg and get closer, my bare chest against his. I kiss him, then prop my head up as our lips part. Never loving nakedness more than in these moments with him, our bodies ebb and flow together in dips and curves. Two sides of the puzzle come together to form a union that seems protected in perfection and unscathed by life. Here, together, we don't have pasts that scar us or baggage that weighs us down with burdens and regrets. Here, together, our flawed souls find solace in each other.

Here, together, we make sense.

22

"I find normal more fascinating than outrageous. I'm surrounded by chaos all the time. Normal is way more interesting." ~Johnny Outlaw

After three weeks on the road, Dalton returns to L.A. and I jump him the minute he shows up at my door. It isn't pretty or romantic. I'm just so damn happy to see him. He drives me crazy like that, so romance flies out the window. I was sore for two days afterward and have absolutely no regrets about it.

It's been blissful to spend five days straight with him. He left for his house this morning to 'take care of business' as he put it, but most of the time, he's at mine. I think he likes the normalness of the neighborhood. No paparazzi or fans have discovered him over here... yet.

"I want to take you to my friends' house today. Are you busy?" Dalton asks me over the phone.

While sitting in my office, I lean back in my chair and swivel to face the window. "I'm free for you."

"I like that."

"I like you."

"Okay, I like that even more."

"I really like that you like that even more." I giggle, feeling silly.

Chuckling, he asks, "With this big like-fest going on, do you have any openings I can fill before we head over? You know, openings in your schedule."

"I have several... openings you can fill. What works best fo—"

"I'm on my way."

Dead air. At least it's for a good reason. The man is insatiable and I love it. Jumping up, I run into the bathroom and freshen up. Thank goodness I decided to take a shower this morning. I put on a little makeup and spritz with perfume. I whip my hair up into a ponytail and rush back into my office to shut everything down.

Dalton arrives in record time. When I open the door, I greet him by saying, "You're a motivated man."

"You know how to motivate me."

"C'mere." Feeling a lot motivated myself, I kiss him hard. He backs me further inside, lips joined with mine, until the back of my legs hit the end of the couch.

Not wasting time, I push down my shorts and pull off my shirt.

"I like this look on you," he says, running his finger over my bare breasts.

"You mean naked?"

"Yeah, naked. I like you naked best." Kneeling before me, he leans forward, his heated breath hitting me right before he kisses me again, but much lower this time. Motivation does funny things to people and we lose the next hour to moans and breathy sighs as pleasure is built and satisfaction is found.

I'm nervous as we drive over to Dalton's band-mate's house. This neighborhood is not where you expect a guitarist from one of the most popular bands in the world to live. It's down-to-earth, not pretentious at all. The house is in the middle of the Valley and most of the homes are similar ranch-style homes, but it suits all the good things I've heard about Cory and Rochelle.

When we walk in, Dalton's hand tightens around mine, which makes me wonder if he's a little nervous too. Introducing me to his friends is stressful stuff and definitely makes us more than just two people who have sex, even if it is a lot of sex. After a few hellos, Dalton continues out the sliding glass door to find the hosts. The backyard is an oasis. Not a rocker's oasis but one many would envy—green grass, vegetable garden in the corner, a nice deck, and a fountain against the house that adds to the casual ambience.

Walking straight across the lush lawn to where a group of people are gathered, Dalton says hi to Cory, "Hey man." They shake hands, but Cory pulls him in with a few hard pats to the back. I recognize him from a CD cover.

Looking back at me, Dalton introduces me, "This is Holli." I note how he doesn't call me Holliday. Looking at me, he says, "Cory's our bassist and writes a lot of the songs, most of the hits actually."

"Hi," Cory says, shaking my hand. "It's nice to meet you. I heard you created that lime."

I Laugh. "Guilty."

"That's cool. It's funny stuff."

I shrug. "It certainly was when I was drunk and thought of it. Now it's taken on a life of its own."

He nods as if he understands. "Yeah, I can see that. The music business can be the same."

A petite brunette—hair highlighted from the SoCal sun, olive skin, big dimples in her cheeks, pregnant—joins us. "You must be Holli."

"Yes, I—"

She hugs me, an embrace that comes with genuine warmth. "It's so good to finally meet you. Johnny has told me so many wonderful things about you."

My eyes meet Dalton's over her shoulder while a sly grin teases the corner of his mouth. "This is Rochelle—the heart of the band," he says.

She turns and smacks him in the stomach. "Stop it. Don't embarrass me. Everyone knows the great Johnny Outlaw is the heart of the band. I'm just a groupie these days."

Dalton reaches forward and wraps his arms around her and she does the same to him. The hug is sweet, the embrace sincere. "How are you feeling?" he asks.

"Big," she replies. "How are you?"

"Happy." His gaze flashes to me, then back to her.

Rochelle smiles. "I like happy on you."

Dalton steps next to me and takes my hand. "So do I," he says, as if the emotion is something he's trying on for the first time. "Rochelle is eight months pregnant. Cory managed to knock her up twice out of wedlock."

Cory laughs, beer in hand. "Ha! Not for lack of trying to shackle her to me. She's the hold-out, not me."

Looking at her, she smiles like she's heard this a thousand times and maybe even a faint blush is hidden in those dimples of hers. "Ask me again when you're not drunk and lonely on the road."

"Done," he says, draping his arm around her shoulders and kissing her on the head. She rubs his stomach over his T-shirt, the gesture loving. They feel so different from what I expected. By the way they look at each other, I can tell they're more than just significant in each other's lives.

Suddenly, the realization that I'm Dalton's current 'other' hits me like a sledgehammer.

"Holliday?" Dalton sounds distant though he's standing right next to me. His hand takes hold of my elbow and he calls me again, "Holliday?" When I look up, his green eyes are curious. "Rochelle just asked if you want something to drink."

Turning to her, still a little shaken, I say, "Yes. Yes, I think that will be nice. I'll go with you." My hand drifts from Dalton's, one of my fingers keeping contact until he's out of reach.

Rochelle smiles at me, and says, "Johnny says you own your own business."

"I do," I reply as we stroll. "It's grown a lot in the last year and I'm expanding the brand."

"Sounds like a lot of hard work. Guess you won't be joining them on the road."

"No, my schedule sucks right now. This afternoon, Dalton had to force me away from my computer."

"I like the name Dalton. I used to call him Jack but it got complicated in public. The masses want Johnny Outlaw. Anyway,

I'm glad you came over. Johnny came over on Wednesday and had dinner with us. Neil, our little guy playing over in the garden, loves him. Calls him Uncle Johnny." She nudges me. "I think Johnny has a soft spot for kids, too."

Kids? That's not a topic I'm ready to broach anytime soon. "Maybe just Neil."

She laughs, knowing I'm trying to change the topic. "Yeah, maybe just Neil."

I'd call Rochelle a modern day flower child, but she has a rock n' roll edge to her that makes her a paradigm to place. The skirt is full and flowy with a knot holding it high above her left knee, exposing her lean legs and bare feet. A simple, man's white tank top fits her pregnant body and exposes a few tattoos. I suspect she has more, but not on display. One tattoo is a ring of wildflowers that adorns her wrist. It's colorful and pretty, reminding me of mine.

She leads me to a light blue metal swing set and she sits. The set is not new and has rust spots and is a duplicate of one I had when I was six. I love that it's not a rich kid's swing set or even one of the large treehouse-type playscapes that fill suburban neighborhoods. I sit down in a swing and push off, my ass feeling way too big for this small seat.

"How did you meet Cory?" I ask, leaning my head on the chain of the swing and watching her.

Her eyes find him across the yard. He's laughing while pushing a popping kid's toy and running from their son. She smiles, then turns to me. "Would you believe I'm from the streets of elite—a goth, Greek girl who grew up in Boston?"

I'm too intrigued to interrupt and I have a feeling most people would feel the same. She has a great energy about her. Her brown eyes are welcoming and her smile warm as she sways on the swing next to me, and continues, "I was born and raised in Boston, Beacon Hill to be precise. Well, raised is relative. I lived there until I was sixteen. I left at seventeen before I graduated." She laughs, pushing herself off, and swinging with her legs out in front of her. "Feels almost stereotypical to say, but my great-grandfather was in shipping and freighting back in Greece and did very well. Very Aristotle Onassis of him. He moved to America, coming over on a luxury yacht, opting out of the rickety sea ships back in those days. He settled in Boston, feeling it was nicer than New York, which was going through an industrial transition at the time."

She stops, her feet dragging in the grass below. "It's my history that led me to Cory." She stands and starts to walk and I follow, catching up with her. "I hear you have tattoos?"

"Just one, right here on my side." I lift my shirt up just enough to show her, suddenly wanting her approval and friendship.

She stops and leans down as much as her baby belly will allow and studies it. "Johnny called it sexy," she says casually. "I'd have to agree. It's very sensual in the artistry of the curves. Does it represent anything special?" She stops and looks me in the eyes, genuinely interested.

"It represents my journey, everything that is my life."

"It's beautiful, Holli, and very you."

"Thank you."

She shakes her head as if a thought just hit her. "Oh, you were asking about Cory. So I decided the Colonial Colonies weren't for me. Yeah, Boston wasn't exactly Plymouth and not quite Massachusetts Bay, but it wasn't me either, so I sat my parents down and had a heart to heart with them. I told them I was moving to the City of Lost Angels because it felt more like the place I was supposed to be."

"And they just let you go?"

Laughter. "Um, no, but I was too determined. I packed one suitcase—five albums and three outfits in it. Pulled on my Doc Marten's and caught a flight to L.A. the next day."

A long story might bore some, but she's so animated that I'm happy to listen till the end.

At the picnic table, she pours herself a glass of lemonade, offering me one, and continues. "My parents gave me a monthly stipend if I worked on my GED, which I did, and I got a full-time job at a guitar store. That's where I met Cory. He was this geeky seventeen-year-old, who had mowed lawns all summer to buy a guitar, hoping to learn how to play and woo the ladies. We became friends because he hung around so much. I was self taught from the age of thirteen and gave him lessons five days a week. I sucked. He knew it, though he won't admit it." She shrugs and smiles again. "I don't know what it was that drew me to him. He had no cool moves and he didn't own a vintage rock shirt to save his life, but he was shy and really sweet when you got to know him. He made me laugh, made me feel pretty, and won me over."

"Wow. That is such a romantic and sweet story."

Her eyes are on Cory again and she smiles. "Just like him."

I follow her gaze. Dalton's talking to Cory, both of them looking our way. He sends a little wave in my direction, and I return one with a smile.

"We met Johnny two years later. He walked into the store with all this bravado and attitude—angry at the world, and very determined. We all got to talking one night over beers in this garage that he was renting and it just came together. The start of the band."

Neil comes from behind her and tugs on her skirt. She looks down and around and a wide grin covers her face. "If you'll excuse me, I have a little monkey to tend to."

"Of course. No problem."

While walking away, she turns around, and says, "I'm glad you came today. It's really nice to meet you, Holli."

"You too. Thanks for having me."

"Anytime." She disappears into the house.

A hand slides around my waist, and a warm whisper tickles my ear. "I've been missing you. That can't be normal, right?"

I turn in Dalton's arms and wrap mine around his neck. "You might need to see a doctor about that?"

He tempts with a lick of his bottom lip, and says, "I'd love to play doctor with you. You have any openings... in your schedule?" One of his hands slinks under my shirt, getting dangerously close to the underside of my boob.

As his thumb strokes back and forth, taunting, teasing, I repeat my earlier invitation, "I have several openings you can fill."

Standing upright as if shocked by my response, he says, "You are a very dirty girl, Holliday Hughes."

"Whatever." I roll my eyes. "You led me straight into that trap."

"I'm gonna lead you into more later. Let's go."

We say our goodbyes and make a quick exit, heading back to his place to fill those openings... in my schedule.

23

"I've discovered the quiet ones are usually the loudest. You just have to take the time to listen." ~*Johnny Outlaw*

I've been good about not searching online for information regarding The Resistance or Dalton. I want to hear *him* tell me about his adventures and where they're traveling. It feels more personal, more real that way. Anytime a story about them comes on TV, I quickly turn the channel. Once, I caught a story about who the press thinks he should hook up with. I felt numb and disconnected from him for hours afterwards. So I avoid the media when it comes to him.

What I can't avoid is business, which is picking up. Tracy is working in my office more to avoid miscommunication and scheduling conflicts. She has access to my online planner, but twenty phone calls a day to confirm or make a decision was getting old, so we started working together in person until we get everything under control.

I also find it easier to focus on work when she's here. Other times, I'll call Dalton or start to slack and daydream. Discovering that bliss comes with a price, my responsible side is being overrun by my ridiculously happy side.

Resting my head on my hand, I look at the calendar pinned to the corkboard in front of me. Two days until Dalton comes home for two weeks. The break was scheduled into the tour so the band can rest before touring France, Italy, and flying to South America. Their schedule makes no sense to me. They're also supposed to record a song they're working on that they want to debut at a big music festival down in Brazil.

"I took Adam back."

Surprised to have the silence broken, I look at Tracy, shocked by her confession. "Okay," I reply.

"I love him and realized I'm punishing him over something that happened too long ago to worry about now."

"That sounds reasonable."

She stands and walks to the patio door. "Don't get me wrong. I put him through the ringer and told him to tell me anything and everything because once this conversation was over, it was over for good and I want to move forward."

"More than a fair request. Logical. I think I'm seeing a new side to you, Trace. You usually run off of your emotions."

"My heart hurt too much, so I started using my head."

"What was his reaction?"

She giggles, revealing her joy. "He said we should fly to Vegas and get married this weekend."

"Really?" I ask, sitting up. "Are you gonna do it?"

"I'm tempted, but I told him no. I still want the big wedding and everyone there. Call me selfish, but I want my special day with all my friends and family with me."

"Eloping is romantic, but you have to do what feels right for you two. I think sharing your day with everyone you care about is beautiful. I'm so happy that something so good has come from the bad."

She sits down on the couch, and pulls her files onto her lap again. "Thanks for not pressuring me about it."

"Pfft." I wave my hand nonchalantly. "I knew you would go back, but I'm glad you did it when it felt right. You guys are gonna have a great life together."

"We already do. Now we just appreciate it more." She grabs her phone and starts scrolling on the screen. "And by the way, the wedding is in seven weeks and you're my Maid of Honor, so get ready."

"Seven weeks. Um... okay." I take a deep breath. "You're gonna have to be very organized. I can help however you need me."

"Thank you. I knew I could count on you. Now," she says, holding up a contract, "we need to get these signed and our banners to the printer for the convention next month."

An exasperated sigh escapes before I can stop it. "Damn, I forgot about the convention."

"It's been on your schedule for six months. It's only one day of face time, but it will be a long one and I need you ready. These are the people we want to carry the brand and they're gonna want to meet you."

I nod. "I'll be ready." I spin back around and start going over the ad designs. "You do more than your job description, you know," I say, casually. "How do you feel about a raise?" I peek over my shoulder and see her smiling.

"Really?"

Shrugging, I say, "Sure, you've earned it. More than earned it actually. Thank you for the hard work you put in. The business wouldn't be the same without you being a part of it."

She gets up and hugs me. "Thank you."

"You're welcome."

When she sits down again, she says, "I have a great product and even better boss, so you make my job easy. Now get back to work. I need those designs approved before my two o'clock call."

"Okay, okay. "

When two rolls around, I sneak out onto the patio, giving Tracy privacy for her conference call. I also have ulterior motives—*Dalton*. He answers on the second ring. "To what do I owe the pleasure?"

"I'm lonely."

There's a pause that might be construed as uncomfortable, but I'm starting to learn that Dalton says what he means. He doesn't talk to fill unpleasant silences. When he does speak, his words are poetic. "Loneliness is a trick the heart plays on the mind."

"So you're never lonely?"

"I didn't say that. Sometimes the mind starts to believe."

A smile crosses my face. I knew he felt more than he was letting on. "It's okay to show emotion, you know."

"I show emotion. Was it not enough?"

"Look, I'll let you off the hook... for now. But when I see you, I expect I-missed-you-so-much-reunion-sex. Okay?"

He chuckles. "Like I'd hold out on you."

"I hope you never do. " Checking over my shoulder, I see Tracy inside on her call. "I should go."

"Hey, Holliday?"

"Yeah?"

"I'm lonely too."

"Thank you," I whisper, my own emotions grabbing hold of me.

"Be at my place on Friday when I get home."

The phone goes quiet just as I reply, "I'll be there."

I'm let in through the gate without question after ringing security. People—maids, security, gardeners—weren't here the other time. It's interesting to see the bustling about the property preparing for Dalton's arrival home. I grab my small suitcase from the trunk and walk inside. A lady with a rag in her hand smiles from across the living room. I say hello, then walk upstairs to his bedroom. I've not been here alone before and it feels different without his energy filling the space.

I sit on the bench at the end of his bed and look around. I use the time to snoop and check out the framed photos. The two on his dresser are pictures he took of the audience at a concert—his view of the show, which is so different from ours of him on stage. They make me wonder what shows these were in particular that warranted framing. The one next to his bed looks like Texas by the landscape, but I'm not sure. I'll have to ask him about it some time.

The bedroom is clean in design. Not modern, but not traditional either. The large bed is covered in deep browns and reds, with hints of gold, not over the top. The view from his home is what I love the most. I open the large doors and walk out onto the balcony. His view of L.A. is incredible and I imagine the city at night must look magical from here. Below is the pool, which makes me think of a secret lagoon with the plants and rocks surrounding it. His property is very private from the surrounding homes.

Walking back inside, I sit on the end of the bed, wondering how much longer he'll be. After a few more minutes, I kick off my shoes and crawl up the mattress to rest my head on his pillow. My eyes grow heavy as the minutes tick by and the sun lowers outside, and I fall asleep.

"Holliday."

I reach my hands out, touching his face, feeling safe with him near.

"Holliday, wake up."

Our lips part and I try to tempt him, grasping to hold on when he starts to disappear.

"Hey there," he says, stroking my hair back.

My eyes open and I see Dalton, his head on the pillow next to mine, making me smile. "I fell asleep."

"So I see."

"You're home."

"I'm home," he repeats, moving closer. Lifting up onto his elbow, he hovers over me. "About that loneliness…"

I come up for air, my wet hair covering my shoulders. Dalton is sitting on the edge of the pool and I swim to him. When I reach the side, I kick my feet behind me as he finishes a phone call.

He lifts my chin, eyeing my mouth. His fingers leave my skin and he looks away. When he stands up, he turns his back and walks toward a chair by the hot tub. "I don't want to. That's why," he says. His voice is low which makes me wonder if he doesn't want me to hear. Irritation takes over. "Fine. In. Out. Appearance only. Now drop it, Tommy."

Pushing off the wall, I swim to the other side of the pool to give him privacy while he talks with the band's manager.

"Do you want a drink?" he asks, calling to me.

I turn around and balance with my arms on the edge. My eyes meet his and I reply, "Sure. Whatever you're having."

His phone rings again as he walks inside and I start to wonder if this is how his days in L.A. will be—here physically, but too busy to invest in us.

I untie my top when he returns. He has what appears to be two whiskey and Cokes. He sets them down near the steps and I toss my top at him. "Come in with me."

His phone beeps with a text and he looks down at the screen. Frustrated, I take my bottoms off and hit him in the chest. Surprised, he looks at me. With a raised eyebrow, he jumps into the pool, clothes and all and comes after me. I splash him, laughing he jumped in fully clothed. Grabbing me to him, he says, "You look good in my pool." His hand slides up my naked body.

"I like your pool a lot." I tug at his shirt. "But you'd look better without these on."

"Wet isn't enough? I can't please you woman," he says, laughing, making me giggle in return. He strips his shirt off, then his jeans come down, but he struggles in the water, so I go under and help him out.

Our bodies come together and he grabs my hair, tilting my head back gently and kissing me. When I wrap my arms and legs around him, I hold him close. Our lips part and our tongues meet. There's something magnetic when we're together, something more powerful, a draw stronger than us.

My back is pressed against the stone side, his erection pressed against me. Dalton's stubble scrapes my skin as his lips caress my neck. The pain mixed with pleasure sends tremors through my body.

"I want you," he whispers, his breath harsh against my jaw.

I stroke the back of his head, my own voice laden with heavy breaths. "You have me."

He lifts up, his eyes locking on mine. "I want to be inside you. Right now."

My breath slows, deepens as I realize what he's saying. My tone dips, and I say, "Dalton—"

"Forget it," he says, pushing away and swimming to the other side of the pool.

"Dalton? Don't leave." I swim after him, but he's already climbing out.

"Don't worry about it." He goes inside, leaving the door open behind him.

I stand in the shallow end of the pool, confused to why he's so upset. Going to the stairs, I get out and hurry across the stone and deck, glad everyone left the house earlier since I'm naked. I chase him upstairs, knowing he's gone to the master bedroom. Leaving a trail of water in my wake, I enter the bedroom. The shower is on. Slowly, I walk inside the large bathroom. His head is tilted back, the water raining down on his face, his hands rubbing his eyes.

I'm tentative when I step in next to him. His eyes open and he glances sideways at me.

With my fingertips, I touch his shoulder, tracing his flag tattoo, and say, "I'm sorry for upsetting you. If you want to talk about it—"

"I don't." He turns back under the water, causing my hand to fall away while he rinses his hair.

I refuse to indulge his mood. "Fine," I reply, turning to leave the shower.

He grabs my arm and I'm suddenly spun and pinned against the cold tile wall. "Stay."

Glaring at him, I'm not sure what I want to do. My stubborn side wants to win, walking out to teach him a lesson. I'm just not sure what lesson that would teach, so I stay, letting him win this round. "What?"

"Don't be like that."

"Me? You don't be like that. You act like me wanting to use a condom wrecked your whole world outside. And you're telling *me* not to be like that?"

"Yeah, I am." His hand slides up my neck, his thumb putting pressure as he moves. He comes closer. His lips are almost on mine, but he stops, and says, "I know your body, Holliday. I know every inch of it, touched it, kissed it, can manipulate your impulses to my will. But sometimes I don't know what you're thinking or what you think about me."

"The fun of a relationship is discovering all those things in time."

He leans back and asks, "What happens after? After you find out too much?"

"Too much, as in, you don't think I'll want you?"

His gaze lowers to his hand on my throat, his thumb pressing against my pulse, seeming to count each racing beat of my heart. "Not when you see the ugly side."

Leaning forward, I kiss the corner of his mouth. "We can't predict the future and there's no reward in that anyway." His hand slides down my wet body, stopping on my hip where my tattoo is. When he looks back up at me, I say, "As for the condom,

I'm not ready to not use one. I'm sorry if that hurts your feelings, but in the moment shouldn't be when we're discussing the issue. It's more complicated than that... and too important to treat casually."

His body before me is hard, the lines of his muscles defined. His eyes match, an edge to them that tells me he doesn't like something I've said. "I'm trying to be faithful to you—"

"Trying?" I don't like that at all. "I don't have to try," I say, keeping my voice steady. "It's easy to do. It's what we decided when you had your unexpected wanderlust."

"You remember that?"

"Of course, I remember that. Do you? Do you remember how you made the same agreement with me as I did you?"

He smiles, the expression much more attractive than the other, though some might disagree. His voice smoothes, becoming more seductive, and he says, "Angel, you're in my home, which means you're in my life. There's no one else if that's what you're asking. I don't break promises and our agreement was a promise." His lips brush against mine. "We can talk about protection again soon, but right now I'm gonna remind you why you missed me so much."

Closing my eyes, I smile just as his lips touch mine. He may have been upset about my reaction to no condom earlier, but I guess he didn't think I would stay mad. He grabs a foil packet from the ledge and we make up by making love under the warm water showering down over us.

24

"It's not a question of if they're a friend or foe. It's really a question of when the friend becomes a foe. At least in my experience."
~Johnny Outlaw

On the eighth day, we rest. We sleep in until two in the afternoon. I haven't slept past nine since I was in college, but with all the making up for lost time we've been spending together, our bodies and our minds need it.

You learn a lot about a person when you lay around in bed all day. Dalton tells me about his family and his childhood and I share my stories. Dalton's dad worked construction and seemed to put all his dreams on Dalton to fulfill. His mother worked at a Texas college in the registrar's office. He said she wanted him to go to that university, to bring baseball to the forefront for the school and win a much needed title. He was too determined to go to the University of Texas or University of Southern California; Those schools are where most pro ball players are recruited, so that's where Dalton wanted to be.

I open my eyes though I've been awake for a while. "Do you ever go back?" I ask.

"To Texas?"

"Yes."

He stays focused on the ceiling. "I haven't been to visit my family since the band got big, but we've played shows in Houston and Dallas."

"Not Austin?"

"I told Tommy no."

"Too close to home?"

He sighs, closing his eyes again. "Too close to everything." Reaching over, he grabs his phone from the nightstand. "I should get going."

"Going where?"

Looking back at me, he says, "I have a wedding to go to."

"What?" I sit up. "What wedding?"

"Remember that ex I told you about? It's her big day." His sarcasm is caught.

"I'm confused. You hate her."

"I don't hate her per se—"

"If you don't hate her per se, that's the same as saying you don't like her either. Why are you going?"

"Because I have to. It's PR that I committed to doing."

After tossing the duvet off of me, I stand up. "Well maybe I don't want you to go to your ex-girlfriend's wedding." I walk across the room to my suitcase. I dig through it and pull out some leggings and a big T-shirt, not caring how I look. I start to put them on while he sits up.

"What do you want me to do?"

Sitting down on the floor, I start to fold my clothes and pack them neatly back in the case. "I'm not gonna tell you what you can and can't do, Dalton. Maybe you should go if you've already committed."

"Do you want to come with me?"

I nod my head. "No, it's not that. I just," I start to say, looking at him, his bare chest distracting. "We've been holed up in this house for a week. The other times we were at my place."

"So you want to go out... like in public? Be seen together?" I notice how he turns away from me when he says this and stares out the window.

"No, I don't need grand statements like that. That would make it about everyone else. I think I need the little ones though. Ones like letting me know that you're going to your ex's wedding before you roll out of bed after making love to me."

"I wasn't hiding it from you. Tommy reminded me yesterday, and I forgot to mention it."

Getting up, I pull the shirt down so it hangs correctly. I crawl onto the bed, pushing him down, and situate myself on top of him, straddling his taut midsection. "I'm glad it meant so little that you didn't think it worth mentioning, but I want to know your schedule. I have a life and I don't want to lose it because yours is so big."

His hands slide up the curvature of my waist and he says, "Come with me. Let me show you off."

Smiling, I run my fingertip over his bottom lip. "That's exactly why I'm not going."

Grabbing my wrists, he pulls me down. With our faces mere

inches apart, he says, "You're different than other women I've dated."

"That's why I'm here and they're not," I whisper, then kiss him.

He rolls on top of me, and says, "That's exactly why you're here and they're not. I think you're really fucking sexy." His hands hold me down as his body starts to grind on top of me.

My body reacts as my mind relaxes, getting lost... until his phone rings. I sigh when he drops his head to the bed next to mine with an angry grunt. "Fuck."

"It's fine," I reassure him, rubbing his back. "Answer it."

When he lifts his head up, his eyes are darker than usual in the low light of the room. "It's not fine." The phone is still ringing while vibrating. He picks it up and is about to throw it, but I grab his arm to stop him.

"Don't. I won't be able to call you until you get a replacement."

He drops it on the bed instead. The ringing has stopped but now texts start coming in. With another sigh, I move to the edge of the bed then stand up. "It's probably Tommy. You should get dressed and go." I walk back to my suitcase, close the top, and zip it up. I'm annoyed. I can admit it to myself at least. I don't want him to go, but I'm not about to tell him he can't.

Dalton watches me, his expression not giving away any of his thoughts.

"Call me later," I say as I wheel my suitcase out the door.

Right before I reach the stairs, he scoops up the suitcase. I see he put jeans on too. He says, "I'll call you when I leave the wedding." We walk the rest of the way to the car in silence. He loads the case into my trunk, then asks, "You're gonna come back, right?" His more boyish side comes out, innocence and hope seen in his eyes. I bet the girls went crazy for him back in high school.

"If you want me to," I reply breezily, though I'm not feeling carefree at all.

He grabs me by the waist. "I want you to."

I lift up on my tiptoes and kiss him quickly before hurrying to the other side of the car and hopping in. He shuts my door as I start the car and roll down the window. "I'll see you later."

With a nod, he shoves his hands in the pockets and I back out, leaving him standing there looking more sexy than should be allowed—shirtless, shoeless, the top button of his jeans undone. I keep my eyes ahead, needing any excuse not to look back at him because if I do, I won't be leaving. And right now, it's best that I don't sit at his house waiting for him to return like a desperate housewife.

Dalton left for the wedding over three hours ago. From our earlier conversation, I was under the impression that it was more of a show your face and then sneak out kind of event, but I guess not since he's still there.

I hate my girly emotions. They make me feel weak and I hate feeling that way. Another two hours pass when a loud show comes on, waking me up. Glancing at the time, it's just past ten. I turn off the TV and sit up. Maybe I should call a friend and go out, but it's still early for the L.A. nightlife scene. I decide to text Dalton. *Going to bed.* I'm irritated and I don't care if he knows it.

I head upstairs to the bedroom and am about to crawl under the covers but I'm too awake to lie around, I text Tracy instead. *Want to grab a drink?*

She responds quickly. *Can't. I'm at dinner with the future In-Laws. This week sometime?*

I type, *I'm game.* I have lots of friends, but I'm not in the high-energy mode I'd need to be with the single ones. And most of my other girlfriends don't do anything without their significant others and I don't want to feel depressed that my significant other is partying without me.

I grab my e-reader from the nightstand and head out onto the patio with a warm, fuzzy blanket. After curling up in a chair, I start to read a book I've been wanting to for ages but haven't had the chance.

"Whatcha readin'?"

Following the voice, my gaze lands on Danny over on his patio. With his off-kilter smile in effect, he seems to be up to no good. "A romance," I say, laughing, sort of embarrassed I've been busted reading a bodice ripper.

"Nice," he says, nodding. "Is it a dirty romance?"

"Yeah."

"Very nice." He leans his elbows on the ledge in front of him, and asks, "So why are you sitting home on a Saturday night reading dirty romances?"

"No better offer, I guess."

"I'm offering." He nods toward the street. "Let's go get a drink. We can walk down to the Mexican restaurant up the block."

"I didn't take you for a margarita man."

He laughs, and once again, I see why the ladies are so attracted to him. He's very handsome, unshaven tonight, and his hair is a little unruly, but in a way that some might call sexy. Okay, I'd call it sexy, too. He says, "I'll have beer and leave the margaritas to you. C'mon, let's go."

"I'm not dressed to go out."

"You're dressed enough to hang out at a local restaurant with a neighbor."

Looking down at my jeans and T-shirt, I figure he's right. "Good point. I'll meet you out front in five." I go inside and brush my hair and my teeth, don't bother with any makeup and then put on my shoes.

Danny is outside waiting when I come out. After locking the door, I shove my key, my phone, and my credit card into my pockets and we walk up the street.

The neighborhood is quiet and I like that normally, but it seems to be adding an awkward tension now. "I did have an offer earlier, but I turned it down."

He smiles. "I was surprised when you said you hadn't. I don't see you sitting at home much. You're too pretty for that."

I put on a big goofy smile. "Eh, not just a pretty face here."

Laughing, he replies, "Yeah." Turning back, he looks ahead as we walk, the restaurant coming into view. "I left out funny and smart too, but those traits shouldn't be discounted."

"Awwww," I say, bumping him with my arm. "Thanks. Just for that, first round is on me."

"Awesome. I should pay you compliments more often."

We're seated in a booth by the front window. I like this spot because I can people watch. Queso comes when our drinks arrive and we dig in while picking up where we left off in the earlier conversation. He asks, "Why'd you turn down your other offer?"

"I didn't want to attend a wedding."

"I thought girls loved weddings."

I sip my drink before responding, "I do, I confess, but this one... I didn't have any interest in. I don't really want to talk about it."

"Okay, I'll change the topic. How's business?"

When I burst out laughing, I have to put my hand over my mouth to keep from spewing my drink everywhere. When I finally swallow it down, I say, "Wow, we went from personal to business just like that."

He shrugs. "That's what you wanted and I'm happy to see the smile again."

"Thanks. Hey, and I'm sorry I'm being so vague."

"It's no big deal. You seem to like your privacy. I don't mean to make you uncomfortable. I just find it odd that you're either completely gone from your place or sitting alone on a Saturday night. I'm not judging. I'm also alone on a Saturday night and glad we could get together. You actually saved me from some bad reality show marathons I've been lost in for two days. It's good to be around people again." I watch as he takes a drink, then he asks, "So since I'm a nosy bastard, tell me, what's your story, Holli? You said you're dating someone, but here you are with me."

"I can have friends, you know. Anyway, he's the one who went to the wedding. It's his ex-girlfriend's and it's complicated. I just didn't want to put myself in an awkward situation."

"So let me get this straight. Your boyfriend went to his ex's wedding tonight instead of spending time with his girlfriend?"

"Well when you put it like that it doesn't sound very good."

He leans back, his fingers on the cold beer in front of him. "Is there a good angle I'm missing?"

"I can't seem to find one." I take another drink, then reach for a chip and dip it. When I'm bringing it to my mouth the queso drips, and lands on my left breast. "Damn it!"

I hear Danny chuckle. "Need help with that?"

My eyes flash up to his, and I smile as I wipe the spot on my T-shirt. "I think I can handle it. Thanks though," I reply sarcastically.

"Anytime."

"So why don't you have a girlfriend, Danny? A single, good-looking, and successful man in L.A. isn't usually lacking for opportunity."

"I have plenty of opportunities. I guess I just don't find them that appealing."

"You like the chase, huh? Why does this not surprise me?"

Resting his hands on the table, he says, "I think you're probably very hard to surprise. You have a cynical side."

His words take me aback, the reality of them hitting me hard. I pause in thought, wondering when I started doubting the good. "Wow, you might be right. When did I become cynical?" He remains silent as I work through my own dating past while staring out the window at a couple passing by. "I've been burned and it sucked, but I thought things were changing. I thought I was changing." My eyes meet his again. "Those guys were jerks. None of them made a real effort in the relationship. Am I just repeating the cycle? Maybe it's time I start making demands of my own."

"Sounds like you deserve more than you're getting."

After downing the remains of my drink, I set my credit card down on the table. "I need to go."

"I'm sorry if I upset you. I didn't mean to."

"You didn't. I just need to clear up some stuff."

"Sounds like you're on a mission—revenge?"

"No. Nothing dramatic. Just need to talk to someone." The waitress takes my card and disappears into the back.

"So that's all it takes to get you motivated, a little queso and a margarita?"

Shrugging, I say, "I'm easy like that."

When the waitress returns, she sets the bill on the table and Danny holds his glass up, and says, "I like easy."

"Ha ha. I just bet you do." I sign the check and we walk back outside. "Don't think I didn't notice how you avoided the girlfriend question."

"I thought we talked about this before."

"I like seeing you squirm under the intense interrogation."

He playfully nudges me. "If this is your version of intense, bring it on anytime."

"Thanks for the drinks."

"You bought the booze, not me," he says.

"When I said drinks, I really meant the motivational speech and the company."

"Then you're welcome... for the drinks."

We stop between our doors, and for a short moment, it feels like the end of a date. He runs his hand through his hair and says, "This was fun."

"Yeah, it was." I look down, then back again. "I guess I should go inside."

"Thought you were going to bed?"

Danny and I turn at the same time.

Dalton's standing on the sidewalk—chin lowered, his chest heavy with each breath he takes, hands squeezing and releasing again and again. "Guess when you texted you were going to bed, you actually meant fucking this asshole."

"Dalton?" His anger is palpable as I walk slowly toward him. "*You* didn't text at all."

"Holli?" Danny says from behind me. "Everything alright?"

With my eyes focused on Dalton, I reply to Danny, "It's okay."

"Actually, it's not fucking okay, Holliday." I can smell whiskey on Dalton's breath. "What the fuck is going on? Did you go on a date with him? Is that what this is? A date?"

I put my hands out slowly. "He's a friend. We had drinks."

"Holli, I think—"

Danny is interrupted when Dalton's arm flies up, pointing at Danny. "Nobody gives a fuck what you think."

"Calm down, Dalton. This looks bad," I say, "but it's not."

He reaches to touch me, but drops his hand to his side instead. Shaking his head defeated, he says, "To think, I thought you were different."

"You're drunk, please don't do this. Nothing is going on here." I step closer, but he steps back.

Danny asks, "Holli?"

Dalton rushes forward, jumping the four lower steps and slamming Danny against the house. "Stay the fuck away from what's mine!"

"Dalton!" I yell, running to try and break up the fight before it escalates any further.

"Keep your hands off me!" Danny shoves him hard enough to send Dalton stumbling back onto my steps.

He jumps to his feet and warns, "I'm gonna kick your fucking ass, motherfucker."

Turning my back to Danny, my palms go flat against Dalton's chest as he pushes forward. "Stop, Dalton!"

Staring down at me in disbelief, Dalton asks, "You're defending him?" He backs up like he's been hit, glaring at Danny, then back at me. After a hard look and tortuous few seconds, he says, "Fuck this," and walks away.

I go after him as Danny calls, "He's drunk, Holli. Talk to him when he's sober."

Ignoring Danny's advice, I don't stop until I reach Dalton. He turns, and with a nod of his head, Dalton says, "Go back to your boyfriend."

"Dalton, listen to me."

He lights a cigarette while glaring at me.

"He's just—" I start but he interrupts.

"He's what, Holliday? Who the fuck is he to you?" When I

don't respond quick enough, he says, "This is why I don't do fucking relationships."

The ash glows bright orange and he walks away, leaving me in a trail of smoke and haze. I stand there watching as he gets in the car and revs the engine. After one glance back, he peels out, the rubber squealing loudly against the pavement. I remain there until I can no longer see the tail-lights. When I turn, Danny is still on the stoop, waiting for me.

I pull my key from my pocket and walk back, feeling dizzy from all the crazy and embarrassed in front of Danny.

"Was that Johnny Outlaw?" he asks just as I approach.

With a heavy sigh, I say, "Yes, *that* was Johnny Outlaw." *Not Jack Dalton.* I walk past Danny and unlock the front door. "Sorry."

"It's not your fault. Are you okay?"

"No." I push the door open and step up. "Don't worry about me. I'll be fine."

"If you need to talk..."

"Thanks." Just before shutting the door, I say, "Goodnight."

"Goodnight."

I hurry upstairs and change into my pajamas. When I climb into bed, I lay in the dark somewhere between angry and hurt. I'm still shocked by how we went from happy earlier today to Dalton accusing me of cheating tonight. I know how it must have looked. What he said to me... I realize him thinking I would cheat hurts deeper than his words. I roll over and snuggle my pillow closer— the one he uses—wanting to cry. But as his words repeat in my head, the anger comes back. I close my eyes and try to sleep, trying to forget this happened.

My phone rings, startling me awake. I grab it from the mattress beside me and see his name.

"Dalton?"

His words are slurred, his voice deep. He only says three words. But those three words are all it takes for me to forget everything that happened earlier. "I need you."

25

*"Sometimes the ones who are the
closest cause the most pain."*
~*Johnny Outlaw*

Dex's house is everything I expect a famous, single drummer's
house to be like. Smoke fills the air, women are everywhere, and
my stomach is tied up in knots, wondering what I've walked into.

Rochelle was not happy about me calling at two-thirty in the
morning, but when I explained the situation, she asked Cory
where Dalton was. After finding the house, here I am. I never
realized how low-key our relationship has been until I start
looking around this party. Dalton and I spend time with each
other, hidden away from the rest of the world for the most part.
This house, this party, and seeing Dex on the couch smoking from

a bong with girls hanging on him is a harsh reality check. Dalton has managed to keep me away from this side of his lifestyle and I'm starting to think it was on purpose.

Waving my hand in front of my face to clear the smoke, I walk through the living room and into the kitchen, searching for him. I see a man in the dining room chatting to a woman. I continue outside to the large deck that seems made for parties like this and look toward the hot tub. I'm relieved Dalton's not in it. Some other guy with a gaggle of girls is though. When I return to the living room, someone puts their arm around my shoulders. "Where you been hiding?" he slurs as I spin out from under him, putting distance between us.

"I'm looking for someone," I reply to discourage him.

"Aren't we all? I can be your someone tonight."

Shaking my head, I say, "I'm looking for my boyfriend."

"If you don't find him, come find me." He's easily distracted by another woman walking by and follows her. I hear him say to her, "Where you been hiding?"

That makes me laugh. What wipes the smile off my face is seeing all the drugs—white powder on the coffee table, the bong next to it, joints being passed as well as little bags of pills everybody's so interested in.

My heart starts racing, worried what I might find if I find Dalton at all. I grab the railing of the stairs, steadying myself as I walk up. I hear laughter in one room I pass on the second floor and a guitar being played up ahead. I follow the sound, the music familiar from times we spent alone and he played for me. I walk under a large archway and into a room painted deep red where he sits, the center of everyone's attention. I stay back, not hiding, but not making a show of my arrival.

Dalton sits on one side of a dark purple, velvet couch, girls next to him—one perched on the furniture's arm, three squeezed onto the cushions. A guy sitting in a throne type chair has his eyes closed with another girl on his lap who's nodding to the music. He seems out of it by the off-beats of his rhythm. There are more drugs on the table and lots of beer cans, a few half-emptied bottles of liquor are next to toppled over cups. At least another eight people linger in the room. Only a few notice me.

I want to be mad at him. I should be, but when Dalton finishes a song he seemed to be escaping into, he looks up unaware of his audience. His gaze lazily glides across the room and lands on me as if he sensed my presence. His smile matches his gaze—lazy in ways that appear beyond alcohol induced. "Angel," he says and everyone in the room turns to look at me. "You came for me." His words come slowly, but his look becomes intense, set on me.

I smile, needing to coax him from this room without making a scene. My tone is soft and welcoming as I signal back down the hall. "I did. Come on. Let's get out of here."

"That's my girl," he announces proud, unmoving from his spot.

I think I gasp like everyone else in the room when he says it—so open and free about it.

"Since when do you have a girl, Johnny?" the girl on the arm next to him asks, running her hand over his shoulder.

He glares at her hand, as if the touch itself is insulting. When he looks up, he says, "Since I fell in love."

My heart stops, skips, then races. I can't believe he just said that in a room full of people. Overwhelmed by a gush of emotions, my mind blurs.

"Angel?"

I look up and right into his eyes, the gawkers in the room irrelevant. "Yes?"

"Come here."

The girl next to him says, "I'm here." She's flirting and I watch as she moves to touch him again.

I step forward and go to him. Offering my hand over the table. "Time to go."

He takes it and stands, moving his guitar into the air as he slides between the others to get out. "It's been real," he says, and walks with me into the hallway. As soon as we're hidden in the darkness of the hall, his body pushes against mine, my back hitting a large wooden door between two bookshelves full of albums. "I want to make you come and then fuck you."

His words are dirty, the look in his eye equally naughty, and as usual my body reacts. Wanting to get him out of here, I make a suggestion. "I'll drive us home and then we can fuck all night."

"I don't wanna wait." The door behind me falls open and I stumble backward. He quickly shuts it, then locks it. Setting the guitar down, he keeps his eyes on me as if I might escape if he doesn't. His shirt is taken off and tossed, his muscles looking hard, tense, almost threatening.

I'm not scared, but deep, way deep down, there's an inkling that wanes, despite my thought. Maybe I should be. He walks forward, not bothering to take off the rest of his clothes, though he does undo his belt and button fly. My legs hit the end of the bed and I take a deep breath. I exhale, and say, "Dalton—"

"Don't you want me?"

"I do, but—"

His hands fly out to the side, the gun tattoos on display, the way he stands full of arrogance. "Everybody fucking wants me, but my own woman."

"I want you." I open my arms wide, the wounded rock star out tonight. "I want you. I always want you. Have I not proved that to you?"

He holds my face—firm, but not hurting—maintaining eye contact. "Let me have you."

"You have me. I'm right here," I say, feeling like we've shared this moment before.

Our lips meet and although his muscles feel ready to fight, his kisses are gentle, ready to love. With a peek over his shoulder, I verify the door is locked once again and then lay back, giving him what he needs and taking what I want—our bodies speaking the language we share together, every caress a way to express our feelings.

Needing to give him all of me, to prove that I can weather his storm. Dalton undoes my jeans and pulls them down, a roughness to the action. My shoes fall from my feet and my jeans are yanked the rest of the way. He climbs on top of me and smirks. "We never had that talk."

"We're not having it now. Condom or no sex," I state firmly.

He digs out his wallet as he balances above me. With one hand, he flips it open and pulls out the packet. So cliché, but I can't say I'm not happy he has it.

Sitting up, he slides the condom on then drops forward again, grabbing my arms and pulling them above my head. He thrusts as he kisses, my head digging into the mattress from the sudden impact. He's lost in his own world, his body trumping mine without care. I start wondering how drunk he is as he starts to take too much, pleasure becoming pain, so I call to him again. "Dalton." I free my hands and push against him. "Dalton!" When he doesn't respond again, I yell, "Johnny!"

He opens his eyes and stops moving.

"You're hurting me," I whisper just as a tear escapes.

His body jerks away and he stumbles backwards.

As images of the drugs I saw downstairs fast forward through my head, I lift up on my elbows and call him, trying to find a way inside his head to the man I know. "Jack?"

"Jack. Jack." He grabs his head, holding it tight. "Don't call me that. It's wrong. All wrong."

I sit up abruptly. His behavior is odd and he starts to fall apart before my eyes, his hands grabbing at the wall as he slides to the floor. I jump off the bed and kneel in front of him. "Dalton? Dalton. Did you take something? What did you take?" He closes his eyes and lowers his head, his body starting to shake. "It's okay. It's okay," I say, trying to calm him.

"Stay back!" he shouts, his hands covering his ears as if it pains him to hear me. Leaning down, his body balls up and he lays there.

"Shit! Dalton. Baby, can you hear me?" When he doesn't react, I get up and pull my pants on, buttoning them as I run out the door—down the stairs, and into the living room. "Dex, I need you."

Dex looks up from the couch with a smarmy grin, and says, "I can squeeze ya in, sweetheart."

"No, Jack needs you."

"Who the fuck is Jack?" Putting his cigarette to his mouth, he sucks long and hard.

I whisper, "Johnny."

"Fuck. Go bother Tommy."

"Tommy's here?"

"Dining room. That way."

I run through the kitchen and into the dining room, finding that same couple I saw talking earlier. "Are you Tommy?" I startle him when I shake his arm, interrupting their conversation. "Are you Tommy? Jack needs you."

"Whoa! What the fuck?"

"Please help me. Dalton needs you. Please. Please help him."

"What?" he asks, standing up.

Looking at the woman, I turn to Tommy again, not wanting to say too much in front of others. "I'm Holli. Please. Help me."

I take off running toward the stairs with Tommy right behind me. I open the door to the bedroom and find Dalton in the same position I left him, but it looks like he's passed out. "Oh my God. Please help him."

"What did he take?" He asks, kicking the door shut.

I lock it. "I don't know. He just started freaking out. I saw pot and um, coke, liquor. I don't know what else is out there."

Tommy struggles to get him upright, then shakes him. "Motherfucking Johnny! Wake up!"

"Should I call an ambulance?"

"No..."

"Dalton?" I say, hoping for a response this time.

He startles awake, jumping away from me. "What the... Where am I?"

His throat sounds dry as he coughs to clear it. I hand him a glass of water and watch as he drinks. Stroking his cheek, I turn my palm out, raising the back of my hand to his forehead. "How are you feeling?"

He's calmer now, leaning against the headboard, when he

replies, "My head hurts. Why are you looking at me like that? You look tired."

"I am."

Looking toward the window in his bedroom, his expression lightens, and he says, "We can watch the sunrise together."

"And the sunset." My statement seems to confuse him. "Are you hungry," I ask. "I can order something. You should eat. You need to eat." I try to settle the nerves rising within me.

"What's going on? Why do you look so worried, Holliday?"

"What do you remember?"

His temper flares. "What the fuck is going on?"

I stand slowly, not wanting to upset him, not knowing the repercussions of the drugs he took. He keeps his eyes locked on mine while I move to the door. "You did drugs. You're coming down. I'm not really sure. I never did drugs."

His head jerks back. "I don't do drugs, not the heavy stuff anymore. Pot occasionally."

"I only know what I saw and was told, Dalton."

"I don't like your tone."

"I don't have a tone."

"The absence of tone is what I don't like. Why don't you have a tone? You look scared of me," he says, tilting his head. "Do I scare you?"

"No. I'll be right back."

"Holliday?" I hear him say just as I shut the door and rush downstairs to find Tommy.

"He's awake," I tell him. "You should talk to him."

I turn to head back upstairs, but Dalton is standing at the top. By the look of his tensed jaw and the hardness of his arms as he grips the railing, he looks pissed. He asks, "What's going on?" Tommy steps next to me, his arm going to the rail in front of me.

My eyes tear up when I realize Tommy is taking a protective stance. With his hands out, Dalton walks slowly down the steps. "What's going on?" he repeats when neither of us answers him the first time.

Tommy starts talking, "You took drugs. You took them when you said you weren't going to do that shit anymo—"

"Not you!" he demands, pointing his finger at Tommy. I jump in response, startled. "I don't give a shit what you have to say. I want her to tell me." Dalton takes a breath and exhales while coming closer. "What's going on, Holliday?"

When he reaches me, I take his hand and tug gently, encouraging him to come with me. "We should talk."

He's hesitant but follows, sitting down next to me on the couch. When I glance over at Tommy, he says, "I'm gonna get myself a drink. I'll be in the kitchen if you need me."

Dalton is quick. "Why would she need you?"

"I meant either of you. If *either* of you need anything. Fuck, Johnny. You make things so damn hard." He walks off, mumbling to himself.

"What do you remember?" I ask, rubbing Dalton's leg to bring his attention back to me.

"I didn't do any," he says. "I remember that much."

Looking at my lap, I bring my hand back and entwine my fingers to keep them to myself. "You were definitely on drugs. We have no doubt about that." I look up, not afraid of him or his outbursts, his darkness or his demons. "Are you saying you were drugged?"

"I'm saying I didn't take any drugs. I remember a crazy dream, but that's it."

"You scared the shit out of me. I thought you were dying and I didn't know how to save you. I had to run through a house full of people looking for someone I've never met who I knew would keep it from becoming a spectacle."

He gaze falls away and he says, "I'm sorry." When he looks back up, his spirit is gone, a sadness replacing it. "Thank you."

"You should tell that to Tommy. He knew what to do."

He nods.

Leaning forward, I touch his cheek and then kiss him. Whispering, I say, "I'm here for you. I'll be whatever you need me to be, but I know my limits and last night got pretty damn close to crossing it when you accused me of cheating and then the drugs."

Turning his head to the side, our eyes meet. "I'm sorry," he says, "I swear I didn't take any drugs."

I search his eyes for the lie I expect to find, but I don't see it, not even hidden in the deep green edges. Finding sincerity instead, I smile and hug him. "I was so scared."

"I'm sorry," he says, hugging me, his hold on me tight.

Tommy comes back out and says, "I went ahead and ordered dinner."

"It's nighttime?" Dalton asks, his expression still a bit confused as he rubs his head.

"You've been asleep all day. I kept checking to make sure you were breathing, but Tommy said you were fine."

He doesn't apologize this time, but I see the regret in his eyes.

Over Chinese food, we spend the evening going over the details of the night before. With his chopsticks in the air, he says, "Dex didn't make me any drinks last night. I drank beer at his house, bottled beer, so I don't think I was slipped anything."

"Did you smoke anything?" Tommy asks, putting a bite of Kung Pao Chicken in his mouth.

"I've cut down, but I bummed a few cigarettes at the reception," he replies. "I needed it."

"I would too," Tommy adds, "if I had that kind of crazy coming after me."

"What kind of crazy?" I ask, sitting upright.

Tommy speaks without thinking. "The lovely bride decided she wanted her present in the form of Johnny."

"Tommy," Dalton warns.

I stare at Dalton as he glares at Tommy. "Tell me what happened," I say, losing my appetite.

Dalton looks at me. "It's no big deal. Nothing happened."

"Something happened or Tommy wouldn't have said that."

"He's talking shit. Nothing happened."

After wiping my mouth with a napkin, I calmly set it down on my plate and push away from the table. I stand up, irritated, and head for the bathroom. Dalton reaches for me, but misses, his fingertips grazing my hand. "Holliday."

My pace picks up. He runs to catch me, jumping in front of me and blocking my way. "Hey. Nothing happened."

I look away. "Okay, nothing happened."

He lifts my chin and directs me to face him. "I don't want you to repeat what I say. I want you to believe me."

Pursing my lips, I bite the inside of my cheek in contemplation. "I've been cheated on, I've been berated, and I've been treated secondary to business, sports, family, and cars in relationships. Through all of the crap I've been through, the one person I knew I could always rely on was me. So if you're standing there asking me to trust you, sometimes I'm gonna struggle."

"She said she'd leave her fiancé if I'd take her back."

My mouth drops open. Closing my eyes, I start to rub my temples. When I open them again, I say, "That sounds like more than nothing, Dalton."

"It was nothing to me."

Just like that... my heart is his again.

There's something about a man who has the ability to knock you off your feet with only a few sweet words. I throw myself on him, holding him tight. With my cheek pressed to his chest, I say, "Last night you told a room full of people that you love me."

I feel him tense, his hands trying to push me away. I embrace him even tighter until his arms wrap around me and he's holding me just as tight.

"I do," he whispers.

My smile returns. His words are not direct, but the message is loud and clear.

26

*"When you fly away, remember to
leave a forwarding address."*
~Johnny Outlaw

We didn't get the answers about the drugs like we wanted, but I made the decision to trust Dalton, so that's what I did. Despite the tabloids announcing he and his ex were 'Secretly dating,' 'Caught in the Act at her Reception,' and 'Married,' I stuck by him.

Although negative press sucks, Dalton leaving me sucks more. "Four weeks," he says, holding my hand. With a smile on his face, he leans down and kisses me. "You can come anytime. I'll fly you to wherever we are in the world." He backs up with a deep breath, exhales, and says, "Goodb—"

My finger goes to his lips, and I say, "No goodbyes."

"No goodbyes." With a little arrogant smile playing on his

mouth, he turns and leaves, shutting the door behind him.

I sit down on the couch and turn on the TV, pretending that my whole world isn't turned upside down again. I click it off, unsettled in my own skin. The truth is my world is turned upside down and it takes too much effort to pretend it isn't.

My phone rings and seeing Dalton's name on the screen makes me smile. I answer quickly, "Hi."

"I miss you already. Does that make me a pussy?"

"Not in my book. It makes you charming."

"I wasn't charming before?" he asks with a chuckle.

"I never said that. Anyway, I like when you say sweet things to me."

"Holliday," he says, the laughter gone from his voice. "I owe you for all the shit that happened."

"No—"

"Please just let me say this." He pauses, then says, "Thank you for being there and staying."

I could make a big deal about it and torture him by going over it again, but I don't for two reasons. One, because I believe him. And two, because I don't want to rehash the negative. I'm liking the here and now too much to ruin it. So I say, "You're welcome," and leave it at that.

When Tracy arrives for work, she brings coffee, just another reason I love her so much. We sit on the patio, enjoying the nice day while working on the schedule.

"I've got a fitting tomorrow," she says. "You can still come, right? I want a second set of eyes that I trust."

"Of course. Can't wait."

"And we chose our baker and caterer. Deposits have been paid. How's your dress shopping coming along?"

Looking at her, I lower my sunglasses. "Not great..."

"You haven't shopped yet, have you?"

"Dalton was here."

"Well he's gone, so get your ass in gear."

"Hey," I say, "I wasn't just sitting around—"

She points at me accusingly. "Oh I know you weren't 'sitting' around.' You two do it like rabbits."

Cocking my eyebrow, I shrug. "I'd love to deny that," I say, then giggle. "But you're right. My sex life has never been better." I shuffle some papers around, realizing I forgot to sign them yesterday. "But besides the sex, I actually did get some work done. I finished all the cards and after I sign this document, I'm all caught up."

"Well, let's keep it that way. I hate being behind. We have some busy weeks ahead, so you might have to squeeze some more work than usual in between the sex sessions. I need that pretty head of yours in the game. Fully in the game."

It seemed so simple, in theory, to stay on top of things... until I had lunch with Rochelle a few days later for a mid-week get together. We sit and chat while Neil is content with toys on the table. It's good to talk to someone who understands the crazy life that Dalton leads. But we mostly talk about our lives because I have a feeling most people don't ask about her life much at all. This vibrant, intelligent woman probably gets overlooked in the shadow of her famous partner. I refuse to do the same.

She paints and gardens, reads with Neil, and cooks. These are the things she says she loves doing. It starts to make me think about the things I love to do besides work. As much as I complain about my work keeping me busy, I love it and have sacrificed a lot of other things in my life for it. But the two things I can think to tell her is that I love the beach—in all forms, from walking it to sitting there watching the sunset. The other is traveling. It's hard to get away these days for fun, but I love it when I do.

"You should visit Johnny in France," Rochelle says while cutting Neil's carrots for him.

"I remember loving France. I haven't been since my parents took me in junior high."

"You should definitely go then. You can surprise him."

"When do they go to Paris?"

"Two days, I think." She scrolls on the screen of her phone, and nods. "Yep, two days." Resting her chin on her hand, she says, "Some days I miss being on the road with them. I hated it when I was gone for months at a time, and then I had Neil, but it was an adventure I'll never forget."

I've been missing Dalton so much and I have a week until the convention... "You really think I should go?"

"I do. Go find your adventure, Holli."

Looking across the table at this woman I've come to admire, I feel butterflies of anticipation building inside. I decide to take her advice. "I'm gonna surprise him. Send me the hotel details, okay?"

Her eyes are bright and I can tell she's excited for me. She says, "This is gonna be so awesome and romantic. When you get back I want to hear all about it."

"Definitely." So I blame her—fair and square—for ending up in Paris.

My hands are sweating I'm so nervous. I release the handle of my suitcase and drag my palms down my thighs. Rochelle hooked me up with the suite number and contacted security so I'd get by. I'm new to all this secrecy stuff that goes into dealing with famous people. He's checked into the hotel under the name Jared Harper. I'm sure there's a story behind that, but for now, I knock on the door and duck to the side.

"Who is it?" That sounds like Cory.

According to Rochelle, he can't keep secrets and will blow it, so I reply, "Room service."

Muffled voices are heard through the thick wood of the old door then it swings open. Dalton is talking before he looks up. "I didn't order any roo—"

Our eyes meet and a big smile spreads across his face when I say, "I had an unexpected wanderlust."

He looks me over from head to toe, then leans against the threshold. "You have the heart of a poet, Ms. Hughes."

"I stole the line—"

"I know a few other things you stole," he says. Reaching forward, he pulls me to him by a belt loop.

"Okay, I confess," I say. "I borrowed the line, but I'm keeping everything else." I'm actually curious to what 'other things' I've stolen might include exactly.

"Keep'em. They're yours anyway." He kisses me, turning us around so I'm inside the suite. With his hands holding my face, he looks at me. "Hi," he whispers.

"So yeah. I'm gonna clear out of here and give you guys some privacy," Cory says, making his way to the door. Cory pulls my suitcase inside the room and then turns back to us. "Guess you're not going anywhere, Johnny."

Dalton looks at me smiling. "Guess not. You're on your own, buddy."

"Next time you see me, you'll be an uncle for the second time."

"And you'll be engaged," Dalton adds.

"What?" I ask, surprised by the news. "Rochelle's having the baby and you're asking her to marry you?"

Dalton laughs. "She went into labor this afternoon when we were in an interview. You should have seen Cory's face when she called. They caught it on camera."

The happiness I feel for this amazing couple is way beyond ecstatic. "Congratulations on the baby and the engagement."

Cory smiles. "Thanks. Two kids, a house with a picket fence, and I'm finally thinking this music thing might just work out. So yeah, I'm gonna ask her." Cory pulls a ring box from his pocket and opens it. "Do you think she'll like it?"

We both lean forward and look, but I gasp, my hand to my chest and a huge smile on my face. When I look up at him, I say, "It's perfect. Rochelle's gonna love it."

The ring appears to be vintage by the intricate detailing. Black diamonds cover the band.

Cory says, "She never was a traditional girl. Maybe that's why she puts up with my shit." Snapping the box closed, he walks over to his suitcase and picks it up. "I should get going. The car should be here soon and the jet is ready from the text I got a few minutes ago."

He hugs me. "It's good to see you, Holli. Don't let this guy get into any shit he can't get out of. Okay?"

"I'll try my best. It's good to see you too." I release him from the hug. "Tell Rochelle I'll be visiting next week and I'm gonna need snuggle time with that new baby."

"Will do." Turning to Dalton, he puts his hand out. "Brother."

"Brother."

With a strong handshake, Cory brings him in for a chest bump.

"Take care, man," Dalton says, then backs up, shoving his hands in his pockets.

"Yeah, and I'll let you know—boy or girl—when I know. Wish me luck."

"You don't need any," Dalton replies as Cory heads out.

The door shuts and we're alone. Feeling on top of the world, I walk to the window and look out over Paris. The evening lights start to flicker on, making it even more magical. Dalton comes up behind me and presses his chest to my back while slipping his arms around my waist. With a whisper, he says, "You're here." He follows that with a soft kiss on my neck.

I turn in his arms, wrapping my own around his neck. "I wanted to see you." I kiss him once, twice, and then add, "I'm starting to despise this touring thing."

"Tour with me then."

The invitation is flat and direct as if it makes all the sense in the world the way he threw it out there like that. "If you're serious, I might stay for a few cities, but you're stuck with me for the week regardless."

"Mmmmm," he hums. "I like stuck, but I prefer willing participant."

"Willing, able, and wanting. Does that work better?"

He kisses me. "Much, much better."

I spy his suitcase near the door, so I ask, "You were leaving?"

Looking over his shoulder, he says, "Ummm, yeah. I was supposed to fly back with Cory, but you're here."

"Oh no, I've ruined your plans?"

Caressing my face gently, he looks into my eyes. "You were my plans. I was flying back to surprise you."

"You were?" I ask, looking up into his deep greens.

"The next two shows were cancelled." He walks to the couch,

sits, and scrubs his face with his hands. Joining him, I'm tentative when I sit next to him as he continues, "Dex needs a few days off, and we're a band. When one goes down, we all go down. It's a motherfucking sinkin' ship around here, but you're here, so none of that matters."

I lean on him, loving the feel of his arm around me as he kisses the top of my head. "You were really gonna come see me?" I ask.

"Cory got the jet since he's heading back for Rochelle and the baby, so I figured I'd come see you. I'd rather that than be here." He makes it sound oh so casual, but I feel the sentiment. His hands slide under my shirt and bra and he kneads my breasts. His lips land on my neck and he kisses and nips his way toward my ear. "Now that we're alone, what do you want to do?"

I tilt my head to the side, enjoying the feel of his lips on my skin again, and reply, "I want to see Paris."

Everything stops—his lips, his kneading, and his hands leave my body. With a nod, he asks, "Unless Paris is code for my cock, not interested."

Rolling my eyes, I say, "You and your code words. I meant the city." Batting my eyelashes, I wait.

After a long pause, he relents. "Okay, if you want Paris, I'll give you Paris. But later, you're all mine. You've got an hour till we leave."

I may have my own money, but I'm not accustomed to living extravagantly. I can definitely get used to this celebrity treatment. The car takes us to the Eiffel Tower and we get rushed in, passed the long line and right into an elevator they're holding open for us.

Being with Dalton in public is different than I imagined. Maybe I just never thought about it beyond the time when the valet guy in Vegas recognized him, or at the beach when we separated. As we stare out across the city, I sneak a peek at him, realizing this is really our first time in public where others are around. We've dated months. *Months...* or have we?

"We don't date, Dalton. We have sex." I pretend the wind made me shiver, not my nerves.

"What?" he asks, looking at me, bewildered by the comment.

"I don't think we've gone on an actual date. I know we've talked about it, but this might be the first time."

He turns away, staring out into the night. Just when I think the conversation is over, he says, "I'm an asshole." Standing up straight, he turns back to me and takes my hand. "I'm sorry, Holliday. You deserve better than that."

"You don't have to apologize. I just... being with you like this is new." I squeeze his hand. "I guess our relationship has been a little unconventional."

"Unconventional," he repeats, rolling the word around in his mouth several times. "I need to make this right."

"I don't need right because what we are isn't wrong. It's us and I like it. It just feels different tonight. That's all."

We're interrupted by two giggling teenagers holding their phones up to him. Two men come from around the corner and start to say something to them, but Dalton stops them and nods. He poses with each, then thanks them. When they leave, the two men remain, checking the premises.

"We should go. Are you hungry?" Dalton asks, taking me by the arm. His grip is firm, possessive.

I stop and resist. Pulling my arm back, I ask, "What's going on?"

He looks around, causing me to look back over my shoulder. The two men are eyeing him and Dalton says, "It's best if we leave now."

The doors to the elevator open and we walk inside. Other people try to get in, but are stopped by the large men. After they step in and the doors close. I ask, "Are they bodyguards?"

Dalton stares straight ahead. "Yes."

"Why do you have bodyguards?"

His reply is a hard glare. My stubborn side takes over, and I venture a guess, "We weren't alone when I thought we were, were we?"

My statement sets him off. "Holliday, I can't be alone in public. You're not dumb. You live in the land of celebrities. You know how this works."

"I didn't know because we've been holed up at my place or yours anytime we've been together. So, although it's very obvious to me now, it just surprised me to see them here." I have a flashback of the first time we met at the bar with that drunk guy who hit on me. The security team that rushed in to escort him out... I look at the men standing in front of me now and it becomes clear. "They were in Vegas."

"They're almost always with me."

The bell dings and the doors open. A few flashes go off, but the bodyguards keep any inquisitors at bay as we head for the car. The door is shut and there we sit in silence in the back of the car as it speeds away.

He sighs. "Are you mad at me?"

"No. I have no reason to be mad. I'm trying to process the

level of your fame that you need bodyguards around you all the time."

"I can't even process it. I can't do normal things. I told you this early on. I can buy whatever I want in the world except my freedom back. The memories of walking down the street and not being recognized are long gone."

"But Cory and Rochelle. Their lives are normal and they don't live in a gated communit—"

"I'm the front man. I'm the face of The Resistance." He's leaning his head against the window, his hand between us. "I pay the price so they can live like normal people. Rochelle helped orchestrate that early on. I didn't mind at the time... I may sound bitter. I'm not." Turning to look at me, he says, "I'll never have what they have, but most days, I'm grateful for what I've been given." He looks out the window. "This is the part where you decide if you can be a part of this life or not."

My hand finds his and I slide across the seat. Leaning my head on his shoulder, I say, "I want to be a part of your life. This side of your life is new. I'm used to the bubble we've been living in."

He wraps his arm around me and holds me against his side. With his lips pressed to my hand, he says, "Let me take you to dinner, a real dinner date."

"I'd like that. But the guards don't sit with us."

He chuckles and it's good to hear. "They're actually good guys and they do protect my ass, but no, the guards won't sit with us."

The car stops outside of a bistro that is packed with people. Dalton hops out first, then offers his hand to help me out. When we enter the restaurant, he walks straight back and to the right to a rounded booth in the corner with glass and wood partitions on two sides. The maitre d' follows quickly behind, greeting us in

French then switching to English for our benefit. "Bonsoir, Monsieur Outlaw et Mademoiselle. Our specials are listed on the menu." He doesn't waste time with chit chat but leaves us alone to peruse the menu.

Dalton sits back and looks around the restaurant. He says, "They have really great soufflés. The black truffle and cheese pasta with smoked chicken is also good."

"Dalton?"

His gaze rises to meet mine. "Yes?"

"Thank you."

"For what?"

"For bringing me on a date."

His smile is charming and light, worry not weighing on his expression. "Thank you for coming to Paris."

The evening is divine and we stay past midnight. Like time hasn't passed, we talk openly and intimately all through dinner and the dessert course.

"That chocolate soufflé was orgasmic," I say, sitting back, feeling full.

"Now I'm competing with a soufflé?"

"Never. You always win."

"Good to hear." He pays the check and we leave.

Back in the suite, I run a hot bath while he opens a bottle of wine and pours me a glass. After setting my glass on the edge of the tub, Dalton comes in and sets a chair in the middle of the opulent bathroom. He starts Led Zeppelin's "Kashmir" and sets his phone on the counter. Sitting down, he takes a sip of his wine, keeping his eyes on me, and says, "Strip for me."

"You want me to strip?"

"Yes," he says, "I want you to strip for me."

With the water filling the tub, I turn to face him, his eyes penetrating my body with an intensity that warms my blood. Without looking away, I take my shirt off and toss it on the counter. Sliding the zipper of my jeans down slowly, exposing my black lace panties, I reveal the tiny hot pink bow in the front. I turn my back to him and slide the denim over my hips and down my legs, stepping out and kicking them to the side.

I pick up my glass and take a large sip, letting my gaze slide over him as he relaxes in the chair, his eyes heavy as they look me over, a calmness settling in. I set my glass down, bending over and slowly rising, letting my own hand slide from my knee up my thigh, grazing over my panties and up my stomach to my lace covered breasts. I sway to the music with my back to him, my hips moving in time to the erotic melody. I see him in the reflection of the mirror. I like the look in his eyes as he takes me in. I like him watching me. With his eyes on my body and his hand over his erection, he says, "Show me your tits. I've missed them."

Reaching around my back, I unclasp my bra and let it fall to the floor before I shut the water off and test it with my finger.

"I want to watch you take a bath," he says. "I don't want to talk. I just want to watch."

When I glance over my shoulder, he licks his bottom lip then bites it.

The music stops suddenly and is replaced by his ring tone. We both look over at the counter, but he doesn't move. With a nod, he encourages me to go on. The music continues when the ringing stops and I slip my panties down, one side then the other, gradually, I can tell too slow for his liking. He sits forward resting his forearms on his knees. He's close, but just out of reach.

I step into the warm water and sink down, relaxing back. His phone begins buzzing on the marble, moving from the vibration. "For fuck's sake." He stands, setting his glass down hard on the countertop and picks up the phone to read his text. He turns his back to me and says, "I need to make a phone call."

He's not asking, so I pull the water up and over my chest and wait.

His eyes are on mine in the mirror as I start to lather with the body wash. He takes in every circle of motion I make. Sitting back down with his glass in hand again, he watches me as he talks into the phone, "What?"

I look down, pouring more body gel into my palm and covering my shoulders, but the chair skids across the slick tiles when Dalton stands abruptly.

I still, not wanting the water to splash, and watch as the depths of his eyes go shallow and confusion takes over. He looks up at the ceiling, and asks, "What did you say?"

His patience wears and his expression hardens as he's told something he doesn't want to hear. "No. No," he says again, shaking his head. "No way. Double check... then check again. There's no fucking way, Tommy. No fucking way."

I rinse the soap off quietly and step out of the tub just as he hangs up, sensing something bad has happened. I grab the hotel robe from the back of the door and slip it on. He drops down on the chair again, sitting there in silence, staring at the empty bath tub. Wanting to know, but treading carefully, I kneel before him. "What's wrong?"

"Rochelle had a baby boy." He stares ahead, his expression blank.

"That's great news," I reply. Moving closer, I touch his arm. "Why are you upset?"

Dalton's face loses all color and his eyes get glassy. The change over something that should be happy shocks me. Suddenly, his wine glass goes flying, slamming into the mirror—

glass shattering into tiny pieces at our feet as the red wine splatters.

"Dalton!"

His eyes turn to mine, all hope gone. His voice is hollow when he says, "Cory was in a plane crash. There are no survivors."

27

"How can you be a star when you live beneath them? There's an amazing freedom that comes with perspective of your place in the universe."
~Johnny Outlaw

After hearing the news of Cory's death, the record label arranges a private jet. Dalton, Tommy, Dex, and I fly back together. There's something going on with the three of them... something other than Cory's death. I can sense it, but I'm kept out of the loop.

I don't deal well with death, but no one does I guess. I've also developed a sudden fear of flying, or crashing rather, but I suspect they have too by the silence. We keep to ourselves for the most part until Dex tries to be funny. "At least I can't be blamed for the tour being cancelled."

Bracing myself for their reaction, I grip the arm rests tightly, and hope Dalton and Tommy will just let it slide.

"What the fuck did you just say?" Dalton pushes up from his chair beside me and stands over him.

Oh no. I unfasten my seatbelt and rush to his side, placing my hand on his wrist, and taking hold. "Hey—"

Dex stands, unafraid, making me even more nervous than the reality that they're about to throw down on this plane. I have a feeling this isn't the first time they've gotten into a fight, but I hope it doesn't happen again. "You heard me," Dex says, sneering. "I know you would've blamed me and now you can't."

Tommy stands. With his arms between them, he says, "Everyone needs to calm the fuck down. We shouldn't be fighting right now."

"So fucking typical," Dalton says, pushing Dex. "You're a motherfucking selfish bastard. It's not about Cory dying, but about you feeling you dodged a bullet of blame."

Dex comes back, spewing his anger forth, "Fuck you! I know how the great Johnny Outlaw works. You would be nailing me with all the tour troubles. You play the altar boy, but you're not so fucking innocent. Well, guess what, your past will catch up with you, then see if you're so high and mighty." He walks past Dalton, hitting him with his shoulder as he passes, going into one of the two back bedrooms.

Dalton stares at the place where Dex stood, then without a word goes into the other bedroom and slams the door. Tommy and I are left there, confused to what really just happened. From Cory's death to Dalton's past, the conversation was shrouded in underlying secrets and threats.

"It's probably best they're separated," Tommy says. "They haven't been getting along lately."

I just spent the last twenty-four hours traveling with only a few hours in Paris before getting right back on another plane. I'm tired and upset, but Dalton needs me, so I say, "I'll check on him."

After knocking three times, I turn the handle. It's unlocked, so I walk in quietly and lay down next to him on the bed. The room only has one small light on the wall, keeping the room dim. Sliding my hand over until I touch his hand, I place my pinky over his.

"He may be an asshole, but he's right," he says. "My past will catch up with me unless I deal with it."

"How bad is it?"

He drapes his arm over his eyes, covering up, but it feels more like he's hiding from me. "I don't think the drugs and partying I've done is gonna surprise anyone or make headlines. Kind of expected of musicians."

"Then what will make headlines?" I ask hesitantly.

His laugh is deep, hardened and cynical when he says, "A father of a famous musician who calls him a slacker sucking off society."

Our fingers entwine, the desire to cover him with my body, to protect him from the world takes over. I move to my side and slide my leg over his, my arm across his chest. The intensity his body showed to Dex minutes before is gone. His arm slips under me, bringing me closer.

I still feel the need to tiptoe with my words, not wanting to upset him, so I whisper, "Your Dad thinks he knows the kid you once were, but I don't think he ever knew you."

"I don't think he ever will." There's a defensive edge, maybe even some anger in there. "It's funny how when you grow up in small town America, you think Hollywood's red carpets and hanging with celebrities."

"Limos and award shows," I add. "I remember thinking the same thing before I moved out here for college, maybe I still thought that even in college. Then one day I went to a party in the Hollywood Hills and saw an actor I'd had a crush on when I was a teenager. He was wasted, drugged out, and hitting on everyone. He was a complete mess and a prime candidate for a *Where Are They Now* article. The bright lights kind of dimmed for me that night."

"My dad thinks it's all druggies and people with no souls. Says it was aptly named. I think I just wanted to prove him wrong, but I don't know if I can." He sighs, then says, "Dex started using again right before Vegas. No one was worried about the light stuff, but Cory and I knew he was doing more. We just didn't want to deal with it. But last night we all went to a bar. He'd been gone for a while, so Cory went looking for him. He found him on the floor in the men's bathroom having seizures. If we hadn't been there..."

I gasp, but push down the other horrifying feelings that start to overcome me. Calming myself for Dalton's sake, I ask, "That's why you had a few days off?"

He nods. "Cory went to the hospital with him. Dex had a severe reaction to some hallucinogens he'd taken. Shit he bought in some alley from a stranger."

"That's awful."

"Tommy got him released a few hours later despite what they wanted. From what we know, the press doesn't know yet. Cory and I were doing the interview while Tommy kept an eye on him at the hotel. That's when Rochelle called to say she went into labor." He sits up and looks into the black sky through the jet windows. "What he said out there... It's bullshit. He loved Cory. That was his guilt speaking, but it still doesn't make it right."

"We all deal with grief differently."

"You haven't mentioned it."

He lets that lie between us, waiting for a response from me. "Mentioned what?"

"That I was supposed to be on that flight."

A trembling sigh escapes me because I'm not ready to think about if Dalton had caught that flight with Cory. But for him, I'll be strong. "Do you want to talk about it?"

"You saved me." He glances over as he slides down onto the bed again. "My bag was packed. Ten minutes. Just ten minutes and I would have been out that door heading for my own death."

"Dalton." Tears pool in my eyes.

"You saved me. I knew you would." A tear slips down my cheek as he nuzzles against my neck, repeating, "You're my angel."

I hold him, thankful to have the opportunity. I hold him so tightly and cry, now knowing Rochelle will never have the chance to hold the man she loves again.

Our breathing evens as we wear down, exhaustion setting in. Just when I think we're going to sleep, Dalton says, "Tommy found out the cigarettes Dex was smoking were laced. That's how he was hiding it from us."

"What?" I ask, surprised by the bombshell he just dropped.

"Yeah, he knew if he was caught using again he'd be out of the band. He's been told several times and there he was getting high right to our faces. It's like a fucking game with him."

"Dex doesn't need you to be the parent. Let Tommy do that. Rochelle, Neil, and the baby need you right now. Focus on them."

He turns out the light and we lay there, silent. I let my mind roll over what he said and try to figure out if I've seen any signs of Dex's problem. Thinking back to the night I picked Dalton up from Dex's house, drugs were everywhere. He wasn't hiding them that night, but I can't say I saw him doing anything other than smoking pot. I also remember seeing him sitting on the couch smoking cigarettes.

Dalton's words from the night I picked him up from Dex's come back to me. *"I bummed a few cigarettes at the reception."*

Rolling on my side to face him, I ask, "What kind of cigarettes did you smoke at the reception?"

His voice is deeper, bordering on sleep. "Huh?"

"The night of your ex's wedding. You said you 'bummed a few cigarettes' from Dex."

Tension fills the room as his body hardens. Dalton flies out of bed and out the door before replying. He's banging on Dex's door yelling one profanity after another.

Dex is wise not to open the door.

Tommy pulls Dalton back and they end up in a heap on the floor while Dalton yells, "He fucking drugged me and he knew it. He fucking knew and let me do it. Bastard!"

They both get to their feet, out of breath. Tommy asks, "What are you talking about?"

"The night at his house when I said I didn't do drugs. It was Dex. He gave me his cigarettes at the end of the reception. I smoked when I was leaving Holliday's."

"Oh shit," Tommy says, his hand in his hair, an expression of disbelief on his face.

"Oh shit is right. He's fucking out of the band or I am." Dalton turns, his gaze hitting mine. I step inside the bedroom cabin and move out of the way as he walks in and slams the door. He locks it as he tries to regulate his breath, his air still coming out harsh.

He kicks his shoes off and takes his jeans down, stepping out of them. After getting in bed, he says, "Let's go to bed. I need this fucking nightmare to go away. Dreams, hopes, they all get destroyed in L.A. I expect it there. But I was blindsided in Paris."

His back is to me as we lay in silence and I let him remain that way, feeling the distance he needs is justified. "Dare to dream," I say, a mere whisper between us in the dark as I press my palm to his back. "For without dreams, we have nothing to look forward to."

He repeats the quote, then asks, "Who said that?"

"I did. It's a motto I live by, the reason I moved out to California and why I have my company today."

"It's good."

I stand up to undress and he rolls over to watch. By the look in his eyes, I know we'll have sex. I'm just wondering if he's going to take his frustrations out or if he wants to make love.

Intimacy with an edge—he takes me two times and shows me both his gentle side that satisfies and the other that defines ecstasy.

Our breathing finally evens and in this tiny room that only fits a bed on a flight across the world, we try for sleep. Just when I'm drifting under, he touches my cheek, and says, "Don't leave me, okay?"

Seeking him out in the dark, I place my hand over his heart, and whisper, "Okay." Exhausted, we sleep the rest of

28

"Memories are best left for the living."
~Johnny Outlaw

Five days feels like a lifetime since Paris. What I tried so desperately to hold onto disappeared without me knowing and everything has changed. There's a growing distance between me and Dalton that I feel deep inside. I hate it. It makes me angry, but I don't push for emotional chats about us. Not right now. I'm trying to be whatever he needs. I'm just not sure what that is, but I'm choosing patience. He's choosing to be numb. I don't like it, but I understand.

The public is mourning Cory's death. The gate at the end of Dalton's driveway is covered in flowers and mementos, cards, and little personal effects that people made to celebrate Cory and the band.

Kneeling next to the tub, I test the water around Dalton's chest. The heat has turned lukewarm, but I decide to leave him be, hoping he soaks some feeling back into his body. I stop in the doorway when he says, "I'm not dead, but I'm being honored like I am."

"They're mourning Cory," I reply, keeping my voice soft, not wanting to upset him any more than he already is.

"Have you seen my house? Seen the memorial fans made outside, the campout, the vigils? I'm already dead." He yells, "The Resistance is dead. Cory's gone and a thousand fans lighting a candle in *his* honor in front of *my* house won't bring him fucking back." His crystal glass goes flying across the room and breaks. The outburst doesn't surprise me. It's good to see him finally react, but I still walk out, shutting the door behind me. Anger surges—his anger over Cory's death and my anger over the feeling that I'm losing him, our relationship strained under the pressure.

When I go back to the living room, Tommy is sitting there. He's been coming by every day, telling me he's just checking in and wants some company. But I've come to realize that it's not what he's telling me that worries me, it's what he's not.

"We need to get the gate cleaned up," I say, sitting down on the couch across from him.

"It's too soon," he replies. "It's a shrine. How do we remove a shrine without causing an uproar? It will seem like he's ungrateful. I haven't figured out what to do yet, so it stays until I do."

"It's a shrine to Cor—"

"No," he raises his voice, but catches himself and calms down. "It's a shrine to one of the greatest bands that ever lived, that will never be again."

"His career isn't over."

"The Resistance is."

Silence fills the room as reality takes over—*what once was will never be again.*

I finally stand up, walking around to the back of the couch. I grip the edge while searching for a solution. "If the shrine can't go, then Dalton has to. We need to get him out of here. He's suffocating in memories and the constant reminders aren't good for him. We can hear the fans out there at night."

"Moving him somewhere else doesn't change the facts."

"But it might give him the reprieve he needs. I'm moving him. Today." I leave Tommy sitting there and go back upstairs to the bedroom.

Dalton's suitcase is still packed from the tour. I move it to the front door then return to get another from the top of his closet. When I turn around, he's there, a towel wrapped around his waist. The man I met—confident and sexy—is not the man standing in front of me now. His shoulders are slumped and the week's emotional damage has sunk into his face, darkened his eyes, and created a frown where none used to be.

I climb down from the step stool, setting the suitcase down and go to him, wrapping my arms around him so tightly that he can't deny me any longer. I need this as much as he does. His arms wrap around me and tighten. I sigh as tears fill my eyes. When sharing the burden, all that felt heavy before feels lighter. For the few minutes we stand there, inside the large closet, the devastation of the last week lifts and momentarily, I feel our bubble form around us again.

After lunch, I drive him to my place. It was mayhem getting him off his property. The police were called to move fans, paparazzi, media, and gawkers from the premises and escort our vehicle from the street. I had to drive twenty minutes out of the way to make sure we weren't being followed. I'm worried about security here at my townhouse. I'm able to work, which is good because I'm falling behind, but if the paparazzi or fans start showing up, we'll have to go somewhere else.

I spend a few hours working in my office with the door closed, not wanting to disturb him with my music. I need the distraction to keep my mind focused on my project and not on him.

Wanting fresh air, I walk out onto my patio and sit on a lounger. Being home again, I realize how strangely normal sitting here is, like nothing bad has happened, like Cory is still alive and Dalton and I are still fine. I try to relish the moment because it feels precious.

Danny's patio door opens and he walks out. I watch him as he moves around not noticing me when he clears some glasses, taking them inside then comes back out.

Feeling a little like I'm spying, I say, "Hi."

He looks up and smiles. Coming to the patio wall that faces me, he says, "Hey there. How's it going?"

"Okay."Not wanting to talk about me, I turn the conversation around. "How are you? Cleaning up after another party?"

"It was small, I promise. And you were invited. Well, I came over to invite you, but you never answered."

"I've been in… and out."

"And shaking it all about."

"Yeah, my life sort of feels like an ongoing hokey pokey these days."

"You've been working a lot," he says.

"Other stuff too, but yeah, I work a lot. Helps to keep my mind off of—"

"The other stuff?" he asks, using my words against me.

I know he's being friendly and I'm just overly sensitive, but I stand anyway, suddenly feeling a little awkward, maybe guilty like me talking to him will upset Dalton. "Speaking of work, I should get back to it."

"Good to see you're alive."

"You too." Right before I step inside, I look back and add, "Bye."

He waves. "See you around."

Inside, I put my headset on and call Tracy to go over the marketing schedule for next month. She sounds good, happy, and I crave that feeling again too. I've been sad since Cory's death, which is to be expected, but I want to feel good again. After we hang up, I send a few emails then my mind starts to wander, so I call it a day. Anyway, I miss Dalton, so I go and check on him. He's napping in the bedroom. The room is dark, the blinds and drapes closed. I climb into bed next to him and curl up, resting my forehead to his back.

He rolls over and brings me closer, holding me to him. "I'm trying," he whispers.

"I know you are," I say, but I don't know if I believe my own words.

"Too many memories. I want them gone. I don't want to remember anything."

I lean back, looking at his face, and say, "You'll never forget and you shouldn't try to. Cory deserves better than to be forgotten just because it eases our pain."

"I can't face Rochelle or the baby. I won't be able to look Neil in the eyes. His father is fucking dead and the kid is only four. Is he coping? Does he even understand? He'll see me and want to know where I dragged his dad off to. It was a joke we used to play. Cory blamed me for taking him away, so Neil wouldn't get mad at him directly. I fucking love that kid and he loves me. I can't look him in the eyes. I'm not ready to destroy him like that."

"You didn't kill Cory. No one is blaming you. Neil won't blame you either. But right now, his father is dead, and you're the next closest to him other than Rochelle, and she's struggling with everything else, including a newborn."

"He was my best friend."

Running my hand over his cheek, I whisper, "I know… I know."

Rolling onto his back, he closes his eyes, and says, "This world wasn't fucking good enough for him. He lives with legends now. It's where he was always destined to be."

"Rochelle needs you, Dalton. Neil and CJ need you."

His eyes meet mine. "CJ?"

"The baby," I say, my voice sounding more somber than I want. "CJ. Cory Jr." Both of us sit up, resting our backs against the headboard. "You may not be ready, Dalton, no one ever is, but you need to go over there. Rochelle understands what you're going through and hasn't said anything, but she still needs you."

Nodding, he knows I'm right. When he looks over at me, he asks, "Will you come with me?"

Leaning my head on his shoulder, I reply, "Of course."

We both get up without any more discussion on the matter. It will be one of the hardest things we'll ever do, but it's the right thing.

When I park in front of Rochelle's house, there are no shrines or memorials set up, and nobody is hanging around. I realize that's why Rochelle chose such a low profile home to raise her family. They're normal people to their neighbors and treated as such, the outside world hasn't discovered their accessibility yet. They're very lucky.

An older woman, with bloodshot eyes, answers the door. She smiles at me, but steps forward to hug Dalton. He whispers, "I'm sorry. I'm sorry."

She pats his back. "Thank you, Jack." When they part, she looks at him with her own sympathy. I have a feeling he'll be getting that a lot from now on. Cory's death affects more than just family and friends. A band, a brand, a business is gone that employees relied on for their paycheck. I know he feels the weight of responsibility as well as the devastation of his friend's death.

The inside of the home is serene like I've walked into the home of any young family with hopes and dreams pinned on their walls with the family portraits and the kid art. I see Neil playing on the back deck with a car, the sliding glass door wide open letting in fresh air. His tiny vroom sounds fill the otherwise quiet living room.

Rochelle is sitting in a chair with her legs curled under her, holding the baby, and watching Neil. Our presence isn't noticed, her mind on other things. When I sit, she looks at me with tear-stained cheeks and watering eyes. She just had a baby a week ago but looks gaunt, too skinny for that to have happened. The roots of her naturally brown hair show, the longer strands still full of the chestnut color she prefers. Her gaze leaves the backyard and land on Dalton, who's standing behind me. Tears escape her eyes and she quickly looks down at her baby.

I go to her, trying to stay strong, and say, "I'm sorry. So sorry, Rochelle." Leaning down, I hug her and she wraps one arm around me, returning the hug.

When I stand back up, she lifts the baby up enough to show me. "I had my baby."

I want to burst into tears, but restrain them. "He's beautiful. Can I hold him?"

She nods, then stands up. Setting him carefully in my arms, she says, "His name is Cory Junior. We call him CJ."

"I love that." Looking down into his little face, I can see both Rochelle and Cory in his features, maybe a little more Cory, or maybe for Rochelle's sake, I'm just hoping there's more Cory. I take over her seat and she walks to Dalton.

They hug, no words, just an embrace that shows they've gone through something tragic, something life changing together. Then I hear her say, "I'm sorry."

"For what?" he asks, looking at her.

Although I feel I'm invading their private moment, I'm glad I hear what she says next, "For your loss."

I stifle a sniffle and glance down at the sweet baby in my arms.

Dalton says, "He was my best friend."

"You were his," she replies with ease and a small lift of her mouth, but not quite a smile.

Rochelle just gave him a gift, she released the burden Dalton was carrying and now he gets to grieve. Peeking at them again, I see the dark lift from his face and a small grin appears. It's been too long since I've seen it, and my heart warms.

29

"It's hard to see the light when you're surrounded by so much dark."
~Johnny Outlaw

"Do you know what it's like to be caught in an undertow?" Dalton asks as we drive away from Rochelle's house.

"Sure. It's like vertigo."

"Yeah, you don't know which way is up and you're fighting to stay alive. It feels pointless to fight so hard and get nowhere—"

"But then you do," I add. "You find your way out." This conversation should worry me, but he's searching for a truth to relate to, so I let him lead.

"Yeah, just like that." He goes quiet, staring out the window at the old sixties style bungalows. As much as I want to throw a million questions at him, I don't and wait for him to speak. When he does, there's a dullness in his tone I've gotten used to hearing over the last week. He looks at me and says, "I'd forgotten what normal was like. This is normal—these houses, this neighborhood, and how we spend our time is normal."

"I like normal."

"I like normal too, but you deserve extraordinary. Normal is all any other guy has ever given you and those guys aren't around anymore."

I reach over and rub his thigh. "I should clarify that I like doing normal with you." We've only dated a few months and most of my past relationships were over by this point.

"You weren't someone I would have normally approached... that night."

I put both hands on the wheel again. "Geez, thanks."

He chuckles. "That's not what I mean. You're hot. You know it," he says, a little smile revealed. "But you were so uptight and business like, pissy, and strong, independent. Believe it or not, that's not the typical type of woman I date."

I want to say something really sarcastic, but I refrain because though there's a lightness to his voice, there's also a seriousness blanketing his words.

He angles his body toward me while tugging on his seatbelt, and continues. "You see my flaws and my good side. You see who I am, not just what others want me to be."

"Your fame doesn't define you, Dalton."

"To you. To you, I'm more than Johnny Outlaw. The world doesn't want to see Jack Dalton. They want whatever they can take and some days," he says, then sighs. "Some days I can give them everything they want, what they crave. Others... since Cory died, I'm left wondering if I'll ever be able to be that person again. Do I even want to or am I done? Life is short. Too fucking short.

Is this how I want to spend the rest of it?"

"You've had a lot to deal with. You've been touring for months and then, well, Cory passing away. I don't think you have to figure out your entire life's plan this week. You have time to think about what you want. Don't make rash decisions based on temporary emotions."

His fingers weave into my hair, a slight tug that makes me turn his way. There's a hint of that arrogant man I know well tingeing the green of his irises when he says, "I've been a part of something great, built an empire. But it's a career I fell into. I've admitted that many times before, but I'm ready to take ownership of it, take control back." His grip loosens. "That means figuring out plan C. You're right. It doesn't have to be today."

I keep my eyes forward, but then my gaze is drawn to him when he adds, "But you still deserve extraordinary."

There's something about the way he kisses. It makes me wonder if he kissed every other woman with as much passion as he shows me. He makes me feel like the only one, but that can't be right. He's Johnny Outlaw and with that name comes groupies and backstage fucks, and everything else that fame brings.

I try to drown out the thoughts that keep me out of the moment by listening to the loud music that fills the room. But it doesn't do the trick.

He stops and looks at me, the moon providing the only light in the room. It's enough to see his concern. "You okay?" he asks.

Seeing his desire makes me feel bad that I can't give him the same back right now.

"You're thinking too much," he adds. "Just feel. Only feel."

"I can't shut my mind off." I lean back, caught up in his reality, in Rochelle's and my mind lost to the sadness.

Expecting an exaggerated sigh or a look of irritation, I turn away. But I don't get any of that. His hand rubs my back and he says, "We don't have to do anything... sexual. We can just hang out."

When I turn to look at him, to my relief, all I see is sincerity. And there's something about a guy being sincere that is incredibly sexy. Call me weak, but I fall for it every time.

Paparazzi surround the cemetery, but are kept out. The funeral is large and Dalton tells me there are famous musicians here, though I don't recognize any.

We stand near Rochelle, but let her family comfort her. It seems to be what she needs. She's too young to be widowed. Sadness permeates the air without effort, everyone letting it envelop the service of a man too young to die. Out of the corner of my eye, I see Dalton's hands at his sides, fingers moving quickly, strumming to a song no else can hear. My heart hurts as I watch him trying to cope in the only way he knows how—through music. I'm not even sure if he's aware he's doing it. His eyes are steady, staring at the casket before us, his shoulders slumped down. The tempo of his fingers picks up and I wonder if he's playing a song I would know or if it's one that will never be heard now that Cory's dead.

Briefly, I debate if I should take his hand in mine, but I don't, knowing it's best to let him play on.

As the mourners walk away, Dalton and I, Rochelle and Neil remain in silence, standing there and watching as the casket is lowered. Neil bends down and grabs a handful of grass and blows. The small breeze sends them into the air, a few blades landing on the dark wood of his father's casket. Neil smiles, looking pleased.

"He knows Cory's not in there," Rochelle says, large sunglasses covering her eyes as she keeps her attention forward. "What he doesn't know is there are no remains to bury. The crash took care of that, but his parents insisted on tradition." She turns to us and lifts her glasses, settling them on top of her head.

Neil takes her hand, and tears fill her eyes as she looks up to the sky, attempting to keep the tears at bay. "Daddy lives in here now," Neil says, patting his chest over his heart.

We stare at the little boy—a little Rochelle, a lot of Cory, just like his baby brother. My heart breaks as I attempt to stop my own tears from falling.

Dalton kneels down, takes Neil's hand, and says, "Your daddy is always with you. He was so proud to be your daddy too. He showed everyone your picture when he was on the road."

When Dalton squats like that, Neil is eye-level. The little boy smiles and asks, "Are you, Uncle Johnny?"

Nodding, Dalton gives him an assuring smile. "I'm very proud of you, too." He hugs him and Neil wraps his arms around Dalton's neck as he lifts him up.

I take Rochelle's hand and the four of us walk to the procession of cars, all waiting on us.

Cory and Rochelle's families and closest friends gather at Tommy's house. They decided it was best to host it here to keep people from discovering Rochelle's home for privacy. Dalton shakes hands, gives hugs, receives lots, and thanks almost everyone for coming. The look in their eyes when they see him is a mixture of sympathy and curiosity. They want to know what will become of him almost as much as I do.

Everyone settles into quiet conversations and snacking. I sit next to Rochelle in the living room, wanting to hold the baby. CJ, although not even two weeks old, has grown so much. I rock him in my arms as Rochelle stares out the window. "I'm moving to Boston," she says.

Surprised, I turn and ask, "You are?"

There's a vacancy in her eyes when she looks my way, the strong woman I met months ago, now gone. "I don't think I can do this by myself."

"You aren't alone."

"I can't rely on friends to replace Cory."

"Cory traveled, toured a lot. You were already doing this on your own most of the time. You love your home and L.A."

She gets up and walks into the kitchen. Her mother comes out and offers to hold the baby. I take the opportunity to find Rochelle again. She's outside on the side of the patio alone. "I didn't mean to upset you," I say.

"You didn't. You reminded me of why I left Boston. Cory grew up here. His family is here, our friends are here." She tilts her head my way while leaning against the house. "I have a lot to think about, but you're right. This is my home. I may not be able to stay in the house, every inch reminds me of Cory, but I should probably stay in L.A."

After taking a sip from a flask, she hands it to me. I take it and sip. Whiskey. Strong like I always knew her to be.

"Don't ever lose yourself in somebody else, Holli. It's hard to remember who you used to be if they disappear."

Sound advice in a genuine moment. "You're stronger than you remember. That feisty girl who carved her own path in life is still in there. You just need to give her time to reveal herself again."

"You're good for Johnny."

I sit down next to her, and say, "We've never spent this much time together."

She laughs. "It'll be fine. You'll see. You just need to get to know these new sides you're both seeing for the first time." We both take another swig from the flask. "Johnny was Cory's best friend, but he also considered him the brother he never had."

"That's one of the last things he called him before he left Paris." Her smile turns as her eyes fill with tears. I hug her. "I'm sorry."

"I'm pissed he left me." She looks up, the anger replaced by a broken heart. "We never fought. He was too good, his soul was compassionate. He loved me through and through, and I knew no one else would ever love me like that. He took me, rough edges and all, and smoothed me out. He was the better one of the two of us. How am I going to raise those boys to be like their father when he's not here?"

We finally let our tears fall freely and with my arm wrapped around her shoulder, I whisper, "You show them the love that you and Cory shared and do your best. You're a wonderful mother, Rochelle. Cory's death doesn't change that."

Sitting up, she nods as she takes a deep breath. "The site investigators found a ring," she says. "They said they traced it back to Cory. He bought it at a shop in Paris."

My heart stops along with my breathing.

She continues, "Do you think Johnny knows anything? I think Cory would have told him about it."

About to break down, I quickly excuse myself. "I'll get him for you."

I rush inside and grab Dalton by the arm, dragging him to a guest room down a long hallway. After shutting the door, I sit down on the bed. His warmth comforts me as he sits down and pulls me to his side. "I'm sorry," I start to say, "I know he was your friend and—"

"It's okay. Today is hard on everyone."

Snuggled into his side, I say, "They found the ring, Dalton. My heart is breaking for her. I couldn't look at her knowing the truth. You need to tell her. She should know."

He holds me, stroking my hair, his inner strength shining through. "I'll talk to her."

30

"Sure I've gotten into some trouble, a few bar fights. I have an ego bigger than Texas and a jealous streak to match." ~Johnny Outlaw

The convention looms and Tracy isn't letting me get out of it. I have to be there. I have too many people counting on me being there today. I leave Dalton in bed at his house, which we retreated back to this week, and tiptoe downstairs. The front door is about to close when I hear Dalton. "Holliday?"

I step back inside and look up at the top of the stairs. He's been holed up for days, so seeing him out of his room surprises me, especially at this early hour. "Hi. You're up?"

He uses his palms to rub his eyes and the sleep away. In the low light coming from the bedroom I'm reminded how handsome he is, even with the sadness that haunts him. "Where are you going?"

"I have the convention today. I reminded you last night."

"I guess I forgot."

"I need to get going or I'll be late."

I feel his gaze harden. His voice becomes stern as if I have to justify myself. "It's four in the morning."

"I have to go back to my place to get dressed first and pick up some stuff. I'm meeting Tracy there at seven to set-up."

He sits down on the top step, his body looking too tired to stand. Rolling his shoulders forward, I can see his mood changing for the worse. "How long will you be gone?" First his body language, now his tone. He's losing patience.

"All day."

"When will you be back?"

"I don't know. Late."

"I need you here," he says, leaning his head against the wall for support.

"Dalton—"

He stands and rushes down the stairs, grabbing me by the arms. "I don't just need you here. I want you here. I want you with me." He pulls me to him, holding me tight. "Don't leave me."

"I don't want to leave you. I want to stay." I whisper, rubbing his back. "But I have to go. Today's important for me and the company. I have meetings I can't cancel last minute."

Cupping my face, he looks into my eyes. His are glassy, desperate. "You don't have to work. You know that. I need you here. I can take care of you."

"I love my job. I do it because it makes me happy."

"Don't I make you happy?" I feel the slight shake of his hands. "I almost died. It should have been me, not Cory."

My heart splinters, hurt from seeing him so broken. I touch his cheek and try to find enough strength within me to share. "You have to choose to live your life." The weight of this tragedy is destroying him on the inside, he's being dragged under. "Don't let the dark win."

He kisses me, holding his mouth hard against mine. When he releases me, he says, "You can't go. You see what I'm going through."

I pull my hands back from him, surprised by his manipulative tactic. "I want to be here for you. I do—"

He raises his voice. "Why are you doing this to me?"

"Dalton, it's early. I'm tired. You're tired. Go back to bed. I'll check on you late—"

"No! You have to make a decision—you stay or go, but you don't get both."

"Please don't do this. It's just one day. I'll be back tonight. I promise."

His hands jerk back like my touch now burns. "You don't have to say it. I can tell you've made your choice. Go. Get out."

"Dalt—"

The sincerity he held minutes before disappears, engulfed by anger. "Fucking go, Holli!" He turns abruptly, runs up the stairs, and slams the bedroom door shut.

I'm left with my mouth agape, caught between pain and my own anger. Picking my heart up off the floor, I try to collect myself, fighting back the tears until I reach my car. There is no traffic at this hour, but the burden of the baggage I brought with me from Dalton's weighs me down.

Holli.

He's messing with me, pushing buttons, picking a fight. I take a deep breath, trying to put it in perspective. He's in so much pain, giving into the dark when I'm fighting to keep him in the light. Cory dying just might be the death of Dalton. That scares me. As much as I want to save him, I might not be the angel he thinks I am. I might not be strong enough to pull him through this. He might have to save himself this time.

Showing up on time doesn't win me the brownie points I thought it would. Tracy is already at the convention center and has set up most of the Limelight products. "I'm surprised to see you," she says.

"I said I'd be here," I reply, too curt, which I hate. Taking a deep breath, I add, "This is important."

"It is. It's your baby. I'm glad you're here."

"I'm here, but I'm useless." I sit down in a chair, my body heavy with worry. Dropping my head into my hands, I say, "He told me to leave this morning."

"What? What do you mean he told you to leave?" she asks, standing there with a box in her hands.

With a sniffle, I say, "We had a fight."

"Oh no, Holli. I'm sorry." She sets the box down and sits in the chair next to me.

I huff. "I feel like I haven't stopped crying since Paris."

"Do you want to talk about it?"

"If I talk about it, I'll lose it again and I don't feel like crying anymore. Can we concentrate on work?"

"Okay." She turns around and points. "There's a box somewhefre over there that's labeled brochures. We need to put those out and I think we're set up."

She starts straightening the T-shirts on the rack out front and I walk behind the display and move boxes around until I find the right one. When I bring it back, I set it down on a chair, and start unpacking while this morning's fight runs through my head and guilt weighs down my heart. I give into my emotions and say, "He wanted me to stay." I peek up at her, expecting judgment.

She stops what she's doing and says, "But you decided to come anyway. Is that why he told you to leave?"

I nod, my throat tightening too much to speak.

"I'm sorry, Holli."

Holli. He called me Holli in his anger. Breathe. One breath at a time, I breathe deeply.

"It's just a fight," she adds. "You've been through a lot of heavy stuff lately, both of you, not just him."

"These last few weeks, I feel like I'm losing myself. His life is big, his depression even bigger. And I can't stop thinking about Rochelle and the kids. The baby will never know his father."

She comes and hugs me. "You care about them and they know that. It's not going to be easy for them, but from what you've told me about her, she's a fighter and she'll fight for the kids to have the life they deserve. She's fortunate to have so many around who love her."

My head drops down and I close my eyes, trying not to cry. I should be out of tears—Cory's death, Rochelle's heartbreak, and Dalton lost in the middle of a tragedy. I've had to be strong when I felt weak and now that I'm away from him, I feel like my emotions will cave in on me if I'm not careful. "I can't lose everything I've worked so hard for—"

"You won't. You're crazy about each other. He'll understand and I know you two will be okay."

Taking her words to heart, I start to believe we'll be okay.

"Thank you," I say, releasing her. I lift my chin, take a deep breath, and when I exhale, I solidify my purpose of being here today—my business. I love my company too much to let it slip to the wayside. So today, I'll be here, fully present, and tonight, Dalton and I can talk. He knows how much my company means to me. He'll understand why I came here today.

"I'm thinking the brochures should go on the sides to capture the attention but not block the product," I say, lining them up.

"I agree," she says.

The morning disappears while I have meeting after meeting with buyers and do some meet and greet type stuff. I could have never predicted a lime would land me where I am today. Why anyone wants to meet the creator is beyond me, but it's flattering.

Right before noon, I see a familiar face heading our way. But even better, it looks like he brought lunch, or I'm hoping he did. "Fancy seeing you here, Danny."

"Eh, I had nothing better to do," he says, shrugging.

"Ha ha." I lean forward, trying to get a peek inside the bags. "What do ya got there?"

"Oh this?" he says, holding the bags in the air just out of my reach, teasing me. "Just some sandwiches. Nothing you'd be interested in."

Tracy returns to the booth, and says, "Holy! Um, hello." Her mouth is open as she stares at him. She sets our drinks down on the table, and asks, "Who's your friend, Holli?"

"Don't stare," I whisper, "his ego is already way out of whack. And this is my neighbor Danny."

"Underwear model neighbor Danny?"

Danny laughs. "I prefer photographer these days, but it's good to know my reputation precedes me."

"Oh here we go," I say, rolling my eyes. "You've done it now, Trace."

"Nice to meet you..."

"Tracy, Danny," I introduce them. "Danny, Tracy."

"Nice to meet you, Tracy."

She replies, "Likewise."

After setting the bags down, he says, "Holli, last week you mentioned you'd be stuck here all day. Thought you could use some food."

"Awesome. I'm starved."

"Wasn't sure how many people would be here, so I have extras. Hope you like turkey or ham."

"Thank you. This is very thoughtful." We find an extra chair for him and eat together, trying our best to not be so obvious to any convention goers.

After filling a buyer's order, I sit back down with them and point at Danny's shirt. "Don't think I didn't notice the tee either. I appreciate you wearing it."

He puffs his chest out. "Have to show my support and it's awesome. A good friend gave it to me."

"She must be very beautiful," I state without smiling, laughing on the inside.

He chuckles and rolls his eyes this time. "She is."

"Stop flirting. I feel left out," Tracy says, pretending to pout.

"Not flirting. She has a boyfriend. A guy she keeps locked up in her basement, hidden from the world. Right, Holli?"

"That is so not true. I don't even have a basement," I say, laughing, but it's short-lived as I'm reminded of Dalton. This conversation, even in jest, hits too close to home for me to enjoy.

"Hey." Danny stands just as we finish, and says, "I should get going and let you girls get back to work."

"Thanks for lunch," Tracy says, digging through her purse. "Let me give you some money."

"Nope, it's on me. My treat," he says, nudging me with his elbow. "You okay?"

"Yeah, I'm okay. Thank you again. Lunch was good—"

"The company better," he adds.

"The company was definitely better. You made me smile, which was starting to feel foreign."

"That's a shame. If you ever need someone to talk to, you know where I live," he says as we hug goodbye.

"I think I remember where you live," I joke, releasing him, but our hands stay together as I look up into his eyes. "Thank you for the offer. I might just take you up on it sometime."

While rubbing his thumb over the tops of my fingers, he leans closer, the scruff of his cheek against my cheek. "But not tonight. I have a date." He winks and with a confident smile says, "I'm hoping to get lucky tonight."

"What the fuck is going on?" I'd know that voice anywhere, but I still jump, shocked by the harsh words, and pull my hand back. When I turn toward the table, Dalton is standing on the other side of it, his hands fisted, fury written across his face. "This is why you said you'd be late? Fuck. I'm such a fucking fool." He gives me a hard stare of disbelief before he turns it on Danny and it changes to hate. "Are you for fucking real with this shit right now? Every fucking time I turn my back, you're right the fuck there on top of my girl."

"Dalton!" I say, surprised to see him and even more so by his anger.

Danny's hands are in front of him in surrender, and he says, "Hey buddy, like last time, nothing's going on here."

Before I can say more, Dalton's rushing forward and grabbing him by the shirt.

"Dalton, no!" I yell. I grab Dalton's arm, trying my best to pull him back, but his strength easily outmatches mine.

Danny's ready to fight this time, his body as hard as Dalton's, and equal in size.

Dalton pushes him in the chest, and says, "Then why the fuck do you have your hands on my girlfriend?"

Danny could fight back, but doesn't. Instead, he puts his hands between them, and says, "You need to calm down. Holli and I are just friends."

As a crowd gathers, I hear the whispers begin. *I hate the whispers.* Phones and cameras are out probably capturing the whole incident to share with the world.

"Just friends," Dalton repeats, angling his body toward me. He points his finger accusingly. "You left. You left *me* to come see *him*?"

"No," I plead, "you've got this all wrong."

Dalton takes a step closer to me, his eyes wild, his actions equally unpredictable.

Danny matches him by moving next to me, his arm out in protection. He lowers his voice, a threat masked in words of peace. "She said you've got this wrong. Now calm down."

Dalton fixates on Danny's hand, which is a mere inch in front of my thigh, then drags his gaze back up, calculating, until his eyes lock on mine. *Betrayal.* He looks at me with hurt and betrayal. Just as I reach out to touch his cheek, he left hooks Danny who falls against the flimsy banner and hits the floor.

I hear the scream. I just don't realize it's mine until I see the look of horror on Tracy's face.

Dalton leans over Danny, and threatens, "She's mine, so keep your fucking hands off!"

"Dalton, what have you done?" I fall to my knees and touch Danny's cheek that's red and already swelling. "Oh my God, I'm sorry. We need to get you some ice."

Tracy leans down, to help Danny up. "Holli, you need to go!"

"What?" I look at her and I see her own anger tinting her cheeks red. "Take him," she says, pointing at Dalton, "and leave. I'll take care of Danny and the booth. You *both* need to go."

"Danny," I say, "I'm so sorry."

He won't look me, but moves away to stand up. Tracy holds his arm as he gets to his feet.

"What?" Dalton asks, standing behind me. "You're sorry? You feel sorry for him?" He looks shaken and confused. His hands are still closed, the veins in his arms pulsing, but there's an innocence in his expression, the hurt coming through. "You're taking his side?"

The whispers aren't whispers anymore. They become louder, embarrassment sets in as: I'm chastised by Tracy, humiliated by Dalton, and feel horrible for Danny.

Security quickly takes Dalton by each arm, using their own threats of removal. He puts his arms up like he's waiting to be cuffed. "I'll go."

Tracy and Danny move behind the shirt stand then walk toward the main hall of the convention center.

A fire has been set, an anger sparked deep within that fuels me. I turn, poking Dalton in the chest. "How dare you come to *my* work, hurt my friends, ruin my business, and make a scene like that! These are buyers, Dalton. This was my chance to grow and you ruined it. Nobody will want to work with me if they think I'm crazy and hanging around insane people."

"Insane? Ha! Everyone loves a good show. They eat it up." With an arrogant smirk crossing his face, he proclaims, "I'm Johnny fucking Outlaw. I just made your business."

And there it is...

While backing away, my breathing becomes harsh, and my thoughts start spinning too fast to keep up. In a rush, I turn and grab my keys from the floor near my purse.

"I'm going. I'm going." He's aggravated, yanking his arms away from the security guards. I dash past him just as he calls to me. "Angel..."

I don't stop. I go. I run, past the crowds, and the other booths. I run out the entrance, bumping into people along the way. I know he's behind me. I hear him calling me. I feel our connection—stretching beyond being saved—his words the breaking point.

He catches me just inside the parking garage. "No. You can't leave me. Holliday, don't."

Turning abruptly, I hit him on the chest, and yell, "You don't get to tell me what to do. You don't own me. I am not your employee, and I don't owe you anything." With a wave of pained emotion, I hit him again. "What you said in there... you took everything—everything—I've worked so hard for and you belittled it like it's a casual hobby of a kept woman."

He grabs my wrist, squeezing so tight I can't escape. "I didn't mean it like that. I didn't. Cory's death has fucked with my head—"

"No! You don't get to use Cory's death and you won't use Dex's drug problem, or the band ending to excuse what you just did to me. I get what you think you saw, Dalton, but you are wrong. I was giving a friend a goodbye hug, thanking him because he was gracious enough to not only come out and support me today, but to bring lunch for us because he knew we wouldn't be able to get away."

"You have money. You can order delivery."

"Oh my God! You don't get it, do you?" I shake my head, but his grip tightens. "You live in your own world. You've said it yourself. I may have money, but everyone doesn't drop their lives for me. You're so caught up in yourself that you've failed to notice you've been losing me." Remembering Rochelle's advice, I refuse to back down. "I can't live like this anymore. I can't live only for you anymore."

"I do things for you. I do, so don't turn this around like I haven't. I have."

"What are you talking about? And what have you done for me? Because where I stand, everything has been about you from the start, starting with the lies you told to get laid back in Vegas."

He stares into my eyes, his mouth slightly open, then he says, "I've flown across the world just to be with you."

I nod, closing my eyes and taking a deep breath. When I open them again, I look down, away from his, not able to reason between how he's hurt my feelings and the love I feel for him. I don't think I'm going to be able to in this parking garage either. I take a step back, but stop because he's still holding my wrists. When I glance over at two women entering the garage, he loosens, then releases his hold.

When I take another step back, he moves closer. "Holliday?"

I don't understand how a man who loves me so much can hurt me so badly. "Don't."

He doesn't listen. He moves and pulls me to him. With our bodies pressed together—one of his hands lands on my lower back, the other on the back of my neck. "I don't want to hurt you, but my life is a whirlwind."

I want to kiss his regrets away, but he needs to feel everything right now. He needs to escape this state of numbness he's been living in since Cory's death. I'm just sorry that him living again is coming at the expense of us. "Your life is a tornado, destroying everything in its path."

The whispers return as a group of teenagers exit an elevator down the row of cars—their giggles getting louder as they hurry in our direction. Their mission accomplished as they point at Dalton.

We head for the car. I get my key ready to help with a quick escape as my steps pick up. But there's a hollowness to the echo from the solo footfalls of my heels hitting the cement. Panicked, I turn around, realizing there's no *we*, but *me* here and *him* over there. My eyes connect with his as he remains where I left him. My heart beats faster as my hand goes out, trying to close the distance. Even though I know the answer before I ask, I do it anyways, hoping to be surprised. "Are you coming?"

"No," he says, "Go on without me, Holliday."

I glance over at the teens with their phones out, squealing in excitement, then back to him. With a small nod and a silent goodbye, he signals for me to leave. I turn back around, standing there a second longer before I walk away from him... and he lets me.

31

"Sometimes what you want and what everybody else wants from you are two different things." *~Johnny Outlaw*

I'm exhausted—today mentally and physically drained me. The tears I cried earlier have dried on my cheeks, so I rinse my face, the cool water feeling refreshing on my hot skin. After changing into boxer shorts and a tank top, I pull my short fuzzy robe on and go out onto the patio. I glance over at Danny's patio door, but it's closed. The light is on, but when I knocked earlier to check on him there was no answer.

Lying back on the chaise, I tilt my head up and stare at the stars. My eyes feel heavy and I close them, relaxing into the chair.

"Clear sky tonight."

Danny. I jump up and go to the short wall of my patio that faces his. "How are you?" Grabbing hold of the stucco wall, the sharp edges and smooth grooves are contrasting like my emotions. I gulp before I speak, worried he's mad at me... or worse, hates me.

"I've gone through two bags of peas and one steak I was planning on having for dinner tonight, but I think I'll live."

I can't help scrunching my nose at seeing the bruising that's already forming and the swelling near his eye.

"Don't look so grossed out," he adds. "You're gonna give me a complex."

Smiling, I say, "Good, the humor's still intact. Danny, I'm sorry." I lean down on my elbows, dropping my head, feeling shame, guilt, and embarrassed. I look up and see his smile, a mixture of understanding and sympathy as I continue."I don't know what to say. I'm just... You've seen the worst of him, but he's not normally like that. We had a fight this morning and left on bad terms, so I'm to blame. I'm sorry you were dragged into it and more sorry that you were hurt. Is there anything I can do for you?"

He presses his palms against the barrier, leans forward, and says, "You know, Holli, I've been in plenty of fights in my life. Today I tried to do the right thing, take the high road, and I ended up with a black eye from a sucker punch. I'm not gonna lie, it took a lot for me not to knock him on his ass, but I didn't for one reason."

"Why is that?"

"You." He stands up and sighs. "I saw your face, the hurt on your face. I just didn't want to add to it."

I lick my lips then scrape my teeth over my bottom one, bringing it in and look down.

"I didn't tell you that to upset you," he says. "I just thought you should know that I didn't hold back for him, because he's famous, or your boyfriend."

Reaching across the space that divides our patios, I place my hand on top of his, and say, "Thank you. Thank you for being a good friend."

His other hand covers mine and with a soft, reassuring smile, he says, "You're welcome, neighbor."

Focusing my eyes up, I reply, "I can see stars forever tonight."

"That's rare for L.A." He pauses, but the silence is broken when he asks, "Want some company?"

"Sure."

He starts to climb up, but stops to ask, "You don't have any crazy boyfriends hiding inside, do you? One black-eye is enough for today."

"Stop," I warn, totally teasing.

"Too soon?"

"Give it a day or two before the crazy boyfriend jokes are unleashed."

"I'll give ya a day." He waves his hands out to move me away from the wall, and says, "Step back and don't try this at home."

"But you're trying this at home."

"I'm a professional."

"You're a photographer, a professional photographer, not a stunt man. You could fall and then where would your underwear modeling career be? It'd be sunk is where it would be."

He raises an eyebrow up at me. "Are you really worried about my modeling career or about my body?" He winks with his hurt eye... yeah, he's gonna live.

With a wry grin, he jumps, landing on my patio. Dusting his hands off, he follows me to the chaises and we sit down. "So how are you really?" he asks.

I glance over at him. He's watching me, so I turn back and look up at the stars. "I've been better."

"Yeah, not a great day for you either."

I laugh, but there's no humor. "No, not a great day."

"Speaking of stars—"

I roll my eyes while resting my head back against the lounger. "Were we speaking of stars?"

"We were. You just mentioned the clear night and stars forever, blah, blah, blah."

"Gee thanks for the blah, blah, blah." I laugh.

"So your boyfriend's famous?"

Rolling my head to the side, I smile. I get the intrigue. I'm still fascinated myself. "He wasn't when I met him."

"Really? Johnny Outlaw's been around a while." When I don't say anything, he adds, "You know I used to think you were hot, when we first met."

Now that makes me laugh for real. "You *used* to?"

"Well," he explains, using his hands to help demonstrate. "I thought you were single that first time, the morning I invited you to the party."

"I *was* single then."

He quirks his head to the side and narrows his eyes. "I thought you just said you've dated Johnny since before he was famous?"

"I said he wasn't famous when I met him. There's a difference."

"I'm confused. He wasn't famous and you were single? Yeah, totally lost over here."

I sigh. "I was single that morning of the invite. I drove to Vegas for a convention and met... Johnny while I was there, but I didn't know who he was." It feels so wrong calling him that. He'll always been Dalton to me.

He starts to laugh. "You're wilder than I thought, Holli. So you hooked up with him that weekend and along the way, started dating?" He shakes his head. "You know, I'm being really fucking nosy. You can tell me to shut up if you don't want to talk about this."

"I'd love to say it's not as illicit as it sounds, but really, it is. We hooked up. I thought it would be a one night stand, but it turned into breakfast then visits... and more. Maybe it should have stayed in Sin City all along."

Another long pause leads into him saying, "I'm not expert on relationships, but I've had a few and I can say I never felt like Johnny did today."

I sit up, bringing my knees to my chest and resting my cheek down. "What do you mean?"

"I mean, I've never felt strongly enough about a woman to fight for her like that. He may have been off base with his assumptions, but his heart was in the right place. In my opinion, that guy loves you."

When he stands up, I lift my head up and ask, "Where are you going?"

"I need to leave. I'm starting to get all sensitive and crap and that just doesn't sit well with me. I'm thinking it's the knock to the head that's done it."

I chuckle. "You're being ridiculous. It was actually very sweet of you to say and a good observation. I hadn't thought of his reaction being because he loves me."

Danny stops just before climbing back on the ledge, and says, "As I see it, his actions spoke louder than his words. I'm not saying how he handled it was right..." He points to his eye. "This is proof it wasn't, but it might not be that wrong either." He hops up and makes the jump. When he lands, he smiles all proud of himself.

"You know you could have used the door."

He pops his hand against his forehead, and says, "Now you tell me."

"Danny?" He smiles when I call his name. "Thanks for the advice, chat, whatever this was. You've given me a lot to think about."

"Don't go buying us bestie necklaces just yet, and let's pretend you didn't hear any of that love talk from me. Okay?"

He's looking a little coy. "I like when you're embarrassed," I say, "but I like that you told me all of that even more."

"I'll be here, calling my buddies over to talk completely inappropriately about women, and to chug some beer in hopes that I grow my balls back."

"Your balls are safe." I whisper, "I won't tell anyone that you actually have a heart. We'll keep them focused on your pretty face instead."

He lifts his shirt and runs his hand over his abs. "Don't forget about the hot body."

"The hot body is definitely unforgettable. Now stop fishing for compliments and go earn your mancard back."

I hear him chuckle.

"Hey," I call to stop him. "By the way, what happened to your date?"

"She got a modeling gig in Paris, but don't worry about me, I'll find another before the night's through. I'm sure there are plenty of women who like to play nurse."

"Oh, I'm sure there are." I laugh.

After sending a nod and smile in my direction, he goes inside, shutting the door behind him. I roll my eyes at the last comment, but let his other words linger a bit.

Settling back down, I look up at the stars again. Despite what happened today, I can't stop thinking about Dalton. He's been hit with a lot lately between Dex and Cory, and now our relationship. Rationally, I know I should cut him some slack, but for Dalton to think I would purposely hurt him, hurts me.

Unlike last time when he tried to pick a fight with Danny, this time he's gone too far. We need to talk and soon. But tonight, it's best we don't. I'm still too mad.

32

"Touring is amazing. I get to see the world and meet the fans. It's incredible, but it's hard on relationships—family, friends, and dating. They all have to pay the price for the career I've chosen."
~Johnny Outlaw

Dalton doesn't call me. It hurts. My strong-willed side tells me I deserve better. My weaker side brings me to tears more than I'd like to admit. I thought I meant more to him, but now I question everything we were, everything he said, every gesture, and the time we spent together. I'm driving myself mad with the lack of answers, so I work all the time, well aware of the days passing by. Both of us too stubborn to give in—

my pride bruised, his ego wounded.

When I'm not working, I help Tracy with the planning of her wedding. I slip on my Maid of Honor dress to show her how it looks, a knock at the door interrupting. I freeze, my breath stopping, my heart clenching, still holding onto hope that Dalton will come around.

Tracy sees my face, and says, "I'll get it." She runs out of the bedroom and down the stairs. But it's not him. A female voice dashes my hopes.

"Holli?" Tracy calls from the living room. "You have company."

I walk downstairs, not caring that the dress is unzipped in the back, my heart deflated.

"Hi. Hope you don't mind me stopping by," Rochelle says with a little wave.

I go to her. "No. No, not at all. Come in." We hug and I say, "It's good to see you. It's been too long."

"It has," she says, smiling. "I don't have long. My mom is visiting for the week and has the kids, so I need to get back soon."

"Okay, what brings you by? Do you mind zipping me up, Tracy?"

Tracy comes around to zip up the dress for me, muttering something about a business call she needs to make and disappears upstairs. Rochelle and I sit down on the couch together. "I wanted to check on you," she says.

Instant guilt overcomes me. "I should be the one checking on you."

"No, everybody else does that. I like that I get to be..." She releases a breath and says, "Normal with you. I don't have to be strong or put on a happy face to make you feel better. I like that and I've just been missing you. Anyway, I didn't come over to talk about me."

I touch her leg, and say, "I've been missing you too."

"You look nice. It's a pretty dress. Are you going somewhere?"

"Thanks. It's for Tracy's wedding. I was showing her." *Surface, keep the conversation surface and don't be the first to bring up Dalton.*

She starts fidgeting with her ring, her engagement ring from Cory, and I look away, hiding the tears I know will come if I don't. Her voice shakes when she says, "I needed to see you. I'm worried about Johnny."

I sigh, afraid that's what this was about. "I can't help you there."

The urgency in her tone worries me. "Why?" she asks. "Why'd you break up?"

"I didn't realize we were."

"I don't understand."

"What I thought was a fight turned into... this."

"What's this?"

"The remains of something that once was," I state flatly.

"And still can be. He's going through a hard time, but he loves you. I could see. I still can. He's spoiled and used to getting his way. He's stubborn—"

"The life of a rock star," I reply casually though I feel anything but that when speaking of Dalton.

She nods. "He was dealing with a lot of baggage when we met him. But the band helped, gave him something to hold onto, something real, that he respected, that fed his drive to be something other than a disappointment. You gave him direction though. You gave him meaning that no one else has, Holli."

"He sucks you in with his charisma and sweet lines, but the

way his life controls him, the heaviness of what's going on inside of him... it spits you out. It spit me out and he hasn't even bothered to call."

"He'll come to his senses. Just give him a little time," she says. I stand and walk to the window, looking out over the street. "Is there still a chance?"

"Did he send you here to talk to me?"

"No. Would you talk to him if he did come over?"

"Rochelle," I say, turning around. "I may have been the one to walk away, but he let me. He hasn't contacted me at all. How much does he really love me if he can go all this time without even a text?"

"Have you called him?"

I shake my head. "I can't. He hurt me. He's going through so much and I tried to be there, but I can't get swept up in his turmoil. Day and night, I was there and he barely noticed. He only took notice when he felt threatened, that's not love. That's possession. If I'm in a relationship, I need to be more than the Great Johnny Outlaw's girlfriend."

"Are you talking marriage?"

"No, I'm talking about being me. I..." I stop, needing to contain the emotions from bubbling over. My tears are wiped before they fall. "No matter who he chooses to be, I need to stay true to me. You told me that."

"You need to be equal. You do," she says, reflective.

"The balance in a relationship shifts all the time. I'm okay with that. I just want him to see me as more than someone who warms his bed at night. I want him to be as proud of me as I am of him."

With a heavy sigh, a small smile appears on Rochelle's face. "You deserve that and more." She stands. "I think you might be the first woman who didn't want to use his fame and connections. It's refreshing to know there's still good in the world." She walks to the door and I follow her outside. "Thanks for letting me barge in."

"Thank you for stopping by and feel free to barge in any time," I say, giving her a tight hug goodbye. "How about lunch next week? Any day, your choice."

"I'd like that. I'll text you." She hurries down the stairs, but stops and turns back. "You've made a bigger impact than you realize, Holli. On all of us."

"Then maybe one day he'll stop by."

She nods, understanding.

I go back inside and see Tracy standing on the bottom step. "You okay?" she asks.

Finally feeling like I'm starting to make sense of things, I reply, "I think so."

33

"Life isn't about right or wrong, but learning to live with your choices."
~Johnny Outlaw

The fallout from the convention has died down in the media. Photos were sold to tabloids, making me relive that day for weeks after. The 'Lime Lady and the Rock Star' makes for interesting press, I guess. I don't see the appeal, but they've finally moved on just like Dalton has. The public's idol is now being tied to every single socialite, starlet, and groupie. The photos showing up online and in the rags at the supermarket don't look incriminating, but the headlines say otherwise. I know how the media twists the truth to fit the story they want to tell.

Or maybe I just don't want to believe that Dalton and I are done for good.

Tracy has the week off to entertain family from out of state and to wrap up wedding details. I'm getting at least five calls a day from the nervous bride and two from vendors, not counting my business calls. So when Danny stops by with beers, I welcome him with open arms, needing the break. I turn off my phone to block out my obligations, kick my feet up on my coffee table, and tip back the bottle. The beer is more refreshing than it should be. "Ahhhh," I moan, closing my eyes as I lean my head back on the couch. "I needed this."

"You look tired."

Lifting my head up, I give him the evil eye. "Gee, thanks, neighbor."

"I didn't mean it like that," he says, laughing. "But the way you're laying there, looks like you might fall asleep on me."

"I just might. I don't sleep well, haven't in a while."

He's about to say something, but he turns back to the TV, watching the quiz show, and takes a drink instead.

"Go on," I say, "get it off your chest."

"What?"

He's playing dumb. "Nice try. Let's just talk about it, so we don't have to talk about it again tonight."

"Still no word?"

"Nope," I emphasize the word.

"Sorry."

"Don't be."

With his foot, he pushes my legs off the table, making me fall on my side. "Dude," I complain, holding my beer in the air so it doesn't spill. "What's that about?"

"You. Look at you in your sweats and baggy tee, holey socks, and your hair..." he says, moving his hand above his head all crazy, "... like that. You need to snap out of this funk. You need to get out of your house and get a change of scenery." He stands and pulls me up by my arm. "C'mon, I'm taking you out. If I remember correctly, I owe you some drinks."

Offended, I put my hand on my hip, and say, "First of all, these are yoga pants, not sweats. You're a model. You should know these things. Secondly, this," I say, swirling my hand above my hair, "is the latest in working-from-home-hairstyles. All the coolest entrepreneurs are sporting this look, don't ya know."

"Yoga instructors, maybe, but not people who have to leave the house on a regular basis."

"But I don't have to leave the house much."

He taps me on the nose, twice. "That, my friend, is why I'm getting you out of here."

"Did you just boop me?"

"What's a boop?"

I tap him on the nose and say, "Boop."

His eyebrow lifts. "Well, in that case, I did just boop you and I'm gonna do it again. Hold still." He boops me again, then says, "Now go change, slacky. I want you lookin' hot."

I want to argue, but I also want to show him how good I can look. I go with the latter. If I'm doing this, I'm doing it right. I shower quickly, and get dressed, pulling on tight, white jeans and a purple tank top that flows over my curves, ending at the top of my hips. I slip on my brown wedges and do my makeup and hair, deciding to let my hair hang free with my natural waves showing.

When I come back downstairs, Danny's standing there with the beer to his mouth, but he stops, and slowly lowers it. "Shit. I was just planning on grabbing drinks down the street. But with you looking like that... I might want to show you off."

"Very funny," I say, getting my purse from the bar. "I see you changed clothes." I walk past him and flick his arm. "Not too shabs yourself. C'mon, let's go." Grabbing a jacket on our way out, we head to the street where his Jeep is parked. "No top today?"

"Do you want the top on?"

"Look, I know I'm not an 'Official' date, but I'd still like to arrive wherever we're going without the crazy hair," I say, pointing at my head.

"Good point. I'll put the top on."

I stand on the sidewalk, tapping my foot impatiently. I actually don't mind the top being down, but I like giving him a hard time like he does me. I also could have offered to drive my car, but when he steps up on the running board and stretches to snap the vinyl in place, I appreciate the view. Then he reaches across the roll bar and his shirt rides up. Since his jeans hang low, his abs are exposed. My gaze follows up and over each muscle that's well defined and keeps him modeling. No one works that hard if you don't want to show it off, and getting paid is a bonus. I have a feeling he's very good at his job.

He claps his hands, proud of himself, and says, "Doors and all, fancypants. Now get in. I've worked up an appetite."

"That didn't take much."

He rubs his belly, unknowingly teasing me with another hint of skin. "I'm a growing boy."

... And my mind goes to the gutter.

I slide into my seat, staying close to the flimsy canvas door and holding tight to the seatbelt after buckling up. *He's my neighbor. He's my friend. That's all. I remind myself.*

The hostess takes us to a table for two against the far wall. Looking over the wine menu, I decide on a pinot noir. After we order, I ask, "I've seen this place before, but I've never been here. Do you come here often?"

"It's my favorite Italian restaurant. I like that it's a mom and pop shop, everything is homemade."

As much as I don't want to, when I look at the man sitting across from me, my mind flashes to Dalton and I wish it was him. I grab a long, skinny breadstick and start munching, hoping to distract myself, but the candle on the table, the dim lights above, and the Italian music sets the scene for a romantic date. It's hard not to get caught up in it. *He's my neighbor. He's my friend. That's all. I remind myself... again.* "How's the photography?"

The waiter brings our drinks and takes our dinner orders. As soon as he leaves, Danny says, "It's going good. I've got a shoot in Cabo next week. I had a model drop out last minute. You want to fill in?"

I burst out laughing. "You're kidding, right?"

By his expression alone, the serious face, I can tell he's not. "Not kidding at all."

I take a big gulp of wine, then shake my head. I start to give him thirty reasons I'm not model material, a list that's like a daily running tally. "I'm not that tall and I have flaws that I refuse to speak of on the back of my legs. I pretend it's not there, but I know it is. It taunts me. And then—"

"You're very beautiful, Holli. I know you can rock a bikini and there are no flaws. Trust me, I've looked."

Always the charmer. "Why are you still single, Danny?"

"Because I want to be."

I tilt my head and glare. "For real."

"The truth is that the girl I like is currently unavailable."

"Interesting."

"Tragic really."

His gaze lays heavy on me and I feel my cheeks heat. I look down, spinning the glass by the stem and watch as the wine rolls up the sides like a wave before sliding back down. When I look back up, I say, "You're such a flirt." I laugh to break the building tension, but fortunately our plates arrive doing a better job of it.

As he speaks with the waiter, I take the chance to look at him, really look at him.

He's handsome, like worthy of a fifty-foot billboard on Sunset handsome. He keeps saying he's not interested in modeling anymore, but the modeling industry isn't ready to let him go just yet. The dimples that reveal his charm, even before he opens his mouth, are there when he looks at me and the plate of spaghetti I ordered. "That looks good," he says.

Holding eye contact, I reply, "Yeah, very good."

With a knife and fork in hand, he narrows his eyes and points at my food. "We still talking about food? You seem distant."

"Food. Right. Yeah."

"Food. Right. Yeah," he teases. "Seriously, what's going on with the caveman speak?"

"Nothing, just—" A phone from the next table rings, interrupting me. The ringtone is The Resistance. Hearing the song breaks my heart all over again.

"Will you excuse me?" I toss my napkin on the table and walk away before he has a chance to respond. *He's my neighbor. He's my friend. That's all. He's my neighbor. He's my friend. That's all. Dalton. Dalton. Dalton. Damn him!*

I push open the door to the women's restroom and hurry to the sink. With my hands flat on the counter, I lean forward, so close to the mirror that my nose almost touches. I'm not drunk, and I don't know what other signs I'm looking for in my reflection, but I can't find anything different. My eyes are hazel, my hair is sandy-blonde, Dalton doesn't love me anymore, and I've got what appears to be a new wrinkle on the outside of my right eye.

Jerking my head back, I stand upright convinced that no one should ever have to look at themselves that close up. But the reality is—I have a few wrinkles, plain brown eyes and dirty blonde hair on a bad day. On a good day, I had Dalton.

I don't have good days anymore.

But I deserve them, so I walk back and sit down across from Danny. "How's your food?"

He takes a sip of his wine, and says, "Really good. Are you okay?"

"I'm fine." I look up and see his concern. "Really. I'm fine and I'm having a good time."

"Good. I aim to please."

"I just bet you do." I punctuate with a wink.

"There she is," he says, raising his glass. "Ladies and gentlemen, the sarcastic and clever girl I've gotten to know is back."

I pull his arm down. "Okay. Okay. I got the message. I'm here. You got me—body and mind, fully present on ole Danny boy."

"I don't know about the 'Ole Danny boy' part, but I like the idea of your body on me."

I roll my eyes for what feels like the tenth time tonight and laugh. "Don't forget my mind—"

"Oh, don't worry. Your mind is one of the things... You know, we should save that conversation for another time, after many alcoholic beverages."

"Okay."

We're definitely going to have to catch a cab home tonight. Danny's just handed me my third shot of tequila and neither of us is in any condition to drive. I don't even know where we are. It's a bar, near the restaurant, but other than that, nada.

The music is loud and the bar packed for a Wednesday. For a few brief moments, the pain I've felt over the loss of Dalton in the last month is replaced... almost. But I'll take it, because it feels good to feel 'almost' normal again.

With a big, cocky grin on his face, and the crowd chanting my name, it's my turn to do a body shot—off of Danny. He pulls his shirt over his head and the women in the bar go nuts, calling his name and whistling. Deep down, I'm confused because I'm starting to feel territorial over him. He's with me... at least for the night.

His shirt hits me in the face, but I'm too drunk to care. I tie it around my neck and step forward as he starts to lie down on top of the bar. He turns my way and says, "Photographic evidence or it didn't happen."

"Yes, we definitely need a picture to cringe over tomorrow when we feel like shit and can't remember anything that happened the night before." I dig through my purse to find my phone.

Just as I pull it out, he adds, "Oh baby, I'll remember every second of this."

I shove a lime in his mouth to pipe him down, which makes him laugh, and hand the phone to a girl who is way too eager to take this picture. I notice it's still off from when I needed peace from work and the wedding vendors earlier in the night. "Hold up. Let me turn it on." I tell the girl to hit the camera icon when the screen loads up. "And tell me when you're ready."

"Okay," she says. "Ready."

At the last moment, I set the shot glass down on his stomach instead of pouring the liquid on him. Using my mouth, I tip it back, then drop the glass into my hands. The alcohol burns as it slides down my throat, but Danny's hand on the back of my arm is warm and comforting, encouraging me to take the lime, which typically ends in a kiss.

My text message alarm goes off, causing me to glance over my shoulder, distracting me from his lips... the lime, I mean. The girl hands the phone back to me and I catch a glimpse of Dalton's name on the screen. Danny pulls me closer, and the boisterous chanting that surrounds me, reminds me of the lime waiting in his mouth. The text ring goes off again, and I look down at it, my heart thundering in my chest, a lump in my throat forming. *Dalton*. I can't put this off. I've waited too long to hear from him. Touching Danny's shoulder, I say, "I'm sorry. I need to check this."

He sits up, the lime falling from his mouth. "Holli?"

But I'm already pushing my way out the door and walking to a secluded part of the sidewalk for privacy. I should be mad after all this time, but my heart hasn't gotten the memo and I anxiously open the message.

Four texts. Four lines—lyrics, a poem, or his inner thoughts. I have no idea, but he sent them to me and now I cling to hope once more.

Love is a sparrow I hold in my hand
An angel believing me a better man
I'm finding my way back to her before she flies away
Hoping she can forgive when I come back to her one day.
"Holli?" *Danny.*

I wipe a tear from my cheek before he has a chance to see it. Turning toward him, I say, "I'm here." He's shirtless, and now I feel guilty for leaving him in there. I unwrap his shirt from around my neck and hand it to him.

"What happened?" he asks, taking the shirt. "Is everything okay?" He pulls it over his head.

"Yeah, yeah, no worries." *Play it off. Don't let him see how Dalton affects you.*

"Hey," he says, bending his neck to look into my eyes. "I'm worried, okay? You're crying. Was it the text? Or me?"

"No, it wasn't you. I'm sorry. I don't mean to worry you. It was the text. I wasn't expecting it. Just caught me off guard."

"C'mon. Here's your purse. I think we should call it a night." I'd like to think I'm reading too much into his clipped tone, but when he turns and walks away from me, I know he's hurt or mad or both.

In the cab, I offer, "I can bring you back to pick up your Jeep in the morning."

"Nah, it's fine."

"Really. No trouble at all."

"I have to go for a run in the morning anyway. I'll just come this way and get it."

"Okay, if you're sure."

"I am." We sit in silence for another minute, staring out our own windows when he says, "It was Johnny, right? The text. It was from him?"

When I look over, his expression is neutral, almost like he saw this coming. I won't lie to him though. He's too good to be lied to. "Yes."

"Just like that? It's a done deal?"

"Right now..." I talk in metaphors to keep things nice, uncomplicated, but it's already complicated, and the truth for him, not so nice. "I'm not open to any other possibility."

"Currently unavailable," he repeats from earlier in the night.

Currently unavailable. The plain truth.

The cab pulls up out front and I give the driver money just as Danny does. We decide to split the fare. As we walk up the first steps, we don't talk, but when we reach the landing, we stop. He says, "This doesn't have to be awkward. We're neighbors. We're friends."

"That's all," we say at the same time. Neither of us laughs at the coincidence.

"Thank you for dinner," I say, "and well, the whole night. Danny, I had fun and I loved it, but mostly, I needed it. I needed a friend. So thank you." I take a step forward and open my arms.

He comes closer, and embraces me. It's tight and filled with sincerity. "Thank you... friend." The last word seems a struggle to say, but he releases me with a smile and walks to his door. With his key in hand, I walk to mine and we open our doors at the same time.

"Goodnight, Danny."

"Holli?"

"Yes?"

"You say you have these flaws, but I want you to know that for every flaw you think you have, I can name three things that make you perfect to me."

I gulp, then my voice cracks with emotion when I whisper, "Thank you." We both go inside and I lock my door behind me. Grabbing the empty beer bottles from the coffee table, I head into the kitchen and throw them in the recycling bin. I get a glass of water and an Ibuprofen and head upstairs for bed.

After turning out the lights, I climb under the covers and lay in the dark. I read the texts at least ten more times before holding the phone to my chest and falling asleep.

34

*"Fuck expectations. They only set you
up for disappointment. I'd rather
believe in the possibility of chance
then die wallowing in regret."*
~Johnny Outlaw

"You're late," Tracy says, our eyes meeting in the reflection of the
mirror as she's getting her makeup done.

I check my watch one last time. "Really? Two minutes. You're
holding two minutes against me?"

"What if I needed you two minutes ago?"

"You had me all morning and I was only gone an hour. I'm
here for you now, beautiful bride. How may I be of service?" I set
a bottle of champagne down on the vanity in front of her, along
with three glasses.

"Okay, you're forgiven. Pour the bubbly."

The makeup artist laughs. "She's been a nervous wreck."

I pop the cork and pour the champagne. "You have nothing to be nervous about. You and Adam are made for each other. You've loved him forever. He's loved you longer."

A smile appears. She takes a sip, and says, "Thank you."

"You're welcome. To a lifetime of memories with the love of your life."

The three of us toast in unison, "Cheers."

Twenty minutes later, I'm nervously standing outside large wooden doors waiting for them to open. The guy holding my arm is single and good looking, but my heart's still having trouble getting over Dalton to appreciate the opportunity.

Right before the doors open, Tracy says, "Wish me luck."

I hug her tight and whisper, "You don't need luck. You've got everything you need already."

Smiling, she steps back and takes her father's arm.

The doors open wide, and we start walking. I want to run, not digging the attention, but the best man, Alex, holds me back from bolting, keeping the right pace. The church is pretty with its stained glass windows catching the light and reflecting the colors into the sanctuary. Tracy surprised me by keeping the list under a hundred guests. It feels more intimate. I see plenty of familiar faces when looking around, but despite the myriad of smiles and big hats, only one person stands out in the crowd—*Dalton*.

My mouth drops open when my eyes meet his. My heart races as all the feelings I once had for him come rushing out from that secret place where hope was hidden deep inside. Tears fill my eyes, thinking I'd lost him forever. He's here. My emotions get the best of me when I see his gentle smile. It's the smile that reminds me of everything good we ever shared—it's happy with the small eye crinkles I missed so much, and my breath hitches... *Hitches*! I thought that was reserved for romance movies and pirate novels until now. My mind starts reeling in disbelief and I close my eyes quickly hoping when I reopen them, he's really here. When I do, I see him again, a quiet laugh shaking his shoulders. It makes no sense for him to be here, and yet, there he is.

The best man whispers, "Keep walking."

I hadn't noticed I'd stopped, but I did. Nodding, I mumble, "Yes, keep walking." My feet move me forward, but my eyes don't leave the deep greens I've fallen in love with, the man who stole my heart and who despite my best efforts to reclaim it, still wholly owns it.

Just before we pass his pew, a sly grin appears then he bites his lower lip. I look toward the waiting minister, suddenly feeling guilty for having naughty thoughts in church. I start to look around at the pretty flowers and wedding decor and smile at Tracy's family sitting in the first row. But it's pointless. There's no way I'm going to get that lip bite out of my head. *Impossible.* Jack Dalton is impossible to forget and completely irresistible. So trying to be a little devious myself, I lower my chin to my right shoulder and steal a peek at the sexiest man I've ever seen.

He sits alone on the bride's side, but doesn't go unnoticed. A few cameras and some cell phones are aimed in his direction. Unlike his usual protective self, here he's unguarded, paying no mind to them. I like seeing him relaxed even with the attention.

Taking the bride's bouquet when I'm supposed to, I concentrate back on my friend and her special moment as they exchange vows. Adam grabs Tracy, dipping her down, and kissing her hard. Their love fills the room and encourages applause and catcalls. They run down the aisle hand in hand and Alex grabs mine to head down after them. I keep my eyes forward, struggling not to look in Dalton's direction because if I do, I won't be able to look away.

Cat and mouse... or maybe cat and cat. Not sure what we're doing, but I enjoy the game, enjoying the chase with Dalton this time. At the reception, we move in circles, keeping our distance while keeping our eyes on the other. I decide to play a little longer, enjoying the anticipation of our reunion.

Time and perspective, becoming more aware of who I am, learning balance while in a relationship—these are the things I've had plenty of time to think about and discover. Dalton didn't take over who I was. I gave myself willingly and got lost along the way. He fell in love with me, all of me, and never asked for anything other than trust in return.

For someone as famous as he is, he's approachable here, taking photos with other guests, while being respectful of the bride and groom. Adam is mesmerized. *Join the club.*

After getting the bride a cocktail, we stand there looking at the party before us. "Do you hate me?" she asks.

"You're hard to hate."

She taps her glass against mine. "*He* called me by the way."

I turn to look at her. She's glowing and happy, a secret hidden in her smile. "Should I be worried?"

"No, everything is perfect." She seems to be referencing the reception, but I know better.

Looking past the dance floor, I spot Dalton across the room, sitting at a table with a group of kids. They're totally engrossed in some story that involves his arms going out like there's a large explosion. The best part is he's equally engrossed in the story, which makes me smile. "You should eat," I suggest to Tracy. "Can I make you a plate of food?"

"I'm good. I've been snacking, but you go ahead."

I walk to the buffet and get in line. It moves along slowly, but I'm not in a hurry. I start placing appetizers on my plate, mainly going for cheese and fruit. I'm reaching for the Swiss when I feel someone press against my arm, and say, "You look beautiful." I freeze, my heart skipping a beat or five just from hearing his voice again. Like I missed him, I've missed his voice, and my shoulders drop as I exhale, all my willpower escaping me with that breath. Three words are all it took. Three words, and like my heart always knew, I am his again. That easy. What we share that powerful. Our hearts bonded even when our bodies weren't.

When I dare to look into his eyes, Dalton's expression is lighter than the last time we spoke, his mood playful. It's a good look on him. He's tanner, appears healthier. His smile is different, less damaged. It's been four weeks and I should probably be offended and hurt we haven't spoken, but it's hard to stay mad at the man you love. Time heals and all that... With a gentle nudge to his ribs, I say, "Fancy seeing a rock star at my best friend's wedding."

I continue moving down the buffet line loading my plate.

"I'm more Jack than Johnny these days." Dalton stays close to my side, but leaves a little distance I wish he wouldn't.

"You look good, Jack."

"Dalton," he says with a little smile that feels special, like one only I can evoke. "You are only allowed to call me Dalton."

"You look good, Dalton."

His smile grows. "I spent a week in Hawaii." He runs his hand through his hair then shoves it in his pocket.

"Any new tattoos?"

He looks down at his arm, his sleeves are rolled up, but not enough to show the hula girl. With a light chuckle, he says, "No. A few drunken nights... Okay, a lot of drunken nights, but no new tattoos." He looks over as the music changes from fast to slow. "So, um," he stammers, shifting his weight. "I know you're about to eat, but I asked the DJ to play a song and I was hoping you'd dance with me."

"Is this the song?" I ask, looking over at the dance floor.

"Yes," he says. "Will you dance with me, Holliday?"

I nod and set my plate down without hesitation. "I'd like that." He doesn't realize I would say yes to anything he asked of me.

He takes my hand and heads for the dance floor, his fingers curling around mine possessively. I'm lost to how warm his skin feels, his touch always more than skin deep. When we reach the dance floor, he takes my other hand and we begin to dance, him taking the lead. He looks down at my face, his gaze hitting my mouth and moving up to my eyes. "I never thanked you properly... when we came back from Paris," he says.

"Thank me for what?"

"For saving me."

Looking down, we turn, keeping our feet moving. "You did once—"

"I'm not talking about the plane crash."

His eyes are fixed on mine, an intensity directed at me when he pulls me closer, cups my face, and he says, "You're the calm to my storm."

Staring up at him, my lips part, my heart thunders in my chest, and my cheeks heat. The song ends and clapping begins. I discover we have an audience, "People are watching."

"I don't care."

That brings my attention back to him. "You don't?"

"No, I don't care about them. I only care about yo—" A loud tapping, a fork against crystal, interrupts him. I'm introduced to give my speech.

His hands fall away and we both look toward the microphone, everyone waiting on me. "Will you stay?" I ask.

"I'll wait for you."

I walk away to make a toast to the bride and her groom, but glance back, missing his touch already. After my speech, I sit next to Tracy while Alex gives his best man's speech. My gaze shifts from Alex to Dalton. Dalton captivates me, and I watch him move to the bar. Loud laughter draws my attention back to the speech, but I missed the joke. Alex wraps up his toast and we all drink in the couple's honor. Tracy leans over, and says, "He told me he wants to start over with you. Do things right this time."

"To me, things weren't so bad the first go round, but I'll take this second chance... maybe it's our fifth at this point. I've lost count and honestly, I don't want to keep track." I know how I want this night to end and I think I know how he feels, so I stand and say, "Wish me luck."

"You don't need luck. You've got everything you need already."

"Using my advice against me, huh?"

"Whatever it takes to get you to see the light."

"You don't play fair, Trace."

"It's not about fair or unfair, right or wrong. It's only about love. Now go get yours before someone else does."

Not wasting another minute, I cross the room. Dalton's leaning on the bar with one arm, his head tilted down. When he sees me, he stands upright, his eyes on me as if he can't resist the temptation. I place my hand on the bar top, getting the bartender's attention, and order, "An Old-Fashioned with extra orange please."

"Coming right up," the bartender replies.

Angling closer, Dalton says, "Rules are made to be broken, but laws, breaking laws can get you into a lot of trouble. Hate to be a dick, but I'll need to see your ID."

Starting over.

I giggle, remembering how a chance encounter has turned my world upside down... and after having time apart, I realize I wouldn't change anything about the start of us. So I play along, and ask, "Are you being serious?"

He takes my hand just as the bartender sets my drink down. Taking a step closer, Dalton says, "You know, expectations can be a tricky thing. You think you know what's going to happen and then something else does entirely, something out of blue. You don't see it in that moment, but later, when you have time to reflect, you realize it was planned all along."

I lean in closer, feeling that connection that binds our hearts, strengthen. "Divine intervention?" I ask, "Fate? Kismet? Destiny?"

"That's the funny thing," he says, keeping his voice low, just for my ears alone. "We try to label it to make ourselves feel less crazy for not being able to predict the outcome. But while we're busy trying to define it, we miss the magic." He closes the gap, his lips to my temple comforting to me, then he whispers, "I don't want to miss the magic. I want you. Any part you're willing to share with me, I'll take. If time and distance is what you need, I won't like it, but I can give you that. I love you, Angel."

Right then and there—that's when I knew I would stay. I knew I could never walk away from him again. I wrap my arms around his neck and close my eyes. Resting my forehead on his shoulder, I inhale, his scent making me whole again as every amazing memory I've been fortunate enough to share with him comes rushing back.

"I love you, Jack Dalton."

Leaning back to look me in the eyes, he asks, "What about Johnny Outlaw? Can you learn to love him too?"

"What's not to love about a rocker with a bad temper, sexy tattoos and a hot ass?"

With a chuckle, he wraps his arm around my waist and brings me close to kiss me, but stops and says, "I knew you couldn't resist me."

"I never could," I say, touching my fingertips to his cheek. He shaved, but I still feel his five o'clock shadow.

His hands comfort me as he holds my face and I feel it, our connection stronger than it ever was before. He whispers, "I'm going to kiss you."

"You're warning me?"

"No, I'm making you a promise. The next time I kiss you, it's gonna be the first kiss of our forever."

I take in a trembling breath, his words filling my soul. I release it and say, "Dalton?"

His eyes have never been more green than they are right now. "Yeah?"

"Kiss me now."

His lips press firmly against mine and when my mouth opens, we come together—warmth, love, and passion engulfing us. My eyes stay closed after our lips part, wanting to live in this dream world with him forever.

"Open your eyes, Angel."

When I do, he says, "I thought Cory's death would destroy me, but I realized it didn't. Waking up without you did. Cory will always remain in the music, a part of me as my brother, but you, you're my soul and I don't want to live another day without you. Marry me."

35

"There's no fun in hard truths, so I
always choose the dare."
~Johnny Outlaw

A jet is on stand-by. We're Vegas bound. No luggage or doubts holding us back. We leave straight from Tracy's reception. As we take off into the night sky, I ask, "When did you book the jet?"

"A week ago."

"You were pretty confident, huh?"

"I was hopeful," he says, cocking a brow while reaching over and taking my hand in his. "I also booked a room."

For some reason that makes me burst out laughing. It feels good to feel light, happy again, the burdens of our time apart lifting from my heart. "Oh Dalton, what am I going to do with you?"

"Marry me. Have lots of great sex and make babies," he says with a completely straight face.

Holy shit! "Babies?"

"One day, not now."

"Yeah, one day," I repeat, the realization that this is him—my future husband and father of my children—hits me and I've never felt happier in my life. "But the great sex we get now, right?"

"Most definitely." He looks out the window briefly and turns back. "But this flight is short, so maybe we can work on that at the hotel."

Facing forward, I close my eyes and lean my head back. "Chicken," I provoke.

"Did you just dare me to have sex with you?"

I shrug, eyeing him up. "Maybe."

"You know that's not really how dares work?"

I like seeing him get all analytical on me, so I ask, "How do they work?"

"Usually, you dare someone to do something they wouldn't normally do, not something that they're happy to do. And I'm more than happy to have sex with you right now if that's what you want."

Teasing him, I say, "No, it's fine. We can wait till we get to the hotel." I start digging through my purse, pretending to be looking for something and a mental countdown begins. *Three... two... one.*

"Stand up, Holliday."

Bingo. "Why?"

"I'm taking that dare. Now stand up."

I slowly unfasten my seatbelt while setting my purse on the floor and stand up. "What now?"

Dalton stands and takes me by the hand as he walks to the

back of the plane. He spins me around quickly, my back hitting the wall, then he drops to his knees in front of me. He places his hands on the back of my calves and slides his fingers slowly up. The warmth and slow pace are already driving me insane. When I look down, he's looking up, watching me, watching my reaction as his hands move under my dress. When he reaches my ass, he squeezes then slides over my hips and under the front of my panties.

With a smirk on his face, he says, "I like you in lace."

My breaths deepen as his hands flatten, heating me. Taking the sides, he pulls them down and I step out. "I thought you were going to rip them."

"I was, but I could tell you expected it."

"So you're teasing me?"

Simple and direct. "Yes."

When he stands up, he kisses me, pressing his body against mine, reminding me how much I missed this closeness. No one makes me feel the way Dalton does. Roaming my hands over his shoulders and up his neck, I hold onto him, never wanting to be away from this man again. I kiss him hard and moan. Breathing rapidly, I say, "Unzip my dress."

"No, I want it on."

I kiss him again as I hear his zipper come down. With his hips pushed against mine, he looks me in the eyes, and says, "I don't have anything on me. I planned this, but forgot condoms, so we don't have to go further if you don't want to." Rubbing my cheek gently, he adds, "I haven't been with anyone else in the last eight months."

"Me either. I want you, all of you."

Fingertips alight every nerve in my body as he slides them down my arm and entwines his fingers with mine. "I want to be tied to you in every way possible."

As I stare into his eyes, I can see his truth staring back at me, and I say, "I want to feel everything with you."

He pushes up without hesitation and my eyelids drop closed, my mouth slacking open as we become one again, the sensations too good to contain silently. "Dalton," I sigh through jagged breaths as he moves within me.

Kisses to my neck soothe against the fast pace of our bodies. His groans of pleasure make me smile while my insides start to tighten and coil. "I missed you. You feel so good," I say.

Pushing my dress even higher, he lifts my other leg, using his strength and determination to hold me there. I flex up, coming back down to meet him thrust for thrust.

"Fuck, I missed you." Each of his words punctuated with a thrust that increases in intensity.

My head goes back, hitting the hard wall as he speeds up, becoming erratic. Fingers touch, my arousal being coaxed until I'm coming, his name escaping me repeatedly.

He follows quickly behind, his body slack as his energy is drained and he sets me down. "I love you, Angel," he says, his voice tired, his eyes searching mine while he leans his forehead against mine. "How are you?"

"Good. So good, but tired."

Turbulence causes us to sway and his hand grabs my arm to steady me. "We should get back to our seats." Stepping back from me, he lowers my dress then pulls my panties from his pocket, handing them to me. When I take the undies, he pulls his pants up. A few minutes later, we're back in our seats, buckled up, and ready to land. Leaning his head back, he turns to face me, and says, "I was thinking we could get married tomorrow night."

"Have you already booked everything for the ceremony?" It's

been a long day, a yawn escapes me.

"Maybe." A devious grin appears. "And no yawning. I have plans for us later."

"Care to expand on that?"

"No. I want to keep you guessing."

"So you're not gonna tell what you have in store for later?"

"My plans include you, only you, naked in bed, under me, on top of me. If I'm lucky, your mouth on me, and being inside of you for the next two days."

I stare at him, not sure what I should say other than, "Wow."

Touching my cheek, he says, "I've slept without you for over a month. I never want to sleep without you again. I want to spend every minute of forever with you."

"Wow."

He laughs. "Again with the wow?"

"I have a feeling I'm gonna be saying that a lot."

With a smile, he tilts his head and kisses me on the neck. "You deserve a lifetime of wows."

The plane lands and we're whisked by private car to the hotel. I try to straighten the wrinkles out of the lower half of my dress as we walk in the doors, but with this fabric, I'm stuck being a wrinkled mess. "I look like I just got fucked," I whisper.

"I know," he says, not whispering.

That's when it occurs to me, and I pop him on the arm. "That's why you wanted my dress to stay on, isn't it?"

He shrugs, not apologizing.

"Next time, why don't you just pee on me?"

Stopping in his tracks, he turns to me. He holds my face and with his thumbs he rubs from my nose to my temples. "Your makeup was smudged." I hold onto his wrists, and he says, "You're damn beautiful and you know I get jealous easily. Do I want everybody in this hotel to know that I just fucked you? Absolutely, doesn't bother me. Is it a trust issue? Not with you. I trust you explicably. It's all these other fuckers in here who already have their eyes on you. They're the ones I don't trust."

I love that he doesn't have a bunch of rehearsed lines. He just tells me how it is, not bothering to hide his flaws. I lift up on my tiptoes and kiss him... and he kisses me—in public for the first time. I take his hand and we start walking again because I no longer care how a wrinkled dress leads to implications and gossip. It doesn't matter. What matters is that I am here with Dalton. We don't need to hide our love... or lust.

When I walk into the penthouse at The Palatial, I smile. "So many good memories." I twirl. "I'm so glad you booked this room."

"We may have met downstairs, but this suite is where we began. Plus..." He looks smug. "... when I look around, I can name everywhere we've fucked. Good memories."

Although I love the changes I see in Dalton, I'm still glad that some of the rough around the edges rocker is still there. It's past midnight and I'm exhausted, so I start tugging at the zipper on my back, pulling it down while I walk toward the bedroom. I stop just inside the doorway and look back. His top few buttons are undone with his tie loose around his neck. His hair is messier, sexier, his shoulders relaxed. "You coming?" I ask, stepping out of my Maid of Honor dress.

"Come here, beautiful."

I go to him in only heels and lingerie. He takes my hand and leads me into the kitchen. Turning me around, my stomach is pressed against the counter and his hands are on my waist. His warm breath hits the back of my neck and he says, "I also remember everywhere we kissed and this was where I tasted your skin for the first time." His lips touch the top of my shoulder and he kisses me gently. I close my eyes, remembering the goosebumps I got in this very spot. When he drags my bra strap from my shoulder, I turn around and his arms trap me between them. With our noses touching, my heart races and just like I did months ago, I place my hand on his chest. He covers mine, and whispers, "I always felt it. I knew when you walked into that bar that there was no other ending for us. You took my breath away and there was no way I could let you leave without knowing you, even if I had to lie."

"I understand why you lied."

"But you love me for who I am, not for what I do. You loved me before you knew."

"I've always known the real you. That was the lie you could never tell. You gave me *you* that first night and now I'll give you all of me every night after. I love you that much."

"I didn't do this back in L.A. but I should have." He bends down, kissing a path down the center of my body, giving me goosebumps all over again, until he's on one knee before me.

My breath catches and my hand covers my mouth as I look down.

"I can't promise you a smooth road. I can't promise you we won't be tested or that your life wouldn't be easier if you had chosen someone without my baggage, because I know it would be. What I can promise you is that if we have faith and trust in each other, nothing else will matter, none of it. I know now that you came into my life when I needed you most," he says, then pauses, looking down briefly before his gaze reaches mine again. "You saved me from more than what you signed on for. You saved me from myself. This ring..." He holds the most beautiful ring I've ever seen in the palm of his hand, offering it to me. "...is a thank you, but it's also a vow I will live by and respect as much as I do you. Will you marry me?"

My hair and makeup is already done when we walk into the Clark County Marriage License Bureau. Dalton is holding my hand tight, both of us aware our secret is out the minute we walk in here. We take the forms and stand off to the side, huddling together to fill it out.

When we leave, we hop in the waiting car and head for the chapel. Once there, I go to the dressing room and slip on the short lacey dress I think he'll love. I attach the flowing tulle skirt that is open in the front and opt to leave my neck bare, no straps or necklaces.

When I hear a knock on the door, I look in the mirror one last time, suddenly realizing, this is it. This is the day I've dreamed about my entire life, and I'm marrying a man that those dreams never did justice to. I slip on my heels, dab a little gloss on and fluff my hair, leaving it down, how he likes it most.

Dalton is in the small chapel room, waiting for me. The marriage officiant clears his throat and Dalton looks up. Shifting, he pulls his hands from his pockets and comes to me. There's a smile on his face, his love shining through as he looks at me. Taking my hands, he leans in and kisses my cheek, then whispers, "You're beautiful."

I lean my head against his, loving the moment we're sharing. "You look so handsome." We walk back to the minister together and when he begins to speak, I take a peek at Dalton. He's the epitome of cool, even when it comes to wedding clothes—his dark grey pants and jacket fitted to accentuate his great body. The white shirt is classic and the black tie, thin but not too trendy.

The vows are traditional, sweet and to the point. Both of us have already shared our deepest thoughts privately. We don't drag it out. We just want to be married.

When Dalton doesn't kiss me right away, the minister smiles and asks what he is waiting for. Dalton replies, "I'm not waiting. I'm memorizing."

Our lips meet in a soft embrace. When we part, I open my eyes and look into my husband's for the first time. *Emerald*—the color of his happiness.

While snuggling in the back of the car, I say, "Last time I was in a Town Car with you, we steamed it up in the middle of traffic."

"Wanna steam up another?"

"Nope. I'm gonna make you wait."

"You never made me wait before," he says all cocky. "And now that you're my wife, I have to wait?"

"Yes. I know it makes no sense. But we haven't done anything traditional in our relationship... maybe we can at least wait to get to the room so I can say I waited until our wedding night."

He laughs. "You mean lie? Cuz, I remember quite vividly having sex with you many times before our wedding night."

"Yes." I hit his leg. "Anyway, it's not a total lie because I'm definitely going to make you wait until we get back to the room now."

Still chuckling, he nods. "If that is what it takes to make you feel more appropriate, you got it."

I slide across the slick seat and smile when I lean my head on his shoulder. "Thank you."

Why am I nervous? We've had sex a million times—in every way and position possible, but this time, I'm nervous. With a full stomach from the dinner he had waiting for us, I take a deep breath and leave. I walk out of the bathroom, not wanting to over think this nerves thing, and I see Dalton half-dressed... or technically undressed. His back is to me as he stands with his arms crossed, staring out the large window that overlooks The Strip.

"Hi," I whisper, leaning against the doorway, feeling better just seeing him.

He turns and my eyes travel down, noticing his pants hanging open. His tattoos show and I can't lie, I missed them. "C'mere," he says, leaning back against the large ledge of the window. When I walk, my skirt flows behind me and this time, his eyes travel down to my exposed legs. "I like the dress."

"Thanks," I reply, wrapping my arms around his neck as his hands slide up and down the outside of my thighs.

"I like it, but I want it off. Do you want to keep it?"

My eyes go wide, and I laugh. "You want to rip my dress off me?"

His right hand slips between my thighs and moves up slowly until he discovers his wedding gift. "No panties?"

What else do you get the man who has everything. "I figured what's the point if they were going to be destroyed anyway." Brushing one of my fingertips across his eyebrows, I say, "I didn't count on the dress being its replacement."

His fingers find the spot that makes me fall apart and he

begins rubbing softly. "I haven't kissed you enough today. That needs to be remedied," he says, pulling me closer by the back of the neck.

Tightening my grip on his shoulders, I kiss him. My tongue tingles when it touches his and I can taste the cinnamon gum he was chewing. He pulls back, his hand leaving me as he slides my skirt up. I'm exposed to him—baring my soul as much as my body. He kisses the apex of my thighs then his tongue tastes me, ending with a kiss. Standing abruptly, he spins us around until I'm the one with my back against the window sill. He lifts me by my waist until I'm perched on the ledge. The lower half of my body is left exposed as the skirt flares out around me.

With his hands, he gently pulls my knees apart, licks his bottom lip then bites it. "You look so fucking sexy like that."

Grabbing him by the loose ends of his belt, I pull him closer until his legs are between mine. Crossing my ankles behind his knees, I trap him. The warmth of his palms roll over my shoulders as one works its way up the back of my neck and into my hair. He pulls my hair together, holding it in his hand then pulls down, causing me to look up. My hazels meet his greens and the desire he has for me shines from within. "Don't ever doubt how much I want you. I always want you so much. Too much." Before I have a chance to respond his mouth crashes into mine and he kisses me hard and deep, frenzied and passionate. He takes and takes, pressing himself against me.

I pull back, resting my head against the cool of the glass, trying to catch my breath. Standing over me, he leans forward, his hands going flat above my head and looking down, trying to calm himself. He's failing. His chest pumps in and out, his fingers tap on the glass, the sound of impatience or lust.

The cold marble under me penetrates the tulle of my skirt,

making me shiver, so I lift up as he stares out over the bright lights of the city. I touch my tongue to his chest and follow the curve of the tiger tattoo. His skin is smooth just bordering on the outside of his light chest hair. Reaching up, I take hold of his shoulders and drag him down. Arms swoop under me, his hands chilled from the glass as he lifts me. Our mouths are bonded until he tosses me on the bed. "I want that dress off. Now."

I sink into the down comforter and watch as he drops his pants to the floor, his prominent erection thick and hard. I detach the belt that holds the skirt on and roll to my stomach. "Unzip me."

Starting at my feet, he wraps his large hands around my ankles. "I like these shoes. Keep them on." I peek over my shoulder and see him moving onto the bed. On his knees, straddling my body, his hands slide over my calves to the back of my thighs. A kiss to each leg leads his warmth to my backside as he pushes the short dress up and over my ass. His breaths deepen. "I want to be inside you."

"Unzip me, Dalton."

The tips of his fingers drag along my back as the zipper comes down with ease. I slink underneath him and sit up on my knees. When I get to my feet, my dress falls to the floor. Wearing nothing but an expensive pair of high heels, I feel provocative, empowered. "You ready for me, my hot husband?"

I'm yanked, landing on my back in the middle of the mattress. Leaning over me, he says, "The question is..." He pulls my arms above my head, and spreads my legs with his, positioning himself over me. "Are you ready for me, gorgeous wife?"

"Always."

His body becomes one with mine, stirring a groan from deep

within his chest while my breath is whisked away. With each thrust, I'm pushed higher as he grips my wrists tighter. In an instant, he releases me and lowers, his mouth finding my breast and covering it, peaking it. He bites and I gasp from the pain, his tongue swirling around to ease the effect. Touching his head, I pull him up to face me, eye-level. His thrusts are still intense despite my efforts to slow him down. "Make love to me, Dalton."

All movement ceases as he hovers above me, his hands on either side of my head. "Make love," he repeats as he lowers, resting his weight down on his elbows. His hands grace my face, and he kisses me. Tongues move then he licks the corner of my mouth, leaving me wanting more, even though I was the one who wanted to slow down. His body is hard, his muscles working above me while making love to me. With his lips against my cheek, he whispers, "Every time we're together we create love."

His words are lyrics he sings to my soul.

"What are you smiling about?" he asks, his own playful smile coming out as he stills.

"This. Life. We're married. Everything."

"It's pretty great, huh?"

"More than great. Amazing."

With a tilt of his head, he starts moving again while watching our connection, taking his time until we're both satisfied.

Except for an excursion to the tattoo parlor, we spend the next day watching movies in bed. It's a perfect day.

As the sun sets on our last night here, I walk to the bedroom window, the drapes wide open. A golden light fills the room, I slowly undress, slipping my lingerie off. He watches me. It makes me feel sexy. *He* makes me feel loved.

"Come over here," he says, his arm behind his head as he lays shirtless on the bed. Moving to the end of the mattress, I kneel between his legs, leaning forward. With my tongue, I leave a trail, tasting him, enjoying what I see. I pull his boxer briefs down, just a little, enough to tease and kiss him once, twice, and again from his hip to his tip, then cover him back up.

His hand grabs my wrist as I start to slide down, stopping me. When I look up, he says, "I want you."

"You want me... how?" I ask, keeping my tone seductive like his. I want to hear him say it. I want him at my mercy.

"I want your mouth on me."

"You, Sir, are a very dirty boy. You know that?"

"I assure you I'm no boy. Why don't you take those boxers all the way off this time and let me prove it to you."

Our eyes hold the stare, and then I smile. "With pleasure."

He proves it twice before we both need a nap.

When I open my eyes, it's dark. I'm on my side facing the window. I roll over to find Dalton, but he's not in bed. I sit up and look around the room. Music comes from the living room. Tiptoeing to the door, I find Dalton on the couch holding his guitar. He has a pencil in his mouth as he stares at the paper in front of him and strums lightly. I watch him for a minute without him knowing, loving the sight of him writing music, playing, healing. His eyes go wide and he takes the pencil from his mouth then jots something down on the paper in front of him. He looks satisfied... happy. It's good to see.

"Hi," he says, looking my way. "Good nap?"

I nod, giving him a smile. "What are you doing?"

Looking down briefly, he appears shy, something I'm not

used to seeing on him. "I was lying in bed, next to you, watching you," he says. "You used to be more restless when you slept... anyway, a melody came to me, so I got up and started writing. I'm trying to get it down before it disappears."

"I love that." I look at the time. Almost eight-thirty. "We slept a long time, or at least I did."

"You hungry?"

"I want you to write."

"I'm almost done," he says, thoughtful. "We can go out or order in. Your choice."

"I'm thinking in. I'm gonna take a bath."

He stands just before I turn, and says, "Thank you, Holliday."

Leaning against the doorframe, I tilt my head, and ask, "For what?"

"For saying yes."

"Thanks for asking."

"For being my inspiration."

"I always wanted to be someone's muse," I say lightheartedly.

"You've always been in here," he says, patting his chest over his heart. "We just hadn't met yet."

Dalton sits down, getting back to his songwriting, not realizing how much he's touched my soul. I savor his words and go take a bath.

In the middle of the night I find Dalton asleep on the couch, a beam of moonlight slipping in and residing across his body. For a moment in time, I forget about demons and darkness. Seeing him like this, with his guitar laying across his chest, all I see is goodness—an angel in his own right. Even if he never sees himself that way, I do.

His hand hangs over the edge, the pencil on the floor beneath it. Walking over, I kneel down. Pressing my lips to his forehead, I grab the guitar by the neck then whisper, "Dalton, come to bed."

His eyes open and focus on mine, a small smile sliding across his face. Covering my hand on the guitar, he whispers, "You're so beautiful." The sincerity in his eyes is clear, a sparkle in the depths. His hand wanders up my back, gentle pressure coaxing me forth, his mouth beckoning me without words.

We kiss. We kiss and like the thousands of kisses we've shared before, there's an unbridled passion that stirs within. He's more than I expected, more than I dreamed possible, and I adore him—body, heart, and soul. Jack Dalton owns me, cherishing while devouring me equally.

I move the guitar to coffee table, and turn back, resuming our kiss as I move on top of him. Both of us squeezed onto the couch together. His hand slips under my chemise and he grabs my breast. "Best tits ever."

His dirty words turn me on and I run my hand over his hardness. His voice is raspy with sleep when he says, "I want you on top of me. I want you to fuck me, Angel."

We both stop and undress, not wanting to lose a second that we can be together. His eyes lock on mine as I lift up. He aligns himself before I slide down, my breath catching.

With my hands pressed to his chest, I close my eyes, sinking emotionally as much as physically into all that is Dalton. I begin to rock, each sensation sparking another. Faster. Faster, needing more, feeling everything. His hands are on my breasts, my hips, and pressing against my tattoo, the new script still tender under the bandage. "Choose the dare," he says from memory. "Dare to dream." His words become moans.

When his eyes close, his body grips me harder and he starts his own rhythm and slam, driving my orgasm out with his name bursting from my mouth. Sitting up, he covers my mouth and my moans, swallowing my passion until he releases.

His head drops to my shoulder and a shiver courses through his body. Warmth from his arms keeps me steady and upright. "I love you," I say.

Dalton looks up, and touches my face, "I love you."

Our bodies exhausted, our minds at ease, our hearts full of love, we fall asleep on the couch together. He stirs next to me as the sun rises. When I wiggle next to him, he says, "Let's get in bed." He takes my hand, helping me up and we climb under the covers. I snuggle into his side with my ear pressed to his chest. His breaths are even, a steady and comforting tempo that I fall asleep to.

In the morning, just as we wake, he whispers, "I want to take you somewhere."

"Okay, where do you want to take me?"

Taking my left hand, he brings it to his mouth and kisses it. "Nothing can top this, but one day I'm gonna take you to Texas."

Suddenly feeling wide awake, I lift up on my elbow and look at him, surprised. "You want to take me home?"

"No, my home is with you," he says, with a small smile. "I need to settle things with my dad. I don't want it weighing down our future. Will you go with me?"

I kiss his forehead, then run my finger down his handsome face, stopping on his bottom lip. "If you're ready to go back, then I'm ready to go with you."

36

Jack Dalton

"It was never about becoming rich. It was about doing something I love."
~Holliday Hughes

When the plane touches down in Austin, I lean over and say, "Stay close to me." I don't want to scare her, but LAX sucked this morning and when I fly commercial, I get a lot of unwanted attention. I don't want Holliday hurt in the chaos that surrounds me.

She's done well with all the media craziness over the last few months. Our elopement is old news now. The press has put their focus on Holliday and what they call a 'bump watch.' She's been doing a lot of fucking yoga lately and can almost do as many sit-ups as me. She doesn't need it. Her body is hot as fuck already, but I think it makes her feel like she has some control over the situation.

Recently, cheating stories have popped up online claiming the honeymoon is over and I'm moving on with this actress or that model. It's all bullshit. We know the truth and don't have anything to prove.

I take her hand just as security greets us as we walk off the plane. We're escorted down the escalator to baggage claim. While waiting, I'm asked for autographs and photos. Even though the band is gone, it's still easy for me to step into the Johnny Outlaw persona. It's a part of who I am, not Holliday's favorite part, but she understands and sees through the act.

To draw the crowd, I separate from her. I continue giving the fans what they want, who they want—Johnny Outlaw— sunglasses, bad attitude, and impatience works well in these types of situations. As soon as our suitcases are retrieved, I get us the hell out of here.

My job as a celebrity is over. I need to protect my wife. Without making a big deal of it, I nod toward the door and our team is on the move. I direct security to cover her first, me second, and keep my eyes on her as much as I can, mindful of her whereabouts as I position myself a step ahead of Holliday with security taking the tail. She doesn't notice she's being sandwiched for safety. I'd be happy if she never had to deal with this, never had to have a second thought about her safety or mine, but with my fame and her growing fame, we have to be aware at all times.

I hear my name being called, then some guy yells, "Outlaw," which gets my attention. He's wearing a T-shirt with our band on it. It's from our last tour when Cory was still alive. The reminder makes me want to escape the scrutiny I feel I'm under to keep producing. The break I've had has been good.

Holliday gets in the car and I quickly follow. The door is shut. The trunk is closed, and we're off. The phrase 'The silence is deafening' is felt within the vehicle. These situations can go wrong fast, but there's also a rush that comes from fans wanting a piece of you. I know it's Johnny Outlaw they want, but it still takes time to come down from the high. Since I've been out of the spotlight, it's gotten easier to separate my job from my real life. It also helps that Holliday gets me. She always did, and gives me the space I need when necessary, but is also there when I fall. She slides her hand across the leather seat, and asks, "You okay?"

Back at LAX, she was called a gold-digging whore twice and accused of using me to further her business. Yet, here she is worried about me. I take her hand, and ask, "Are *you* okay?"

Shrugging, she says, "It is what it is."

"Don't listen to them."

"It's kind of hard not to when they're yelling at me."

I angle my body toward her, and say, "Don't ever believe what they say. Believe me."

Squeezing my hand, she smiles. "That's easy to do."

I lean over and kiss her before sitting back and staring out the window the rest of the ride. My parents aren't expecting me. I thought it was best this way, but now I'm having doubts. This could backfire and it will be humiliating if it does in front of Holliday.

We check into the hotel and go up to the room. As soon as the door closes, she drops her purse on the bed and walks to the window, checking out the view. With her arms crossed, she asks, "Does it get easier?"

The drapes frame her body, her curves highlighted from the outside light. Walking up behind her, I touch her shoulders.

"What do you want me to say?"

"I want the truth."

"No, it doesn't get easier, but you do get more used to it, if that makes sense."

Her voice is soft, too quiet. I hear the sad realization in her tone. "When you have a good day, the paparazzi turn them bad." Turning around in my arms, she says, "But your fans make it good, right?"

With a small nod, I say, "Yeah, they make it great. They get my art. They understand what I'm trying to do."

"So maybe one day, people will accept me as your wife."

I touch her face, hearing the question deep down that she's asking. "Don't do that. You're my wife because I love you. That will never change. Block the static and focus on the truth."

She leans her head against my chest and nods as I hold her. "Block the static," she repeats.

As we drive into town, I notice that Elgin has changed a lot since I left ten years ago. What used to be a small Texas town, stereotypical with its open fields, cowboy hats, and pickup trucks, is no more. Now it's full of strip malls, coffeehouses, and a few more liquor stores. I pull up and park in front of one of them, cutting the engine. Looking at Holliday, I say, "No one shows up at my dad's house without a twelve pack of Lone Star. Want anything?"

"I'm good. I'll wait here."

I walk in and straight back to the beer cooler. Out of the corner of my eye, I see Old Joe running the counter just like he did when I was in high school. He watches me as I walk and I'm pretty sure he recognizes me. I grab the beer and head back up. Just as I pass the sodas, one catches my eye and I go back to grab it for Holliday. I remember her saying one time that it was her favorite. "Joe," I say, setting the drinks down on the counter.

"Jack Dalton, Jr. Long time."

"Yeah. You doing okay?"

"Yep," he says, typing on the cash register. "Holding down the fort like always. How bout you?"

Setting two twenties down on the counter, I reply, "Going good. Keep the change." He hands me a receipt and bags the soda. "Thanks, Joe. Have a good one."

Right as I reach the door, he says, "We're proud of you, Son. You've done well for yourself."

"Thanks." I get in the SUV and set the beer in the back. Handing the bag to Holliday, I say, "For you."

She looks inside and smiles, her eyes showing her happiness. "You got me Big Red. I just might have fallen even more in love with you if that's possible."

With a wink and smile that I know drives her wild, I say, "I know how to woo the ladies alright."

When I pull off the single lane road onto the dirt road that leads to my house, I spot the old barn up ahead. *His domain and escape.* My fingers flex around the steering wheel as the demons get louder in my head—failure, disappointment, weak, sissy, and the worst he ever said to me—ashamed you're my son.

"Dalton?"

Just as the chorus to an Ozzy song kicks in, I jump, startled by Holliday's hand on my arm. "What?" I reach over and turn off the music.

"What's going on?"

"What?" I'm short with her, but I don't mean to be.

"Suddenly you turned the music up so loud that the windows were vibrating."

I put the car in park and look down at the stereo. "I didn't realize. Sorry."

"It's okay," she says. "I was just worried. Guess we're here."

Looking over my left shoulder, I see the garage nearby and the house beyond. There's the field where I played baseball and helped with the crops, and the barn where I wasn't allowed to go once I got injured. I turn to Holliday. "Let me lead okay?"

"Okay."

I get out and go around, helping her down. Hearing a screen door slam shut, we both turn to find my mom squinting her eyes in our direction.

"Is that your mom?" she asks.

Not able to stop the smile, I say, "That's her. C'mon."

My mom hurries down the front porch steps with her own big grin. "Jack Dalton, give your mama a hug."

It doesn't matter how long you've been gone, how much money you've made, or even how famous you are, when you come back to the place you grew up, you feel like the kid you once were. My mom doesn't treat me like a rock star or millionaire. When I reach her, she hugs me so tight that the air constricts in my lungs. I hug her back just as tight, realizing how much I've missed her. "You're too skinny," she says. "You can't survive off sprouts and sunshine out in California. A boy needs hearty food to grow."

"I don't think I'm growing anymore, but I won't turn down your home cooking."

She eyes Holliday and with a gracious smile, says, "You must be my son's wife."

Taking her hand, I pull her close and introduce her properly. "Mom, this is Holli."

My mom's arms go wide as she welcomes her into the family. "The wedding was all over the news for months and I've seen stuff online about you, but it's nice to finally meet you in person."

Holliday hugs her, and says, "Thank you. It's so nice to meet you too, Mrs. Dalton."

"Call me Judy. All my friends do." She smiles, wrapping her arm around Holliday's shoulders. "Let's go inside and get some iced tea. JD, your dad is out back working in the barn."

I glance at Holliday and she smiles at the nickname. "I'll introduce Holliday to him and then we'll come inside. Give us a few minutes."

She walks ahead with a nod. "I'll get the tea ready and then you can fill me in on the wedding I wasn't invited to and what brought on this surprise visit."

We hold hands and walk in silence to the barn out back. A country song is coming from inside. I assume it's Hank or George, his favorites. Country music wasn't my thing. I can feel my palms sweating, my anxiety getting the best of me. I just hope Holliday doesn't notice. When we stop in front of the open doors, a man— an older version of the dad I once knew, an older version of me, sits on a barstool at his workbench.

He briefly glances up, then back in thought before he sets down his pliers, and asks, "What brings you here?"

I can't help being disappointed, though this is the reunion I expected.

"Thought it was time for a visit."

Tinkering with the pliers again, he says, "Your mom's inside."

"I came to visit both of you. I got beer out in the truck."

Dad looks at us out of the corner of his eyes. "You shouldn't let good beer go to waste in the heat. I take it this is the wife, Junior?"

Fucking Junior. I haven't heard that in years. "Yes, this is Holli."

Holliday steps forward and puts out her hand. "It's a pleasure to meet you, Sir."

"Good to meet ya," he says, shaking her hand. "The son of a bitch always could get the lookers." He starts walking toward the SUV, stepping around me. "You better have brought the good stuff, Son."

Signaling for her to come with us, I say to my father, "I brought your favorite."

An hour later, my dad is the asshole he's always been. Plain and simple. I'm now old enough to know he's not changing for me or anyone else.

"Saw Patty O'Toole the other day," he says, eyeing me, ignoring Holliday. "She's got three kids now." His head lulls, the alcohol starting to sink in. "Why'd you two break up again?" His eyes meet mine, then his gaze lands on Holliday. "Patty was a looker too... and Homecoming Queen."

My mom smiles, trying to lessen the tension building on the back porch where we're sitting, by saying, "Not as pretty as you, Holli. You and JD make a beautiful couple."

"Well, I'm no Homecoming Queen," she replies, "but I get by."

"You more than get by," I snap, pissed he has the nerve to say that to her. "Ignore him."

"Ignore me?" he laughs.

Glaring, I remind him, "Isn't it Patty Brouchard now?"

"Oh Holli," my mother interrupts. I'm thinking on purpose. "My son was so handsome standing center field in his tuxedo with that crown on his head. I should show you the pictures. And I still want you to tell me about the wedding." She glances over at me and I can see the hurt in her eyes.

Holliday smiles. "I'd love that." Nudging me, she says, "I didn't know you were Homecoming King?"

Bumping my shoe against hers, I say, "I can't seem to shake the title, no matter how hard I try. The press loves shit like that."

"JD," Mom admonishes.

"Sorry." I laugh, enjoying that some things never change.

Mom starts for the door, and says, "Come inside, Holli. Let's give the boys some time to talk. I'll show you some embarrassing photos of my son."

I can already tell Holliday's going to be using this against me later when we're alone. But I love that she's smiling too much to argue. She says, "I can't wait to see those." As soon as the door closes, I turn and face out over the porch railing, putting my back to my dad. I feel the confrontation between us brewing.

And then it bubbles over. Sitting in his rocking chair, he says, "You could have had a good life here. Patty has a good life. She's settled. Her husband is the high school baseball coach. Her oldest plays little leag—"

"And?" I turn to face him. "What the fuck does it matter what Patty or Ricky are doing?"

"That could've been you," he says, pointing a finger. "You had so much potential. You could have pushed through the pain. You chose to wuss out, to cry on your mother's apron like that would make it better. Locking yourself in that room all day, listening to that damn rock music."

"You should have come to the doctor's appointment. You know," I say, standing upright. "The one you chose to not show up

349

for. I was never gonna play again, not like I did. Not college ball or pro ball."

"See? You admit it. You could have played. You could have worked hard to get back to the shape you were in."

When I was a kid, he was my hero. Today, he stands before me a bitter shell of the man I once admired, but I'm too pissed to feel sorry for him. "You just don't get it," I say, shaking my head. "Do you not realize who I am?"

"I realize who you aren't."

He always did know how to hit where it hurts most. I don't even know why I care anymore, so I stop trying to please him, and fight back. "I'm a fucking rock star." Raising my voice, I say, "I have millions of fans and more money than I can spend in two lifetimes. I own three homes and have the most beautiful fucking wife in the world. If I want, I never have to work another day in my life—"

"That might be wise since the news said your friend had all the talent."

My arm flies back, ready to deck him. But he stands to his full height and warns, "If you throw that punch, you better knock me out, Son. Cuz if you don't, you're not gonna wake up in the hospital the same man."

"Dalton?" Holliday calls from the doorway. She comes closer, the creak of the door drawing my gaze to her. She touches my arm, and whispers, "You don't need to do this. You don't have anything to prove."

"And what does a woman from Cal-I-forn-I-A know? You probably spend your days spending his money. He could be here, where he belongs, raising a family with a good girl, going to a respectable job five days a week. Instead, he's out there raising hell and doing drugs. Look where that got the other guy. It got him buried six feet under before the age of thirty."

My heart thumps heavy in my chest, my head filling with the bad or what Holliday calls the demons, I fight. I've been good over the last few months. I can't let him drag me back under—the undertow is too hard to fight a second time. She stands in front of me, her hands on my chest. "Don't listen to him. He's trying to provoke you. Don't let him win."

"Listen to her new age crap," he says. "And run back to Pretend Land. The rest of us will be here."

"What is your problem?" Holliday asks. "Why are you doing this?"

"A real woman knows her place," he says, turning on Holliday.

"Don't, Dad. I'm warning you."

"You're warning me?" He laughs. "You're a fool. You had everything here and you let it slip away. That family of Patty's could've been yours. The coaching job, this place when I die, but no, you left, proving me right about you all along. You're weak."

"I left so I wouldn't end up like you." I feel the pressure of Holliday's hands holding me back when I say, "So if you think that makes me weak, so be it. But what you think of me doesn't matter anymore. All that matters is what this woman thinks. She not only loves me for who I am, but believes in me, something you never really did."

"You lost your roots along the way to La La Land, Junior," he says, snidely.

"You act like you're mad because I left, but you're the one who drove me to the county line and dropped me off at the bus stop. So I didn't lose my roots, I had them ripped out from under me because I ruined your dreams of playing pro ball."

"You were great. The greatest. You had a billboard in the

center of town your senior year. You could have been someone, a real player. Instead, you decided to sulk in your room and listen to that noisy music. Your mind was made up and your bag was already packed. I just saved you the trouble of walking the eight miles."

Looking down into Holliday's eyes, her eyebrows together in worry, I say, "This was a mistake. We shouldn't have come."

"No, honey," my mom says, letting the door slam behind her. "I'm glad you did. I've missed you terribly." She hugs me. "I had no idea you were planning on leaving for good and even less of an idea that your dad drove you."

"He drove me away is what you mean—literally and figuratively," I say, my bitterness coming back. My mom has tears in her eyes, so I hug her even tighter, thinking it might be the last time I ever do. "I never meant to hurt you."

"I never meant for you to leave," she says, "I love you."

"Love you too, Mom." I turn, and leave, rushing to the field I used to play ball in, the one I once loved. My dad used his best crop field to make that baseball field, to learn, to make him proud of me one day. Like the field, I've outgrown it, him, this life. I run through the tall grass to a log I dragged out here after the injury. It's where home plate once was, it's where I came to think, where I was when I decided I needed to leave, and where I sit now, knowing I'll never return.

Lying down, I stare up at the blue sky, a few clouds drifting by in the unseasonal breeze. I close my eyes and try to remember all the good I had here. A shadow darkens my eyelids. When I open my eyes, Holliday is standing over me, blocking the sun, a halo around her. *My angel.*

"Why'd I come back?" I ask, sitting up, so she can sit down.

She sits close to me, leaning forward and pulling tall blades of grass in thought. Then she says, "We're told that dealing with our past will free our futures. But I call bullshit. It's never as easy as it's sold to us."

Staring out into the distance, I say, "It doesn't matter what I accomplish. He'll only see my failures."

"His perspective is screwed up. You getting injured and not being able to play baseball is not a failure, Dalton."

"What is it then?"

Taking a moment to think about it, she looks me in the eyes, then says, "Destiny. You were never meant to be a professional baseball player or you would be."

I smile because she has enough faith for the both of us. "Does that make you a part of my destiny?"

"I believe we were meant to be. Even when we were apart, my heart hung onto you."

Wrapping my arm around her, I kiss her head, and say, "You didn't have to become a firefighter to become a hero."

She looks surprised. I bump her knee with mine, and add, "You've done more for me than a trip back home could ever do. I don't need Texas. I have you." I stand up and look around, surveying the land one last time. "It's time to go."

The tips of the wild grass graze my fingertips as we make our way back to the truck. The screen door opens and two figures appear on the front porch as we approach. "Stay for dinner. I'll make your favorite," my mother offers.

"Can't, Mom, but thanks."

She comes down the stairs. "Stay. Don't leave like this."

I hug her like I should have the last time I left, hugging her tight enough for her to know I'll miss her when I'm gone. "I'm sorry about the wedding. It was spontaneous. No one was invited. It was just the two of us."

"I can tell she really loves you." She brushes my hair back and smiles. "I'm proud of you."

My dad lingers on the front porch—him and his stubborn pride will rot together. "If you go now, don't bother coming back again," he yells.

"Dalton, you can't leave like this," Holliday starts to say, but my dad cuts her off and says, "He needs to do what he needs to do. We haven't been a consideration in his life for years now."

"Honey," Mom says, "Please don't leave."

"What he said," Holliday starts. "It's not about consideration, it's about love. Your son has a hole in his heart that taints his success. He's worked hard to get to where he is. So he didn't play baseball. So what? Most baseball players want to be rock stars. Your son is talented and is loved by millions. Yet, all he wants is his parents' approval."

"He expects it," my dad says, standing his ground a few feet away. "It should be earned like respect."

"Holliday, it's okay," I say.

But she's pissed, and I love her for it. She says, "Love is given. It doesn't come with a list of qualifications. You should try to let go of the dreams you had for him and let him live his. I know you'd be proud. And, if you ever want to get to know your son for the man he's become, call me." She turns and gets inside the car.

I hug my mom one more time, then get in the vehicle. "I love you, Mom."

"I love you, too. Ignore your father and don't let it be so long next time. I've missed you."

"Okay." I get inside the SUV and ask Holliday, "You ready?"

A nod suffices.

A few hours later, we've checked out of the hotel a day early and are pulling up to the airport. "Don't forget your Big Red. I know how much you love the stuff."

Security is curbside waiting for us. We're rushed through the doors and past the long row of check-in desks and through another door. In a private security room, we're scanned from head to toe. They check our carry-ons and ask about the brown bag. "Damn," Holliday replies, "I didn't even get a sip."

"Drink some now."

She chucks the bottle into the trash can. "You know what? I don't need reminders of the past. I've got a future to look forward to with you."

After we settle in on the plane, she takes my hand and brings it to her lap, and asks, "Are you sure you're okay with how everything was left? I know it didn't turn out how you hoped."

"I'm fine. I've got everything I need right here."

37

Holliday Hughes

*"Someone special once told me to dare
to dream. For without dreams, we
have nothing to look forward to. I'm
starting to believe her."*
~Johnny Outlaw

Dalton aptly named the ranch he bought for us, Peaceful Resistance. The name just as contradictory as the man. The air is cleaner, the real world far away... or at least over an hour away. I love it out here. It's earthy and the grounds are beautiful. But there are plenty of luxuries as well, like the huge infinity tub I'm currently soaking in.

"Are you gonna be in there much longer?" he asks, leaning

against the arched doorway that leads to the bedroom.

With my back to him, I lift my leg up, and tempt. "You sure you don't want to join me? There's plenty of room in here."

"You know we have people arriving soon, right?"

I hear him move closer, taking the bait. "I do, but they know us," I say, shrugging.

His footsteps are heavy against the wood floor as he comes closer. Grabbing the stool, he moves it front and center to the bathtub, eyeing my body through the sudsy water. I've been in here long enough for most of the bubbles to disappear, leaving me exposed.

He licks his lips and releases an exasperated sigh. "What am I going to do with you?"

Leaning my head back, I rest it on the edge, close my eyes and smile. "Just love me."

"Done." He dips his hand beneath the water's surface and drags a finger down my body until he's between my legs.

Soft circles gain momentum and the pressure increases. My smile falls away as pleasure takes over. Water splashes over the edge as he maneuvers closer, covering my mouth with his. Our tongues meet and a mutual moan harmonizes between us.

Deft fingers slip inside as one remains on the spot he knows will send me under... underwater, under bliss, the undertow as he once labeled emotions that overwhelm. He lifts up, his hand still skillful in the action, bringing me closer, coaxing me to the edge. I open my eyes, a heaviness surrounding my lids, so I close them again and feel, listen, then sink.

His persistence pays off and I embrace the ecstasy. After kissing me on the shoulder, he leaves, leaving me to piece myself together as I come to. I use the time, relaxing in the bath, then get out and get dressed.

Joining him in the kitchen, I rest my head on his arm as he pours me a glass of wine. "You spoil me," I say lazily.

"I give you what you deserve. *You* spoil me."

"I do, but I like to," I reply with a gentle laugh.

His arm stretches around my waist, and he says, "I think I'm ready to play live again."

Surprised, I move between him and the kitchen island. With my hands on his chest, I ask, "What?"

"Nothing big. I was thinking a small club or something to get my feet wet."

"Solo?"

"I don't know. Is there a band without Cory?" Looking down, he seems to disappear into his own thoughts momentarily. When he looks back up, he says, "I need to figure out who I am on stage without him before I can go back. I'm thinking maybe a few solo shows. But even with all the shit with Dex, I still think I want to play together again one day."

"As Johnny Outlaw?"

That makes him smile. "I dunno," he replies with a shrug, looking amused. "Maybe as Jack Dalton. I'm not sure what I want yet."

"I'm proud of you," I say, smiling.

"For what?"

"For not giving up on something you love so much."

"If I did that, you wouldn't be here."

"You say the sweetest things," I say, resting my cheek on his chest.

The sound of cars pulling up to the front of the house, the tires crunching against the gravel driveway draws his focus over my head. "They're here. You ready?"

"I'm ready."

Two hours later, everyone is sitting around the large fire pit. Neil is running around the lawn chasing bubbles while Rochelle holds baby CJ, who has fallen asleep from the excitement of the visit. Tommy has his feet kicked up on a tree stump that's currently serving as his ottoman, and telling Adam about this 'one time' in Amsterdam. Dalton is listening, content sitting on the sidelines when Tracy and I walk out with another bottle of wine and two beers—one for Adam and one for Tommy. As I refill Rochelle's glass, she looks up at me and smiles. "We need to get together for lunch soon, no kids. Or better yet, a girl's night out."

"Yes, we do." I sit down next to her, once again admiring the engagement ring on her finger, always reminded of the first time I saw it in Paris when Cory showed it to me. I don't say anything, but a lump forms in my throat.

Her hand covers mine, giving it a squeeze. "It's alright."

When I look into her eyes, I see a peace has settled there, similar to the one she used to carry with her, but not quite the same. The carefree days before Cory's death have disappeared altogether, but I'll take the peace that today offers. I nod and we don't talk about it, moving back into the greater conversation of the group.

"Dex gets out of rehab next week," Tommy says. "I told him we're gonna be talking about things when I pick him up."

"What'd he say to that?" Dalton asks, picking at the label on his bottle.

"He said he'll do whatever he has to do to get the band going again."

Dalton's eyes flash to Rochelle, but she remains looking down at the baby. He stands up and downs the beer, then tosses it into a bucket nearby. Walking into the grass a few feet away, he leans against an old Oak tree and stares out toward the sunset.

We've had the band conversation many times over the last six months. Dalton feels The Resistance died when Cory did, but he also feels a responsibility to Dex. He's torn.

"Johnny?"

All of us, including Dalton, turn to Rochelle when she calls his name, not expecting to hear her, not expecting her to call him Johnny. None of them do anymore. It's been Jack for months now.

She stands and walks with the baby to the stroller under the pergola, then sets him down to sleep. When she rejoins us at the fire, she takes her wine in hand, and says, "The Resistance is one of the greatest bands that has ever lived. You have three gun tattoos to prove it. Cory may never get another, but you still can." Raising her glass, we follow suit as she looks Dalton straight in the eyes—a look of determination on her face that captures all of our attention. "Cory may be gone, but Johnny Outlaw lives on."

A year later, the lights go down and the chanting begins. Eighteen-thousand people are crowded into this arena in the City of Lost Angels to watch the return of a living legend, one that could have disappeared, but chose to rise again.

A spotlight hits Dex, drumming, as he kicks off the beats of the first song. I know it well, Dalton playing it over and over again when he wrote it for the new album. The audience goes wild, and the chanting begins, "Outlaw! Outlaw! Outlaw!"

As the energy from the room starts to spread throughout my body, I look around until I see two people that seem entirely out of place—his parents. They wave and I wave back. They want to surprise him. They've done a good job of surprising us all by showing up this afternoon to support Dalton to see their son do what he does best—entertain.

Two guitarists walk out—one a bassist, Cory's replacement on stage. The other needed to round out the sound for the new direction of the band. Rochelle filled in on the studio recordings for the CD. Dalton thought it was only right since she taught Cory how to play and knew every song. She opted not to join the band on tour, choosing to stay with her kids instead.

Although I've seen a few rehearsals, as soon as the band stops playing and the lights go down, my heart starts thumping heavily. Like everyone else who came to see The Resistance reunite, my excitement builds.

I know it's coming, but when a single spotlight hits the Rock God standing center stage—the music kicks in and I know he's right where he was always meant to be. *His destiny.*

Throwing my hands into the air, I scream in exhilaration, knowing the world may own Johnny Outlaw, but Jack Dalton is all mine.

The End

A Personal Note

"Time stood still for just a little while.
Then I crashed into it head first."
~Johnny Outlaw

Very much like the quote above, this project blossomed from a seed to a full grown tree before my very eyes. I dedicated my days and nights to writing and editing. My world stopped for half a year as I engrossed myself into Holliday and Dalton's world. I got to know these characters through rhythm and words, their emotions, and through time. It wasn't fast, but a slow love affair that led me to a grander destination. I'm so honored to share this story with you and hope the destination is worth the journey.

It was a true privilege to work with Heather Maven on this novel. She has great insight, enthusiasm, and a fantastic head of hair. Thank you for giving your time, attention, and love to The Resistance (and me).

My team is everything to me. I count on them for way more than I should. But I truly value and trust their commitment, guidance, and honesty, and feel my story is better because of having their eyes on it. But these lovelies are not just editors, readers, and team members, they are true friends. Thank you: Daisy, Danielle, Hillz, Irene, Jenn, Kandace, Lisa, and Marla for working your magic and sharing your thoughts.

Life is a bowl of chocolate and these ladies deserve all of it because they make my world go round with their endless support. This makes no sense. Just humor me. These loverlies mean the world to me. Thank you: Jennifer, Kerri, Kirsten, Mary, Nina, Ruth, S & L's, Sonia, Suzanne, Tracy, Tricia, and my TL & R girls.

All my love to my family. XOX

About the Author

Always interested in the arts, S. L. Scott, grew up painting, writing poetry and short stories, and wiling her days away lost in a good book and the movies.

With a degree in Journalism, she continued her love of the written word by reading American authors like Salinger and Fitzgerald. She was intrigued by their flawed characters living in picture perfect worlds, but could still debate that the worlds those characters lived in were actually the flawed ones. This dynamic of leaving the reader invested in the words, inspired Scott to start writing with emotion while interjecting an underlying passion into her own stories.

Living in the capital of Texas with her family, Scott loves traveling and avocados, beaches, and cooking with her kids. She's obsessed with epic romances and loves a good plot twist. She dreams of seeing one of her own books made into a movie one day as well as returning to Europe. Her favorite color is blue, but she likens it more toward the sky than the emotion. Her home is filled with the welcoming symbol of the pineapple and finds surfing a challenge though she likes to think she's a pro.

Scott welcomes your notes to <u>sl@slscottauthor.com</u>

30150627R00223

Made in the USA
Charleston, SC
07 June 2014